A VINEYARD
IN ANDALUSIA

A
VINEYARD
IN
ANDALUSIA

MARIA DUEÑAS

Translated by Nick Caistor and Lorenza García

SCRIBE
Melbourne • London

Scribe Publications
18–20 Edward St, Brunswick, Victoria 3056, Australia
2 John St, Clerkenwell, London, WC1N 2ES, United Kingdom

Originally published in Spain in 2017 by Planeta as *La Templanza*

First published in English by Scribe in 2017
Reprinted 2017

The moral rights of the author have been asserted.

Interior design by Dana Sloan
Printed and bound in the UK by CPI Group (UK) Ltd, Croydon,
CR0 4YY

Scribe Publications is committed to the sustainable use of natural
resources and the use of paper products made responsibly from
those resources.

9781925322422 (Australian edition)
9781911344469 (UK edition)
9781925548365 (e-book)

CiP data records for this title are available from the National Library
of Australia and the British Library.

scribepublications.com.au
scribepublications.co.uk

For my father, Pablo Dueñas Samper,
who knows about mines and enjoys a good wine

CONTENTS

Part I

MEXICO CITY, 1861

1

Part II

HAVANA

121

Part III

JEREZ DE LA FRONTERA

231

Part I

MEXICO CITY
1861

CHAPTER ONE

❧

What goes through the mind and body of a man accustomed to triumphing over the odds when one September evening his worst fears are confirmed?

Nothing changed in his demeanor. There was no outburst, no telltale gesture. Only a fleeting, imperceptible tremor that coursed through him from head to foot when the disaster he had already anticipated was finally confirmed. Undaunted, with one hand resting on the sturdy walnut desk, he fixed his eyes on the two women who had brought him the news, registering their lined, exhausted faces and desolate mourning attire.

"Please enjoy your hot chocolate, ladies. Forgive me for having put you to this trouble, and thank you for your consideration in coming all this way to inform me in person."

The moment the interpreter had finished translating, the two North Americans did as they were told, as though obeying an order. Their country's embassy had provided them with this intermediary so that the women, overwhelmed with fatigue, the bad news they were bringing, and their lack of Spanish, could make themselves understood and thus fulfill the purpose of their journey.

They raised the cups to their lips with little enthusiasm, merely out of a sense of respect, in order not to offend the man. However, they left untouched the biscuits made by San Bernardino nuns, and he did not insist. While the two women were sipping the thick liquid with barely concealed discomfort, a silence that was almost palpable slithered into the room like a reptile amid the polished wooden floor, the European furniture, the paintings of landscapes and still lifes.

The interpreter, a smooth-cheeked young man of no more than twenty, sat there rather uneasily, his clammy hands clasped awkwardly on his lap as he wondered what on earth he was doing in that place. Meanwhile, a thousand sounds floated on the air. From the courtyard came the echo of servants rinsing the tiles with laurel water, and from the street beyond the wrought-iron window bars, the thudding hoofs of mules and horses, the laments of mendicant lepers, and the cries of a street vendor hawking cream empanadas, tortillas stuffed with cheese, guava jelly, and sweet breads.

As the clock struck half past five, the ladies dabbed their lips with the exquisite Dutch napkins. Beyond that, they had no idea what to do.

The owner of the house put an end to the tension.

"Permit me to offer you my hospitality for the night before you undertake your return journey."

"Thank you kindly, sir," they replied, almost in unison. "We already have a room booked at an inn that the embassy recommended."

"Santos!" he cried out in a booming voice.

Even though it wasn't directed at them, both women flinched.

"Have Laureano accompany these ladies to collect their luggage and transfer them to the Iturbide Hotel. Charge it to my account. Then go and find Andrade. Haul him out of his game of dominoes and tell him to come here at once."

The young bronze-skinned servant received the orders with a simple

"As you wish, sir." As if he hadn't already had his ear to the door and learned that the world of Mauro Larrea, until that day a wealthy silver miner, had suddenly been turned upside down.

The two women rose, their skirts rustling ominously like the wings of crows as they followed the servant out of the room and onto the cool veranda. The one who had said she was the sister went first, while the other, the widow, brought up the rear. They left behind the papers they had brought: documents confirming in black-and-white the truth of his premonition.

The interpreter made to follow them, but the owner of the house stopped him, placing his big gnarled hand on the American's chest with the firmness of someone who knows how to command and is certain he will be obeyed.

"Just a moment, young man, if you please."

The interpreter barely had time to respond before the older man spoke again.

"Samuelson you said your name was, didn't you?"

"That's right, sir."

"Very well, Samuelson," said Larrea, lowering his voice. "I hardly need tell you that this conversation has been strictly confidential. One word about it to anyone and I'll make sure that within a week you'll not only be deported but conscripted back in your own country. Where are you from, my friend?"

The young man's throat felt as dry as a desert hut.

"From Hartford, Connecticut, Señor Larrea."

"Better still. That way you'll be able to help the Yankees defeat those damned Confederates once and for all."

⁓

As soon as Larrea calculated that the two women had reached the front entrance, he lifted the heavy drape before one of the balconies and observed them as they left the mansion and climbed into his carriage. The coachman, Laureano, geed up the mares, and they set off at a brisk pace, weaving their way past well-dressed passersby, ragged barefoot children, and Indians wrapped in serapes who in a chaotic chorus of voices were peddling tallow and mats from Puebla, salt meat, lard, avocados, flavored ices, and wax effigies of the infant Jesus. After the carriage turned into Calle de las Damas, Larrea pulled back from the balcony. Elias Andrade, his agent, would not be there for at least another half hour, and he knew exactly what to do until then.

Protected from the gaze of others, Mauro Larrea angrily removed his jacket and proceeded to make his way through the rooms as he pulled off his necktie, undid his cuff links, and rolled the sleeves of his linen shirt up past the elbows. Upon reaching his destination, he took a deep breath and spun the billiard cue rack, which was shaped like a roulette wheel.

Holy Mother of God, he muttered to himself.

There was no apparent reason why he chose the cue he did. Others were newer, more sophisticated and valuable, acquired over the years as tangible proof of his spectacular rise. And yet, on the evening that blew his life asunder, as the light quickly faded and his servants lit oil lamps and candles in every corner of the big house, while the streets were still pulsating with energy and Mexico as a whole remained stubbornly ungovernable due to seemingly endless squabbles, Larrea rejected the obvious choice. Opting instead for the rough old cue that connected him to his past, he set about furiously combating his private demons at the billiard table.

As the minutes ticked by, he played his shots with ruthless efficiency, one after the other, with the only sound that of the balls rebounding off the cushions and the sharp smack of ivory on ivory. He remained in control, calculating and decisive as always. Or almost always. Until he heard a voice from the doorway behind him.

"Seeing you grasping that cue makes me suspect bad news."

Larrea kept on playing as if he had heard nothing: flicking his wrist for an unerring shot, raising his fingers in a solid bridge for the hundredth time, revealing the stumps of two fingers on his left hand, and the dark scar rising from the base of his thumb. War wounds, he used to say ironically. The consequences of his passage through the bowels of the earth.

Of course he had heard the well-modulated voice of his agent, a tall man of exquisitely outmoded elegance, his skull as smooth as a river stone and his brain both shrewd and vibrant. In addition to looking after his finances and his interests, Elias Andrade was his closest friend: the elder brother he had never had, the voice of his conscience when the uproar of tumultuous days robbed him of the serenity required to make wise choices.

Leaning athletically over the green baize, Mauro Larrea struck the last ball firmly, bringing his solitary game to a close. Replacing the cue in its rack, he turned unhurriedly toward the newcomer.

They looked each other in the eye, as they had done so many times before. For good or ill, that was how it had always been between them. Face-to-face. Without mincing words.

"I'm ruined, my friend."

His trusted friend shut his eyes briefly but made no comment. He simply took a handkerchief from his pocket and mopped his brow, for he had begun to sweat.

While awaiting a reply, the miner raised the lid of a humidor and took out two cigars. They lit them from a silver brazier and the air filled with smoke; only then did the agent respond to the dreadful news he had just heard.

"Farewell to Las Tres Lunas."

"Farewell to everything. It's all gone to hell."

Having lived between two worlds, whenever he spoke Larrea mixed expressions, at times sounding like a peninsular Spaniard, at others more Mexican than Chapultepec Castle. Two and a half decades had passed since his arrival in Mexico, by then already a fledgling republic after a lengthy and painful struggle for independence. He had brought with him a broken heart, two unavoidable responsibilities, and the urgent need to survive. Nothing could have predicted his path would cross that of Elias Andrade, last descendant of an ancient Creole family as aristocratic as it was poor following the collapse of Spain's colony in Mexico. But, as so often happens in cases where the vagaries of chance intercede, the two men first met at a notorious bar in a mining camp at Real de Catorce when Larrea's business affairs (he was twelve years younger) were just starting to prosper, and Andrade's dreams had hit rock bottom. From then on, despite the thousand reversals that both men encountered, despite all the disasters and triumphs, the joys and disappointments, that fortune held in store for them, they had never parted ways.

"Did the gringo cheat you?"

"Worse. He's dead."

Andrade's eyebrow arched into a question mark.

"Killed by Confederates at the battle of Bull Run. His wife and sister came all the way from Philadelphia to bring me the news. That was his dying wish."

"What about the machinery?"

"Requisitioned by his associates for their Lackawanna Valley coal mines."

"And we paid for the whole lot . . ." his agent whispered in amazement.

"Down to the last screw; we had no choice. But not a single machine was loaded on board ship."

Without a word, the agent went over to one of the balconies and opened the shutters wide, perhaps in the vain hope that a breeze might blow away what he had just learned. But only the usual voices and noises rose from the street: the never-ending bustle of what until only a few years earlier had been the biggest metropolis in the Americas. The richest and most powerful city, the old Aztec capital of Tenochtitlán.

"I warned you," Andrade growled, gazing abstractedly at the hub-bub below.

Mauro Larrea's only reaction was to draw deeply on his cigar.

"I told you that opening that mine again was too precarious: that you shouldn't take on the concession or invest so much money in foreign machinery, that you should look for shareholders to mitigate the danger. That you should get that wild idea out of your head."

A firecracker went off close to the cathedral; they could hear two coachmen quarreling nearby and a horse neighing loudly. Larrea's only reply was to blow out smoke.

"I told you a hundred times there was no need to risk so much," Andrade insisted in an increasingly angry voice. "And yet, against my advice, and against simple common sense, you insisted on risking everything you owned. Mortgaging the Tacubaya estate. Selling your land in Coyoacán, the ranches at San Antonio Coapa, the stores on Calle Sepulcro, the farms at Chapingo, the cattle pens by Santa Catarina Virgen y Martir church."

He reeled off the list of properties as if he was spitting out bile.

"But that wasn't all: you cashed in all your stocks, sold off your government bonds and securities, drowned yourself up to your ears in debt. I don't see how you think we can confront what's about to hit us."

Larrea finally spoke up.

"We still have something left."

He spread his hands as if to indicate the room they were in, and by extension the entire mansion and its contents.

"Don't even consider such a thing!" howled the agent, burying his head in his hands.

"We need capital to pay off the most urgent debts first, and then for me to get going again."

Andrade's face turned suddenly alarmed.

"Get going where?"

"I don't know yet, all I know is that I have to leave. There's no other way, brother. I'm done for here; I'll never be able to rebuild anything."

"Wait," insisted Andrade, trying to inject some calm into his friend. "For heaven's sake, wait. First we need to weigh up everything: we may find a way to pull the wool over people's eyes for a time while I go around putting out fires and negotiating with creditors."

"You know as well as I do that will get us nowhere. At the end of your accounting, all you'll find is despair."

"Stay composed, Mauro, restrain yourself. Don't meet trouble head-on and, above all, avoid putting this house in jeopardy. It's the last thing you own outright, and the only thing that could help you keep up appearances."

Formerly a baroque palace, the imposing colonial mansion on Calle San Felipe Neri had been purchased by Larrea from the descendants of the Count of Regla, once the wealthiest miner in the viceroyalty. The property had confirmed Larrea's social status in the most sought-after area of the city. It was the only possession he had not mortgaged to obtain the monstrous amount of hard cash needed to reopen Las Tres Lunas mine; the only thing remaining of the wealth he had accumulated over the years. Above and beyond its monetary worth, both men knew the true value of his residence: as the only means whereby Larrea could prop up, however precariously, his public reputation. In holding on to it, he would avoid ridicule and humiliation. Losing it would broadcast his failure to the entire Mexican capital.

An intense silence fell over them again. These two men who had once been so blessed by good fortune, so admired and respected, now gazed at each other like two souls cast without warning into a treacherous sea.

"You were a damned fool," Andrade declared eventually, as if by restating his opinion he could somehow lessen the impact of the disaster.

"You accused me of the same thing when I told you how I planned to get started with the La Elvira mine. And when I invested in La Santa Clara. And then La Abundancia and La Prosperidad. I ended up striking it lucky in all of those mines, pulling out silver by the ton."

"But back then you weren't even thirty, just a young savage on the far side of the world with nothing to lose, you idiot! Now that you're three years shy of fifty, do you really think you'll be capable of starting again from nothing?"

The miner allowed his agent to go on venting his frustration.

"You've been asked to join the boards of some of Mexico's foremost companies! Liberals and Conservatives alike have wooed you—you could lead either party if you showed the slightest interest! There's no salon where your presence isn't coveted, and the most prominent people in the nation have dined at your table. And now you're throwing it all to hell through sheer obstinacy. Your reputation is about to go up in smoke, you have a son who without your money is no more than a fool, and a daughter whose social position you're on the verge of destroying!"

Having finished his rant, Andrade crushed the half-smoked cigar in a quartz ashtray and headed for the door. At that very moment, the silhouette of Santos Huesos, the indigenous servant, appeared at the threshold. He was carrying two cut crystal glasses on a tray, along with a large bottle of Catalan brandy and another of whiskey smuggled from Louisiana.

Andrade did not even let him set the tray down on the table. Stepping in front of him, he brusquely poured himself a glass, drained it in one gulp, and wiped his mouth with the back of his hand.

"Let me go over the accounts tonight, to see if there's anything we can salvage. But, for God's sake, don't even think about getting rid of this house. It's all you have left if you want anyone to have faith in you again. It's your lifeline. Your shield."

Mauro Larrea pretended he was listening, and even thrust out his chin in agreement, but by now his mind was already racing ahead in a completely different direction.

He was convinced he would have to start all over again.

And for that he would need hard cash and some time to think.

CHAPTER TWO

A fter Andrade had departed through the veranda's majestic arch-way muttering curses, Larrea found he had no appetite for food. Instead, he decided to take a bath and reflect without his agent's voice pricking his conscience.

As he soaked in the tub, Mariana was the first image to flash through his mind. As always, his daughter would be the only one to hear straight from his lips what had happened. Despite the fact that she no longer lived under his roof, the two saw a great deal of each other, and scarcely a day went by when she didn't call at her old house or take a stroll with him down Paseo de Bucareli. The servants were overjoyed whenever she crossed the threshold, especially in her present condition; they would tell her how beautiful she looked and urge her to stay awhile, offering her meringues, brioches, and other sweets.

Nicolás was going to be another matter entirely, and Mauro Larrea's worst nightmare. Mercifully for them all, news of the catastrophe would reach him in France, at the Pas-de-Calais coal mines, where an old friend had taken him under his wing with the aim of getting him away from Mexico for a while. Larrea's son was a strange combination of angel and devil: smart and selfish, reckless, unpredictable in his actions. His own good fortune as well as his father's protective shadow had followed him always, or at least until he began to go too far. At nineteen he had developed a sudden infatuation for a congressman's wife, and months later a wild spree ended with a ballroom floor caving in beneath him. By the time his son reached twenty, Mauro Larrea had lost count of the scandals he had been obliged to bail him out of. Fortunately, despite all this, he had arranged a favorable marriage between his son and one of the Gorostiza daughters, and in order for him to finish his apprenticeship before joining his father's business, as well as to avoid any further shameful episodes prior to his marriage, he had persuaded Nicolás to spend a year overseas. From now on, however, everything would be different, which was why each move Mauro Larrea made required the utmost consideration. In confronting his imminent ruin, one of his most pressing concerns remained his son, Nicolás.

Closing his eyes, Larrea tried to empty his mind of problems, at least momentarily, setting aside all thoughts of the dead gringo, the machinery that would never reach its destination, the colossal failure of his most ambitious project to date, his son's future, and the abyss that had opened beneath his feet. What he needed to do now, urgently, was to move forward, to advance. Having weighed up the options from every angle, he knew there was only one surefire way out. *Think twice, sonofabitch,* he told himself. *Like it or not, you have no other choice. There's nothing you can do in this city without giving yourself away. The only solution is to leave. So, damn it, decide once and for all.*

Like many men shaped by ceaseless struggle, Mauro Larrea had developed an astonishing ability to seize life by the horns. His character had been forged in the silver mines of Guanajuato during his early years in the Americas: toiling endless days in the bowels of the earth, grappling with the rock face by torchlight, dressed only in a pair of scanty leather pants, a soiled bandanna covering his brow to protect his eyes from the vile mixture of dirt, sweat, and dust. Pummeling rock with brute force for eleven hours a day, six days a week, in that dismal, godforsaken place had instilled in him a permanent tenacity.

Perhaps that was why now there was no trace of bitterness in him as he sat steeping in that magnificent enameled bathtub imported from Belgium, something that on his arrival in Mexico would have been a dream to which he never dared aspire. During those early years he would wash under a fig tree in a barrel of rainwater, and in the absence of soap he scrubbed the grime off his skin with a rag. For a towel he used his shirt and the sun's rays, and for toiletries the harsh wind. His only luxury was a crude wooden comb, and the lemon-scented hair oil he purchased in quarter-liter bottles on payday, which helped tame his thick, unruly locks, which back then were chestnut-brown. What terrible times those had been! Eventually, when the mine began to take its toll on his body, he decided the moment had come for him to move on.

And now, with this rotten luck, the only way for him to avoid absolute ruin was by revisiting his past. Notwithstanding his agent's sound advice, if he wished to keep this hidden from the circles he moved in— if he wanted to move on before everything came out and there was no way for him to pick himself up—he had only one recourse. Despite the intervening years and life's vicissitudes, he was now forced to travel down murky pathways populated by shadows.

He opened his eyes. The water was growing cold, and so was his heart. Stepping out of the tub, he grasped the towel. Drops of water trickled down his naked skin to the marble floor. Time had treated him kindly, as if his body wished to honor the titanic efforts of bygone days. At forty-seven, besides a few old wounds, including the still-visible scar on his left hand and two mutilated fingers, his arms and legs were sinewy, his belly firm, and he possessed the same broad shoulders that never went unnoticed by tailors, enemies, and ladies alike.

He finished drying himself, shaved hastily, rubbing Macassar oil blindly onto his jaw, then selected the clothes most suited to his purpose. Dark and resilient. He dressed with his back to the mirror, buckling on the protection that always accompanied him in situations such as the one he anticipated now. His knife. His gun. Lastly, out of a desk he retrieved a folder tied with red ribbon and removed from it several documents, which he folded without reading and tucked away close to his chest.

Only when he was completely ready did he turn to face the large mirror on the wardrobe.

"This is your last shot, compadre," he declared to his reflection.

Snuffing out the oil lamp, he shouted for Santos Huesos and stepped into the corridor.

"Tomorrow at dawn, walk to Don Elias Andrade's house and tell him I've gone where he would never want me to go."

"To Don Tadeo?" Santos Huesos asked uneasily.

But his master was already striding toward the stables, and the youth had to break into a run to keep up with him. His question remained unanswered as the instructions continued to flow.

"If Mariana comes here, not a word of this to her. And if anyone calls asking for me, tell them the first thing that enters your head."

The servant was about to speak when his master took the words out of his mouth:

"No, my lad, this time you're not going with me. Regardless of how this madness ends, I'm going into it alone, and coming out of it alone."

It was past nine o'clock, but the streets were still filled with hustle and bustle. Wrapped in a Querétaro cape and seated astride a criollo horse, his face partially hidden beneath a wide-brimmed hat, Larrea purposefully avoided the busiest intersections and alleyways. He used to enjoy the swarming crowds, usually because they preceded his arrival at an interesting gathering or a dinner that might prove beneficial to his business interests. Sometimes a rendezvous with a woman. However, that night, he longed only to leave everything behind.

Gringo sonofabitch, he muttered to himself, spurring his steed on. But he knew the gringo wasn't to blame. A former officer in the US Army Corps of Engineers, and moralistic to the core, he had honored his side of the bargain. He had even had the decency to provide his wife and sister to tell Larrea what he would never be able to say to him in person, buried as he was in a common grave, one eye blown out and his skull shattered. *That filthy war, those accursed slavers*, Larrea muttered.

How could this string of mishaps have come to pass? How could fate have dealt him such a rotten hand? These questions were pounding his brain as he galloped down the Calzada de los Misterios.

❧

Despite his flash of resentment, Mauro Larrea was fully aware that Thomas Sachs, otherwise known as the Yankee, had been an honest, upright Methodist and never a scoundrel. Thirteen months earlier, Sachs had come to him on the recommendation of an old friend from San Luis Potosí. He had arrived just as Larrea was finishing his breakfast, when the house was barely ready to receive guests, and the prattle of young servant girls chopping onions and milling corn reached them from the depths of the kitchens. Santos Huesos showed the visitor into the study, where he was asked to wait. The gringo did so standing, swaying from one foot to the other as he gazed at the floor.

"I hear you might be interested in purchasing some machinery for one of your mines" was his greeting when he saw Larrea enter the room. The miner contemplated the man before replying. He was stocky, with a complexion that reddened easily and a tolerable level of Spanish.

"That depends on what you're offering."

"A state-of-the-art steam engine, manufactured by Lyons, Brookman and Sachs at our factories in Harrisburg, Pennsylvania. Custom-made to our purchasers' requirements."

"Capable of pumping out water at two thousand feet of depth?"

"More: up to twenty-eight hundred feet."

"In that case I'm interested."

As Mauro Larrea listened, he became aware once more of the murmur of something that had lain dormant inside him for many years. To resurrect the old mine Las Tres Lunas, to return her to her former splendor.

The potential of the machinery Sachs was laying before him was tremendous. Nothing like this had ever been attempted before in Mexico, not by the Spanish miners during the time when it was a colony, nor by the English who had settled in Pachuca and Real del Monte, nor even by the Scots in Oaxaca. Larrea knew from the outset that what Sachs was proposing was something different. Immensely promising.

"Give me a day to think it over."

He received the Yankee the following morning, extending his beefy miner's hand. Sachs knew his type well: he was one of those intrepid, intuitive men who understood that his profession was an endless round of successes and failures. Who had a confident, unwavering way of taking challenging—even risky—decisions, constantly tempting fate and providence. Who were possessed of a tremendously pragmatic approach to life, and a keen, instinctive intelligence. The gringo was used to doing business with such men.

"Let's discuss the details, my friend."

They closed the deal. Larrea applied for the relevant licenses from the Mining Board and drew up a risky financial plan, to which Andrade was steadfastly opposed. And, from then on, Larrea began to lay out large sums in the agreed installments until he had used up his capital and investments. In return, every three weeks, he received like clockwork progress reports from Pennsylvania: about the intricate machines being assembled, the tons of material piling up in warehouses. Boilers, gantries, auxiliary equipment. Then one day, the letters from the north stopped arriving.

࿇

Just one year and a month had gone by between those days brimming with optimism and this night, when his dark outline sped along stark roads beneath a starless sky as he searched for a solution that might at least offer him some breathing space.

The sky was already growing light when he came to a halt outside a heavy wooden portal. His body was aching, his mouth parched, and his eyes red; he had scarcely given his horse or himself a moment's rest. Even so, he dismounted swiftly. Moments later, the forelegs of the animal buckled and it slumped to the ground in exhaustion.

Dawn was breaking over a small valley at the foot of San Cristobal hill, a stone's throw from the Pachuca mines. No one was expecting him at the lonely hacienda: Who would have imagined anyone arriving at such an ungodly hour? The dogs, on the other hand, immediately detected his presence, and a chorus of frenzied barks shattered the peaceful morning.

Almost instantaneously, Larrea heard footsteps, a cracking sound, and a voice commanding the dogs to be quiet. As their uproar died down, a youthful voice demanded brusquely from within:

"Who goes there?"

"I've come looking for Don Tadeo."

Two bolts, heavy and thick with rust, screeched as they were drawn back. Then a third began to grate before stopping halfway, as if the person opening it had changed their mind. After a few moments' silence, he heard footsteps padding away across the beaten earth.

Three or four minutes later, he became aware of another human presence on the far side of the door. Instead of one person, there were now two.

"Who goes there?"

The same question, but a different voice. Despite not having heard it for over a decade, Mauro Larrea would have recognized it anywhere.

"Someone you never imagined you'd see again."

The third bolt was suddenly drawn back and the door opened. As though impelled by the devil himself, the dogs started up their frenzied yelping again. Amid the din came the sound of a gun being fired into the air. Still slumped after its long gallop through the night, Larrea's horse lifted its head and rose to its feet. Four or five mangy dogs slunk away from the entrance, tails between their legs, whining pitifully.

The men stood waiting for him, feet set slightly apart. The youngest, a night watchman, was holding the half-cocked blunderbuss he had just fired. The other man's rheumy eyes drilled into Larrea. Beyond them, at the far end of a broad path, the outline of the house was slowly becoming silhouetted against the morning sky.

The older of the two men peered at Larrea. Dimas Carrús, gaunt and melancholy as ever, with at least a week's worth of stubble on his face, had been roused from the straw mattress that served as his bed. His lifeless right arm dangled at his side, maimed after a beating his father had given him in early childhood.

Finally, still staring at Larrea, he mustered a belch, which erupted like a gob of phlegm. Then came his greeting.

"My God, Larrea. I never thought you'd be crazy enough to come back here."

A cold gust of wind blew around them.

"Wake your father, Dimas. Tell him I need to speak to him."

The man shook his head, in a gesture of disbelief rather than refusal. At seeing him again after all that had happened.

He started toward the house without a word, his arm drooping from his shoulder like a dead eel. Larrea followed him as far as the inner courtyard, the gravel crunching beneath his boots, then waited while the heir of all this disappeared through one of the side doors. Larrea had only stepped across the threshold once since the days of the Real de Catorce mine had come to an end. The house was as he remembered it, although even in that dim light Larrea could tell it was dilapidated. The same large crude building with thick walls and few refinements. Discarded tools, various types of debris, and animal excrement.

Dimas soon reappeared in a different doorway.

"Come in and wait. You'll hear him arrive."

CHAPTER THREE

❧

The low-ceilinged room where Tadeo Carrús conducted his business deals appeared unchanged by the passage of time. The same rustic table cluttered with papers and open files. Half-dried-up inkpots and tattered quill pens, an old set of scales with two pans. And on the brown flaking wall was the same image of the dark-skinned Virgin of Guadalupe surrounded by faded golden rays, her hands folded across her chest, a moon and cherub at her feet.

He heard slow shuffling footsteps on the clay tiles out in the corridor, without even imagining they belonged to the man he was waiting for. Larrea scarcely recognized him when he entered the room. Once a tallish man, he appeared to have shrunk by a good twelve inches and his body had lost its former vigor and compactness. He couldn't yet have been sixty but gave the impression of a decrepit ninety-year-old. Ashen-faced, crooked, and frail, Tadeo Carrús was dressed in ragged clothes and was protected from the cold dawn air by little more than a threadbare shawl.

"After so many years of not remembering me, you might at least have waited until noon to show up."

Mauro Larrea's memory flooded with images and sensations. The day the moneylender had sought him out at the mine he intended to exploit; the small-goods store he ran back then, next to the Real de Catorce mine shafts. As they sat on stools facing each other, an oil lamp and a jug of pulque between them, the moneylender had made an offer to the ambitious young miner. *I'm going to back you to the hilt, Spaniard,* he'd said, placing a heavy paw on his shoulder. *You and I are going to make big money together, you'll see.* And although Larrea was perfectly aware how unfair the contract was, his lack of funds and surfeit of dreams had led him to accept.

Fortunately for both men, the profits from the mine were so huge he had been able to keep his side of the bargain: 70 percent of the silver for the moneylender, 30 percent for him. Then came another promising venture, and again he invested Tadeo Carrús's capital. This time he suggested a fifty-fifty split. *You lay out the money. I lay out the work. My instinct. My life,* he said. The moneylender laughed out loud. *Have you lost your mind, boy? Seventy-thirty, or there's no deal.* On that occasion, too, Larrea had struck it lucky and made a handsome profit. And once more the division of the spoils was heavily one-sided.

When it came to his next venture, however, Mauro Larrea sat down to do his sums and realized that he no longer needed help from anyone: he could take care of himself. He told Carrús as much in the same store, over two fresh glasses of pulque. But the moneylender didn't accept the parting of ways with good grace. *If you don't ruin yourself first, sonofabitch, I'll do it for you.* He proved himself to be a fearsome adversary, resorting to threats, harassment, skulduggery, obstruction. Blood was spilled among both men's followers. Carrús's men hobbled Larrea's mules; they tried to make off with his iron ore and quicksilver. Several times they held a knife to his throat, and one rainy afternoon he felt the barrel of a gun brush against his neck. The avaricious moneylender moved heaven and earth to make him fail, but did not succeed.

It was years since Larrea had last seen him. And now, instead of the unscrupulous, corpulent bully he had been determined to confront, he discovered a walking skeleton, ribs jutting out obscenely from his chest, skin the color of rancid butter, and breath so foul he could smell it at five paces.

"Sit wherever you can," Carrús ordered as he slumped behind his desk.

"There's no need. This won't take long."

"Sit down, damn it!" exclaimed Carrús in a strangulated voice, lungs whistling like a two-holed flute. "If you rode all night, you can afford to spend a quarter of an hour with me before turning back."

Larrea gave in and sat on a narrow wooden chair without leaning back or giving the slightest impression of getting comfortable.

"I need money."

Tadeo Carrús made as if to laugh, but the phlegm impeded him and set off a loud coughing fit.

"You want us to be partners again, like we were in the old days?"

"We were never partners, you merely invested in my projects hoping for an ample return on your money. Which is more or less what I'm asking you to do again now. And as you're still baying for my blood, I know you won't refuse."

The old man's wizened face took on a skeptical look.

"I hear you've done remarkably well for yourself, Spaniard."

"You know this business as well as I do," Larrea replied impassively. "It has its ups and downs."

"It has its ups and downs . . ." the moneylender repeated sardonically, trailing off until only the intermittent whistling of his lungs could be heard.

A sliver of morning seeped in through a crack in the shutters. The light sharpened the contours, adding to the lamentable aspect of the setting.

This time there was no attempt at laughter.

"And what will you pledge in return for my money?"

"The deed to my house."

As he spoke, Mauro Larrea raised his hand to his chest. He retrieved the documents from among his clothes and placed them on the table.

Tadeo Carrús inflated his bony chest with a sharp intake of breath, as if to muster his strength.

"You must be in one hell of a tight spot, you sonofabitch, if you're prepared to wager your finest possession in this way. I know perfectly well what that former palace of the goddamned Count of Regla is worth. Although you weren't aware of it, I've kept track of you over the years."

Larrea had suspected as much, but didn't wish to give the money-lender the pleasure of saying so, and let him continue.

"I know where you live, the circles you move in, and how you invested your money. I know you married your little Mariana off well and that you're engineering another favorable alliance for your boy."

"I have no time for this," Larrea interrupted abruptly. He didn't wish to hear the old man talking about his children, or to discover what if anything he knew about his last failed business venture.

"Why the hurry, if I may ask?"

"I have to go."

"Where?"

As if I knew myself, Larrea thought sarcastically, but replied:

"That's none of your business."

Tadeo Carrús's mouth twisted into a rapacious grin.

"Everything about you concerns me now. What other reason did you have for coming?"

"I need the sum specified in the document. If I fail to pay back the amount to you by the date we establish, the house is yours. With all its contents."

"What if you succeed?"

"I'll refund the entire loan, together with the interest we agree on today."

"I usually charge my clients fifty percent, but in your case I'm prepared to make an exception."

"How much?"

"As it's you, a hundred percent."

A rotten miser from the day he was born, Larrea reflected. *What were you thinking, that time would have turned him into a saint?* He knew Carrús couldn't resist now having him once more in his clutches.

"I accept."

A pair of invisible hands seemed to be tying a thick rope around his neck.

"Then let's talk about the repayments," the moneylender went on. "I usually allow twelve months."

"All right."

"But in your case I'll make an exception."

"You tell me."

"I want the money in three installments."

"I'd prefer to pay it all at the end."

"But I don't. I want a third of the money four months from today, another third in eight months' time, and the final payment in a year."

Larrea could feel the imaginary rope tighten around his jugular, threatening to strangle him.

"I accept."

The dogs barked excitedly in the distance.

Thus ended the nastiest deal Larrea had ever made. The old swindler was now in possession of the deed to his last remaining property. In exchange, in two dirty leather saddlebags, he took away with him enough money to pay off his most pressing debts and to take the first steps toward a tentative resurrection. How and where, he did not yet know. As for the longer-term consequences that ruinous agreement might lead to, he preferred not to contemplate them just yet.

No sooner had they signed the contract than Larrea slapped his thigh vigorously.

"All right, then," he announced, gathering up his cape and hat. "You'll hear from me in four months' time."

He had almost reached the door when the wheezing voice blasted him from behind.

"You were nothing but a dirt-poor Spaniard with gold fever, like all those other fools from the goddamned mother country."

Larrea responded without turning.

"It was my legitimate right, wasn't it?"

"You'd never have gotten anywhere without me. I even fed you and your kids when all you had to eat was a handful of beans."

Patience, he told himself. *Don't listen to him. He's just the same heartless scoundrel he always was. You have what you came for, don't waste another second. Get out of here.*

But he couldn't stop himself.

"All you ever wanted, you old devil," he retorted, turning slowly around, "was to keep me in your debt forever, the way you had dozens of other miserable wretches, all your life. You offered loans at exorbitant rates, exploited and cheated, demanded absolute loyalty, while all you did was suck our blood like a parasite. Especially mine, because I made you richer than all the others. That's why you fought to stop me setting up on my own."

"You betrayed me, you sonofabitch."

Larrea walked back to the table, slammed his fists onto it, and leaned forward until he was only inches away from the old man's face. The stench that reached him was putrid, but he barely noticed it.

"We were never partners or friends, and I disliked you as much as you disliked me. So stop throwing these pathetic accusations at me and make your peace with God and your fellow men in what little time you have left on this earth."

The old man shot him a black look, seething with rage.

"I'm not dying, if that's what you think. I've lived for over ten years with these diseased lungs, much to everyone's astonishment, starting with my useless son and ending with you. Although don't imagine that I'd care much if the grim reaper came for me at this stage of the game."

He raised his eyes toward the dark-skinned Virgin, his lungs rattling like a pair of snakes.

"But just to be on the safe side, I vow by all that's holy to say three Hail Marys every night to see you groveling in the mud before they lay me in my grave."

The silence congealed.

"If in four months from today you aren't here with the first payment, Mauro Larrea, I won't hold on to your palace. No," he paused, gasping for breath, rallying his strength. "I'll raze it to the ground. I'll dynamite it from top to bottom, the way you did those caves when you were no more than an ignorant ruffian. And if it's the last thing I do, I'll stand in the middle of Calle San Felipe Neri to watch your house collapse, wall by wall, and with it your name and what's left of your reputation."

Tadeo Carrús's loathsome threats floated in one ear and out the other. Four months. That was what remained imprinted, as though with a branding iron, on Mauro Larrea's brain. Four months to find a way out. Four months, like four explosions resounding in his head, as he walked away from that piece of human refuse, mounted his horse, and set off on his return journey toward whatever lay in store for him.

It was already dark by the time he crossed the threshold of his own home and called out to Santos Huesos.

"See to the horse, and tell Laureano to have the coach ready in ten minutes."

Without stopping, he strode across the huge courtyard on his way to the kitchens, shouting for water. Sensing their master's mood, the flustered servants hurriedly obeyed. "Come on, stir yourselves," he urged them. "Fetch the buckets and bring up clean towels."

Although his aching body cried out for rest, he had no time to languish in the tub. Water, soap, and a sponge were what he needed. He furiously scrubbed away the thick coating of dust and sweat that stuck to his skin, then directed the straight razor along his cheeks and jaw. In quick succession he patted his face dry, tamed his unruly locks, and slipped into his shirt and trousers. Buttons, collar, shiny leather shoes. He finished knotting his tie in the passageway and pulled on his tailcoat as he reached the stairs.

A short while later, as Laureano, the coachman, pulled up the carriage amid the clamor outside the Gran Teatro Vergara, Mauro Larrea straightened his cuffs, smoothed his lapels, and ran his fingers once more through his still-damp hair. His return to the present, to the excitement of an opening performance, required his full attention: greetings he had to reciprocate, names he had to recall. His objective was to be seen and not to arouse suspicion.

He strode into the foyer tall and erect, impeccable in his tailcoat, purposefully adopting a vaguely supercilious air. He ran the gamut of polite gestures with seeming ease: exchanging courtesies with statesmen and budding politicians, brisk handshakes with the titled, the moneyed, those with potential or social standing. Amid the dense smoke of the splendid foyer was the usual diverse mixture of prominent people. The descendants of Creole elites who had split away from old Spain hobnobbed with nouveau riche entrepreneurs. Scattered among them was a plethora of decorated military men, dark-eyed beauties whose cleavages were bathed in buttermilk, and a large contingent of diplomats and high-ranking civil servants.

After clapping the shoulders of the men who really mattered, Larrea politely kissed the gloved hands of a number of ladies who were smoking cigarettes as they chatted animatedly, festooned with pearls, silks, and feathers. And as though his world were still spinning on the same axis, the once wealthy mining tycoon behaved exactly as was expected of him: no differently from any other evening among the elite of Mexico City's society. Nobody of course realized that each step he took required a monumental effort.

"At last, my dear Mauro, where have you been hiding?"

He just had time to add another layer of affectation to his charade.

"Too many engagements and invitations, you know how it is . . ." he replied, giving the new arrival a hearty embrace. "How are you, Alonso? How are you all?"

"Fine, fine, still waiting . . . although the convention that frowns upon expectant mothers attending social gatherings is something of an ordeal for Mariana."

The two men chuckled, and if the laughter of the son of the Condesa de Colima was genuine, Larrea's appeared no less so. He would rather die than reveal even a hint of his concern to his daughter's husband. He knew that when he was eventually forced to explain she would be discreet, but all in good time, he reflected.

Two other men with whom Larrea had once done business came over at this point, putting an end to their private conversation. The four men broached various topics until Alonso was called over to another group; then the governor of Zacatecas approached Mauro Larrea, followed by the Venezuelan ambassador, the minister for law and justice, and soon afterward a widow from Jalisco swathed in crimson silk, who for months had been pursuing him whenever their paths crossed. Time slipped by as they spoke of political scandals and their concerns for the incomprehensible fate of the nation. At last the ushers began to announce that the performance was about to begin.

As he made his way to his box, Larrea continued to greet this and that person, searching for an appropriate phrase or timely compliment for each of them. Then the lights went down, the conductor raised his baton, and the theater filled with the strains of the orchestra.

Four months, he said to himself once more.

Concealed now amid the dramatic overture to *Rigoletto*, he could finally let down his guard.

CHAPTER FOUR

◈

H e stopped off at Andrade's house opposite the Santa Brígida Church to spoil his early morning coffee.

"If you've decided to string yourself up like that, there's little I can do" was his agent's curt reply. "I just hope you won't regret it."

"This way we can square away the most urgent debts, and I can take whatever's left and invest it."

"I suppose what's done is done," his friend concluded. He decided to channel his fury into something more constructive. "Let's get to work, then. We'll begin by emptying the estate at Tacubaya; it's far enough away from the city for us to do so inconspicuously. The furniture and fittings will fetch a tidy sum. When we've finished, I'll have a quiet word with Ramón Antequera, the banker. I'll explain that we're no longer able to make the payments and that the property now belongs to him. He's a discreet fellow, he'll know how to deal with the matter without making tongues wag."

A few hours later, two faithful servants pushed along a massive chest of drawers while Santos Huesos guided them toward a cart stationed in the circular driveway. A double wardrobe and four oak bedsteads had already been loaded onto it, while on the ground waiting to join them was a full set of studded leather dining chairs that in their day had seated eighteen guests.

At a distance both nearby and yet removed from these domestic activities, Mauro Larrea had just informed his daughter of the sad news. *Financial ruin, departure, quest, an uncertain destination*—these were the words that remained floating in the air. Mariana understood.

He had called for her on his way back from Andrade's, sending a message ahead to ask her to be ready. Together they had traveled in the coach to their holiday residence, and were now conversing beneath a pergola in the large front garden.

"What are we going to do about Nico?"

Mariana's first response was a question enveloped in a whisper. She was concerned for her brother, the third element of the uneven number to which their family had been reduced the day he was born back in Spain when puerperal fever snatched the life of the young woman who until then had been their rock: Elvira, the mother of Mariana and Nicolás, and Mauro Larrea's steadfast companion. He would give her name to his first mine a few years after her death, and would hear that name echo in his mind when he lay awake at night, until with time it faded and finally disappeared. Elvira, the daughter of a Castilian farm laborer who never accepted her becoming pregnant by the illegitimate grandson of a Basque blacksmith, or marrying that young lad at dawn without any witnesses, or living with him until her dying breath in a miserable foundry on a dirt track at the outskirts of their village in Castile.

"Keep it from him, of course."

❧

Safeguarding Nicolás had always been the watchword between father and daughter: protecting the motherless child, fragile as a bird. That was why Mariana had grown up fast; there was no choice. She was nim-

ble as a hare, plucky and sensible the way only someone could be who
had spent her fourth birthday among the cargo, rats, and stevedores
in the port of Bordeaux, cradling her brother in her arms while her
father carried their meager belongings in two bundles. At a time when
tensions between Spain and Mexico were running high, the family was
about to board a dilapidated French vessel that went by the romantic if
somewhat ironical name of *La Belle Étoile*, transporting iron from the
Basque country and wine from La Gironde. And yet there was nothing
romantic about the arduous seventy-nine days it took them to cross
the Atlantic, oblivious to the fate that awaited them. Life's vagaries,
together with enthusiastic reports from a handful of Welsh miners they
met at the Mexican port of Tampico, made them head inland for Guanajuato. That was where they would get started.

By the age of seven, Mariana was already in charge of looking after
the miserable gray adobe shack they lived in close to La Valenciana
mining camp. Each day she prepared their simple meal in the communal kitchen, alongside much older girls. When they or one of the
miners' wives offered to keep an eye on little Nico, she would hurry
across to the school, where she learned to join up letters and, more im-
portantly, to add and subtract, so that the owner of the grocery store,
an old Spaniard from Aragon, would be unable to cheat her out of the
housekeeping money her father gave her every Saturday.

Eighteen months later, they gathered up their possessions once
again and moved farther west to Real de Catorce, lured by the second
rush of silver fever that had broken out in that far-flung mountainous
region. Exactly a month after they arrived, Mauro Larrea went missing
for four days and four nights, trapped in the bowels of Las Tres Lunas
mine, his hand crushed between two rocks, up to his neck in water. Of
the twenty-seven men working hundreds of feet belowground when
the massive explosion occurred, only five survived to see the light of
day. Mauro Larrea was one of them. The others were hauled to the

surface, bare chests adorned with scapulars and medals of the Blessed Virgin that had failed to protect them, the tendons in their necks bulging, their bluish faces wearing the contorted features of the drowned.

The catastrophe meant Las Tres Lunas was shut down, its ropes cut, according to the industry term. From then on, the mine remained in the collective memory as an accursed place that nobody would risk exploiting. However, Larrea never forgot that its depths were rife with the finest silver, even though for the time being any thought of resurrecting the place that had almost taken his life was out of the question.

What he gained from that terrible ordeal was a steely determination to change his destiny. He refused to continue being a simple mine worker and decided to take the plunge. Rumors were flying about rich seams being struck in the middle of nowhere; more and more shafts were being dug, and hopes were running high. So he ventured blindly into setting up his own modest enterprise. *Advance me the money I need to start excavating, to buy mules and hire a few men, and we will split the raw minerals I find like this, half and half,* he would say, revealing a gray clod in his calloused palm and blowing on it until it shimmered. That was the offer he bandied about in the canteens and bars among the encampments, at every crossroads or tiny hamlet. Then he would add:

"And each will refine his own mineral however he chooses to."

It wasn't long before a seedy opportunistic investor, a two-bit cardsharp, took a gamble on his venture, if indeed the waterlogged hole in which Larrea had placed all his hopes could be called that. However, the miner's instinct told him that if they dug to the west they might strike it lucky. And so he named the new mine after his dead wife, whose face had all but faded from his memory, and set to work.

That was how he set up the operation in La Elvira, proceeding the way the old-timers said his countrymen, the Spanish miners of the colony, had in bygone days. By trial and error. He determined the shafts guided solely by instinct, the way a dog follows its nose. Based upon sheer guesswork rather than halfway logical calculations, and without any scientific rigor whatsoever. He blundered about recklessly, sustained only by his stubborn determination, rugged physique, and the two other mouths he had to feed.

It was during his next venture, La Santa Clara, that Tadeo Carrús entered his life. Two projects, three years, and many setbacks later, Larrea managed to get free of the moneylender and make his own way. Despite Carrús's threats and underhanded attempts to bring him down, there was no stopping him. And although during that time he suffered further disappointments, took foolish risks, even exposed himself to danger through being too hasty, the geological goddess of fortune was on his side, placing veins of silver among the folds of the earth upon which he trod. In La Buenaventura, fate smiled upon him threefold; in La Prosperidad he learned that when an excavation became dangerous, beating a timely retreat was best. The silver he extracted from La Abundancia was of such quality that even some independent refiners from other areas went there to buy from him.

But he was not the only one to shine. After decades of inactivity, the region of Real de Catorce was once again pounded with the sound of debris flying, drilling, and detonations as it had during the days of Spanish rule. It was a chaotic, savage, tumultuous place where notions of peace and order were a pipe dream. The money that flowed from the resurgence of silver in that rich subsoil inevitably gave rise to myriad conflicts: fierce tensions and ambitions, constant outbreaks of violence, knifes carried openly, stabbings between partners. Until one Saturday evening, as he dismounted in high spirits after selling a consignment of silver to a German dealer, he was greeted by an unholy row from inside his house, accompanied by Mariana's screams and Nico's howls.

After his first successes, Larrea had bought a halfway decent house on the outskirts of the town, hiring an old cook, who went home to her family in the evenings, and a maid. That night the maid was off dancing at a fandango party and a young Otomí Indian girl with lustrous black hair named Delfina was left in charge of his children, although they had already learned to look after for themselves. But what he heard as he arrived home made him realize that they needed far more protection than this gentle girl could offer.

He leapt up the stairs, dreading what he would find when he saw the furniture upturned, the curtains torn from the rails, and an oil lamp burning on the floor. The actual scene was far worse than he had feared. On his own bed, a man with his trousers down was thrusting like an animal atop the inert body of the young Delfina. Meanwhile, trapped in her room, Mariana, her nightdress torn open, a bloody scratch on her neck, was jabbing a poker furiously at a clearly drunken second intruder. Nicolás, half-hidden behind a woolen mattress his sister had propped up in the corner as a defensive wall, was wailing and howling as though possessed.

With unbridled strength and rage, Mauro Larrea seized the assailant by the scruff of his neck and repeatedly slammed his face into the wall. Again and again, with dull but resounding thuds, and then yet again, while his children looked on in a daze. Eventually, he let the man slide to the floor, and a trickle of blood, dark as the night seeping in through the balcony, oozed onto the innocent floral wallpaper of Mariana's bedroom. Having swiftly ascertained that his children had no other injuries, he hastened into the adjacent room and seized Delfina's attacker, who was still panting and writhing on top of the terrified girl. The procedure was the same, with a similar outcome: the assailant's face was smashed in, his skull crushed and thick blood flowing from his nose and mouth. It all happened so fast that he didn't know or even care whether those two animals were dead or just unconscious.

He didn't wait to find out but promptly took hold of his children and, clasping the sobbing Delfina to him protectively, abandoned the house with the intention of leaving them in the care of a neighbor.

Alarmed by the noise, a crowd of onlookers had gathered outside. Among them was a long-haired Indian who had been working in his shafts for a couple of months; a smart, reserved youth, he was doubtless on his way home from a local dance on his evening off. Larrea couldn't remember his name, but recognized him when he stepped forward resolutely.

"At your service, *patrón*, if I can be of any help."

With a jerk of his chin he gestured to the youth to wait a moment. Then he found a couple of women to take care of the three youngsters before concocting a story for the benefit of those present about how the miscreants had escaped through a window. Once he was sure that the crowd had begun to disperse, he looked for the youth in the darkness.

"Two men are inside—I don't know if they're alive or dead. Take them out through the backyard and deal with them."

"How about I just leave them to rest in peace outside the cemetery wall?"

"Don't lose another minute; jump to it."

This was how Santos Huesos Quevedo Calderón came into his life; from that moment on he ceased to toil belowground and became Larrea's shadow.

While the youth was completing his first task on that sinister dawn, Mauro Larrea rode off to see the man who by then was in charge of his accounts and his workforce. Rousing Elias Andrade from sleep, he charged him with two tasks: to return Delfina to her parents with a bag of silver as useless recompense for her defiled virtue, and to take his children away from the town that same night, never to return.

❧

"But surely Nicolás and Teresita's nuptial agreement still stands?"

Years later, the same Mariana who had clambered onto a cart, bruised and grubby in her nightdress, was now wearing a dress of embroidered silk over her swollen belly, plucking a cigarette out of her mother-of-pearl case.

Around them, the sounds of the house being dismantled continued: shouts and commotion, hurrying back and forth between the magnolias and garden fountains. Andrade was directing the servants: "Take everything out, pack it up, and get it ready. Lift your feet, you lazy oafs, put those cabinets on a different cart, and for the love of God be careful with those alabaster stands!" Even the pots and pans were removed. To be hocked or hawked—whatever it took to obtain enough quick money to start plugging the holes. As Andrade fired off orders, father and daughter went on conversing beneath the pale light filtering through the vines covering the pergola. She sat on a chair someone had rescued from the move, hands resting on her rounded belly. He stood.

"Alas, the engagement can be broken off by either party. Especially if there's a good reason."

Mariana was nurturing a life in her belly that was nigh on seven months old. The same length of time Nicolás had spent gestating before he was born prematurely in that country, Spain, to which they had never returned. The village in the north of Old Castile, and the dazzling smile of the young woman who had abandoned them, writhing on a straw pallet drenched with blood and sweat; the iron cross driven into the cemetery earth one fog-bound morning. The shock, bewilderment, and grief: fragments of memory that were seldom revisited.

Mexico City eventually became Mauro Larrea's universe, the place of his day-to-day existence, an anchor for all three of them. And Nico had changed from a skinny tadpole into a lively, impetuous youth—a born seducer whose ability to charm was equaled only by his recklessness and errors of judgment. As a result, his father had shipped him off to Europe to prevent him getting into any further scrapes before his marriage to one of the city's most eligible young ladies.

"I bumped into Teresita and her mother the other day at a stall near the Porta Coeli," Mariana went on. "They were purchasing Genoese velvet and Mechlin lace. It seems they've started preparing the wedding trousseau."

Nico's fiancée, Teresa Gorostiza Fagoaga, was descended from two aristocratic families dating back to the viceroyalty. She wasn't particularly pretty or charming, but she was extremely pleasant. And sensible. And head over heels in love. In Mauro Larrea's opinion, exactly what his wayward son needed: a commitment that would give him the security to settle down, while at the same time reaffirming his family's privileged place in society, which he himself had won through his hard effort. The vast new wealth of an affluent Spanish miner united with a reputed Creole family stretching back generations: What better alliance? Except that this auspicious plan had just been derailed: while the Gorostiza family had pedigree to spare, the vagaries of a distant war had caused the Larrea family's fortune to go up in smoke.

And, without any money to his name, or an account at the best tailor in Calle Cordobanes—with no satin upholstered carriage in which to arrive at the salons, parties, and dance halls; no spirited horse on which to show off in front of the young ladies; and lacking his father's tenacious character—Nicolás Larrea would be finished. A handsome, affable young man without profession or income: a dandy, a fop. The son of a bankrupt miner who had come and gone.

"The Gorostizas mustn't find out," muttered Larrea, gazing off into the distance. "Nor must your husband's family. This remains strictly between you and me. And Elias, naturally."

Ever since Elias Andrade whisked them away from Real de Catorce that dreadful night, the man who had been their father's accountant became the closest thing to family that Mariana and Nicolás had known. It was his idea to take them to Mexico City, to the place he hailed from, whose codes and customs he knew well. He proposed that Mariana attend El Colegio de las Vizcaínas while installing Nicolás in Calle de los Donceles with a relative, one of the last members of the illustrious Andrade family, whose former glory had crumbled to dust.

Oblivious to their conversation, the agent continued to reel off an unending list of commands: "Pack those Talavera plates properly in linen so they don't break. I want the mattresses rolled up; can't you see that rocking chair is about to fall over, idiots!" The servants, cowed by Don Elias's rage that morning when nothing was as normal, ran to and fro, trying to comply with his orders, until the house and gardens of what had once been a splendid country retreat looked more like a besieged garrison.

Mariana arched forward, clasping her back to relieve the discomfort caused by her heavily pregnant belly.

"Perhaps you should have been less ambitious. We might have been happier with less, with a simpler life."

He shook his head in disagreement. He had never wanted to emulate those celebrated miners from colonial times, determined to secure their position among the nobility by means of bribes and kickbacks to greedy viceroys and corrupt officials. The purchase of titles and conspicuous displays of wealth were common at that time. But Mauro Larrea belonged to a different era. He was made of sterner stuff and his ambition was simply to succeed on his own terms.

"By the time I was thirty I had triumphed in the silver business. And yet I hadn't toiled to accumulate all that wealth only to remain an unscrupulous, ignorant brute. I had no desire to live surrounded by savages in a luxurious mansion I only returned to for sleep, or to strut around bordellos in front of whores and braggarts, ignorant of how to behave or of world events. You and Nico were living in Mexico City by that time, and I didn't want you to be ashamed of me."

"But we never—"

"For years I suffered from nightmares. I never managed to rid myself completely of that dark dread that lingers in the soul when one has stared death in the face. Perhaps that's what drove me to seek retribution, to defy that mine that showed me its fangs, and almost left you and Nico orphans."

He inhaled the clean, dry air that had made Tacubaya a favorite retreat for the city's elites. They both knew they would never return to the splendid estate, where they had enjoyed so many wonderful moments: her debut in society, raucous gatherings of friends, conversations on cool evenings amid weeping willows, honeysuckle, and lime trees while people in the city were shriveling up from the heat. Just then they heard artillery fire, from which direction they couldn't tell, and yet no one gave a start; they had become accustomed to the sound during the tumultuous period of the Reform War. Seemingly oblivious to everything, Andrade was firing off another volley of cries: "Clear the main entrance, get out of the way! On the count of three, pick up that chest!"

Mauro Larrea finally emerged from beneath the shelter of the pergola and walked the short distance to the balustrade along the terrace. Mariana followed close behind, and together they contemplated the valley with its imposing volcanoes. She linked her arm through his, resting her head on his shoulder as if to say, *I'm with you no matter what.*

"It isn't easy, you know, to watch things from a distance after so many years spent struggling. The body craves other challenges, other adventures. You become ambitious, you don't want to stop."

"But this time it slipped through your fingers."

His daughter's voice contained no hint of reproach, only calm, honest reflection.

"That's what this game is all about, Mariana. I didn't make the rules. Sometimes you win, sometimes you lose. And the higher the stakes, the bigger the fall."

CHAPTER FIVE

❧

Mauro Larrea wasn't a man given to public displays of affection, neither with his children nor the women who happened to pass through his life. And yet that afternoon, upon their return to the city, he couldn't stop himself. After helping his daughter out of the carriage, he clasped her shoulders and planted a kiss on her forehead. Then he embraced her. Perhaps because seeing Mariana pregnant was something that he still couldn't get used to. Or because he was aware that their time together was running out.

Unlike on other occasions, he left his daughter's palatial residence on Calle Capuchinas without greeting her mother-in-law. Not because he wished to avoid the Countess of Colima, with her musty title and her tempestuous character, but simply because he had more pressing matters to attend to. It was urgent that he regroup; that he find a solution that would bolster him should news of his ruin leak out. So that he would not be left naked if his pitiful truth became common knowledge, the source of endless gossip. And no doubt celebrated by some, as was usually the case when others failed. The allotted time Tadeo Carrús had given him was already ticking by.

His next port of call was Café del Progreso, in the early evening. It was at its busiest then, before everyone left to dine with friends or family, and before it filled with nocturnal revelers who hadn't been invited anywhere better. The Café del Progreso was the fashionable place to be, patronized by important people such as himself, the wealthy and powerful. Except that the majority were still solvent.

He had not arranged to meet with anyone, although he was fairly certain about who he wanted to find there and who he preferred to avoid. His idea was to listen and to gather information. Possibly let slip the odd morsel himself, if the opportunity arose.

The city's most affluent men sat about on sofas and brocade armchairs, smoking and drinking black coffee as if their lives depended on it. They browsed newspapers, engaged in heated political debates, discussed business and Mexico's constant state of bankruptcy, world events, the laws that constantly changed depending on which of the nation's dignitaries was in power. Even love affairs, infighting, and society rumors, if they were considered of sufficient interest.

As Mauro Larrea entered, he sized up the situation with a swift glance around the room. The majority were regular customers, people he knew. He was relieved to see that his son's future father-in-law, Ernesto Gorostiza, was apparently not among them. So much the better, at least for now. In contrast, he was vexed not to see Eliseo Samper. Nobody knew more about current governmental policy on finance and loans than him, so sounding him out might have been a good option. Nor could he spot Aurelio Palencia, another prominent person, well versed in the intricacies of the banking system and its tentacles. On the other hand, he did make out the formidable figure of Mariano Asencio. *Let's start with him,* he thought.

With seeming nonchalance, he sauntered over to the table where Asencio was sitting, greeting others on the way, pausing from time to time, and ordering a coffee when approached by a waiter. Until he reached his objective.

"Larrea, old man!" boomed Asencio, his cigar still in his mouth. "Where have you been hiding?"

Since his return, the former Mexican ambassador to Washington had been involved in various business deals with his neighbors from the north, as well as anyone else who crossed his path. This, together with the fact that he was married to an American half his size, meant he was better placed than most to keep abreast of events across the border. As it happened, the civil war there was the subject of their current conversation.

"The South is fighting on its own territory, which gives them a huge advantage," someone at one end of the table declared when the discussion resumed. "They say their soldiers are fearless fighters and that morale among the troops is excellent."

"But they are far fewer in number," another offered.

"True. And they say that the Union can triple its recruits at the drop of a hat."

Mauro Larrea, who cared little about troop numbers or morale, feigned interest until he was able to drop in a timely question.

"How long do you think their war will last, Mariano?"

Larrea was perfectly aware that all indications suggested it would be a protracted and bloody conflict. Yet, in his desperation, he clung to the futile belief in a swift resolution. If the war ended soon, he could try to recover his equipment—or at least part of it. He could sail there, track down his property, hire a gringo lawyer, demand compensation . . .

"I fear it will drag on, my friend. For a good few years, certainly."

Muttered agreement could be heard around the table, as if they were all certain.

"The struggle is a lot more complicated than it appears from where we're sitting," added the giant. "This is a battle between two conflicting worlds, two philosophies of life, two radically different economies. They're fighting over something that goes much deeper than slavery.

What the southern states want is outright independence. Now we can honestly call those idiots the Disunited States of America."

They all chuckled at this: the wounds inflicted by the US invasion of Mexico less than two decades earlier were still raw, and nothing gave Mexicans greater pleasure than seeing their neighbors attacked head-on. However, none of this interested Mauro Larrea; the conversation had merely confirmed what he already knew, that his fight was lost. Never in his wildest dreams would he recover so much as a nut or bolt from his equipment, or the smallest portion of his investment.

Most of the others were preparing to leave, when suddenly Mariano Asencio clasped him by the elbow with a bearlike paw, holding him back.

"I've been hoping to bump into you for days, Larrea. But our paths never seem to cross."

"True, I've been busy recently. You know how it is."

Platitudes, but what else could he say? Fortunately, Asencio ignored them.

"There's something I want to ask you about," he said.

Only after the others had gone off in their different directions did the two men leave the café. Larrea's coachman was waiting for him with his carriage, but there appeared to be no carriage awaiting Asencio. Larrea instantly discovered the reason.

"That quack Van Kampen—the damned German physician whose gibberish my wife forces me to listen to—insists I need exercise. And so she has taken it upon herself to command my coachman not to wait for me anywhere."

"I can give you a lift wherever you wish . . ."

Asencio declined the offer with a wave of his hand.

"No chance: she caught me red-handed the other night arriving home in Teófilo Vallejo's landau, and you wouldn't believe the dressing-down she gave me. What possessed me to marry a blond Episcopalian from New Hampshire, I'll never know," he protested with a hint of irony. "But I'd be most grateful if you'd walk with me, my friend, assuming you're not in a hurry. I live on Calle de la Canoa; it won't take us long."

Larrea sent his coachman on ahead to the new address and, as the empty carriage drove away, prepared to listen to this man who had always aroused conflicting emotions in him.

Throngs of people of diverse complexions filled the streets, bustling to and fro as they did every day. Indigenous women carrying huge bunches of flowers, their infants wrapped in shawls on their backs; dark-skinned men balancing on their heads big earthenware jars brimming with sweetmeats or lard; beggars and soldiers, honest citizens and charlatans—all moving about ceaselessly from morning to night.

Asencio sailed through them like a galleon, using his cane to push aside vagabonds and lepers who moaned and whimpered as they begged for alms in the name of the holy blood of Jesus Christ Our Savior.

"A group of British investors has contacted me. They were all set to participate in a promising mining venture in the Appalachians, but the war has obviously put a stop to that. They're considering moving their capital here to Mexico and have asked me for information."

A joke. A bad joke played on him by fate was Mauro Larrea's first thought when he heard the news. This distant conflict had plunged him into poverty, and here was Asencio telling him that these Englishmen, former brothers of the gringos who were now so busily killing one another, were considering investing in the very sphere that his financial ruin was forcing him to relinquish.

Oblivious to the anxiety gnawing away at his companion, Asencio continued talking as he made his way, swaying from side to side like a pachyderm as he lashed out pitilessly with his cane, sweeping aside blind men with empty eye sockets and cripples boldly displaying their stumps and deformities.

"I tried to persuade them that now isn't the time to invest a guinea in Mexico," he snorted. "Despite the assurances given by the various governments in recent years to attract foreign investors."

"Their fellow countrymen from the Company of Merchant Adventurers already tried that in Real del Monte and Pachuca," observed Larrea, doing his best to sound natural despite the anguish assailing him. "But they couldn't get used to the Mexican way of working, and refused to pay their share . . ."

"They're fully aware of that," Asencio cut in. "But apparently they're better prepared now. The machinery is in Southampton just waiting to be loaded. If they shipped it over here, it would be a godsend for me, because I could use the same vessel to transport my merchandise to England. All they need are good fishing grounds, if you'll forgive the expression—and pardon my ignorance of your business. A good mine that hasn't been exploited recently, they say, but with guaranteed potential."

Larrea had to stifle a sardonic, bitter laugh. Las Tres Lunas, his dream project, was exactly what those damned English sons of bitches were looking for without even knowing it.

"I promised them I'd make some inquiries," his gigantic companion continued. "And it occurred to me to ask you. Steering clear of any conflict of interest, naturally."

The biggest irony of all, Larrea reflected, was that, according to the laws governing mining concessions, Las Tres Lunas didn't actually belong to him. Had that been the case, he could have sold or leased it to the English investors for a significant sum. Or invited Asencio to be his partner in this hypothetical future venture. However, he owned no title deeds to the mine, since this was prohibited by the old bylaws dating back to the time of the viceroyalty, which were still valid. What he had was a temporary concession, entitling him to take possession of and exploit the mine. However, in accordance with the same law, unless he started to do that soon, the concession could be revoked, leaving the way clear for whoever else showed interest in it.

Asencio seized his arm once more, this time to suggest they stop on a corner by an old street vendor. On a filthy-looking brazier, a woman was heating up the tortillas she had kneaded in her bony hands with their long, black fingernails. From among the hordes of food vendors lining the streets, he couldn't have chosen a more wretched stall had he done so deliberately.

"That idiot Van Kampen has also managed to persuade my wife that I should eat less. Between the two of them they're starving me to death." Asencio promptly rummaged in his waistcoat pocket for a few pesos. "I'd have done better to marry a nice Mexican doña, the kind who always has the table laid when you get home. How about a pork taco, my friend? Or a nice corn tortilla dripping with lard?"

They continued on their way, Asencio staving off the beggars with admirable dexterity even as he wolfed down the food he had bought and went on talking nonstop, his shirtfront becoming soiled with specks of grease.

"I imagine this war must also be affecting you negatively," Mauro Larrea then ventured. "With the Confederate ports in the south blockaded by the Union."

"On the contrary, my dear man," Asencio replied. "Due to the blockade, the southern states are beginning to trade through the port of Matamoros, where I have some business interests. And since the North no longer buys the South's cotton, which was the main commerce between them, I've started to provide the Yankees with that, too; I have a few plantations up there that I bought for next to nothing before the hostilities broke out."

With this, he swallowed the last morsel of his third taco and gave a loud belch. "Pardon me," he added perfunctorily.

"So, returning to the matter at hand. What would you advise me to tell the subjects of Her Gracious Majesty? They're expecting to hear from me soon, and are champing at the bit. Naturally, for my part, I'll keep looking into things. You must know Ovidio Calleja, the superintendent at the Mining Board. He owes me a few favors. I'll see what he has to say. That rascal never misses a trick, especially if there's something in it for him. But I'd appreciate your opinion. Between you and me, silver mining is still a safe investment, isn't it?"

"I wouldn't be so sure about that." Larrea was thinking on his feet. "There are more and more problems. The costs often outweigh the profits: the price of quicksilver and gunpowder, which are bought by the ton, changes every day. Banditry is rife, to the point where we are having to pay army patrols to escort the shipments. There is less and less quality silver left in the ground, and the workers are becoming more and more belligerent . . ."

This wasn't a lie, simply an exaggeration. These problems were nothing new. Larrea had been dealing with them for years, ever since he entered that world.

"In fact," he added, embellishing as he went along, "I myself am considering investing abroad."

"Really? Where?" said Asencio with unabashed curiosity. Besides his knowledge of North American affairs, his impetuous opinions, and the extravagant diversity of his businesses, the big man was also known for being quick to seize any opportunity that came his way.

Mauro Larrea had never been duplicitous; he was a straight talker. And yet, finding himself in a tight corner, he had no choice but to hurriedly invent a pack of lies based on snippets of conversation picked up here and there.

"Nothing concrete. I'm looking into several possibilities. I might choose to go south and invest in indigo plantations in Guatemala. An old associate of mine has also suggested doing something related to cacao in Caracas. And then there's—"

At that instant, the weight of Asencio's leaden paw on his arm brought Larrea to a sudden stop.

"If yours truly here had as much capital as you, Mauro, do you know what I'd do?"

And without waiting for a reply, the former ambassador drew his mouth reeking of onion, chili, and pork close to Larrea's ear and muttered a few words that gave the latter pause for thought.

CHAPTER SIX

A ndrade was waiting for him, with his shiny bald pate and his spectacles perched on his nose, in front of a mound of documents.

"Damned opportunist," Larrea muttered, slamming the door behind him as he entered his home.

His agent looked up from the accounts he was going over.

"I hope you aren't referring to me."

"I'm talking about Mariano Asencio."

"The big fellow?"

"The big pirate!"

"Nothing new under the sun."

"He's negotiating with a group of Englishmen, a company of adventurers eager to invest wherever he tells them. They are solvent and have fresh capital, and won't want to risk wasting their time exploiting untouched mines. That devil knows they'll follow his advice. He'll move heaven and earth to offer them something tempting, ensuring himself a large slice of the pie."

"Undoubtedly."

"He's just told me he plans to start by sniffing around at the Mining Board Office, where he'll find no end of projects."

"Most of which are too trifling to suit these people's ambitions. Excepting . . ."

"Excepting ours."

"Which means . . ."

"That as soon as Asencio sees we have started work at Las Tres Lunas, he'll put them on our trail."

"And wherever you've sniffed out the possibility of finding silver, they'll be there like a shot."

The silence grew tense, like a catapult ready to be fired. Andrade was the one who broke it.

"The worst of it is that they'd be acting within the law, because we've overrun the time limits on the concession," he said somberly.

"By a lot."

"And that means Las Tres Lunas can be declared . . ."

They uttered the two sinister words in unison:

"Abandoned and available."

In mining terms, this jargon did not bode well, since if within a given time works did not commence, or were suspended for lengthy periods without reasonable grounds, anyone could apply for a fresh concession that allowed them to take possession of the mining site from its previous owners.

"The same as when the King of Spain's permission was required to install a goddamned winch on royal properties," muttered Andrade.

Mauro Larrea closed his eyes for a few seconds, pressing his fingertips against his eyelids. In the momentary darkness an image appeared of the eleven folios stamped with the Mining Board Office seal that he had signed and deposited in the archive. In accordance with regulations, they contained his application for an official concession to exploit the abandoned Tres Lunas mine, together with detailed plans of how he would go about it: the exact surface area and the direction in which he proposed to explore, the depth, the shafts he intended to open.

As though reading his thoughts, Andrade's lips moved silently: "God help us . . ."

One group of foreigners had already precipitated Larrea into bankruptcy by making off with his machinery. Now, unless he found a quick solution, others were poised to steal his ideas as well as his know-how, his last possibility for redemption if one day the tables turned in his favor.

The two men nodded silently as their eyes met with the same decision floating through their minds. They must at all costs retrieve their application from the archive to prevent it from falling into the hands of Asencio or the English investors. But they would have to be extremely careful not to arouse any suspicions in doing so.

They resumed their conversation that evening when Andrade returned after making a few inquiries. He brought Larrea up to date at the billiard table, where the latter had spent a couple of hours dueling with himself: the only way to calm his demons while he made certain decisions.

"Calleja is away for several weeks on his annual visit to the regional offices."

Ovidio Calleja, the superintendent of the Mining Board, was an old acquaintance of theirs in the mining business. Years ago, they had clashed with him more than once over boundary lines between mines, shipments of quicksilver, and the like. Calleja never emerged the winner from these encounters, and so, despite the intervening years, Andrade and Larrea were aware that their former adversary still bore them a grudge. They certainly couldn't expect any favors from him.

Following a spate of unfortunate investments, Calleja had given up mining before finally securing his current post. Although he didn't command a large salary, a lack of scruples allowed him to gain certain perquisites from the job.

"Perhaps his absence will work in our favor," Andrade reflected.

"If he knew we wanted to retrieve our application, he might make up some excuse to delay giving it back while he had a notary make a copy, or jot down the details to keep for himself."

"Or to share with anyone who expressed interest."

"Undoubtedly," replied Andrade, lifting to his lips the half-finished glass of brandy his friend had left on the edge of the table. He didn't ask Larrea's permission. He didn't have to.

Their two minds were working as one. Frantically.

"We could take advantage of his absence to bribe one of his minions," said Larrea. "The skinny fellow with the wispy beard, for example, or the one with the tinted spectacles. Request that they discreetly remove our application from the file, entice them with the offer of a choice morsel: a valuable painting, perhaps, or a pair of solid silver candlesticks, or two fine mares, before we've sold everything but the clothes on our backs . . ."

Andrade appeared to focus all his attention on replacing the crystal goblet exactly on the moist circle on the mahogany where it had stood moments before.

"Those two clerks you mentioned are the only ones who work for Calleja. He has them trained like a couple of performing monkeys, and they never do anything behind his back. They wouldn't dare bite the hand that feeds them. Unless you offered them the treasure of Montezuma, which I find highly unlikely, they stand to gain more from remaining loyal to their superior."

Larrea didn't need to ask how his agent had come by this information: within the obscure workings of the city's bureaucracy, it was possible to find out anything if one asked the right questions.

"In any event, let's wait until tomorrow," Larrea said finally. "Meanwhile, there's something else Mariano Asencio told me that I'd like you to know."

With that, he repeated to Andrade the last piece of advice to issue from the giant's mouth, adding that he thought this might not be such a bad solution after all.

As was his custom when he observed his friend walking in darkness along the edge of a precipice, Andrade took out his handkerchief and raised it to his brow. He had broken out in a sweat.

◆

Not wishing to betray any urgency, they arrived at the Palacio de Minería that housed the Mining Board Office at around half past eleven the next morning. As if they just happened to be passing the imposing edifice where the archive was kept, or had found an unexpected free moment during their busy schedule. Armed with the usual paper scrolls that were a feature of their trade, together with a folder containing dozens of supposed documents, they appeared self-assured and debonair in their English wool frock coats and freshly pressed ties, each sporting a top hat, which they removed upon entering. The way they had looked when lady luck was still favoring them.

Few mining projects were being registered in those days, and so the place was deserted. They encountered only the two clerks they had expected to find, immersed in their work, protected from ink spots and blotting powder by muslin sleeves, surrounded by floor-to-ceiling glass cabinets. Crammed into these were thousands of mostly yellowing folders, documents, and deeds, which offered to anyone with the patience to read them a detailed description of the lengthy history of Mexican mining from colonial times to the present day. The two visitors could see at a glance that the cabinets were securely locked.

They greeted the two clerks with the grudging familiarity that characterized their customary visits to the mining office at least twice a year. Although they didn't usually have actual dealings with the clerks, but rather with Ovidio Calleja, who treated them with an exaggerated courtesy that betrayed his open distaste.

The two clerks stood up to greet them.

"The superintendent isn't here."

Larrea and his agent made a show of being put out.

"Perhaps we can be of some assistance, gentlemen . . ."

"I suppose so: clearly, Don Ovidio places his utmost trust in you, and I'm sure you know this office as well, if not better, than he does."

Andrade cast the first hook, using flattery as bait, while Larrea reeled them in.

"We need to consult a document regarding a mining claim. It's in my name, Mauro Larrea. I have a receipt here with the archive number, if that makes it easier to find."

The taller of the two clerks, the one with tinted spectacles, cleared his throat. The other, the small, skinny one, clasped his hands behind his back and lowered his gaze.

A few awkward seconds elapsed, during which only the pendulum of the clock above the absent superintendent's desk could be heard.

The first clerk cleared his throat once more, then uttered the words they were by now expecting to hear.

"With the utmost regret, gentlemen, I'm afraid that won't be possible."

The two others feigned surprise, Andrade arching an eyebrow, Larrea knitting his brow.

"How can that be, Don Mónico?"

The taller employee shrugged with an air of powerlessness.

"The superintendent's orders."

"I find that hard to believe," Andrade retorted pompously.

The skinny man spoke up in defense of his colleague:

"Orders we have no choice but to obey, gentlemen. Why, we don't even have any keys at our disposal."

Not so much as a quill pen could be moved in that office without Ovidio Calleja's express authorization, and his minions weren't prepared to budge from that practice, not even at gunpoint.

What do we do now? the two men wondered silently. They had no other plan, and so their only option was to make a humiliating retreat. Empty-handed. Good Lord, at times events took such a complicated turn that anyone might think an emissary of the devil himself was manipulating them at his whim.

They were still debating whether to insist or to accept defeat, when they heard a door creak at the far end of the room. Grateful for a momentary break in the tension, all four pairs of eyes moved toward it as though drawn by a magnet. No sooner had it started to open than three cats slipped into the office as rapidly as a gust of wind. Then the hem of a mustard-colored skirt appeared, until finally the door swung open and a woman of indeterminate age entered. Neither young nor old; neither pretty nor ugly.

Andrade took a step forward, his face contorting into a fox-like grin that concealed his enormous relief at having found an unexpected excuse to delay their departure.

"What a pleasure it is to see you, Señorita Calleja."

For his part, Mauro Larrea stifled the urge to remark sarcastically to his friend: *You* have *done your homework well, sonofabitch.* Not only had Andrade discovered the names of Calleja's subordinates, he had also found out there was a daughter.

It was clear from the puzzled expression on the newcomer's face that she hadn't expected to find anyone else there at that hour. Doubtless she had popped in for a moment from the apartments the superintendent and his family occupied in the same building. Her hair had been left unpinned, and she was not dressed to go out.

In spite of this she had no choice but to return the courtesy, and she greeted them somewhat sheepishly.

Andrade took another two steps forward.

"Don Mónico and Don Severino were just informing us of your esteemed father's absence."

She had a round face and wore her hair pulled back in a bun. She was well into her thirties, and possessed a rather ungainly body, encased in a frumpy day dress with a pale stiff collar. A woman like hundreds of others, who make little impression when a man's eye alights on them in the street, but who arouse neither dislike or disgust. This was what they saw when they looked at Fausta Calleja: a plain woman.

"Yes, my father's away on a trip," she replied. "Although we're expecting him back soon. Indeed, I came to ask whether he has sent word confirming this."

"We still haven't heard anything, Señorita Fausta," replied the clerk with the tinted glasses. "No word has arrived."

Apart from the steps Andrade had taken toward the superintendent's daughter, all of them stood motionless, as though nailed to the wooden floor, while the cats moved freely between the legs of the furniture as well as those of the two clerks. One, a flame-red ginger tom, leapt up onto one of the desks, casually treading over papers and documents.

Once again, it was Andrade who picked up the thread of conversation.

"And your esteemed mother, how is her health these days?"

Had it not been for the enormity of the situation he faced, Mauro Larrea would have burst into a peal of laughter. *Where did you get this sudden interest in the family of a man who'd rather cut off his ear than lend us a hand, you old devil?*

Naturally, the daughter was oblivious to the deceitful nature of his question.

"She's a lot better, thank you, Señor . . ."

"Andrade, Elias Andrade, at your disposal. I am a devoted friend of your father, as is this other gentleman, Don Mauro Larrea, a prominent mine owner, and widower, whom I am privileged to introduce to you. A man whose honor, kindness, and decency I would stake my life on."

Have you lost your mind, brother? What are you trying to achieve with this prose worthy of a romantic novel? Why are you misleading this poor woman as to our relations with her father, revealing details of my private life, and lavishing me with ridiculous praise?

No sooner had his eyes met those of Fausta Calleja than he realized what his friend was up to. He could read it in her gaze, the intense scrutiny she gave to his figure, his clothes, his face, his demeanor. *Crafty sonofabitch. So you discovered that Calleja's daughter was a spinster, and all at once it occurred to you to offer me up on a platter as a potential suitor in a desperate bid to improve matters.*

"We are truly pleased to hear that your mother is feeling better, Señorita. What was ailing her, if I might be so bold as to ask?"

Employing the same pompous rhetoric, Andrade resumed the absurd conversation where he had left off. Fausta quickly averted her eyes from Larrea like someone caught in the act.

"A bad cold, from which she is now fully recovered, thank heavens."

"Let's hope to God it does not return."

"Indeed, Señor."

"And . . . er . . . is she well enough to receive visitors?"

"Indeed; why, only this morning some of her women friends came by."

"And . . . er . . . do you think she might also agree to receive a visit from your humble servant? Accompanied by Señor Larrea, of course."

It was Larrea who now seized the initiative. *Oh, well,* he told himself. *There's too much at stake for any scruples.* Of the four accursed months he'd been allotted to revive his fortunes, he had already wasted two days. If the two clerks refused to be cajoled into handing over the document, it was possible the wife or daughter could come to their aid.

Unabashed, he mustered all his poise and directed a forceful, lingering gaze to the superintendent's daughter.

Startled, she lowered her eyes. The flame-red tomcat was rubbing itself affectionately against the folds of her skirt, and she stooped to pick him up. Cradling him in her arms, she petted his nose as she muttered something to him under her breath.

As they awaited her reply, the two friends' courteous restraint belied the ceaseless workings of their brains as voices hammered inside their heads: *Come on, come on, for God's sake, woman, say yes!*

At last she stooped to put down the cat. As she straightened up, her cheeks faintly flushed, she uttered the words they were so desperate to hear.

"Gentlemen, you are welcome to visit our humble abode at your convenience."

CHAPTER SEVEN

⤞

Mother and daughter were halfway through their lunchtime meal of beef stew when they received the sumptuous visiting card. Señores Larrea and Andrade announced their arrival that very evening at six o'clock.

Two hours later, her finest ornaments dotted about the living room, the superintendent's wife clasped the envelope to her ample bosom for the umpteenth time. Could it possibly be true . . . ?

"You wouldn't believe the way he looked at me, Mama. You wouldn't believe it."

Her daughter's words when she came back in a daze from the office were still resounding in Doña Hilaria's ears.

"Moreover, he's a widower. And so good-looking."

"And he has money, my girl. Money."

But cautiousness obliged her to rein in her hopes. Since her husband had taken up his present position, scarcely a week went by without some proposal or other arriving at their door: invitations to luncheons and dinners, a huge tray of pastries, or a small bag of gold coins. Only a few months ago, to her surprise (pleasant, she had to admit), they were presented with a carriage. All in exchange for her husband, among the dozens of papers that passed through his hands daily, simply stamping or erasing the odd date, mislaying a document, or turning a blind eye when he should have been paying attention.

That was why his wife's initial response was to be skeptical.

"But are you really certain, daughter, that he looked at you in *that* way?"

"As sure as I am that night follows day, Mama. At my eyes first. And then . . ."

She entwined her fingers, modestly.

"And then he looked at me the way . . . the way a real man looks at a woman."

Doña Hilaria remained unconvinced. *He's up to something*, she pondered. *Why else would a man like Mauro Larrea give Fausta a second look?* According to her husband, the man was a force to be reckoned with. He and his faithful friend Andrade had been together for years, and drooled like wolves when they smelled an opportunity. She also knew that he moved with ease in the most distinguished circles, among the sophisticated upper classes to which, alas, the Calleja family did not belong. Doubtless there were plenty of candidates among those circles willing to rescue him from widowerhood. No, if Mauro Larrea was making eyes at her daughter, she was sure he must be after something. Something only her husband could provide him with. *That Spanish bastard*, her Ovidio would say whenever his name came up. Like a hungry predator, he could smell a good deal a mile off. And nothing escaped him when he went in for the kill.

But . . . what if . . . She felt giddy with doubt as she rummaged in the wooden chest for the most suitable tablecloth. The Scottish linen one with the cross-stitch edging? Or the one with the cutwork embroidery? What did it matter if his only aim was to further his own interests? she reflected. What were a few favors in exchange for her daughter to have lifelong security and a virile body in her humdrum life and her frigid bed? A husband, for heaven's sake! At this late stage!

She would find a way to persuade her Ovidio to forget his clashes with Larrea. Which weren't negligible, she recalled as she polished a silver spoon. Indeed, the poor man had developed terrible ulcers and even coughed up blood during those tense disputes over mines, or shipments of quicksilver, or whatever it was. In any event, that was all in the past, she mumbled to herself as she lifted the lid off the sugar bowl they used on special occasions. They had to seize the opportunity while Ovidio was away. It would be easier to convince him if the affair prospered. What was done was done.

While Doña Hilaria was going over all this in her mind, Fausta, a mixture of almond paste and barley water smeared on her face to bleach her skin, gave instructions to the kitchen maids on how to iron the muslin on her finest dress. A few blocks farther south in the city, oblivious to the preparations taking place in his honor, Mauro Larrea was shut away in his study wearing neither frock coat nor tie. Sunk in an armchair, cigar clasped between his fingers, he had deliberately thrust aside all thoughts of the afternoon tea that awaited them and was mulling obsessively over the closing moments of his encounter with Mariano Asencio the previous day.

His prevailing memory was of the man's gestures, his booming voice, and the reek of chili and pork; he could almost feel once again the weight of the man's paw falling on his arm. "If yours truly here had as much capital as you, do you know what I'd do?" That was the question posed by the colossus, who had supplied the answer himself: the name composed of four letters, which was still going around in Larrea's head. The same possibility he had discussed with Andrade the night before. True, Asencio was an opportunist, capable of selling his own father for a plate of beans, but he knew how to fight for his own interests wherever he smelled a profit. *What if Mariano is right?* Larrea murmured to himself for the umpteenth time, puffing on his half-smoked cigar. *What if my fate lies there?*

The sound of knuckles rapping on wood brought him back to reality. The door opened at once.

By then he had made his decision.

"Why are you still lounging in your shirtsleeves, smoking?" Andrade roared when he saw him.

It was six o'clock on the dot when they stepped out of the carriage on Calle San Andrés, around the corner from the vast façade of the palace that housed the Mining Board.

A servant was waiting for them at the main gate, which was open. He broke off his animated exchange with the doorman as he saw them approach, and steered them past the majestic staircase, across the central courtyard, to the west wing. Although the two men were accustomed to finding their way around the public corridors of the labyrinthine place, they had never ventured into its private apartments, and would have been lost without their guide. The young indigenous lad glided over the smooth floor, snakelike in his bare feet, while in their English ankle boots the two men's swift, rhythmical steps echoed loudly on the gray flagstones.

The building was practically deserted at that time of evening. The students, whose lectures on underground physics and the chemistry of minerals had finished by then, were doubtless flirting with young ladies in nearby Alameda Central Park. Their professors and other staff members would be getting on with their own lives, having finished their working day, and both Larrea and Andrade were relieved not to bump into the rector or vice-rector, either.

"Don Florian could have helped us out if he were still here."

However, faced with the new secular airs circulating through Mexico, the chaplain, an amusingly duplicitous old curmudgeon they knew from their days at Real de Catorce, had long since hung up his cassock.

"Perhaps we should have brought the girl a gift" was the next thing Mauro Larrea said between gritted teeth as they walked along an empty corridor.

"Such as?"

"How should I know, compadre?" There was a tone of exasperation in his voice, and more than a hint of indifference. "Camelias, or sweets, or a book of poetry."

"Poetry? You?" Andrade stifled a sarcastic laugh. "Too late," he said in a hushed tone. "I think we're almost there: be on your best behavior."

A small staircase led them up to a mezzanine floor, where they were confronted by a row of doors belonging to the staff apartments. The third one on the left was open a crack, and a young indigenous girl with shiny braids emerged to show them into the living room.

"Good afternoon, dear friends."

In her role of convalescent, Señora Calleja did not get up from her capacious armchair. Dressed in black, with a modest string of pearls about her neck, she limited herself to extending a hand, which both men kissed ceremoniously. Two steps behind her stood Fausta, fingers clasped amid the folds of a plain-looking dress that was still warm from the smoothing iron.

The greetings concluded, they sat down in strategic positions decided upon beforehand by Doña Hilaria.

"Don Elias, you come over here, next to me," she said, patting the arm of a nearby chair. "And, if you will, Señor Larrea, install yourself on the chaise longue." Needless to say, Fausta followed suit, perching on its right-hand corner.

A swift glance about them was enough for the two men to assess the scene: a discreetly furnished room that was neither spacious nor high-ceilinged but that, here and there, betrayed a hint of opulence: a pair of cut-glass cornucopias on a cedar-wood stand, a splendid alabaster vase ostentatiously placed. There was even a piano, shiny as a young bride. Both men could guess the source of these trappings. Tokens of gratitude in exchange for favors granted by Señor Calleja: turning a blind eye, acting as intermediary, passing on information that as super-intendent he was entrusted not to divulge.

As was to be expected, the conversation that ensued was of a trivial nature. Doña Hilaria provided a blow-by-blow account of her current state of health while the two men pretended to be interested, each casting sidelong glances at the wall clock. It was in citronella marquetry and undeniably splendid, doubtless another reward for favors granted. The clock went on chiming every quarter hour as the elaborate litany of symptoms and remedies floated interminably through the air, reminding them that time was passing and they were getting nowhere. After finishing the enumeration of her ailments, Doña Hilaria continued to monopolize the conversation by giving detailed accounts of the most sensational local news stories, including the unsolved crime at the Lagunilla Bridge and a recent spate of robberies in the Porta Coeli market.

The early evening drained away in these fascinating perambulations until the clock chimed a quarter past seven. Mauro Larrea, unable to conceal his irritation at such empty chatter, started to bounce his right leg from side to side as if it were on a spring. Andrade, on the verge of breaking into a sweat, retrieved his handkerchief from his top pocket.

At that moment, as though in passing, Doña Hilaria decided finally to get to the point.

"But let's stop discussing such irrelevancies. Tell us, gentlemen, what plans do you have in the offing?"

Before his agent had a chance to come out with one of his intricate deceptions, Larrea said:

"A trip."

The two women gazed at him as one while Andrade, who was now perspiring freely, wiped his shiny bald head with his handkerchief.

"Soon, although I don't know the exact date."

"A long trip?" inquired Fausta, a catch in her voice.

Prevented by her mother's verbosity, she had barely managed to get a word in until then. Mauro Larrea took the opportunity to gaze at her as he replied, attempting to give his words an optimistic ring:

"I trust not, I'm going away on business."

She gave a relieved smile, which only faintly illuminated her plain face. Larrea felt a pang of remorse.

Then Doña Hilaria, unable to resist seizing the reins of the conversation once more, blurted out:

"And where is this trip taking you, Don Mauro, if you don't mind my asking?"

The noise of the cup, teaspoon, and saucer crashing to the floor brought the conversation to an abrupt conclusion. Thick brown splotches of chocolate covered the tablecloth as well as Andrade's right trouser leg.

"Goodness, how clumsy of me!"

Although it had all been a subterfuge to prevent his friend from talking, Andrade made every effort to sound sincere.

"Forgive me, Señora, I'm a dreadful oaf."

The aftermath of the staged mishap dragged on for a few long moments: Andrade stooped to retrieve the pieces of broken crockery from beneath the table despite the lady of the house's protestations, then rubbed furiously at his trouser leg with a napkin to try to remove the stain while Doña Hilaria told him he was only making it worse.

"Fausta, call Luciana and tell her to bring a bucket of water and some lemon juice."

But Fausta, taking advantage of the sudden commotion, and annoyed by her mother's insistence on stealing the limelight, had devised a strategy of her own. She would have liked to bawl at her: *They came here to see me, Mother; let me enjoy my moment of glory,* but instead she simply pretended not to hear her mother's command and leaned over to pick up a piece of broken porcelain that had landed at her feet. While Mauro Larrea was wearily contemplating the ludicrous tug-of-war between the lady of the house and his agent over the spilled chocolate, Fausta, still leaning over, her hands hidden by the folds of her dress, purposefully slid the sharp edge of a piece of cup across the tip of her thumb.

"Goodness gracious, I've cut myself," she whispered, sitting up straight.

Only Larrea, sharing the same chaise longue, appeared to hear her. He turned his attention to her, leaving the other two engrossed in their battle with the stains.

She showed him her thumb.

"It's bleeding," she said.

Indeed it was. A little—just enough to let a single drop fall onto the rug.

Concerned, Larrea fumbled in his pocket for a handkerchief.

"Please, allow me . . ."

He clasped her small, limp hand, carefully bandaged her thumb with its blunt nail, and squeezed it gently.

"Keep pressing; the bleeding will stop in no time."

He could sense that Andrade was watching out of the corner of his eye, and it came as no surprise when he prolonged his absurd discussion with Doña Hilaria to divert her attention away from them. "So, you'd advise against rubbing the fabric?" Larrea heard Andrade say, as though household chores and garment care were of supreme concern to him. It was all Larrea could do to stop himself from letting out a loud guffaw.

"I've heard that saliva is the best cure."

It was Fausta speaking again.

"To stem the bleeding, I mean."

Her voice sounded calm. Calm but firm, resolute.

My God, he thought, seeing her intention. By then she had loosened the handkerchief around her thumb and, like Salome proffering John the Baptist's severed head on a platter, held it out to him.

He had no choice but to place it in his mouth. They were running out of time and Andrade's acting skills had reached their limit. Whether as a way of rebelling against her mother's exuberant verbosity or because she wanted proof of Larrea's desire for her as a woman, Fausta needed this contact with his hands and mouth, a sensual encounter however fleeting. He knew he couldn't disappoint her.

And so, pressing his lips to her thumb, he ran his tongue over the wound. He looked up to see her eyes half closed. He paused for a few seconds, then repeated the action. A stifled groan rose in her throat. *You're an utter cad,* an accusatory voice rang out somewhere in his conscience. Ignoring it, he put the tip of her thumb between his lips and once again ran his moist tongue over the wound.

"I hope that helps," he said in a low murmur, releasing her hand.

Before she had time to respond, a loud cough from Andrade made them turn around. Doña Hilaria was contemplating them with a frown, as if to say: *What is afoot? What have I missed?*

Night was closing in, and there was little more they could glean from that wasted evening.

"We shan't intrude on you a moment longer," Larrea said, accepting defeat.

"Thank you for the splendid tea: you've been most hospitable," added Andrade.

While the two men let out a string of meaningless pleasantries, the mother insisted they prolong their visit. They wondered what the devil they should do next.

Unsurprisingly, the superintendent's wife took matters into her own hands.

"My husband is on the point of concluding his business in Taxco," she said with deliberate slowness as she lifted herself with some difficulty out of her armchair. "We found out only this afternoon that he will be returning to Mexico City in three, possibly four days at the very latest."

This was an obvious warning, or so they understood it. *Hurry up, gentlemen*, she seemed to be saying. *If you don't wish the superintendent to send you packing, you'd better hurry up and make your intentions toward his daughter clear before he is able to interfere.*

A dark hallway led them to the front door of the apartment, where once more Andrade and Doña Hilaria exchanged empty phrases.

Just as they were about to step out onto the landing, the ginger tomcat approached them, mewling, from one end of the corridor. Fausta made to pick him up with the same affection as she had that morning. *This is your last chance, compadre*, Larrea told himself as he saw her stoop. He quickly imitated her gesture as though motivated by a keen desire to stroke the cat. And in that position, both half crouching, he whispered in her ear.

"I'll come again tomorrow night, when everyone is asleep. Send me a note telling me how to get in."

CHAPTER EIGHT

᪥

Twenty-four hours after he had left the Callejas' apartment, Mauro Larrea was raising his glass and preparing to announce his plans to a carefully selected audience. Exactly the opposite of what his agent and prudence advised.

"My dear Countess, my dear children, dear friends . . ."

The stage in the dining room was set to perfection: two dozen lights from the ceiling chandelier shone onto the silver and crystal ware, the wines had been decanted, the elaborate French meal was about to be served up.

"Dear Countess, my dear children, dear friends," he resumed. "The reason I have asked you here tonight is because I wish to share with you a pleasant piece of news."

As host he was sitting at the head of the table. Facing him at the far end, dressed in black, proud and imposing as ever, sat his daughter's mother-in-law, the magnificent Countess of Colima. In reality, she was no longer a countess, nor could she claim any aristocratic title in the Mexican republic, and yet she was determined to be known in this way. To his right sat Mariana, her husband, Alonso, and Andrade. On his left, two wealthy, distinguished acquaintances accompanied by their wives, expert gossipmongers in Mexico City high society. Exactly what Larrea required.

"As you all know, the situation in this country is far from reassuring to businessmen like myself."

This wasn't entirely untrue; he was simply adapting the facts to suit his own interests. There was no doubt that measures introduced by the Liberals in recent years had been detrimental to the old Creole nobility, the landowning elites, and some businessmen. But not those who knew how to adapt. Several had even developed a flair for turning the stormy political situation to their advantage, procuring generous rewards and public contracts. This wasn't so in exactly Mauro Larrea's case, although he hadn't done at all badly. Nor was he opposed to current Liberal measures, although he preferred to be cautious and avoid taking sides in matters that inflamed people's tempers because of what could ensue.

"The constant unrest forces us to reconsider our options . . ."

"That atheist President Juárez will be the ruin of us!" cried the countess, interrupting him. "That Zapotec devil is leading this nation toward damnation!"

Dangling from her ears, an impressive pair of diamond earrings swung furiously in rhythm to her outburst, glinting in the light of the candles. The wives of the other male guests nodded and made approving noises.

The countess went on angrily:

"Where did that savage learn to sit at a table and eat with a spoon, to wear shoes, and speak in Spanish? Why, in a seminary, of course! And now he spouts all this nonsense about civil marriage, seizing Church property, expelling monks and nuns from their convents! God help us, where will this all end!"

"Mama, please," Alonso chided her long-sufferingly, all too accustomed to her inappropriate outbursts.

The countess grudgingly fell silent, then raised her napkin to her mouth and muttered a few more angry remarks into the square of linen that none of them could hear.

"Thank you, dear Úrsula," Larrea resumed calmly. He was well enough acquainted with the old lady not to be shocked by her vehement interruptions. "As I was saying, without needing to discuss any deeper political issues," he added tactfully, "I wish to announce that, after giving the matter much reflection, I've decided to embark on new business ventures beyond the borders of our republic."

An astonished murmur issued from the mouths of most of the company, with the exception of Andrade and Mariana, for whom this was not news. He had told his daughter about it that very morning as the two of them rode along Paseo de Bucareli in the open-topped carriage she liked to travel in. The young woman's face had shown surprise, followed by comprehension and approval, which she blessed with a smile. "It's for the best," she said. "I know you'll succeed." Then she caressed her belly, as if with the heat from her hands she wished to transmit to her unborn infant the serenity she was feigning for her father's sake. Her many misgivings she kept to herself.

"My dear Countess, my dear children, dear friends . . ." Larrea repeated for the third time, pausing deliberately for dramatic effect. "After considering at length the various options, I've decided to move all my investments to Cuba."

The murmurs became loud declarations, and the astonishment approval. The countess gave a mocking laugh.

"Well done, Mauro!" she howled, banging the table with her fist. "Go to the colonies of the mother country! Return to Spain's dominions, where law and order still rule, where you can respect our queen, and the right people are in power!"

Expressions of surprise, applause, and congratulation flew around the room. Larrea exchanged a fleeting glance with his daughter. They both knew he still had a long way to go. Nothing had been remedied yet. This was merely a first step.

"Cuba is full of opportunities, my dear fellow," said Salvador Leal, a textile magnate. "You've made a wise choice."

"If I could persuade my brothers to sell our estates, I would follow you, surely," added Enrique Camino, who owned vast grain farms.

The conversation continued in the drawing room, where liqueurs and coffee were served, and speculation and predictions succeeded one another until midnight. Without lowering his guard for an instant, Larrea attended to his guests with his usual affability, fielding dozens of questions with vague assertions. Yes, of course, he had liquidated the majority of his assets; yes, naturally, he had excellent contacts in the Antilles; yes, he had been planning this for months; yes, certainly, for a while now he had been predicting that silver mining in Mexico was on an irreversible downward course. Of course, right, absolutely.

Finally, he accompanied them to the mansion entrance, where he received still more hearty farewells and congratulations. Only when the clip-clop of horses' hooves had disappeared into the early morning, bearing with it the last of his guests in their carriages, did he return inside. Halfway across the courtyard, he came to a halt, plunging his hands in his pockets, inhaling deeply, and gazing up at the sky. He held his breath for a few long seconds, then exhaled without lowering his gaze, hoping, perhaps, to discover one star among the many that would shed some light on his uncertain future.

He remained like that for a while, in the center of the gray stone colonnades, without taking his eyes from the heavens. He was thinking of Mariana, about how it would affect her if he failed to revive his fortunes and ended up completely bankrupt; about Nico and his troubling unpredictability, and his future marriage that had seemed so secure and now felt dangerously uncertain.

All at once, he sensed soft footsteps and a presence behind him. Without needing to turn around, he knew who was there.

"So, you overheard everything, didn't you, lad?"

Santos Huesos Quevedo Calderón, his companion on many an adventure, the virtually illiterate Chichimec Indian who, through some extraordinary twist of fate, bore the surnames of two Spanish literary giants. Here he was, protecting his back, as ever.

"Loud and clear, *patrón*."

"And you have nothing to say about it?"

The reply came instantaneously:

"Only that I'm waiting for you to tell me when we leave."

Larrea smiled, a look of bitter irony on his face. Loyal unto death.

"Soon, lad. But before that there's something I must do tonight."

He would go alone. Without his servant, coachman, or agent. He knew he was taking a blind leap and was prepared to improvise, depending on whatever willingness Fausta Calleja showed. At midmorning he had received a violet-scented note from the superintendent's daughter with instructions on how to enter the Mining Board palace through a side entrance. She had ended the message with the words: *I'll be waiting*. And so, blindly, Larrea ran the risk of getting caught somewhere he had absolutely no business to be. As if he hadn't enough problems.

He preferred to walk: his dark shadow would be less conspicuous than the carriage. When he reached the chapel of Nuestra Señora de Belén, he slipped down a dark side alley, enveloped in his cape, hat lowered over his face.

What if one of Mariana's suitors had behaved like this? Larrea reflected as he made his way there. What if some scoundrel had aroused his daughter's naïve hopes and used her for his own ends only to toss her away like a cigar butt once he had got what he wanted? Doubtless he would have pursued the man and gouged his eyes out with his bare hands. *Stop thinking about it,* he scolded himself. *Things are how they are, and this is your only way out. Surely at your age you're not going to get sentimental.*

He walked on a few paces until the faint glow of a streetlamp revealed what he was looking for: a simple side door through which the staff could gain entry to their apartments—far removed from the imposing gates at the front of the building on Calle San Andrés. The door looked closed, but he realized it wasn't when he gave it a gentle push and it squeaked open.

He made his way up stealthily, feeling for the wrought-iron banister, careful on the wooden stairs, which he was unable to see and which creaked beneath his feet. Not even a meager candle illuminated the stairs, so when a loud whisper reached him from the floor above, he froze.

"Good evening, Don Mauro."

He chose not to reply. Not yet. He took another step, then another. Before he reached the next floor, he heard the rasp of a match. A tiny flame instantly sparked a bigger one. Fausta had lit an oil lamp. He remained silent, but she spoke once more:

"I wasn't sure if you'd come in the end."

He looked up and saw her at the top of the stairs, illuminated by the orangey light. *What the devil are you doing here, compadre?* demanded the stern voice of his conscience when he had but four steps to go. *Don't complicate matters. It isn't too late; find some other way of solving your problems. Don't give this poor woman false hopes.* However, driven by the relentless urgency of his predicament, he thrust aside his scruples once again. Reaching the top step, he mentally gave his conscience one last kick in the pants before deploying his most insincere gallantry.

"Good evening, dear Fausta. What a pleasure it is to see you again."

She gave a startled smile, and yet still he saw no sparkle in her eyes.

"I brought you a gift. A modest token; I hope you'll forgive me."

Shortly before dinner, while the servants were seeing to the final preparations and scurrying through the rooms and corridors of this mansion with jugs of iced water and bouquets of flowers, he had entered Mariana's bedroom for the first time since she had left home. It still contained many of her belongings: china dolls, an embroidery hoop, her desk with its many drawers. Doing his best not to give in to feelings of sadness, he went over to the cabinet containing dozens of small trinkets. The glass doors tinkled as he jerked them open. *How about the bead purse he had brought back from Morelia for her years before? Or the tiny mirror with a turquoise frame—a gift on her sixteenth birthday?* Without giving it much thought, he seized a carved horn fan, which he stuffed in his pocket.

Fausta's hand trembled as she took it from him.

"Why, Don Mauro, it's beautiful," she murmured.

Once again he felt troubled by his emotions but, having no time for pity, he pressed on.

"Have you thought of somewhere we can go?"

They hadn't moved from the landing, and were speaking in whispers.

"I was thinking we could go to a study hall on the first floor. It overlooks an inside courtyard, so no one will be able see the light."

"That's an excellent idea."

She gave a shy look.

"Although it occurs to me we might consider somewhere more discreet, more private," he suggested artfully. "Less accessible. I say this more than anything because I'm thinking of your reputation."

The girl pursed her lips, pensive.

"The archive, for example," he blurted out hastily.

"The archive . . . ?" she echoed, in surprise.

"Exactly. It's a long way from the apartments and the students' quarters. No one will hear us."

She reflected cautiously for what seemed like ages. Then at last she murmured:

"That's not such a bad idea."

He felt a quiver of excitement course through him. It was all he could do to avoid saying: *Get a move on, then, my lovely. What are we waiting for?*

"Having said that, I'm sure your papa performs his duties to the letter and has a lock on the door."

"Two locks, to be precise."

Always makes sure to protect himself, the bastard, he muttered under his breath, recalling the superintendent.

"I see . . ." He gave a slight cough. "And would you . . . would you be able to obtain the keys?"

She hesitated, calculating the risk.

"I only ask because I'd like us to feel more at ease. More relaxed." He paused for a few seconds. "The two of us. Together."

"It won't be possible tonight; he keeps the keys in a drawer in his bedroom chest. My mother is sleeping there now."

"Tomorrow, perhaps?"

She pursed her lips again, unconvinced.

"Possibly."

He raised his hand slowly to her pale cheek. Eyes half-closed, she smiled, abandoning herself to his caress.

Stop right there, you scoundrel, his conscience cried out once more. *There's no need.* But Tadeo Carrús's four accursed months minus three days were steadily ticking away.

"Then I'll come back tomorrow," he whispered in her ear.

His words brought Fausta abruptly back to reality.

"Are you leaving already?" Her mouth was half open in surprise.

"I'm afraid so, my dear." Larrea reached inside his waistcoat pocket for his fob watch, remembering that he would probably have to sell that, too. "It's almost three in the morning, and I have a difficult day ahead of me when I wake up."

"I understand, Don Mauro, I understand."

He stroked her cheek once more.

"You needn't keep calling me Don Mauro. Or talk to me so formally."

She pressed her lips together again, and with a slight quiver of her chin seemed to say yes. At that, he started back down the stairs, sure-footedly now, eager to breathe in the cool, early morning air.

Just before he reached the street, he heard her call after him. He halted and wheeled around. Fausta began descending the gloomy staircase, almost at a trot. *What the devil do you want now, woman?*

"Sleep well, dear Mauro, and have no fear, I'll make sure I get the keys for you," she said breathlessly.

Then, seizing one of his hands crushed by the mines and by life, she gently pressed his open palm to her chest. Yet he felt no throbbing, no quickened pulse, only a sagging breast, bereft of any firmness it might once have possessed.

Suddenly she raised herself on tiptoes and drew close to his ear.

"I wonder what you will do for me in return."

CHAPTER NINE

"I bid you good morning, my dear," said the countess. "I trust I didn't wake you with my summons."

"Far from it, dear Countess. I'm usually an early riser."

He had barely slept two hours. After he got back, he had lain awake until daybreak, head resting on his bare arms folded on the pillow, staring into space, his mind spinning with memories and sensations: dogs barking at dawn; chocolate melting on the floor; Nico, ever unpredictable; Fausta Calleja's graceless features; the outline of an island in the Antilles; an unborn child.

As a result, he had remained sleeping until Santos Huesos entered his room shortly before eight.

"Señorita Mariana's mother-in-law has sent word saying she wishes to see you, *patrón*. At her house in Calle Capuchinas, as quick as you can."

Larrea arrived at about nine, when the servants were hurriedly emptying the chamber pots and the chime of bells from the nearby church filled the air.

Tall and thin to the point of being emaciated, her thick white hair immaculately brushed, Úrsula Hernández de Soto y Villalobos received him in her private chamber, wearing a black lace dress with a cameo at the neck and teardrop pearl earrings. Over her bony chest hung a monocle on a gold chain.

"Have you breakfasted, my dear? I've just finished my chocolate, but I shall ask them to bring more at once."

He refused the offer, mentioning a delicious breakfast that in fact he hadn't touched. The knot in his stomach had barely allowed him to sip his coffee.

"At my age, one sleeps less and less," the countess went on, "which is useful in many ways. At this hour when young women are still in the arms of Morpheus, I have attended Mass, settled my accounts, and summoned you here. I imagine you must be wondering why."

"Indeed, especially since we took leave of each other only a few hours ago."

He always addressed the countess with exquisite politeness and a friendly manner, without ever permitting her to look down on him. He had never been daunted by the character and lineage of the illustrious Bruno de la Garza y Roel's widow, legitimate heir to the title conferred on her grandfather a century before by King Charles III of Spain in exchange for several thousand silver coins. A title she stubbornly insisted on using, despite the fact that it was rendered invalid when, after the country gained independence, the fledgling Mexican republic abolished with the stroke of a pen all titles granted during the viceroyalty.

"And so here I am," he added, ensconcing himself in an armchair, "ready to listen to what you have to say."

As if she wished to impart a touch of solemnity to her words, the old lady cleared her throat before speaking, even as she made sure that her cameo was straight with twig-like fingers. Behind her, an enormous Flemish tapestry depicted a confused battlefield scene, full of clashing weapons, bearded, powerful soldiers, and a great number of headless

Moors. The other walls were lined with portraits of her ancestors: imposing military men bedecked with medals, and elegant ladies whose noble lineages had long since vanished.

"You know I'm fond of you, Mauro," she said at last. "Despite our differences, I am fond of you. And I respect you, too. You belong to that tradition of great mining men from New Spain, who helped boost this nation's economy in colonial times. Their vast wealth stimulated our industry and commerce, put food in the mouths of thousands of families, built palaces and towns, almshouses, hospitals, and numerous charitable institutions."

Where is this leading? Why the long speech, you old witch? he thought to himself. But he allowed the countess to continue with her evocations of the past.

"You're a clever fellow like your predecessors, although less given to acts of charity, and you barely show your face in church."

"The only thing I believe in is myself, dear Úrsula, and even that is starting to wane. Had I been a God-fearing man, I'd never have gone into this business of mine."

"You also share their grit and ambition," she went on, ignoring his blasphemous remarks. "I knew it the moment I met you. Which is why I understand, and applaud, your decision to leave. However, I suspect you weren't being entirely truthful with us last night."

He responded to the provocation with feigned nonchalance. His splendid suit of Manchester wool may have matched his proud demeanor, but his stomach clenched in a knot. She knew. His daughter's mother-in-law had found out that he was ruined. Somehow, somewhere, someone had given the game away. A servant, or perhaps one of Andrade's contacts, had been eavesdropping and blabbed. The accursed sons of bitches.

"I know you aren't leaving Mexico because of internal tensions in this crazy country, or because the silver mining business is going through a bad moment. It has been very profitable for you until now, and mines don't dry up overnight—even I know that. No, you're leaving Mexico for a very different reason."

Mariana would be subjected to people's impertinent stares every time she left the house; Nico would continue his wild ways and become a laughingstock when his engagement was broken off; the collapse of the family fortunes would become a subject of scandalous gossip in all the best houses, social gatherings, and cafés. Even the fierce warriors in the Flemish tapestry seemed to have halted their battle with their enemies to turn their gaze upon him, swords poised in the air, eyes oozing contempt. *So, you're ruined, you Spaniard*, they seemed to be saying.

From somewhere deep inside, he mustered a vestige of aplomb.

"I've no idea what reason you are referring to, dear countess."

"Your own daughter put me on the track."

Larrea knitted his brow, at once incredulous and puzzled. Impossible. Out of the question. Mariana would never reveal to the countess what he was struggling so hard to conceal. She would never betray him in that way. Nor was she careless enough to have let slip something that serious by accident.

"Last night, on our way home in my carriage—and your agent can testify to this—she made a remark that set me thinking. She reminded me that although all these years you have resided on this side of the ocean, you are still one hundred percent a Spanish subject."

This was true. Despite living there for so long, Larrea had never applied for Mexican citizenship. There was no particular reason for this: he was neither proud nor ashamed of his roots. Whatever his passport might be, everyone knew that he had been born in Spain, and he had no qualms about admitting it, even though he was aware that nothing tied him to his distant country of origin.

"And you really believe that has something to do with my plans?"

There was a surprisingly aggressive note to his voice, but the old lady was unruffled.

"Indeed. A great deal. You know as well as I do that President Juárez has suspended all foreign debt repayments, and that affects Spain, France, and England. But above all Spain."

"The foreign debt has nothing whatsoever to do with me, as I'm sure you're aware."

"No, not the debt itself, I agree. But perhaps the consequences of its remaining unpaid. I've heard rumors that Spain might go as far as to take measures against Juárez's decision: that there could be reprisals, that the mother country might even be considering invading her old viceroyalty. Reconquering it."

He interrupted her brusquely:

"For heaven's sake, Úrsula, how can you believe such arrant nonsense?"

"And, as a consequence," the countess persisted, raising her hand to demand his patient attention, "these wicked Liberals we have in government could take revenge on you, the Spanish subjects residing here. It wouldn't be the first time. There have been at least three expulsion orders against the Spaniards, who within four days found themselves on the other side of the border. I saw with my own eyes entire families broken up, fortunes lost . . ."

"That was over thirty years ago, before Spain finally accepted Mexico's independence. Certainly long before I arrived."

Indeed, that was how it had been: a bloody war of independence followed by years of denial until the Spanish crown finally recognized the emerging Mexican nation; from Father Hidalgo's Cry of Dolores to the Treaty of Peace and Friendship in 1836. After that, a policy of reconciliation was pursued between Spain and the young republic, in an attempt to overcome the old mutual mistrust between the Creole settlers and the peninsular Spaniards from the days of the colony. For centuries the Creoles viewed the Spaniards as a band of greedy thugs, proud and tyrannical, who came to plunder their land and riches. For their part, the Spaniards viewed the Creoles as inferior merely for being born in the Americas, fickle and prone to idleness, wastrels with an exaggerated penchant for leisure and self-indulgence. And yet, when all was said and done, they were siblings, and as time went by they became neighbors, fell in love, intermarried endlessly, produced thousands of offspring together, grieved over one another's passing, and inevitably infused each other's lives with traces of their own identity.

"Everything can always go back to the way it was, Mauro," she insisted brusquely. "It can. If only it would. If only the old order could be reinstated, we could go back to being a viceroyalty."

At last the tension in his muscles relaxed, and he let out a guffaw of pure relief.

"Úrsula, you wallow in nostalgia."

Each time the old countess dusted off her memories of bygone colonial days, those around her cringed—partly because of her stubborn opinions, her closed-mindedness, but also because she was quite capable of spending hours delving into a past that for most Mexicans had ceased to exist half a century before. On this occasion, she could have gone on praising the imperial dream until she was blue in the face: all that mattered to Larrea was that he was safe. Untarnished. She had no inkling of his financial ruin but was under the false impression that the reason for his hasty departure was to remain one step ahead of a hypothetical political edict that would doubtless never come to pass.

"You're mistaken, Mauro."

With her bony hand she reached for her jewel-encrusted gold cigarette case while he held up a lighted match.

"I'm not nostalgic in the least," she went on, blowing the smoke out of the corner of her mouth, "although I will confess that I belong to a different era, and that I detest the one we are currently obliged to endure. However, I'm nothing if not pragmatic, above all in matters of finance. As you know, I've been running the family's pulque business in Tlalpan and Xochimilco since my husband passed away thirty-two years ago."

Of course Larrea knew this. He would never have given his blessing so readily to Mariana's union with her son, Alonso, had he not known of the healthy state of the countess's finances, that her maguey plantations in the countryside and pulquerías in the capital were thriving. And the countess knew that he knew. Both were fully aware that this marriage had brought mutual benefits.

"That's why," she went on, "I've decided to ask a favor of you."

"I'll do everything I can, as always . . ."

"I want you to take some of my capital with you to Cuba. To invest over there."

His response was unequivocal.

"That's out of the question."

She pretended not to hear him.

"To invest alongside your own money," she repeated vehemently. "I believe in you."

Just as he was about to reiterate his refusal in the strongest terms, Mariana entered the room, her protruding belly encased in a muslin shift, her hair tied back loosely, giving her a casual air that accentuated her natural beauty. She looked drowsy.

"I woke up to learn that you two have been talking since early this morning. Good day to you both. God bless you."

"I've just told him the news," the countess cut in.

Mariana planted a fleeting kiss on her father's cheek.

"A splendid idea, isn't it? Our two families united in a common venture."

With this, she stretched out languidly on a velvet chaise longue while her father gazed at her uneasily.

"You'll enjoy special privileges in Cuba," the countess continued. "The island still belongs to the Spanish crown, and as a native Spaniard many doors will be open to you."

"It isn't a good idea for me to take your money, Úrsula," Larrea insisted. "I appreciate your trust, but the responsibility is too great. Perhaps when I've established something more solid."

The old lady hoisted herself up, arms braced against the chair. Deaf to his protests, she walked over to the balsawood table she used for all her business affairs. On the desk, watched over by a magnificent ivory cross, were piles of documents and ledgers, proof that the countess devoted her time to other things besides charitable works and dusty reminiscences. She rummaged among them, continuing to talk without looking up.

"I could have followed my friends' example, taken my capital out of Mexico and invested it in Europe, in case the disastrous situation into which this foolish nation is plunged grows even worse."

While the countess's back was turned, Mauro Larrea took the opportunity of catching his daughter's eye. He shrugged his shoulders, spreading his hands in a clear gesture of puzzlement, a look of alarm written all over his face. She limited herself to lifting a finger to her lips, signaling *Hush*.

"God knows I've never been one to engage in speculative ventures," the countess went on, still with her back turned. "The pulque business has always brought us a steady income: maguey grows like a weed, the extraction process is simple, it ferments by itself, and it is drunk day and night by Indians, mestizos, and bona fide Christians alike. And the advent of bottled pulque has given the business another boost."

She turned around, having finally found what she was looking for: a pair of bulky leather pouches, which she held out to him. Meanwhile, as though at a distance from what was going on, Mariana remained supine, reclining on the chaise longue, caressing her belly.

"We've been making good returns for years, but in the present climate I don't see how to make our money grow. That's why I wish to hand part of it over to you. As mother-in-law to your daughter and future grandmother of the child my son has given her—in short, as a member of your family—I'm asking you to invest this money."

He refused outright, shaking his head from left to right. She persisted with steely determination.

"Naturally, you will keep part of the profit, as I once heard you explain is the case with your mines. I believe the usual amount is one-eighth."

"That's correct, one-eighth. But this has nothing whatsoever to do with mining. This is an entirely different matter."

"Even so, I am offering you twice that amount for your pains, for acting as my intermediary. You will keep a quarter of any profits you obtain from investing my capital."

Both stood firm, the countess in her insistence, Larrea in his refusal. Until Mariana intervened, with an air of casual distraction, as though oblivious to the implications of what was going on.

"Why not accept, Father? You'll be doing Úrsula a huge favor. Isn't it an honor that she has such confidence in you?"

With this she gave a long, drawn-out yawn before adding nonchalantly:

"I'm sure you'll invest it wisely. It's only a small amount to start off with, but if all goes well more could follow."

Larrea gazed at his daughter in astonishment, while the old lady gave a smile tinged with irony.

"To be absolutely frank with you, Mauro, the naked truth is that in the beginning your daughter's dowry interested me more than her beauty or her virtue. But as I have gotten to know her, I have come to realize that, besides the considerable material wealth she has brought to this marriage, as well as making my son happy, Mariana is a clever woman, and she gets that from you. As you see, she is already concerned with establishing economic ties between our two families. Were it not for her, I might never have thought of asking you to do this."

A servant entered, excused himself, and distracted his mistress with a hurried account of some small domestic accident that had occurred in the courtyard or the kitchens. Two other servants arrived offering different versions and explanations. The countess went out into the gallery muttering to herself, and for a few moments gave her full attention to the matter.

Larrea took the opportunity to stand up and stride over to Mariana.

"What on earth led you to come up with this absurd idea?" he murmured hastily.

Despite her advanced pregnancy and apparent sleepiness, Mariana sat upright on the chaise longue as agilely as a young cat, glancing sideways to make sure that her mother-in-law was out of earshot, busy issuing orders in her usual high-handed manner.

"So that you can begin your new life on firm ground. Or did you think I was going to let you go off here, there, and everywhere without any support?"

Although it broke his heart to oppose his daughter, he was determined to leave the countess's palace empty-handed.

CHAPTER TEN

❧

H e had a bitter taste in his mouth as he left the mansion on Calle
Capuchinas and returned home. For having refused upset Mariana, for refusing the matriarch of the family to which she now belonged.

"Santos!"

His command brooked no argument.

"Start packing. We're leaving."

Everything had been decided, and properly arranged. Now he only
had to resolve the problem of the documents, but with his foolish game
of seduction he had Fausta practically eating out of his hand. Something would need to go terribly wrong for him not to achieve his objective that night.

In the meantime, he had no time to lose. And to that end he shut
himself away in his study with Andrade to deal with the last few important matters. Since his return from the countess's house, they had
toiled ceaselessly over legal documents, bulging files, open ledgers,
half-finished cups of coffee.

"There are still some outstanding debts," said his agent, swiftly running his quill pen over a page of figures. "We can pay them off by auc-
tioning or pawning fixtures and fittings from the estate at Tacubaya. As

for the palace here on Calle San Felipe Neri, we'll leave behind enough furniture to keep up appearances and sell the most valuable objects: the Bohemian crystal, the best paintings, sculptures, ivory carvings. The same applies to any personal possessions or clothes that won't fit in your luggage: more money with which to plug the gaps. From now on, Mauro, your only possessions will be what you travel with."

"Be discreet, Elias, I beg you."

Andrade looked up at him over the tops of his spectacles.

"Have no fear, compadre. I intend to place everything with people I trust, with moneylenders and pawnbrokers in the provincial towns. I'll dispose of each item separately, using middlemen: no one will question where it comes from. Your initials, stamped or embroidered, will be removed; I'll do my best to leave no trail."

They heard a knock at the door. Before permission to enter was given, a head poked through.

"Don Ernesto Gorostiza has just arrived, *patrón*," announced Santos Huesos.

The two friends' eyes flashed at one another. Of all people. What damnable bad luck.

"Show him up, of course."

The agent bundled the most compromising documents into drawers while Larrea straightened his tie and stepped outside into the corridor to receive the newcomer.

"Ernesto, let me begin by apologizing for the deplorable state of my house," he said, extending his hand. "Doubtless you have heard that I'm about to leave the country. Indeed, I was planning to pay a farewell visit to you and your wife, Clementina, and our beloved Teresita."

He was absolutely sincere: he couldn't possibly have left the city without saying good-bye to his son's future in-laws, and to the young woman who was pining for his foolish boy Nicolás. But of course now wasn't the best time.

"Why, half of Mexico knows by now, my friend. Don Cristóbal had scarcely finished pronouncing the *Ite missa est* first thing this morning when the countess started spreading the word outside La Profesa Church."

This doesn't bode well, Larrea said to himself. His agent, to whom the newcomer had his back turned, raised a forefinger to his temple to mimic shooting himself in the head.

Had rumors of his bankruptcy reached Gorostiza? Had he come to break off their children's engagement? The most sinister imaginings assailed Larrea like ferocious dogs: Nico subjected to public ridicule after being spurned by his fiancée's family; Nico knocking on doors that remained firmly closed; Nico in rags, with no prospects, transformed into one of the dandies who were hounded out of cafés every night.

Despite everything, Mauro Larrea's exterior scarcely revealed his anxiety. On the contrary, genial as ever, he offered his guest a seat, which he accepted, and a coffee, which he declined.

"What about a glass of papaya juice? Or a French anisette?"

"A thousand thanks, my friend, but I shan't detain you. I can see that you're busy."

Andrade excused himself on some vague pretext and left the room, closing the door noiselessly behind him. Once they were alone, Ernesto Gorostiza began to speak.

"Look, I'm here on a matter that combines the material and the personal."

He was impeccably dressed and took his time over every word, pressing his fingertips together as he formed each sentence. Fingers that couldn't have been more dissimilar to Larrea's: tapered, with the appearance of never having handled any implement besides a letter opener or a fork.

"I don't know whether you're aware that I have a sister living in Cuba," he went on. "Carola, the baby of the family. She was married very young to a Spaniard recently arrived from the peninsula, and they left for the Antilles together. We haven't seen them since, and we don't know much about them. But now . . ."

Larrea was tempted to fling his arms around the man, overcome with a pang of emotion. *So you didn't come here to ruin my son; you aren't going to humiliate my foolish boy; you still think he is worthy of your family. Thank you, Ernesto, my friend, thank you from the bottom of my heart.*

". . . Now, Mauro, I need a favor."

Larrea's huge sense of relief at discovering that the motive for Gorostiza's visit was in no way related to his son, Nico, merged with a sense of unease when he heard the word *favor*. *Curses, here comes the catch.*

"Some weeks ago, we sold my mother's hacienda in El Bajío—you will recall that she passed away recently."

How could he have forgotten the pomp and ceremony of that funeral? The splendid hearse drawn by four horses sporting black feather plumes, the cream of Mexico City society paying their last respects to the matriarch of an illustrious clan.

"Now that her estate has been sold off, I am obliged to give Carola her share, which as one of five siblings amounts to a fifth."

Larrea, who was beginning to see where this was headed, said nothing.

"You know as well as I do that the current economic climate in Mexico is unfavorable for investment, and yet we're talking about a not-inconsiderable sum. I was thinking of sending her the money via an intermediary, but when I heard of your intentions, it occurred to me that if you, who are virtually one of the family and someone in whom I have complete trust, could take it for me, I would be infinitely grateful."

"Consider it done."

The calm assurance Larrea intended to convey with his words was understandably at odds with his true feelings. *What damned luck! More commitments. More burdens. Less freedom to move.* And yet, if by agreeing to this favor he strengthened the ties between Nico and the Gorostizas, then God be praised.

"We've had little contact with her over the years. She was married young, to a Spaniard. Did I already tell you this?"

Larrea bobbed his chin discreetly, not wishing to embarrass his guest by making too much of the fact that he was repeating himself.

"He was a good-looking young man who arrived in the Americas with a solid amount of capital behind him. Reserved, although extremely polite, he came from a distinguished Andalusian family, with whom for some reason we never found out he had cut all ties. Alas, he showed no interest in forging any with us, for we would have welcomed him with open arms, as we will your son when he weds our Teresita."

Larrea nodded once more, this time with a look of gratitude, even though his stomach was churning. *May God hear you, brother. May God hear your words and shine upon you so that you never regret what you just said.*

"Despite the offer of their own apartments at our palace on Calle de la Moneda, he preferred to cut loose and set sail for Cuba. Naturally, Carola accompanied him. Perhaps you will understand better if I tell you in confidence that my sister fell pregnant before they were betrothed, and the wedding was brought forward to avoid a scandal. Although she subsequently lost the baby, within three months of meeting they were already man and wife. A week later we were waving them good-bye as they sailed for the Antilles. Later on, we heard that he bought a coffee plantation, they moved into a good house, and they adapted to the social life of Havana. And there they remain to this day."

"I see," Larrea murmured, unable to think of anything else to say.

"Zayas."

"Sorry?"

"Gustavo Zayas Montalvo is the husband's name. I'll give you their address when I deliver the money to you."

At this, Gorostiza clapped his hands together languidly before rubbing his palms.

"Good. You can't imagine my relief."

As the two men descended the staircase, they decided that their respective agents should handle the details and delivery of the money. Out in the courtyard, their final exchange turned to Nico's sojourn in Europe.

"By the time he comes back, he'll have grown into a conscientious young man," Gorostiza said. "Theirs will be a match made in heaven. Teresita spends her days praying that all will be well."

Larrea felt his stomach churn once more. Finally, at the entrance, they took their leave of one another with a hearty embrace.

"I am forever in your debt, my friend," Gorostiza said.

"Anything for you and your family," Larrea replied, clapping his shoulder.

The moment he saw the carriage roll away, he returned to the courtyard, calling for Santos Huesos at the top of his lungs.

He had to finish the preparations as quickly as possible and leave immediately to avoid any further demands that might hamper his mission.

It is said that man proposes but God disposes, and in this instance the proverb was borne out by an unexpected second meeting with the old countess after lunch. As was her custom, she arrived unannounced, when the house was still in disarray. On being told that she was on her way upstairs, Larrea gave an angry snort. He hadn't finished going through the paperwork, his hair was unkempt, his shirt half-unbuttoned. *What the devil does she want now, the old crone?*

"I imagine you knew I wouldn't take no for an answer."

She was carrying the two bags of gold he had refused hours before. One after the other, she deposited them on the table with a thud that emphasized the weight of their contents and the coins chinking inside.

Then, before her host could offer her a seat, she swept aside some documents on a nearby armchair and, smoothing her skirts, sat down.

Larrea stood watching her, arms folded, making no attempt to conceal his irritation, a stern look on his face.

"May I remind you, Countess, that as far as I'm concerned I resolved this matter this morning."

"Precisely, my dear, you resolved it, but I didn't."

He gave another angry snort. What with the house in turmoil, and his own disheveled appearance, he no longer had time for social niceties.

"For God's sake, Úrsula, will you please leave me in peace."

"I'm asking you to help me."

For once, the pompous old lady's voice sounded almost humble. Suppressing his irritation, Larrea let her have her say.

"I'm going to be honest with you, Mauro, in a way that I haven't been with my own son. I feel frightened. Terribly frightened. A deep, instinctive fear."

He contemplated her with disdain. Frightened, this fierce, proud noblewoman, who was accustomed to having the world at her feet? Whoever would have thought it?

"My family has always remained loyal to the Spanish crown. I grew up dreaming of crossing the Atlantic, visiting Madrid, the Palacio Real, the splendors of Toledo, the Escorial . . . Until everything collapsed when we broke away from Spain. Of course, we had no choice but to adapt. And now . . . now this nation is starting to fill me with dread: its crazy governments, the excesses of its leaders."

"Not to mention Juárez's profanities and his attacks on the Church. You're singing the same old song, Countess."

"I trust no one, Mauro: God only knows where this madness will end."

She lowered her gaze, entwining her long, twig-like fingers. For a few tense moments neither of them uttered a word.

"Mariana put you up to this, didn't she?"

Confronted with her silence, Larrea crouched down until his face was level with hers. They made an odd couple, the distinguished old lady in her perennial widow's weeds and the miner in his shirtsleeves, squatting in an effort to bridge the distance between them.

"Tell me the truth, Úrsula."

She clicked her tongue as if to say, *Curses, he found me out.*

"That daughter of yours certainly has her head screwed on, my boy. Ever since you left she's been insisting I come here, and she succeeded in convincing me."

Mauro Larrea gave a mocking laugh, hands on his knees as he straightened himself up. Mariana, resourceful and determined as ever. He had very nearly been persuaded that the countess was turning into a timorous old woman when in fact his daughter was pulling the strings.

"After all," she went on, "everything I own will one day belong to Alonso, and therefore to your daughter. Your daughter, and the child they are expecting, the pure mixing of our two bloods."

Silence floated in the air as each thought about the young Mariana in their own way. The countess contemplated her through the eyes of a shrewd businesswoman, beginning to see her as an admirable promoter of the family's interests. Larrea for his part did so as the father who had been present at every stage of her life, from the moment he cradled her tiny newborn form, wrapped in a rough towel to keep her warm, until the moment he led her up to the Altar de los Reyes to the strains of the organ in Mexico City's cathedral.

Stop denying your own daughter, you sonofabitch, he told himself. *Not only is she intuitive and clever, above all she's protecting you. Why dig in your heels in confronting this deluge of catastrophes while insisting on shutting her out? Do this for her. Show your trust.*

"All right, Úrsula. I'll do my best not to disappoint you."

After all, Gorostiza had already burdened him with one commission. Why not make it two?

The countess rose to her feet with some difficulty, muttering, "*Accursed rheumatism.*" Then, much to his surprise and embarrassment,
she took two steps forward and embraced him. He could feel her sharp,
arthritic bones as he registered the scent of lavender, and of something
else he couldn't identify. Perhaps it was simply old age.

"The good Lord will reward you, my son."

Almost at once, regaining her usual haughty air, she added:

"Several of my friends were keen for you to invest their capital, too,
you know. But you needn't worry, I dissuaded them."

"You've no idea how grateful I am for your consideration," he replied, with ill-concealed irony.

"It's time for me to leave; I can see I'm disturbing you."

He made to open the door for her.

"You needn't accompany me: my maid, Manuelita, is waiting for
me in the courtyard, and my coachman is outside."

"Naturally, Countess."

He knew there was no point insisting. The sly countess had returned
to normal; how could he ever have imagined she had been transformed
into a fearful, defenseless old grandmother.

She was about to step out of the room when she came to a halt as
though suddenly remembering something. Looking him up and down,
she gave a faint smile.

"I always wondered why you never remarried, Mauro."

The answers he might have given to her impertinent question were
many and various: because he liked his own company, because the
brutal life in the mining camps was no place for any decent woman,
because there was no room for another in the trio formed by himself,
Mariana, and Nicolás. Or because, despite being romantically involved
with several women after Elvira, he had never met anyone who made

him want to take that step. The figure of Fausta Calleja floated like an ominous shadow across the room.

But before he could open his mouth, the aristocratic, tyrannical, nostalgic ex–Countess of Colima, erect as a broom handle inside her magnificent black lace dress, gripped the ivory handle of her cane and, brandishing it aloft like a foil, declared:

"If we'd met when I was thirty years younger, by God, I'd never have let you get away!"

CHAPTER ELEVEN

ॐ

H e strode down the Betlemitas alleyway that ran alongside the Palacio de Minería and bounded up the stairs. There was no longer any time for caution or regret: either he achieved his objective that night, or he would have to sail away leaving a black hole behind him. It would be only a matter of days before superintendent Calleja allowed Asencio and the Englishmen to slip into it, dealing a fatal blow to his most ambitious project.

"Did you manage to get the keys?"

He even posed the question brusquely, driven by a sense of urgency.

"Did you doubt my word, Don Mauro?"

Fausta, illuminated as before by the oil lamp, had gone back to addressing him formally. He didn't bother to correct her. She could call him "Your Excellency" if she so wished; by now, all he cared about was gaining access to that accursed office.

"We'd better hurry."

He followed her down a maze of small passageways that led off the central hallway and the main corridors. They scarcely spoke as they made their way stealthily, hugging the walls, until at last they reached the far side of the building. Then from among the folds of her dress the superintendent's daughter took out a metal hoop containing two identical-looking keys. Mauro Larrea had to restrain himself from snatching them out of her hands as she jangled them before his eyes.

"You see?"

"Well done. I trust Doña Hilaria won't notice that they—or you— are missing."

She gave an awkward grin in the dark. As if she'd been rehearsing all afternoon in front of the mirror.

"I doubt that. I added a few drops to her tisane."

Larrea refrained from asking what these were.

"Shall I open the door?"

Fausta shook her head even as she raised the first key to the uppermost of the two locks. He held the oil lamp up for her. The key wouldn't fit.

"Try the other one," he ordered.

His tone was unintentionally harsh. *Careful, sonofabitch. Don't mess things up when we're still in the antechamber.* Then the second key entered easily, and he thought he could hear a choir of angels. One down, and one to go.

Fausta was about to insert the second key when something made her hesitate.

Far off down the deserted passageways, they heard a person whistling in the distance. Someone who was coming their way, crudely warbling the melody of a popular dance.

"Salustiano," she whispered. "The night watchman."

"Open the door quickly."

But, confronted with this unexpected presence, Fausta lost her nerve and couldn't fit the key into the right lock.

"For God's sake, hurry up."

The whistling was coming steadily closer.

"Let me . . ."

"No, wait . . ."

"No, let me . . ."

"Wait, I've nearly . . ."

As they were wrangling, the hoop with the keys on it fell to the floor, skittering over the flagstones. The clatter of metal on stone made them freeze. The whistling stopped.

Holding his breath, Mauro Larrea lowered the lamp until it was almost touching the ground. Fausta, flustered, made as if to crouch down and search for the keys.

"Don't move!" he hissed, seizing her arm.

He swept the lamp about them, illuminating his boots, the hem of her skirts, the cracks between the flagstones. But there was no sign of the keys.

The whistling resumed, like a sinister warning.

"Lift your skirts," he whispered.

"For goodness' sake, Don Mauro."

"For the love of God, Fausta. Raise your skirts!"

Her delicate hands began to tremble in the flickering lamplight. Mauro Larrea, with a sudden flash of insight, sensed she was about to scream.

Three swift movements were all he needed. One to cover her mouth, another to set the lamp down on the floor, and a third to lift her skirts abruptly above her knees. Petrified, Fausta closed her eyes.

There were the keys, on the floor between her satin slippers.

"I just wanted to find them, and here they are, you see?" he whispered hastily in her ear, his hand still clapped over her mouth. "And now, please don't make a sound. We're going to enter. Agreed?"

She nodded, trembling. Meanwhile, the whistling was getting closer by the second. Just as discordant, but livelier. Closer.

Larrea cursed as he placed one of the keys randomly in the second lock, without success. The droning melody grew ominously louder as the second key finally went in. One turn, then another, done. He pushed Fausta inside, then hurried in after her, his body almost pressing into her back. The watchman's whistles and footsteps were just reaching the corner when he silently closed the door. He held his breath as he leaned against the hardwood panel in the gloom, the superintendent's daughter beside him.

The darkness inside was cavernous, with no trace of moonlight seeping in through the windows. They spent a few anxious moments while the watchman and his insistent whistling swept past the door outside, until at last they could no longer hear him.

"Forgive me for assaulting you like that," Larrea apologized.

They remained propped against the door shoulder-to-shoulder. She was still trembling.

"Your interest in me isn't genuine, is it?"

He was so close to achieving his goal, if he could only win back her trust. Make her believe in him once more, restore her naïve fantasy. The rich, handsome widower surrendering to the spinster for whom all hopes of marriage were a distant dream: with a few caresses and some more lies, he could have her eating out of his hand again. But something stopped him.

"My aim was to get in here."

Confronted by this sudden outburst of honesty, his own conscience instantly bombarded him with questions. *What will you do now, you utter fool? Tie her to a chair, gag her, knock her out while you find what you're looking for? Or did you put on this ridiculous spectacle only to end up playing the Good Samaritan?*

"I confess that at first I was foolishly happy," said the girl. "But afterward, in the cold light of day, I realized that this was impossible. Men like you never court women like me."

He didn't respond, and he had a bitter taste in his mouth.

"I, too, have had suitors, do you know, Don Mauro?"

Her voice sounded calm, although still a little tremulous.

"When I was seventeen, a young tailor with whom I only exchanged billets-doux," she went on. "Years later, a captain in the militia, the cousin of a childhood friend. And finally, in my late twenties, a draftsman, before everyone considered me an old maid. But my parents thought that none of them was good enough for me."

As she spoke, she moved away from the door and began to approach the desks and chairs. By now they could both see enough in the dark to distinguish the outlines of things in the room.

"They were too poor, their families too humble . . . There was always some reason why my parents weren't satisfied. My last suitor, the draftsman, resided here in the palace, and we would meet secretly in his rooms. Until one ill-fated day he made the mistake of asking my father if he could go for a stroll with me on Paseo de la Alameda. A week later, he was posted to Tamaulipas."

By now she had reached the superintendent's desk. For his part, Larrea remained motionless, listening intently to her to judge how she was going to react.

Fausta rummaged in the drawers and cubbyholes. Seconds later, the flame from a match cut through the darkness, and with it she lit the oil lamp that stood at one end of the enormous table.

"So, you see, you aren't the first, though you're certainly the most suitable, at least in my mother's eyes. My father would protest, but she would make it her job to persuade him."

The archive had filled with a wavering light that cast shadowy shapes.

"I'm truly sorry for my behavior."

"Nonsense, Don Mauro," she said sharply. "You're not at all sorry; you are where you wanted to be. Now tell me what it is you're looking for."

"A document," he confessed. Why keep up the pretense?

"Do you know where it is?"

"I have a rough idea."

"In one of these cabinets, perhaps?"

Raising the lamp level with her chest, Fausta began walking toward a long row of glass-fronted wooden cabinets. With her free hand, she seized an object he couldn't see from the nearest table where the clerk with the tinted spectacles worked. She smashed it against the glass, causing a cascade of shards to fall to the floor.

"For God's sake, Fausta!"

He was too late to stop her.

"Or perhaps what you're looking for is in here?"

Another blow, another shower of glass on the stone floor. She was using a quartz paperweight. *In the shape of a cockerel's head,* it seemed. *Or was it a fox? What did that matter,* he thought even as she took aim once more.

He reached her in two strides and tried to restrain her, but she wriggled free.

"Stop, woman!"

The third blow produced the same effect.

"The watchman will hear! Everybody will hear!"

At last she curbed her frenzied activity and turned toward him.

"Find whatever it is you're looking for, my dear. Help yourself."

For heaven's sake, what the devil is going on?

"All this destruction will have been worth it to see the look on my father's face." Her laughter was bitter. "And my mother's? Can you imagine her face when she discovers that I spent the night in here with you?"

Be calm, my friend, be calm.

"I see no reason why they should find out."

"Possibly not, but I do."

He took a deep breath.

"Are you sure about that?"

"Absolutely. It will be my small revenge. For their not having allowed me to live the life of a normal girl, for rejecting those men who showed a real interest in me."

"And what about me . . . where do I fit in to all this? How will you explain my presence here to your parents?"

She lifted the lamp level with her eyes and contemplated him with a mocking expression. At last there was a spark in her eyes.

"I haven't the faintest idea, Don Mauro. But I'll think of something. In the meantime, take what you want and leave before I change my mind."

He didn't wait to be told twice. Snatching the box of matches she had left on the desk, he began his search like a man possessed.

He had a vague notion where the document might be but wasn't absolutely sure. Doubtless at the end, with the most recent ones. Moving from left to right, striking one match after another, lighting his way with them until they burnt down to his fingertips, he ran his eyes quickly over the shelves. Many documents were in bundles, classified by a subject or date written on the broad ribbon fastening them.

His eyes and brain hunted frantically. March—it was March. Or was it April? Yes, April, April of last year, definitely. Finally, in the sputtering light of a dying match, he found the cabinet that contained the files from that month. But the door was locked. Should he ask Fausta for the paperweight? No, best not provoke her, now that she had apparently calmed down.

Without further ado, he smashed the glass front with his elbow. Her laughter tinkled behind him.

"I hardly dare imagine my father's shock."

Larrea grabbed a whole bundle and put it down on the young clerk's desk. With trembling fingers, he started rifling through the documents. Not this one, or that one, or this other one. Until he could've howled for joy. There it was, with his name and his signature on it.

He could still sense her behind him, breathing heavily.

"Satisfied?"

He wheeled around. Strands of her hair had escaped from the tight bun she wore it in.

"Look here, Fausta, I don't know how to—"

"There's a trapdoor that leads down to the basement, from there you can reach the alleyway opposite the hospital. I imagine it won't be long before someone arrives; the watchman must have roused half the building by now."

"God bless you."

"Do you know something, Don Mauro? I don't regret my naivete. At least it allowed me an illusion."

He hurriedly rolled up the documents and slipped them inside his frock coat.

Glass crunching beneath his feet, he cupped her cheeks in his hands and kissed her as if she were the greatest love of his life.

CHAPTER TWELVE

M auro Larrea's departure on his journey into the unknown took
place in a manner befitting his social status, as though his
world had not been split in two like a gigantic watermelon. He set off
in his own carriage accompanied by Andrade, Santos Huesos, a pair of
trunks, and an escort of twelve strong men, Chinaco soldiers, armed
to the teeth to protect them against any lurking bandits. All were on
horseback, rifles resting crossways on their saddles, pistols holstered;
fighters hardened during the Reform War, paid for every penny by
Ernesto Gorostiza.

"The least I can do to show my gratitude, dear friend, is to pay for
your protection as far as Veracruz," he had written in a message to Larrea. "Banditry is part of our everyday life, but neither you nor I should
expose ourselves to any unnecessary risk."

The mansion had become a hive of activity the moment he returned
from the Palacio de Minería in the early hours, the papers relating to
Las Tres Lunas tucked safely under his frock coat. *Get a move on, Santos, we're leaving! Wake the servants, we haven't a moment to lose.* The two
trunks, travel capes, food and water for the coach journey—everything
was prepared. Soon came the whinny of horses, loud whispers, foot-

steps crossing the stone courtyard, and the many servants, still sleepy-eyed, anxious in the realization that their master was actually leaving.

Larrea was reminding the housekeeper to ensure the upstairs rooms were securely locked, when behind him he heard someone call his name. He felt the blood pulsing in his temples, and he tensed.

He knew who it was without having to turn around.

"What the devil are you doing here?"

&

The man now gazing at him with doleful eyes had been waiting a day and half for this meeting: crouched against a nearby wall, wrapped in a filthy blanket, the brim of his hat pulled down over his face. Warming himself at a meager fire and eating street food, just as so many other souls with no home and no master did day in and day out in that crowded city.

Dimas Carrús, the moneylender's son who always had the look of a dog beaten by his father and by life, took a step toward Larrea.

"I came to the capital on an errand."

Mauro Larrea frowned, every muscle in his body alert. He drew closer to the other man.

"What errand, you wretch?"

"To size up the dimensions of your house. The number of openings, windows, and balconies it has. How many servants you employ."

"And have you done that?"

"I even had a scrivener note it down in case it slipped my mind."

"In that case, get out of here."

"I've brought a reminder, too."

"Santos!"

The servant was already behind him, also on alert.

"Of the four-month period you've been given to pay the first install-ment—"

"Throw him out!"

"—you have already used up—"

"By force, if necessary."

That consumptive figure with his dangling puppet's arm possessed neither his father's ruthless ambition nor his fiery temper. And yet Mauro Larrea was aware that his scrawny frame concealed an equally despicable soul. Like father like son. And that if Tadeo Carrús breathed his last gasp before receiving the agreed sum, one way or another his son Dimas would make sure the debt was paid.

As the clatter of hooves on cobblestones commenced, Larrea lowered his head inside the carriage and gazed at his home for the last time: the magnificent century-old mansion built by the Count of Regla, once the wealthiest miner in the colony. His eyes glided over the ornate façade made of red volcanic rock and carved stone, with its splendid gates flung open wide. At first sight the house might have appeared a simple reminder of the grandiose days of the now-defunct viceroyalty, the residence of a great man who belonged to the privileged class. And yet, where Larrea's own life and destiny were concerned, it had a far deeper significance.

Two enormous cast-iron lanterns flanked the entrance, their light distorted by the uneven glass of the carriage window. Despite this, Larrea could see him: Dimas Carrús, leaning up against the wall to the right, watching his departure fixedly as he scratched the muzzle of a mangy greyhound.

They stopped off in Calle Capuchinas, where word had been sent ahead to Mariana and Alonso. They were waiting in the hallway with tousled hair, coats on over their nightclothes. But they were young and handsome, and what on others might have looked like an incongruous jumble, on them it had an air of natural grace.

Upstairs, oblivious to everything, the countess snored thunderously, contented at having got her own way.

The instant she saw him, Mariana flung her arms around her father. Once again he felt disconcerted by the taut belly that came between them.

"All will be well," she whispered in his ear.

Larrea nodded weakly, pressing his chin into her shoulder.

"I'll write as soon as I've settled."

They stepped back and, lit by a pair of flickering candles, exchanged a few last words about Nico, the house, various unresolved matters she would see to. Until they heard Andrade clear his throat outside. It was time to go.

"Keep this somewhere safe," he said, reaching among his clothes and taking out the papers concerning Las Tres Lunas. What better custodian than his own daughter?

She asked no questions: if this was what her father wanted, she required no further explanation. Then, seizing his big hands, she placed them on the dome of her belly. Rounded, full, still sitting high. "We'll be waiting for you," she said. He wanted to smile, but couldn't. This was the first time he had touched that throbbing life with his fingertips. He closed his eyes for a few moments, sensing it. He felt a lump in his throat, something indescribable.

He was halfway out of the door when Mariana embraced him once again, murmuring words only he could hear. He pressed his lips together as he climbed back inside the carriage; the sensation of the flesh of his flesh had touched his heart. His daughter's parting words echoed in his ears. *Don't hesitate to use Úrsula's money if you have to.*

The grid-like streets gradually gave way to dirtier, narrower, less noble thoroughfares, until names and lights were no longer visible, and they left behind the city of palaces, setting off along the eighty-nine leagues of the Camino Real that stood between them and their destination.

Ahead of them lay three days and nights of rocky trails, being bumped and jolted, wheels getting stuck in potholes, sometimes in sweltering heat. They traversed vast, empty landscapes, bluffs, and ravines where the horses lost their footing as they scaled craggy slopes covered in tangled briars. From time to time they would glimpse a hacienda or shack, a solitary cornfield, and numerous scenes of devastation in villages and churches that had suffered decades of civil war. Occasionally they came upon a town, which they would bypass, or a ranch hand on horseback, an Indian selling pomegranates to quench the thirst with, or a wretched adobe hut where an old woman sat with a faraway look in her eyes as she stroked a hen on her lap.

They paused only to rest and water the horses and to allow the men escorting them to sleep. For his part, Larrea would have carried on without stopping. They could have stayed the night at one of his friend's haciendas, where they would have slept on wool mattresses with clean sheets, enjoyed tasty food, white wax candles, fresh water to wash away the dust and dirt. But he preferred to press on relentlessly, dining on simple tortillas with salt and chili wherever they came across an Indian woman crouched over a brazier who was willing to sell them some; lowering a gourd into streams to drink; and sleeping on palm mats on the bare earth.

"Working the night shift in Real de Catorce was worse, compadre, or have you forgotten?"

Larrea lay with his back to Andrade, a small blanket draped over his large frame. Beneath his head was a large leather pouch containing the money entrusted to him by the countess and Gorostiza. He had his boots on, a gun tucked in his belt and a knife within reach. Just in case. Fixed in the ground around them were a handful of lighted pine pitch torches to keep the coyotes at bay.

"We should have stayed at the San Gabriel hacienda; it's only a few leagues away," grumbled Andrade, unable to get comfortable.

"You're going soft on me, Elias. Sometimes it's not a bad thing to remember where we came from."

Why does this sonofabitch never cease to amaze me? thought Andrade, eyelids beginning to droop from exhaustion. And he meant it: even though he knew Larrea well, he couldn't help being astonished at the way he had borne this colossal setback. In the uncertain world they'd lived in for decades, both he and Andrade had witnessed many a casualty: men at the top who on their way down had lost their reason and committed all kinds of blunders; those whose spirits swayed like reeds in the wind the moment they were divested of their riches.

Rarely had he seen anyone respond the way Larrea did when misfortune sank its teeth into him so mercilessly and unexpectedly. Faced with the unpredictable and devastating vicissitudes of the mining business, he had never known anyone lose so much and lose it so calmly as the man asleep beside him, deprived of all comfort. Like the mule drivers, and the animals themselves, like their Chinaco escort, those peasants who had turned into fighters overnight, brave as they were unruly, fierce as they were loyal.

They had scarcely entered Veracruz when they became aware of the ravages of yellow fever, endemic in that coastal region. A putrid smell laced the air, half-rotting carcasses of mules and horses lay about, and the ubiquitous buzzards, large, black, and ugly, were perched on posts and rooftops, waiting to dive on the animals' remains.

The coachman drove to the Diligencias Hotel without stopping, as if they had the devil on their tail.

"Holy Mother of God, it's hot!" exclaimed Andrade as he stepped onto the dusty ground.

Mauro Larrea removed the neckerchief covering his nose and mouth, then wiped his brow with it. He carefully surveyed the street before openly feeling for his gun to make sure it was where it should be. Afterward, tightly clutching the leather bag containing the money, he shook each of the Chinacos' hands by way of a farewell.

Andrade and Santos Huesos saw to the luggage and stabling the horses while Larrea, in a pointless failed attempt to look respectable, straightened his rumpled clothes and smoothed his hair before entering the hotel.

An hour later he was waiting for his agent in the magnificent entrance, amid an anonymous group of fellow guests. Ensconced in a wicker armchair, he was slaking his thirst with water out of a large jug. He had doused himself with the contents of an entire barrel shortly before, scrubbing himself vigorously to remove the traces of his grueling three-day journey. Afterward, he had donned a clean white linen shirt and the coolest suit he owned to combat the lingering effects of the heat. At last, his damp, tousled hair in place, dressed in casual clothes, he no longer gave the impression of an escaped convict, or an eccentric big-city dweller out of his element.

He had left the hefty bag beneath his bed with Santos Huesos guarding the door, pistol tucked into his belt, and now felt greatly relieved. And, on reflection, he doubtless felt calmer having finally left Mexico City, with its pressures, demands, and lies.

They had agreed to spend the time left before his departure discreetly settling more of his affairs. They would sell the carriage, the horses, and some of his possessions. They also intended to inquire about the situation in Cuba, which had strong ties with Veracruz, and if possible learn of any new developments in the civil war in North America. They even considered throwing a lavish farewell party as a tribute to the old days and to invoke favorable winds for the more-than-uncertain future.

However, the wait for his departure proved shorter than expected.

"I've just come from the port. You sail tomorrow."

Andrade was walking toward him in his usual brisk manner, still dusty from their journey. And yet, despite his grimy appearance, crumpled clothes, and exhaustion, he still managed to exude an air of elegance.

After slumping into the chair next to Larrea, he ran his handkerchief over his shiny bald head. He picked up his friend's water glass and, as was his custom, lifted it to his lips without asking permission, draining its contents.

"I have also been inquiring about whether we've received any mail; all correspondence from Europe comes through Veracruz. I've distributed a few pesos and they'll let me know tomorrow."

Larrea nodded even as he beckoned to the waiter. Afterward, the two men sat in silence, each immersed in his own thoughts, which, given their knowledge of one another, were probably more or less the same.

What had become of the days when they were a handsome silver mining entrepreneur and his dynamic agent? How had all that glory slipped through their fingers? Now, facing each other silently in that port of entry to the New World, they were simply two weary souls dusting themselves off after their fall from grace, searching blindly for a way to build a future from nothing. And, perhaps because the only thing both men had kept more or less intact was their presence of mind, they chose to stifle the urge to hurl angry curses into the air, kept their composure, and accepted the two glasses of whiskey their waiter had just placed on the table.

"All the way from Bourbon County, the best in the house for our fine guests newly arrived from the capital," the young lad declared without any hint of irony.

Shortly afterward, he brought their supper, and the two men went to bed early, each to do battle with his own demons.

Larrea slept badly, as he had virtually every night during the past few months. He breakfasted alone, waiting for his agent to come down from his room. But when at last Andrade did appear, it was through the main door to the hotel, rather than from upstairs.

"I finally managed to get the mail," he announced without sitting down.

"And?"

"Tidings from across the sea."

"Bad ones?"

"Dreadful."

Larrea sat up erect, a shudder running through him.

"Nico?"

Andrade nodded solemnly, then sat down beside him.

"He has abandoned Christophe Rousset's home in Lens, leaving only a note. In it he explained how stifled he felt in that small town, that he had absolutely no interest in coal mining, and that he would see about discussing with you what to do next when the time is right."

Mauro Larrea didn't know whether to let out the bitterest, most savage laugh of his life, or curse like a condemned man before the firing squad; whether to upend the table with its cups and saucers, or knock senseless one of his blameless fellow guests, sleepily sipping their first hot chocolate of the day.

Faced with this dilemma, he struggled to remain calm.

"Where did he go?"

"They believe he took a train from Lille to Paris. One of Rousset's employees saw him at the railway station."

Come on, brother, he felt like saying to Andrade. *So what if it's eight in the morning: Let's repair to a local bar, the two of us, and get dead drunk. We're bound to find one that's still open. Let's play a last game of billiards, bed some whores in the brothels down by the harbor, gamble away the little we have left at the cockfights. Forget that the world exists, and with it all the problems overwhelming me.*

With a great effort, Larrea summoned what little sangfroid he had left, and as the blood beat at his temples like a drum, he reassessed the situation.

"When did we last send him money?"

"Six thousand pesos with Pancho Prats, when he and his wife went to take the waters at Vichy. I imagine they must have arrived there a few weeks ago."

Larrea clenched his fists, his nails digging into his flesh.

"And the moment he got his hands on it, the scoundrel made off with it."

Andrade nodded. Undoubtedly.

"But when his money runs out he might get the notion to return to Mexico, so as soon as I'd read the letter I made a deal with the port customs official, who supervises all the cargo and passengers arriving from Europe. It'll cost us a fortune, but he assures me he'll keep a lookout for him."

"And if he sees him?"

"He'll detain him and send me word."

Gorostiza and his unwed daughter sending up prayers to the Almighty for his fool of a son; his mansion half shut up; Tadeo Carrús—all of them returned to his mind like phantoms out of some gruesome nightmare.

"Whatever you do, brother, don't let him return to Mexico City while I'm not there. He mustn't see or speak to anyone; he mustn't get into any scrapes or ask questions about my reasons for leaving. Inform Mariana the minute you get home: tell her to listen for any rumors spread by people coming from France."

Andrade, who felt toward the boy as though he were his own son, simply nodded.

❧

As midday approached, the dense mass of slate-colored clouds above the port made it impossible to see where the sky ended and the sea began.

Everything took on a depressing gray tone: the faces and hands of the porters, the sails of anchored vessels, the cargo and nets, his spirits.

Even the cries of the stevedores, the water lapping against the ship, and the creaking oars all seemed to echo the mood. The boards on the jetty rose and fell beneath his feet as the distance separating him from his beloved friend grew, drawing him ever closer to the tender that would take him aboard *El Flor de Llanes*, the brig flying the flag of that Spain whose concerns were so remote to him now.

From on deck he contemplated Veracruz for the last time, with its buzzards and sand dunes. In the days of the viceroyalty it had been the gateway to the Atlantic for people and wealth, a silent witness to the aspirations of all those who for centuries had been arriving from the far side of the ocean in pursuit of foolish ambitions, a future with more dignity, or a simple chimera.

On its outskirts stood the legendary Castle of San Juan de Ulúa, now almost completely abandoned. The last outpost of the metropolis, from which the dregs of the Spanish army—starving, diseased, defeated, and in rags—finally departed years after Mexico's declaration of independence, having foolishly struggled to keep the former viceroyalty yoked forever to the crown.

Elias Andrade's parting words came back to him in the tender.

"Take care of yourself, compadre. I'll look after the problems left behind. You just have to try to repeat your own history. Remember, you weren't yet thirty when you excavated mines where no one else dared. You earned the respect of your own men as well as that of the old miners. You behaved honorably when necessary and showed grit when you had to. You became a legend, Mauro Larrea, don't you forget that. There's no need for you to build an empire; you only have to start over again."

Part II

HAVANA

CHAPTER THIRTEEN

They recognized each other from afar, although neither gave any sign of it. Seconds later, when the introductions were made, their eyes met briefly, as if to confirm silently: so it's *you*.

And yet, extending her gloved hand to him, she affected a look of icy indifference.

"Carola Gorostiza de Zayas, pleased to meet you," she said neutrally, as one might rattle off a dusty poem or a response at Sunday Mass.

She bore only the faintest resemblance to her brother, perhaps the way their lips appeared to form a square when they spoke, or the narrow bridges of their noses. She was undeniably beautiful and exaggeratedly opulent, thought Mauro Larrea as his lips brushed her silk glove. A cascade of topazes adorned her bosom, and from her thick, dark, gathered tresses protruded a pair of colorful ostrich feathers that matched her gown.

"Gustavo Zayas, at your feet."

These were the next words he heard, although Zayas wasn't actually at his feet but rather facing him, next to his wife. He was tall, with watery blue eyes, and wore his once fair hair brushed back. And handsome as well, younger than Larrea had expected. For some reason he had assumed Zayas would be roughly the same age as Ernesto Gorostiza, who was seven or eight years his senior. But the man standing before him wasn't much older than forty, although his gaunt face betrayed signs of having suffered the sorts of vicissitudes that others might never have experienced in a hundred lifetimes.

There was scarcely time for more: no sooner had the couple finished their polite greetings than they turned around and made their way through the crowd to the ballroom. One thing was perfectly clear: Carola Gorostiza had no intention of revealing the identity of the newcomer to her husband.

At your orders, if that's how you want things to be, Señora. I'm sure you have your reasons, reflected Mauro Larrea; *I only hope you inform me sooner rather than later what the devil you expect from me*. Meanwhile, he continued to shake hands with the other guests as they were introduced to him by his hostess, the lady of the house, forcing himself to memorize the names and faces of that dense network of influential Creoles and peninsular Spaniards who navigated the two closely connected worlds. Arango, Egea, O'Farrill, Bazán, Santa Cruz, Peñalver, Fernandina, Mirasol.

"Pleased to meet you . . . yes, from Mexico . . . delighted . . . no, not entirely Mexican, Spanish . . . the pleasure is mine . . . delighted . . . how kind . . . so nice to meet you, too."

A lavish atmosphere permeated the splendid villa in El Cerro, the area where numerous members of the Havana upper classes had chosen to build their magnificent residences, having abandoned the decaying palaces in the older quarters of the city that had been inhabited for generations by their ancestors. Extravagance and luxury were palpable in the fabrics and jewelry adorning the ladies, in the gold buttons, braid, and honorary sashes sported by the gentlemen, in the tropical hardwood furnishings, heavy tapestries, and dazzlingly bright lights. *The colossal wealth of the crumbling Spanish Empire's last bastion*, thought

Larrea. *God only knows how long the crown will manage to retain its hold on all this.*

The ballroom floor filled with couples moving to the rhythms of an orchestra of black musicians; at the periphery, clusters of guests were engaged in conversation. An army of gold-braided slaves weaved among them, serving a constant stream of champagne and holding aloft trays laden with delicacies.

Mauro Larrea was content to merely contemplate the scene: the lissom waists of the beautiful young Creole girls bending to the rhythm of the melancholy music, the seductive languor of their swaying skirts. And yet he had no real interest in any of this, but was simply waiting for Carola Gorostiza, despite her initial show of indifference, to give him a sign.

He wasn't mistaken: less than half an hour later, he felt a womanly shoulder brush rather audaciously against his back.

"You don't appear very keen to join in the dancing, Señor Larrea; perhaps a turn in the garden would do you good. Leave discreetly, I shall be waiting for you."

After whispering her message in his ear, the Gorostiza woman sashayed away, flapping her bright feather fan to the strains of the orchestra.

Larrea swept the ballroom with his gaze before following her orders. He could see her husband at the center of a group of guests. He seemed distracted, to be only half listening, as if his mind were in some faroff place. *All the better.* Larrea made his way toward one of the exits, slipping through the stained-glass doors that separated the house from the night outside. Amid the tropical foliage, draped over balustrades or seated on marble benches, couples were speaking in hushed tones in the darkness: flirting, quarreling, making their peace, or swearing undying love.

A few steps farther on, he could make out the unmistakable figure of Carola Gorostiza: her billowing skirts, wasp waist, and generous cleavage.

"I imagine you already know that I have something for you," he began straightforwardly, not wishing to delay matters.

As though deaf to his remark, she started toward the far end of the garden without bothering to check whether or not he was following her. Once she was satisfied that they were far enough from the house, she wheeled around.

"And I have a favor to ask of you."

He might have guessed: he'd felt apprehensive since receiving her note that morning at the guesthouse in Calle Mercaderes. He had taken up lodgings there the previous day after disembarking in Havana following several days of rough seas. He could have chosen a hotel; there were plenty of them to choose from down by the port, where a multitude of souls arrived and departed daily. But when someone pointed him to a guesthouse that was both comfortable and central, he decided that would be ideal: more economical for an open-ended stay, and possibly better located for taking the pulse of the city.

Early in the morning of his first day on the island, still struggling with the humidity and keen to free himself of his obligations, he had sent Santos Huesos to look for Carola Gorostiza's house on Calle Teniente Rey, bearing a note. In it he requested an audience with her at the earliest opportunity, and was expecting to be received promptly. To his dismay her reply was a firm refusal written in an exquisite hand: *My dear friend, I deeply regret that I am unable to receive you this morning . . .* Following a string of vapid excuses, he had been surprised to find an invitation to a ball, that very evening, at the private residence of Señor Barrón's widow, who was a close friend of hers, the letter explained. A horse and trap belonging to the hostess would call for him at his lodgings at ten o'clock that evening.

Reexamining the note as he sipped his second cup of coffee amid the lush palms in the patio where the guests were served breakfast, he puzzled over its meaning. Reading between the lines, he concluded that Carola Gorostiza's overriding desire was to keep him away from her own home. Yet she clearly wished to see him, and had therefore selected a more neutral, less intimate setting.

Midnight was approaching when they finally stood face-to-face in the shadowy garden.

"All I'm asking is that you wait," she went on. "That you hold on to what my brother sent me for a while."

Despite the darkness, Larrea's gesture of irritation couldn't have escaped her.

"Two or three weeks at most. My husband is settling a few business matters. He's . . . he's considering whether or not to make a trip. I'd rather keep this from him until he has decided."

So that's what this is, he thought. *Damned marital problems—just what I needed.*

"In the name of the friendship that unites our families," she insisted after a few moments, "I beg you not to refuse, Señor Larrea. From what Ernesto told me in his letter, which I received only yesterday, you and my brother are soon to forge a family bond."

"I trust so," he replied bluntly, feeling a sharp pang as he recalled Nicolás's disappearance.

A bitter half smile was now visible on her perfectly powdered face.

"I remember your son's fiancée, Teresita, when she was born, swaddled in lace, lying in her cradle. She was the only one who later came to see me off the day I left Mexico. None of my family approved of my marrying a Spaniard and leaving for Cuba."

As she unashamedly shared the same confidences her brother Ernesto had already told him about, Carola Gorostiza now and then glanced toward the mansion. In the distance, amid the warm lights of the chandeliers and candelabra, they could make out the shapes of the guests through the tall stained-glass windows. Snatches of voices, tinkling laughter, and the mellow rhythms of the *contradanza* filtered out to them on the breeze.

"To avoid further complications," she added, returning to the present, "it's essential my husband remain ignorant of your connections with my family in Mexico. I beg you therefore to make no attempt to contact me."

Her voice was abrupt, with none of the flourishes of her handwritten note that morning. Presenting him unceremoniously with both a requirement and a fact.

"And to compensate for any bother my request might cause you, I propose to offer you, say, a tenth of the sum you have brought me."

He stifled a guffaw. At this rate, he would recoup his losses without having to lift a finger—first the countess and now this other mysterious woman.

He gazed at her through the shadows. Elegant, undeniably attractive, with her audacious neckline and sumptuous appearance. She didn't look like the victim of a tyrannical husband, yet he knew nothing of marital strife. The only woman he had truly loved had died in his arms, drenched in sweat and blood after giving birth to her second child when she was not yet twenty-two.

"Very well."

Even he himself was surprised by his hasty acceptance of her offer. *You utter fool, what on earth were you thinking?* he reproached himself. But it was too late to back out now.

"I agree to be discreet, and to take care of what belongs to you for as long as necessary. However, I want no financial compensation."

Her expression hardened.

"What, then?"

"I also need help. I came here in search of business opportunities, a way of making money quickly that doesn't require much investment. You know this society, you move in wealthy circles. Perhaps you can tell me where there might be profits to be made."

She responded with a sour laugh, her black eyes glinting in the dark.

"If making a fortune overnight were that easy, my husband would doubtless have left Cuba by now, and I wouldn't be forced to sneak around with such damned caution behind his back."

Larrea had no idea where her husband was intending to go, nor was he interested. But he felt increasingly uneasy at the unexpected turn their conversation was taking, and he was keen for it to end. Voices could be heard nearby, and doubtless they weren't the only ones hiding from prying eyes and ears in the darkness of the garden.

"Let me make some inquiries," she whispered at last. "But don't come looking for me; I'll contact you. And remember: you and I have never met."

In a swirl of shimmering taffeta, Carola Gorostiza made her way back toward the lights, the music, and the throng. Larrea stood motionless amid the dense undergrowth, hands in his pockets, watching her until he saw her step through the glass doors and become swallowed up by the party.

Only when he was alone did he become aware of his predicament: rather than ridding himself of a burden, he had taken on an even heavier one. And he could see no way out. He wished the transfer of the inheritance had been settled once and for all, freeing him from his obligation. He would have celebrated by dancing with the first caramel-skinned beauty he stumbled upon, even if he had first to negotiate the price of her caress. He wished the ground felt firm beneath his feet.

But instead, like a fool, he had recklessly struck a bargain with a disloyal wife who had long ago burnt her bridges with her own family and was now intent upon deceiving her husband over some money he had hidden at the back of his wardrobe. *For heaven's sake, brother, have you lost what little sense you had left?* he thought he could hear Andrade's prodigiously sensible voice echo in his head.

He went back into the mansion just as the last guests were leaving and the weary musicians were yawning and packing up their instruments. On the marble floor, where a myriad steps had been danced, lay a mixture of crushed, half-smoked cigars, the flattened remains of sweetmeats, and fallen plumes from the ladies' fans. Beneath the high ceilings of the ballroom, amid the stucco and mirrors, some of the household slaves burst into laughter as they downed the dregs of champagne.

There was no sign of Señor and Señora Zayas Gorostiza.

CHAPTER FOURTEEN

⁂

He awoke mulling over the events of the previous night. Weighing things up, debating with himself. Until he resolved to stop thinking: time was short, he needed to act. Becoming bogged down in what had already been done would lead nowhere.

He and Santos Huesos went out early. His immediate concern was to find a safe place to deposit the countess's money and his own meager capital, as well as Carola Gorostiza's inheritance, with which he was still burdened. He could have asked the proprietress of the guesthouse, but he didn't wish to attract attention. Since nothing about this port city seemed straightforward, he preferred to reveal no more than was necessary about himself.

He soon realized how inappropriate his fine English wool suits were for the tropical climate as he crisscrossed the heart of Havana. Despite the familiar Spanish names of the streets, such as Empedrado, Aguacate, Tejadillo, and Aguiar, and plazas such as San Francisco, del Cristo, La Vieja, and de la Catedral, they bore no resemblance to those he was familiar with in Mexico City. Everything seemed thrown together in an eclectic mingling of humanity and architecture where vendors selling salted cod occupied the ground floors of the finest town houses, where

junk shops and hardware stores stood shoulder to shoulder with grand
noble mansions.

He turned down Calle del Obispo, teeming with people conversing and pungent aromas, then Calle San Ignacio, which led him to the
fashionable Calle O'Reilly, where it was rumored each square yard cost
an ounce of gold. In the thick, humid air among the grid of narrow
streets there hovered a smell of the sea and of coffee, of bitter oranges
and the sweat of a thousand perspiring bodies mixed with fish, salt,
and jasmine. A frenzied clamor of cries and laughter arose from every
corner, carriage, and balcony.

The store awnings, large strips of colorful fabric strung from side to
side, created a welcome shade from the harsh light. Weaving his way
along, he dodged children, dogs, porters, messengers, fruit sellers, and
tinkers. He saw shop assistants emerging from stores laden with goods
destined for ladies and adolescent girls who sat waiting in carriages
without having to alight to make their purchases.

After trying a couple of commercial houses, which did not satisfy him instinctively, his third attempt bore fruit: a large, ramshackle
building on Calle de los Oficios with an enamel plaque bearing the
words *Casa Bancaria Calafat*. The proprietor, a fellow with a bushy
mustache, cottony white hair, and a good many years' experience behind him, received Larrea at a magnificent mahogany desk. Above him,
an oil painting of the port at Palma de Mallorca evoked the now-distant
origins of his surname.

"I wish to deposit a certain amount of capital temporarily," Larrea
announced.

"I don't believe I'd be boasting if I said that you couldn't have come
to a better place on the entire island, my friend. Please, if you will, take
a seat."

The two men discussed fees and interest rates, each politely arguing on his own behalf. After reaching an agreement, they proceeded to

count the money. Then came the signatures and the preamble to their taking leave of one another, having made a deal in which both stood to gain and neither would lose.

"It goes without saying, Señor Larrea," declared the banker once the transaction was concluded, "that should you require advice on any local matters relating to business that you might be planning to pursue here, I am entirely at your disposal." He had sensed that this fellow with a Spanish passport, the build of a stevedore, the speech of both a Spaniard and a Mexican, and the commercial savvy of a Jamaican buccaneer had the makings of a good steady customer.

I'd sell my soul to the devil to know what those businesses might be, Larrea thought.

"We'll speak again," he replied evasively as he rose. "For now, I'd be grateful if you could direct me to a good tailor."

"The Italian Porcio, in Calle Compostela, without a doubt. Tell him I sent you."

"I will. Much obliged."

Larrea rose to his feet and made to leave.

"And when you have satisfied your sartorial requirements, Don Mauro, I wonder whether you'd be interested in having me recommend a profitable investment," said Julián Calafat.

Larrea could have burst out laughing. *Shall I tell you something, my good man?* he wanted to say. *Of all the capital I've left in your safekeeping, which gives you the impression that I'm a prosperous foreigner with money coming out of his ears, less than one-fifth is really mine. And to obtain that, I had to mortgage my house to a miserable moneylender whose sole desire is to see me rolling in the mud.* But, consumed with curiosity, he held back and allowed Calafat to continue.

"Needless to say, investing in a few well-chosen ventures would give you an excellent return."

Instead of pressing for an immediate answer, the crafty old banker gave Larrea a moment to reflect while he plucked a pair of Vueltabajo cigars from a nearby box. He squeezed them gently to test their humidity, then sniffed them slowly before finally offering one to Larrea, who, still on his feet, accepted.

Without saying a word, both men clipped their cigars with a silver guillotine. Afterward, immersed in a lengthy silence, they lit them using the same long cedarwood match.

Concealing the unease assailing him, Mauro Larrea sat down once more at Calafat's desk.

"Please proceed."

"As it happens," the banker resumed, exhaling a first puff of smoke, "one of our silent partners has pulled out of a deal at the last minute, and I thought the business might interest you."

Larrea crossed his legs, one elbow propped on the arm of his chair. Having adopted the pose, he drew on his cigar. Emphatically, protractedly, as if he were the master of the universe, successfully disguising his frail resolve behind a façade of self-assurance. *Let's hear it, then, old man*, he thought. *I've nothing to lose by listening.*

"I'm all ears."

"A refrigerated vessel."

"I beg your pardon?"

"The remarkable invention of a German fellow; the English are attempting the same thing but have yet to perfect the technique. Used for transporting fresh beef from Argentina to the Caribbean. Perfectly conserved, no need to salt the stuff, unlike that revolting jerked beef they feed their slaves."

Larrea drew on his cigar once more. Anxiously.

"What exactly are you proposing?"

"That you invest one-fifth of the total capital, which would make you the fifth partner. If not, I shall put up the money myself."

Larrea had no way of knowing the potential of such a venture, but, judging from the sums involved, which the banker went on to explain, it was significant. Larrea's first instinct was to trust Calafat blindly. Thus he made a few swift calculations, but as he had expected, he didn't have enough—not even if he invested both his and the countess's money.

And yet, there was a way. On top of Calafat's table, the gold sovereigns contained in the leather pouches Ernesto Gorostiza had given him seemed to draw him with a force akin to that of the Earth's core.

What if he suggested to Gorostiza's sister that she put up half the money, become his partner?

Are you out of your mind? Andrade would have yelled had he been there. *You can't take that risk, Mauro; don't get involved in something you can't afford. For the sake of your children, compadre, for their sakes I implore you to start off small, don't hang yourself from the first tree you find.*

Stop urging caution, compadre, and listen, he silently rebuffed Andrade's imaginary supplications. *This might not be as crazy as it first appears. Something is troubling that Gorostiza woman; I could see it in her eyes last night. And yet she doesn't appear desperate for the money. She simply wishes to conceal it from her husband, for reasons I prefer not to know. Doubtless she fears he will squander it or take it with him on his purported trip.*

But what if her brother Ernesto finds out? What if she confides in him? Andrade would have countered, to which Larrea also had an answer. *She has nothing to gain from doing that. And if I'm mistaken, well, I'll deal with him when the time comes: I believe he has more faith in me than in her. I can offer his sister a good return on her money without anyone in Havana finding out about it; I can keep it out of her husband's clutches for good, invest it wisely. In short, I can look out for her interests in secret.*

As he mused on the arguments he would have used on his friend, Larrea continued listening to Calafat.

"Look, Larrea, let me be frank with you. It won't be long before this island of ours goes to the devil. Before that happens, I aim to start moving my business abroad. People here live under the happy illusion that we are, and always will be, champions of the New World until kingdom come, persuaded that our glorious sugarcane, tobacco, and coffee will supply us with riches for all eternity, amen. Only a handful of visionaries seem to understand what awaits the largest jewel in the Spanish crown. All her overseas colonies, with the exception of those in the Caribbean, have become independent; they are forging their own paths, and sooner rather than later we, too, will have to sever that umbilical cord. The question is how, and where will we go from there . . ."

Inside Larrea's head, mathematical calculations were still dancing. *How much money do I have? How much do I owe? How much can I lay my hands on?* Cuba's future was of no concern to him at that instant. Even so, if only to appear polite, he feigned interest.

"I see. I suppose the situation is comparable to Mexico before independence: the mother country demanding extortionate taxes, ruling with a rod of iron, subjecting everyone to laws that they dictate at their whim."

"Exactly. However, geographically, socially, and economically this island is far less complicated than Mexico. It's really quite simple: we only have three possible options. And, to be honest, I'm not sure which of them is worst."

The investment, Don Julián. The refrigerated vessel: Stop digressing and talk to me about that, for God's sake, However, Calafat clearly lacked the ability to read minds, and so, oblivious to the concerns of his new client, he continued his discourse on Cuba's uncertain future.

"The first, favored by the upper classes, is to maintain our ties with Spain ad infinitum while gaining greater self-rule and representation in the Spanish parliament. In fact, the wealthiest men on the island already spend a fortune buying influence in Madrid."

Once again, out of politeness, Larrea felt obliged to express an opinion.

"But surely the rich would benefit most from independence; they'd no longer have to pay taxes or levies and would be able to trade more freely."

"No, my friend," Calafat said firmly. "Independence would be the worst option for them, because it would mean the end of slavery. Not only would they lose their investments in the slave trade, but without the prodigious African manpower toiling from dawn to dusk on their plantations, their businesses would collapse within weeks. Do you see the irony? In a sense, by failing to pursue independence because of their slaves, they make slaves of themselves."

"Does no one want independence, then?"

"Of course, but as one might want a utopia, a Platonic fantasy: an anti-slavery, liberal republic, secular if possible. A beautiful ideal espoused by patriotic dreamers in Masonic lodges, secret meetings, and clandestine publications. Alas, I fear we have neither the power nor the institutions to live freely. We would soon fall under the yoke of a fresh oppressor."

Larrea raised an eyebrow.

"Why, the United States of America, my dear friend," Calafat went on. "Cuba is their prime target outside the continent; they have had their sights trained on us for some time now. Presently, their plans are on hold due to their own civil war, but the moment they stop killing one another, united or not, they will turn their gaze on us once more. We are strategically placed off the coast of Florida and Louisiana; three-quarters of our sugar production travels north; over here they are admired and feel at home. In fact, several times they have offered to buy us from Spain. It vexes them immensely how many of the dollars they pay to sweeten their tea and biscuits end up in the coffers of the Bourbon kings in the form of taxes, if you follow me."

Those damned gringos again.

"Perfectly, Señor Calafat. In other words, the dilemma for Cuba is whether to remain yoked to the avaricious mother country, or pass into the hands of those money-grabbers in the north."

"Unless the worst were to happen."

Calafat removed his slender gold-framed spectacles as if they were bothering him. He placed them carefully on the table, squinting at Larrea, then explained:

"An uprising, my friend. A slave rebellion like the one in in Haiti at the turn of the century that led to their independence from France. That is the specter haunting the entire Caribbean: the fear that the Negroes will slaughter us."

Larrea nodded.

"So, whichever way you look at it, we're buggered," said the Cuban, "if you'll pardon the expression."

Larrea did not flinch at this use of the word but was shocked by the banker's blunt depiction of the various possibilities.

"And in the meantime," Calafat went on with a hint of mockery, "here in the Pearl of the Antilles we continue to cavort in our luxurious ballrooms dancing *contradanzas* night after night, jaded by indolence, our love of posturing, and our blindness. This is what life on this island is like: reckless, morally bereft. There is always some reason, some pretext or other. We are simply a colony of frivolous, irresponsible people who think only about the present: no one here cares about giving their children a proper education, there is no such thing as a small enterprise, nearly all our merchants are from abroad, fortunes are rarely handed down to second generations but are squandered at the gaming tables. We are a vibrant, sociable, generous people—passionate, even—but our own insouciance will be our undoing."

Fascinating, reflected Larrea. *A concise, intelligent portrait of the island. And now, Señor Calafat, please be so good as to get to the point.*

His silent plea was finally answered.

"That's why I'm suggesting you become a partner in this venture.

Because you are Mexican—or Spanish-Mexican, as you described your-self. But that's all the same to me. What matters is that your money comes from Mexico, our independent sister nation, which is where you plan on returning."

"Forgive my ignorance, but I fail to see the connection."

"Because, my friend, if I give you a helping hand now by making you my business partner, I feel sure you will return the favor should I need to expand into other territories if and when the situation over here deteriorates."

"If you'll permit the observation, the current situation in Mexico isn't propitious for any large investments."

"I'm perfectly aware of that. However, things are bound to settle down. And Mexico still has a wealth of untapped resources. These are my reasons for wanting you to join our enterprise. A favor for a favor, as the saying goes."

Decades of civil strife, the state coffers gathering cobwebs, bitter tensions with the European powers—this was the true landscape he had left behind in his adopted country. But he didn't press the point. If the banker wished to envisage a bright future, why should he open the man's eyes to his own detriment.

"How long before we see any profit from these shipments of refrig-erated meat?" he broke in, steering the conversation back to a more practical course. "Forgive my candor, but I've no idea how long I will be staying in Cuba, and I need this information to help me decide."

"Three months, possibly three and a half, before we receive the first shipment, depending on the sea. Otherwise everything is in place: the equipment, the necessary licenses . . ."

Three to three and a half months. Almost exactly the time he had left to pay the first installment on his debt. An image flashed into his mind of the miserly consumptive Tadeo Carrús praying to the Virgin of Guadalupe to let him live long enough to see Larrea's downfall. Of

Tadeo's maimed son, Dimas, counting the number of balconies on his house in the dead of night. And of Nico, drifting around Europe, or possibly homeward bound.

"And what sort of profits are we talking about, Don Julián?"

"Approximately five times our original investment."

He was about to roar, *Count me in, old man.* This could prove to be his salvation, for the idea sounded promising and authentic, like Calafat himself. And the timing was perfect: he could take the money and return to Mexico. Numbers and dates danced about incessantly in his head even as he heard his agent's voice booming at him from afar. *Bribe a customs official for information about a shipment, or start dealing in contraband if you have to—we've done worse things in our time, cheating like devils to obtain the quicksilver for our mines. But don't drag a woman you hardly know into this venture behind her husband's back, you fool. For the love of God, don't play with fire.*

"How soon do you need an answer?"

"In forty-eight hours, I'm afraid. Two of my associates will be sailing for Buenos Aires then, and everything has to be decided before their departure."

Larrea rose to his feet, struggling to stifle the clamor of numbers and voices inside his head.

"I'll let you know as soon as possible."

Calafat extended his hand.

"I shall be waiting, my dear friend."

Hush, Andrade, damn it! Larrea yelled at his conscience as he stepped out again into the heat, squinting from the harsh noonday light. He took a deep breath and could detect the trace of iodine from the sea. *Shut up, brother, and let me think.*

CHAPTER FIFTEEN

෧

Mauro Larrea continued making calculations while being fitted for the two beige linen suits and four cotton shirts he had ordered. The Italian tailor, Porcio, to whom Calafat had sent him was as skilled with a needle as he was endlessly loquacious in discussing the island's fashions. As he took precise arm, leg, and shoulder measurements, he elaborated in a singsong voice on the vast differences between the Cubans' way of dressing, with their lighter fabrics, brighter colors, and looser fits, and that of the peninsular Spaniards, who, despite traveling back and forth to their last great colony, were wedded to their broad-lapelled frock coats and thick Castilian cloth.

"And to top it off, sir, I would suggest a pair of Panama hats."

Over my dead body, Larrea muttered under his breath. He had no intention of trying to pass for an islander but rather to ward off as best he could that sweltering heat while his fate became clearer. However, for the sake of his own well-being, he relented somewhat, finally swapping his staid, narrow-brimmed European felted hat for a lighter, floppier version with a shallower crown and a brim wide enough to protect him from the midday sun.

Having accomplished this task, he devoted himself to reflection and observation. He continued to analyze Calafat's offer as he scrutinized his surroundings, paying particular attention to any stores he came across to see what was being sold and bought in Havana, how transactions took place, where the money was, where he might find the refuge of an affordable business. He had already learned that copper mining wasn't an option, since large American companies had bought up the few unproductive mines that still existed after the Spanish crown had relaxed the regulations thirty years earlier. He had also discovered that Cuba's principal source of trade was sugar. The white gold, as it was known, moved millions: vast sugarcane plantations, hundreds of mills, and more than 90 percent of production continually leaving Cuba's ports for overseas consumption, only to return in the form of vast revenues in dollars, pounds sterling, and duros. The output of coffee plantations and abundant tobacco plantations came a close second. The result was the creation of an extremely wealthy upper class of Creoles who, although they complained bitterly about the excessive taxes exacted by Spain, never seriously entertained thoughts of independence. And the necessary driving force generating this torrent of wealth was the tens of thousands of slaves toiling from dawn until dusk.

Larrea's wanderings took him past the old city's wall through the Montserrate gate to the more modern, spacious part of the city. Following the shade cast by the trees in the Parque Central, and the rumbling of his stomach, he arrived at the entrance to a café called El Louvre, where marble-topped tables and cane chairs had been set out for lunch. He sat down at a table vacated by three uniformed officers and signaled to the waiter that he would start off with the same drink that he had just set down before a foreign couple at a nearby table, something refreshing to help combat the oppressive heat.

"One mamey juice in no time at all, Señor," said the young mulatto.

In the meantime Larrea kept thinking, thinking, thinking.

"Will you be ordering any food, Señor?" asked the waiter, seeing him drain his glass in two gulps.

Why not? he thought.

As he sipped his drink while waiting for his spicy chicken stew to arrive, accompanied by two glasses of claret, he continued to ruminate. About Calafat's proposal. About Carola Gorostiza. About how alien to him all these agricultural businesses such as sugarcane, tobacco, and coffee were, not to mention the added vexation they entailed in having to wait for the natural cycle of the harvest.

As the city began sinking into its afternoon torpor, he remained racked by doubts and decided to return to the guesthouse.

"Just a moment, Señor Larrea," the proprietress called out when she heard him reach the shady upstairs balcony.

His fellow guests were dozing contentedly in hammocks or rocking chairs, shielded from the sun by white cotton drapes. He had dined with them the night he arrived: a Catalan salesman of stationery products, a burly American who polished off a pitcher of Portuguese red wine all by himself, a wealthy businessman from Santiago de Cuba who was passing through the capital, and a plump Dutch lady whom no one could understand and whose reasons for being on the island were a mystery to all.

Doña Caridad intercepted him before he could reach his room. A mature, rather buxom woman with black hair peppered with gray, dressed in white from head to foot like most females in Havana, with the air of a woman accustomed to carrying herself with self-assurance, despite her noticeable limp. Larrea had been told she had been the lover of a surgeon-general in the Spanish army. Upon his death, in lieu of a widow's pension, she had inherited this house, much to the annoyance of his legitimate family in Madrid.

"This arrived for you before lunch," she said, handing him a sealed envelope. The front bore his name; the back was blank.

"A coachman handed it to one of my mulattas. That's all I can tell you."

Feigning indifference, he slipped the letter into his pocket.

"Will you be taking coffee with the other guests, Don Mauro?"

He made up some feeble excuse, eager to read the letter.

No sooner had he entered his room than his intuitions were confirmed. Carola Gorostiza had written to him again, enclosing a ticket to the Teatro Tacón for a play that very evening: *La hija de las flores o Todos están locos* by Gertrudis Gómez de Avellaneda. *I hope you like romantic drama*, she wrote. *Enjoy the performance. I will come and find you in due course.*

In fact, he neither liked nor disliked romantic drama, and wasn't even curious to see the Teatro Tacón. Generally hailed as magnificent, it was named after a former captain general in the Spanish army, a veteran of the Battle of Ayacucho whose memory survived in the Antilles three decades after he was deposed.

"Are you attending another ball at El Cerro, Señor Larrea?"

The question rang out behind him a few hours later, after nightfall, when the first candles had been lit on the balcony, and the scent of freshly watered plants filled the courtyard. *How on earth does this good lady know all about my comings and goings?* he thought as he swung around. But before he had a chance to reply to Doña Caridad, she herself, after casting a slow, approving eye over him, furnished a response.

"In Havana, my dear Don Mauro, everyone knows everyone else's business. Especially where an elegant gentleman of substance such as yourself is concerned."

He was freshly bathed and dressed once again in his frock coat. His hair was still damp and his skin smelled of soap. *Mind your own business, Señora, and leave me in peace,* he wanted to tell the proprietress, but it would have jarred with his appearance, and besides, he sensed that she might make a good ally should he ever need one.

"Alas, this elegant gentleman of substance, as you refer to him, regrets to inform you that he isn't going to a ball tonight."

"Where, then, if you don't mind my asking?"

"To the Teatro Tacón."

She took a few steps forward, dragging her leg unself-consciously.

"We have a saying here in Havana, which everyone who comes here ends up learning."

"I can't wait to hear it," he replied.

"Three things in Havana must be seen by everyone: El Morro, La Cabaña, and the chandelier in Teatro Tacón."

Sailing into Havana on board *El Flor de Llanes*, he had contemplated El Morro and La Cabaña—the two fortresses that greeted and bade farewell to all those who arrived or departed from the port—and had done so again when his wanderings had taken him down to the bay earlier. And now he would see the enormous French cut-glass chandelier hanging from the ceiling in El Tacón. He had only to wait for the hired trap to drop him at the theater.

A short while later, following the instructions in the note he had received, he took a seat in a box, nodding politely to those either side of him, before observing his surroundings. He was not overwhelmed by the white and gold ornamentation on the five magnificent balconies, or the guardrails upholstered in velvet; even the famous chandelier left him cold. Carola Gorostiza's face was the only thing he was looking for among the hundreds of theatergoers slowly filling the seats. Intently he scanned the boxes, the orchestra, the parterre, the balconies, and finally the stage itself. He considered asking his neighbor, a voluptuous older woman, to lend him the mother-of-pearl theater glasses lying on her brocaded lap as she whispered sweet nothings in the ear of her companion, a young man with curly sideburns, fifteen or twenty years her junior.

His instinct commanded him to desist. *Calm down, compadre*, he told himself. *Have no fear. Sooner or later she will make her appearance.*

She didn't. But her words did, delivered by an usher just as the huge auditorium started to grow dim. He quickly unfolded the note, managing to read it before the last lights went out. *The foyer outside Count Casaflores's box. Intermission.*

He would have been unable to say whether the performance was sublime, passable, or dreadful; the only description that occurred to him was intolerably long. Or so it seemed to him, since, absorbed in his own thoughts, he paid scant attention to the intricacies of the plot or the actors' declamatory voices. As soon as applause began to ring out around the auditorium, he rose to his feet in relief.

The foyer where Carola Gorostiza had asked him to meet her was a moderately sized but sumptuous salon where it was the custom for season ticket holders to invite friends and acquaintances to take refreshment during the interval. No one asked who he was or who had invited him when, with contrived aplomb, he pushed aside the heavy velvet curtain. Black slaves passed around silver salvers bearing liqueurs, jugs of water with floating chunks of ice, and long-stemmed glasses of guayaba and cherimoya juice. The author of the message soon appeared. Dressed in a dazzling coral-colored satin gown and wearing a splendid ruby necklace, her black locks wreathed in flowers, she had made sure she would not go unnoticed. Especially by Larrea.

If she had spied him waiting for her, she disguised it well, ignoring him for the first few minutes. For his part, he was content to wait, every now and then exchanging greetings with someone he had met at Casilda Barrón's ball at El Cerro, or whose face looked vaguely familiar.

Finally, accompanied by two friends, she made her way toward him, expertly steering her group to the side of the room. The four of them exchanged polite greetings and pleasantries about the performance, the splendor of the auditorium, the beauty of the lead actress. After a few similarly trivial comments, Señora de Zayas cleared her throat as a signal to her companions, who vanished amid the crowd in a swirl of silk and taffeta. And then at long last Ernesto Gorostiza's sister satisfied his burning curiosity.

"I've been told about something that might interest you. It all depends on what scruples you may have."

He arched an eyebrow quizzically.

"This isn't the place to go into details," she added in hushed tones. "A meeting will take place tomorrow night at Casa Novás, the crockery store on Calle de la Obrapía. Be there at eleven o'clock. Tell them Samuel sent you."

"Who is Samuel?"

"A moneylender from outside the city walls. Everyone knows Samuel and no one will doubt your word; you might as well tell them the bishop or the captain general sent you."

"Provide me with some clue."

She gave a sigh, which revealed a somewhat more risqué décolleté than was customary at social gatherings in Mexico City.

"You'll soon learn the details."

"What about you and your husband?"

She blinked, as if she hadn't expected such a direct question. The sound of popping corks and the tinkle of laughter and the chink of glasses surrounded them; a hundred voices floated in the air, hot and sticky as honey.

"What about us?"

"Will you be taking part in this venture?"

She stifled a curt laugh.

"Not on your life, dear sir."

"Why not, if this is such an excellent opportunity?"

"Because in theory we have no funds at present."

"Permit me to remind you of your inheritance."

"Permit me to remind you that I intend to keep that a secret from my husband, for reasons which I prefer to keep to myself."

And long may it stay that way, my good woman. Far be it from me to interfere in your marital problems, he thought. *All I need right now, Carola Gorostiza, is your money. I have no interest in your husband, his predicaments, or his comings and goings, and that is how I want to keep it.*

What he actually said was "I can invest it on your behalf without arousing any suspicions. Make it grow."

The smile froze on her lips. A bloodless smile, an expression of astonishment.

"I am proposing that we put our capital together, and that I act on behalf of us both," Mauro Larrea explained without waiting for her to reply. "I'll look into that other matter you mentioned in good time, but first let me tell you that I have my sights set on a different scheme. Something solid and lucrative. Guaranteed."

"Your proposition is extremely risky . . . I barely know you . . ." she whispered.

She accompanied her unease with a brisk wave of another impressive fan made of marabou feathers, a deep coral pink that matched the color of her dress. Then, equally swiftly, she appeared to regain her composure, the stony smile returning to her face as she greeted people to left and right.

Oblivious to her eagerness to keep up appearances before the other guests, he persisted. Determined, convinced. He had only one card left. And this was the perfect time to play it.

"In approximately three months we will begin to see a profit; our investment will appreciate, and in the meantime I can guarantee you absolute confidentiality. I think I've already shown you that I'm a man of my word: had I intended to swindle you out of your money, I could have done so by now; there have been plenty of opportunities since your brother entrusted me with delivering it to you. I'm simply suggesting a way for you to invest your money anonymously by adding it to my own capital. Rest assured, we will both end up profiting from this venture."

A hundred times I've seen you place a gun on the table before a band of hardened soldiers in a stubborn attempt to negotiate the price of safe conduct for your silver. I've seen you do battle with the devil himself to obtain the concession for a mine you had your eye on; I've seen you ply your adversaries with drink in whorehouses to wheedle information out of them regarding the location of promising veins of ore. But I never thought you'd stoop so low as to inveigle a woman into handing over her money to you, you sonofabitch. Andrade's voice hammered again at his conscience with the same tenacity that he himself had battered the rock face in his day. Their long years together had taught him to anticipate Andrade's responses, and now, like a deadweight, he was unable to prevent them from interfering with his own thoughts.

I'm not deceiving anyone, brother, he protested silently while Carola Gorostiza chewed her lower lip, struggling to digest his proposal. *This woman is no innocent dove like Fausta Calleja; she's no gentle lamb whom a man seduces so that he can take her to bed or steal her heart. She knows what she wants and what her interests are. And remember, she tried first to obtain something from me.*

What about her husband? Andrade's voice went on. *What will happen if that alligator Zayas finds out about the shady dealings between you and his wife?*

I'll think about that if and when the situation arises. In the meantime, be off with you, by the souls of your departed. Get the hell out of my head!

"Take some time to think it over," he told Carola. "Our partners are men of substance." Leaning toward her ear, he lowered his voice to a deep whisper. "Trust me."

As some hidden instinct led him to take his lips away from her face, he turned toward the entrance. At that instant, he saw Gustavo Zayas part the velvet curtain before crossing the threshold. He stood erect, a cigar in his mouth, the shadow of something indecipherable on his face: at once troubled and melancholy.

The two men's gazes did not meet but rather slid over one another almost imperceptibly. Slantwise, tangentially. Then they both whisked away.

By now the foyer was a crush of people, and Carola Gorostiza had vanished from his side. Bodies jostled against one another with no concern for propriety: shoulders and chests rubbed against backs, women's bosoms brushed against men's arms in a chaos of humanity that no one seemed uncomfortable about and in which it was difficult to tell who was engaging with whom, in which group, in which conversation, and in which latest piece of tittle-tattle.

Amid the throng, perhaps Gustavo Zayas had not noticed his wife conversing intimately with that stranger, away from the other guests. Or perhaps he had.

Mauro Larrea did not stay for the second half of the performance: he accepted a last drink and stood aside to let the others back through. Vexed at not having obtained a definite answer from Ernesto Gorostiza's sister, he contemplated the pictures hanging on the walls: pen-and-ink drawings of lotharios and buffoons, operatic baritones and handsome youths, weeping into the tangled tresses of languishing maidens.

When he could sense that everyone had taken their seats—when he was certain that the famous chandelier had dimmed and that silence had enveloped the auditorium like a magnificent cloak—he slipped noiselessly down the marble staircase and disappeared into the tropical night.

CHAPTER SIXTEEN

❧

Mauro Larrea spent the better part of the next morning pacing up and down Calle de la Obrapía, with Santos Huesos acting as scout. This was the fourth time they had walked past the crockery store.

"Now, go inside and tell me what you see," ordered Larrea.

"I think I need to have a reason for entering the place, *patrón*," replied the young servant with his usual deliberate caution.

Rummaging in his pocket, Larrea handed him a few coins.

"Buy something," he replied. "Anything. A sugar bowl, a water pitcher, whatever takes your fancy. The important thing is that you tell me what, and above all who, is in there."

Santos Huesos slipped through the glass door. On it was a sign: *Casa Novás, Local and Imported Ceramics*. To the left, a glass cabinet lined with shelves presented a variety of earthenware objects. Stacked plates, a large soup tureen, washbowls of differing sizes, a statue of the Sacred Heart of Jesus. Nothing of any value: ordinary tableware that any normal family with a house of their own would use all year round.

It was a while before Santos Huesos emerged carrying a small package wrapped in a page of *El Diario de La Marina*. Larrea was waiting for him on the corner of Calle Aguacate.

"Anything to report, lad?" he asked in his usual friendly manner as they strolled off together: a clean-shaven, relatively youthful Don Quixote without his nag, and a slender, dark-skinned Sancho Panza; two men proceeding with caution in a territory alien to them both.

"Four shop assistants and a gentleman who could have been the owner."

"Age?"

"I suppose the same as Don Elias Andrade, give or take a year or two."

"Fifty-something?"

"I think so."

"Did you hear him speak?"

"No, *patrón*; he had his nose buried in a ledger the whole time I was in there. I didn't see him look up once."

Jostled by the dozens of people thronging the streets, they continued walking beneath the brightly colored awnings screening them from the sun.

"What about his clothes? How was he dressed?"

"Well, like a gentleman."

"Like me, you mean?"

Early that morning, when Larrea had received his first suit from the Italian tailor, he was so pleased at how light and cool it felt to the touch that he had slipped it on right away. Before he left, Doña Caridad had given him a glowing look of approval. *It must look all right, then*, he thought.

"Yes, of course, dressed up just like you, like a real Havana regular. A pity Miss Mariana and Master Nicolás can't see you now."

Without slowing pace Larrea removed his hat and gave the young man a playful rap on the head.

"One word of this when we get back, and I'll have your guts for garters. Anything else?"

"The shop assistants all wore a sort of gray topcoat, buttoned from head to toe."

"Were they black or white?"

"White as chalk."

"What about the customers?"

"Only a few, but they had to wait, because there was only one assistant serving."

"What were the others doing?"

"Filling boxes, sealing parcels. Preparing orders for delivery, I guess."

"What was on the shelves and cabinets?"

"Crockery, crockery, and more crockery."

"Like the good sort we had in San Felipe Neri, or the rough bowls we had at Real de Catorce before we moved to the city?"

"Like neither, I'd say."

"What do you mean?"

"Not as fine as the first or as humble as the second. More akin to what Doña Caridad uses in her guesthouse."

Larrea was assailed with doubt. What kind of profitable business venture could that harmless establishment be engaged in? Surely Carola Gorostiza wasn't suggesting he become the partner of a producer of vases and chamber pots, the associate of an elderly shopkeeper, in the hope he might inherit the business? And why ask him to go there at eleven at night, when throughout Havana people were starting to carouse, packs of cards were being opened, and musicians were tuning their instruments in preparation for the dancing?

He had to wait roughly twelve hours to find out, until twenty minutes to eleven, when he set off from the guesthouse in his usual sober attire. The streets were crowded even at that late hour; Larrea had to leap aside several times to avoid being run down by one of the typical open-top carriages that raced through the Cuban night, carrying to their places of entertainment the city's most distinguished gentlemen, accompanied by dark-eyed Havana beauties, laughing gaily, bare-shouldered, their flowing tresses wreathed with flowers. A few gazed at him shamelessly, one gesturing with her fan, another smiling.

⌘

Santos Huesos was with him once more, but this time he remained outside.

"Stay right by the door, understood?" Larrea had told him on the way there.

"Sure, *patrón*. I'll wait for you until daybreak, if need be."

At two minutes after eleven, Larrea pushed open the door.

The store was dark and appeared deserted, although from somewhere at the back a glimmer of light and the sound of muffled voices reached him.

"Your name, sir."

He felt instinctively for his gun, which was tucked in his belt as a precaution. But the relatively amiable tone of his interlocutor, probably a slave, reassured him.

"Or just tell me who sent you."

"Samuel," he recalled.

"In that case, come in and make yourself at home, sir."

Before arriving at the meeting place in the rear, he had to cross a wide corridor filled with wooden crates. The walls were lined with bales of straw, which he assumed were for packaging. Then he came to a courtyard, on the far side of which stood two open gates.

"May God grant you a good evening, gentlemen," he said somberly as he crossed the threshold.

"Good evening to you, too," the company replied as one.

His senses on high alert, he glanced around the room.

Firstly, his eyes took in the shelves, which in this part of the store were stacked with what was clearly the main stock-in-trade of the business—behind the façade of washbasins, cheap vases, and crude figures of miraculous saints. Instantly appreciating the quality of the goods, he glimpsed dozens of fine pieces of porcelain china from halfway around the globe. Derby and Staffordshire figurines diverted from their original destination in British Jamaica, Meissen fawns and pastoral scenes, biscuit dolls, busts of Roman emperors, majolica wares. There were also urns, screens, and Cantonese figurines shipped from the Orient via Manila to bypass the strict custom controls the Spanish crown had established in its remaining colonies.

His nose told him that this reeked of contraband.

The men gathered there, all of whom looked decent and respectable, had stopped speaking, waiting for the newcomer to introduce himself.

He removed his hand from his revolver, acquired years before from an arms trafficker in Mississippi in circumstances no less shady than what appeared to be going on at present.

Smuggling fine ornaments: so this is the business Señora Zayas wishes to involve me in. It certainly wouldn't offend my morals, nor would it seem excessively dishonest or ignoble. But with so many partners, I can't see it being very profitable. Such were his thoughts as he extended his arm to shake hands with the group of seven men. *Mauro Larrea, at your service; Mauro Larrea, at your disposal.* No point in concealing his identity: any one of them could have found out who he was the next day.

They did not hide their credentials, either: an army colonel; the proprietor of Le Grand, a fashionable French restaurant; a tobacco planter; two high-ranking Spanish officials. To his surprise Porcio, the garrulous Italian tailor who had made the linen suit he'd been wearing most of the day, was also there. And last but not least, the host, Lorenzo Novás, owner of the business.

Despite the obvious value of the items around them, the room was little more than a storehouse with ashen-colored walls. In keeping with the décor, the furniture consisted of a rustic table flanked by benches. The only provisions on offer were a flagon of rum and a few half-filled glasses, a sheaf of cigars bound with red ribbon, and a pair of tinder lighters—courtesy of the house, he assumed.

"Well, gentlemen . . ."

Novás rapped the table ceremoniously with his knuckles to catch their attention. The voices died down, and everyone became seated again.

"To begin with, I'd like to thank you for placing your trust in me, for agreeing to listen to what I offer you in this promising venture. That said, permit me to go straight to the point by outlining the pertinent facts all of you will want to know. Firstly, I'd like to inform you that our ship has docked at the Regla quay: a brigantine built in Baltimore, fast and well made, like the majority of vessels that came from that port before the Yankees went to war. They glide like swans in a fair wind, and hold their own in rough seas, not like your coastal sloops or the old schooners they used in the siege of Pensacola. She is a worthy vessel, I can assure you, and comes equipped with four new cannons as well as a hold that has been remodeled for maximum capacity."

The company nodded, giving murmurs of approval.

"I'm also pleased to inform you," he went on, "that as of now we have a captain from Malaga who besides knowing the business has important contacts among the agents and stewards in the area, and is completely trustworthy—a quality that's fast disappearing in this day and age. He is busy hiring officers and engineers: navigators, a chief mate, a ship's surgeon, and so forth. In no time at all, the pennant will be raised and the boatswain will assemble a crew. In this line of business, as you know, they are usually a mixture of—"

"Bunch of riffraff," muttered one of the company.

"—tough, experienced men, which is exactly what we need," Novás retorted. "I wouldn't want them to woo my daughters, but they are perfectly equipped for the task at hand."

A sardonic half-smile appeared on some of the faces, while the Italian, Porcio, gave a chuckle. Larrea, for his part, listened with clenched jaw.

"Forty plucky fellows, in any case," Novás went on, "each of whom will receive a monthly wage of eighty pesos and, as is the custom, an extra seven silver coins for each item that arrives in port undamaged. Also, to be on the safe side, I've urged the captain to make sure he hires a good cook: a well-fed crew is less inclined to mutiny."

"Why not provide him with a few exquisite recipes from Le Grand?" quipped Porcio, attempting to raise a laugh.

No one obliged, least of all the restaurant owner. Ignoring him, Novás took the floor again.

"A cooper is making two hundred barrels for water, and the rest of the provisions will be purchased over the next few days: casks of molasses and liqueurs, tubs of lard, and sacks of potatoes, rice, and beans. The magazine will be well stocked with gunpowder, and a smithy is busy making what we need to . . ." He paused before clearing his throat. "To adequately secure the cargo, if you follow my meaning."

Nearly all of them nodded for a third time.

"When do you expect the ship to be ready?" asked the restaurant owner.

"Three weeks at the most, we hope. And to avoid arousing suspicion, she will be authorized to sail for Puerto Rico, although afterward she will head for the other destination we have discussed. However, upon her return, instead of docking in Havana, the ship will proceed to a quiet inlet close to a sugar mill, where we have arranged for it to be received and its merchandise unloaded."

"Not wishing to jump too far ahead, but may I ask how it will be unloaded?" This time it was one of the Spaniards who wanted more details.

"By all means: into canoes. We investors will travel overland by carriage and divide up the merchandise. Afterward, we will either scuttle or set fire to the vessel, or, if she is still seaworthy, refurbish and sell her."

Too many precautions, reflected Mauro Larrea after listening intently.

In Mexico far less care was taken over such clandestine operations. He supposed that such measures were required because of the far-reaching tentacles of mainland bureaucracy, which were more present in Cuba.

"As for the proceeds," Novás continued, "let me remind you that the total sum of the merchandise will be divided into ten parts . . ."

Mauro Larrea's brain was busy making calculations. His own money alone wouldn't be enough. He needed more. A fair amount more.

". . . of which, as the owner of the vessel, I propose to take three."

Upon hearing Novás's declaration, the company murmured their acceptance, while Larrea continued his conjectures. He did not have enough. But if Carola Gorostiza were to agree . . .

"How long will the expedition take from start to finish?" the colonel then asked.

"Three to four months, approximately."

He felt his heart pounding: exactly the same as the refrigerated vessel. If Carola Gorostiza played along, he might succeed. It was risky, but he was trapped in the vise-like grip of Tadeo Carrús's hateful demands. And, despite that, there was a slim chance.

"Of course, a lot depends on sailing conditions," the vessel owner went on, even as Larrea forced himself to interrupt his reverie to listen. "Generally, each crossing takes no longer than fifty days, but the precise duration depends on whether loading takes place on dry land or from floating platforms off the coast. And on how much merchandise is available at the time: sometimes, if we are lucky we make an excellent purchase without even having to go ashore."

"At what price?"

"That depends on the supply. In the past you could barter for a few barrels of rum, or bolts of colorful fabric, or a half dozen powder kegs; even a sack full of looking glasses and beads would buy you a substantial shipment. Not any more: the agents drive a hard bargain as middlemen, and there's no way around them."

"And how many . . . items do you estimate will reach the port in acceptable condition?" asked one of the officials in a thick Castilian accent.

"Assuming a ten percent loss during the voyage, about six hundred and fifty."

Novás appeared to have an answer for everything: he was certainly no novice in the smuggling business.

"And the profit over here?" another asked.

"Approximately five hundred pesos apiece."

There was a general murmur of dissatisfaction. *Accursed moneygrubbers*, Larrea thought. *How much did they think they would make?* Needless to say, for him five hundred pesos was a not-insubstantial sum. Once more, his brain began to make rapid calculations until the shipowner's voice pierced his thoughts.

"Of course, the profits could be greater. As you know, the price varies according to age, height, and overall fitness."

Some of what Novás was saying puzzled him, but he preferred not to interrupt before he had finished.

"While others may fetch less, usually because the merchandise is damaged—although still intact, I hasten to add."

This went without saying. Who would want a punch bowl with a handle missing, or a one-armed cherub?

"By which I mean alive. And those with child sometimes fetch double."

The others nodded, and Larrea knitted his brow. *What the devil?*

So porcelain goods weren't the real object of Novás's business, or indeed the merchandise being transported in the hold of the brigantine from Baltimore. Now he understood, and it was all he could do to stop himself from crying out in terror: *Holy Mother of God.*

These men weren't trading in figurines of shepherds and cherubs. The merchandise they were talking about was the bodies of living, breathing people. They were involved in the slave trade.

CHAPTER SEVENTEEN

H e glanced nervously through the open gates as he waited for the banker Calafat to put in an appearance. So far, only a couple of clerks and three young slave girls armed with brooms and rags had entered the premises.

He had spent half the night awake and, to counter the effects of his insomnia, had drunk three coffees at La Dominica, a fashionable café on the corner of Calle O'Reilly and Mercaderes, a few blocks from the banker's office.

He was just beginning to curse the aversion the moneyed classes in La Habana had to rising early, when a few minutes after half past nine he glimpsed the old man's unmistakable visage.

"Señor Calafat?" he boomed as he crossed the street in three strides.

The banker seemed unruffled by his presence.

"It's good to see you again, my friend. And if you've come to give me a favorable response to my proposal, I shall be a very happy man. This very afternoon the message bearing our names will be dispatched to Argentina, and . . ."

Larrea clenched his fists. This business was slipping away from him.

The banker's proposal was slipping through his fingers. Another might be opening. Perhaps. Or perhaps not.

"For the moment, I only came here to ask you a quick question," he said evasively.

"At your service."

"It's quite straightforward and shouldn't take long; I simply require some information about another matter. I expect it will come as no surprise to you that I'm weighing several options."

They entered the office and sat down on either side of the large mahogany desk, in the cool shade provided by the half-closed shutters.

"Fire away. Whether or not you end up going into partnership with me, I am still managing your capital, and therefore entirely at your disposal."

Larrea went straight to the point.

"What do you know about the slave trade?"

Calafat responded just as straightforwardly.

"That it's a dirty business."

The adjective hung in the air. *Dirty. A dirty business*, with all the attendant connotations.

"Please go on."

"The slave trade is still legal under Spanish law as applied here in Cuba, although in theory it has been proscribed in accordance with the British, who were the first to abolish it. That is why English frigates police the Atlantic and Caribbean seas, to make sure their law is upheld."

"And yet the practice continues in Cuba."

"Less so than before, but, yes, I believe it still goes on. The trade's glory days, if you'll pardon the grotesque expression, were at the turn of the century. Although everyone knows that the Africa run still exists, and that thousands of poor wretches continue to be shipped to these shores."

"They're known as ebony shipments, aren't they?"

"Ebony or coal."

"What sort of people invest in this trade?"

"The sort with whom, if I am to judge from your questions, you are already acquainted. Anyone who can afford to fit out a vessel and bankroll a run. Merchants for the most part, or business owners of various kinds. Even the occasional opportunist willing to take a gamble. People acting alone or with others. All sorts."

"What about the wealthy sugar, tobacco, and coffee planters? Don't they take part in it, given how much they profit from slave labor?"

"Strange as this may sound, the sugar barons and the other planters are increasingly opposed to the slave trade. However, don't be deceived: they are motivated not by compassion but by fear. As I already mentioned, this island has a huge African slave population, and the more they keep arriving by the shipload, the greater the risk of a revolt. Believe me, that is their biggest fear. And so they have adopted the position that best suits their own interest: they oppose the slave trade while refusing to countenance any talk of abolition."

Larrea frowned as he took a few seconds to digest this information.

"Anyone can pursue this activity, Don Mauro. You or even I would have no difficulty setting ourselves up as slave traders if we so wished."

"But we don't."

"Naturally, I haven't the slightest intention of doing so. I cannot speak for you."

With the objectivity of a man in his profession, but without a trace of melodrama or any fake compassion, the old banker added: "It can be a profitable business, certainly. But an unscrupulous, evil one."

Where the devil are you when I need you, Andrade? Where are your reproaches? Here I am, walking barefoot on the brink of something as sinister as a newly sharpened knife, and not a peep out of you. Have you nothing to say to me, brother? No criticisms, no recriminations? His conscience was still trying to summon his agent even as Calafat accompanied him to the door.

"You alone can decide where you wish to invest your money, my friend. Just bear in mind that my offer still stands."

Calafat glanced up at the clock that hung on one of the walls.

"For a few more hours only," he added. "As I mentioned before, two of our partners are sailing tonight for the Río de la Plata; after that it will be physically impossible to change the terms of the enterprise."

Mauro Larrea fingered the scar on his hand again.

"A simple signature would suffice," Calafat said finally. "Your money is already safe with me; for you to join us, all I need is your name on a piece of paper."

A single idea hammered inside Larrea's head as he left the banker's office: he had no choice but to convince Carola Gorostiza. Convince her that this investment was worthwhile, that they could both make a handsome profit without having to go anywhere near the abominable slave trade.

As he contemplated how best to contact her, he wandered down the sidewalk, accompanied by Santos Huesos, almost oblivious to where he was headed. And yet he already seemed to observe his surroundings through different eyes.

Approaching Plaza de Armas, they walked past dozens of black women with their tiny Creole charges, cuddling them, suckling them, cooing over them. Down on the quayside they saw a mass of dark bodies wearing only breeches; sweat-covered muscles moving back and forth between cargo and boats, to the rhythm of a booming chant. In the crisscross of shopping streets, beneath the bright awnings that filtered the sun, they watched young mulatto girls swaying voluptuously as they flirted with the many men of differing colors, who threw compliments at them as they passed.

Beneath the arches of La Plaza Vieja, in El Mercado del Cristo and La Cortina de Valdés, outside cafés and churches, at all hours of the day and night, they saw Africans everywhere: indeed, Larrea had been told they accounted for nearly half the population now. Women selling tripe were leaning against the house fronts, exchanging banter and bawdy jokes. Trap drivers shouted amid the clamor of hooves, brandishing their whips, proudly vying with one another in the smartness of their attire and the liveliness of their steeds. Cart pushers clad in rolled-up trousers and palm hats, and bare-chested street vendors— from knife-sharpeners through to peanut sellers—hawked their wares in the same melodious tones. And behind the walls and gates of the wealthy and middle-class residences, Larrea intuited the presence of numerous domestic slaves: twenty, thirty, forty, as many as sixty or seventy souls, he had been told. Well nourished and well dressed, with few chores and plenty of room to languish on rush mats during the hottest part of the day, chatting or dozing, combing each other's hair as they laughed and joked, or idling as they waited for their master. *My mulatica* or *my negrilla* were common terms of affection used by their owners. Some would even show a degree of respect, with an occasional *Señor* Domingo or *Señora* Matilde.

They don't appear to have such a hard life, Mauro muttered to himself in an effort to make these innocuous scenes sweeten the cruel business in which he had been invited to take part. *The miners in Mexico had a far worse job, despite not being owned by their employers and receiving a daily wage*, he reflected. These were the thoughts occupying Larrea's mind when, in the middle of Calle Teniente Rey, he saw him emerge.

At that precise instant, Gustavo Zayas, dressed in a fine beige linen suit, appeared from what Larrea assumed was the entrance to his house, cane tucked beneath his arm as he donned his hat. Under the brim, his face wore the usual tense, solemn expression, his jaw clenched; Larrea had never seen the man smile.

Fortunately, the everyday crowds in the streets of La Habana prevented Zayas from noticing his presence on the pavement opposite his house. Not wishing to take any chances, Larrea grabbed Santos Huesos by the arm and ducked into the entrance to a pharmacy, where they stood side by side.

"Is that where Don Ernesto's sister lives?"

He didn't need his servant to confirm the information.

Turning his head discreetly, Larrea followed with his eyes the tall, distinguished figure of Gustavo Zayas making his way through the multitude before disappearing around the corner. He waited a few moments until he reckoned Zayas had gone far enough not to return for some item he might have left behind.

"Come along, lad. We're going in."

They crossed the street and walked through the open gates into the courtyard. Once inside, they asked a skinny young mulatta girl shaking a rug where her mistress was.

"Are you out of your mind?" Carola Gorostiza yelled, no sooner than the door closed behind him.

Far from inviting him upstairs to the family living quarters, she dragged him into what appeared to be a storage room on the first floor containing some sacks of coffee and pieces of junk. Her black tresses hung loose halfway down her back, and she wore a bright blue chiffon dressing gown tied casually at the waist. She had no jewelry or makeup on, and without these superfluous adornments she looked several years younger. Doubtless she had just arisen from bed; when he had asked the mulatta girl to call her mistress, she had told him Carola Gorostiza was having breakfast.

"I need to talk to you."

"How could you be so foolhardy as to come here?"

From behind the door they heard the shrill barks of a little dog demanding to be let in.

"Don't worry, I've just seen your husband leaving the house."

"But . . . but . . . for the love of God, have you lost your mind?"

A fist rapped on the other side of the wooden panel and a man's voice rang out: one of the household slaves, he thought. The man asked his mistress whether everything was all right. The dog barked again.

"If you refuse to listen to me now, name a place and I will meet you there, but I need to speak with you urgently."

Attempting to calm herself, she gave a couple of anxious sighs as her scantily clad bosom rose and fell.

"In La Alameda de Paula. At midday. Now please leave."

❧

The splendid boulevard overlooking the bay was all but deserted; she had made a wise choice. After sundown, when the heat had abated, it would fill up with couples, families, soldiers, officers, young Spaniards newly disembarked in search of a fortune and pretty Creole girls old enough to woo. At midday, however, only a few solitary figures were scattered along the promenade.

He waited for her, elbows propped on the fanciful iron balustrade separating land from sea, tiny waves lapping at his feet. She arrived by trap, more than half an hour late, her image of a well-dressed woman having been restored: her face powdered, her hair gathered up, and the heavy fabric of her canary-yellow dress spread out on either side of the seat, leaving the lace trim on the hem of her skirts a few inches from the floor. On her lap, a silk ribbon between its ears, sat the little dog that had barked like a devil outside the door of the room where they had spent a few minutes together.

For Carola Gorostiza, in common with the ladies from her adopted city as well as many of her own Mexican countrywomen, to allow her silk slippers to touch the dusty ground when stepping out of a carriage onto a public thoroughfare was almost as irreverent an act as standing naked before a cathedral altar. And so, after the vehicle came to a halt, she dismissed her driver with a gesture and did not move from the trap.

Mauro remained standing, on guard.

"Do me the honor of never coming to my house again. Ever."

This was her greeting.

Larrea didn't mince his words, either.

"Have you considered the proposition I put to you at the theater?"

Instead of replying yes or no, Gustavo Zayas's wife posed another direct question, in the brisk tone that reminded him of the countess.

"How did you fare at Novás's store?"

"The meeting was merely informative."

"Am I to understand from this that you're thinking about it?"

Carola Gorostiza was cold and calculating, and he needed to keep his nerve. He instantly went back to the subject that interested him.

"Have you considered my offer of investing in the refrigerated vessel?" he repeated.

She paused for a few moments before replying as she ran her fingers through the lapdog's thick fur. Fondling the animal's head, she gazed at Larrea with those dark, inscrutable eyes, which weren't exactly beautiful but oozed a steely determination.

"Yes and no."

"Do you mind being more precise?"

"I'm willing to accept your offer of a partnership, Señor Larrea. I agree to combining our capital for our mutual benefit."

"But?"

"But not in the business you are proposing."

"Which, I can assure you, is an extremely profitable one."

"That may well be, but I prefer the other . . ." She cast a sidelong glance at her driver, a slender mulatto clad in a crimson dress coat and stovepipe hat, seated on a stone bench a short distance off, finishing his cigar. "I wish to invest my money in the ebony trade. Only then will I go into business with you."

"Firstly, allow me to explain, Señora."

Her reply rang out like a cannon shot from El Morro.

"No."

A pox on the goddamned Gorostiza family, and on that villain Novás! A stream of abuse more befitting the coarse language of miners than a man of his standing passed through Mauro's head. As the waves gently lapped against the rocks and his mouth remained in a firm line, he shook his head slowly from left to right, from right to left, then back again. *I won't do it.*

"Why not?" she asked with a hint of disdainful surprise. "Why do you refuse to take part in this venture with me? My money is worth no less in one business than in the other."

"Because it displeases me. Because—"

A bitter laugh rose from her bejeweled throat. She had chosen aquamarines that morning.

"Don't tell me you are another of those lily-livered abolitionists, Larrea. I believed you to be a man of fewer prejudices, my friend, with all your elegance and seeming self-possession. I see now that appearances can be deceptive."

He chose to ignore her remark and instead to employ all his powers of persuasion in the matter that really interested him.

"Permit me to go into more detail about the business I am proposing: we have little time before they embark."

She sighed, evidently irritated, then clicked her tongue to emphasize her vexation. The little lapdog seemed to bark in agreement as its mistress's ample bosom rose and fell.

"I thought that in Mexico and Cuba everyone spoke the same language. Do you genuinely not understand the meaning of the word 'no'?"

He took a deep breath, hoping the sea air would lend him the patience he sorely needed.

"All I ask is that you reconsider," he insisted, adopting a neutral tone to conceal his anxiety.

Deaf to his pleas, she turned her head haughtily toward the bay.

"If you change your mind, Señora, I'll be at my guesthouse all afternoon, awaiting your final answer."

"I doubt you'll receive it," she hissed without looking at him.

"Even so, you know where to find me."

He doffed his hat, marking the end of the conversation, then walked off along La Alameda. Carola Gorostiza remained perched on the trap, face set in a grimace, eyes stubbornly fixed on the brigantines' masts and the unfurled sails of the schooners.

Depending upon her decision, as though hanging from a thread as fine as that of a spider, Mauro Larrea would either succeed in making money with a minimum of dignity, or continue to stare into the abyss.

CHAPTER EIGHTEEN

❧

The guests started to rise from the table after lunch, heading for the rocking chairs on the balcony. Two dark-skinned girls carried dishes containing the remains of stuffed turkey and rice pudding out to the kitchen. Both were young and beautiful, with slender naked arms and generous smiles, and wore brightly colored scarves gracefully wrapped about their heads like turbans.

However, neither of them brought a message for him or for Doña Caridad: he had heard nothing from Carola Gorostiza since their meeting hours earlier.

"It amazes me, Don Mauro, how much you get around after only such a short time here in Havana."

Accustomed by now to Doña Caridad's indiscretions, he limited himself to murmuring something under his breath, and put down his napkin as he made to rise from the table.

"Not just dances and the theater," she continued undeterred, "but late-night trysts as well."

He shot her a look sharp enough to cut a lemon in two. Despite this, he decided to remain seated even though he had been about to get up. *Very well*, he seemed to say to her. *Carry on, Doña Caridad; speak your mind. After all, I have little left to lose.*

She played for time, issuing needless orders to the slave girls until the last diners had left.

As soon as they were alone he blurted out: "I confess to being surprised by your apparent interest in my affairs, Señora."

"Not in any profound way, I assure you; gossip soon reaches me when one of my guests ventures onto treacherous ground."

"Whether it reaches you or not, I don't think what I do outside your establishment is any of your business. Or is it?"

"No, Señor, it isn't. You're absolutely right. However, since you do me the honor of remaining seated at my table, allow me to take up a little more of your time . . ."

She paused for dramatic effect, her lips curving into a smile as sweet as it was false.

". . . So that not only do I get to know a bit more about you, but you also learn about me," she added.

Go to hell, he was tempted to retort, sensing this was a trap. But he didn't move a muscle.

"I am a quadroon," she went on. "From Guanajay, daughter of a Canary Islander from La Gomera and a slave woman from the San Rafael sugar plantation. *Quadroon* means a quarter Negro; that's to say, my father was white and my mother was a mulatta. A beautiful mulatta she was, the daughter of a black girl just arrived from Gallinas, impregnated at the age of thirteen by the master of the house, who was fifty-two. He took her by the waist while she was out chopping cane; lifted her up like a feather, she was so slight. Eight months later my mother was born. Since the planter had no children because his wife was barren as a desert, they decided to keep her, as you might a straw doll. And to prevent her little black mother, my grandmother, from becoming attached to the child, they sent her to a different plantation. There, unable to see her own daughter grow up, she became increasingly rebellious until finally, at age seventeen, she took to the hills. Do you know what becomes of slaves that take to the hills, Señor Larrea?"

"I'd be lying if I said I did."

Nor had it occurred to him that Doña Caridad, whose skin was the same color as his, had African blood in her veins. Although, now that he looked closely, some of her features might have given him a clue: the texture of her hair, the breadth of her nose.

Mauro Larrea continued to sit at the table, cleared by now of plates and cutlery, listening to the proprietress of the guesthouse with feigned indifference.

"Three possible fates await a runaway slave—or *cimarrón*, as they are called here, in case you didn't know that, either: they are slaves who dare to escape from their masters, who demand sixteen hours' hard labor each day in exchange for a few plantains, a morsel of yucca, and some scraps of dried meat. Would you like to know what those three fates are, Señor?"

"Of course; tell me if you wish."

"The lucky ones reach Havana, or some other port, where they manage to get passage on a boat sailing for anywhere in the Americas where slavery has been abolished and they can live freely. Or they are caught and subjected to the usual punishments: locked away for a month in the darkest corner of a hut; whipped to the point of losing consciousness . . ."

"And the third?"

"They are torn apart by dogs—hunting dogs specially trained to track, and often kill, *cimarrónes*. Would you like to know which fate befell my grandmother?"

"Please."

"So would I. Alas, no one found out. Ever."

The two of them sat alone around the tablecloth, Doña Caridad at the head and Larrea to one side, his back to the white awning that kept out the sunlight and screened them from the courtyard. For a while, all was quiet. The two young slave girls were washing the dishes, the guests dozing amid the vines and bougainvillea.

"Are you going to tell me the moral of this story, Doña Caridad, or must I work it out for myself?"

"Who said anything about a moral, Don Mauro?" she retorted, a hint of mockery in her voice.

He could have picked that moment to tell her to go to hell. But she spoke first.

"It was merely an episode I wished to relate to you, one of many. To show you how slaves outside the city live: those in sugar estates, on coffee and tobacco plantations. Those you do not see."

"And you have done so, for which I am grateful. May I retire to my room now, or do you have any more lessons in morality to impart?"

"Would you like your coffee to be served here at the table?"

Despite his outward composure, Larrea felt a twinge of unease in his gut. Best make himself scarce.

"I'd prefer to retire, if you'll excuse me," he said rising at last. "All this coffee is starting to disagree with me."

He was already on his feet, one hand leaning on the back of his chair, when he contemplated her once more. She was no longer young, nor was she beautiful, although she might once have been. Now, well into her fifties, her waist had thickened, she had deep, coal-black shadows under her eyes, and her cheeks had started to sag. And yet she was mature, serene, possessed of the natural wisdom of one who has met people from all walks of life. Two decades earlier, she had turned the villa her former lover left her into an exclusive guesthouse, and by now Caridad Cervera was more than accustomed to holding her own in an argument, even into the small hours.

Without thinking about it, Mauro Larrea sat down again.

"Since you know so much about me and appear eager to instruct me regarding the shadier side of my business, perhaps you could help me shed some light on another matter."

"Naturally, if I'm able."

"Don Gustavo Zayas and his wife."

The corner of her mouth twisted in a mocking grin.

"Who are you more interested in, him or her?"

"Both. Either."

She gave a soft, silent laugh.

"You don't fool me, Don Mauro."

"Far be it from me to even try."

"If the husband were the object of your inquiry, you wouldn't have taken the opportunity this morning to sneak in to see his wife after he had left his house."

This time it was Doña Caridad's turn to rise, limping over to the nearby sideboard. *Damned gossipmonger*, he thought as he watched her. Scarcely a few hours had passed since he had ventured into the Zayases' residence and she already knew about it: her network of informers must extend to every corner of the city.

Returning to the table with two small tumblers and a carafe of rum, she sat down again.

"You can pour. Courtesy of the house."

He obeyed, filling both glasses. One for her and one for him.

"I know the couple," she said at last. "Everybody knows everybody in Havana. Only by sight, mind you, not to greet them; we aren't acquaintances. But, yes, I know who they are."

"Tell me, then."

"A married couple like any other. With their ups and downs. The usual thing."

She raised her glass and took a tiny sip of the strong liquor. He followed suit, taking a larger swig. Then he waited for her to go on, convinced she would reveal more than these platitudes.

"They have no heirs."

"That I already know."

"But they have a reputation."

"For what exactly, might I ask?"

"Her, for being difficult and extravagant: you only have to look at her to see that money slips through her fingers like water. Perhaps she is independently wealthy; I have no idea."

He did. Only too well. But he was careful not to share that information with Doña Caridad.

"What about him?"

"He has a reputation for being rather volatile, both in his ventures and his finances, but that's nothing new over here. People have arrived empty-handed from mainland Spain and within five years have built business empires, while the heads of wealthy Creole families have fallen by the wayside and lost everything in the blink of an eye."

Five years to make a fortune: an eternity. But, as Andrade had told him when they parted company in Veracruz, he needn't build an empire; he had only to make enough to pull himself from the quagmire, to start breathing again.

However, at the moment they were discussing the Zayas couple. He would do well to keep focused.

"So tell me, Doña Caridad, what is their current financial situation?"

Her lips curled again in a half smile.

"How much money do they have? My knowledge doesn't extend that far. All I know is what I see in the street, and what my friends tell me when they come visiting. As you've seen for yourself, they are invited to the best houses: he with his appearance of a man of substance, she dressed to the nines by the extremely expensive Mademoiselle Minett. And never without her bichon."

"I beg your pardon?"

"Her bichon, the little dog she takes with her everywhere."

"I see."

"However, certain recent events concerning the couple have become common knowledge, so it wouldn't be an indiscretion for me to tell you about them . . ."

She raised her glass to her lips and took a second sip.

"In fact, truth be told, this is merely one of many such incidents that occur on this unpredictable island, where everything changes depending on which way the wind blows. Do you follow me, Don Mauro?"

"Of course, dear lady."

Doña Caridad gave him a knowing look. She could go on.

"They came into an inheritance recently. Some properties, or so I heard."

Another pause.

"In Andalusia, apparently."

Frustrated at receiving the information in dribs and drabs, Larrea refilled his glass.

"Do you know who they inherited from?"

"They had a guest staying with them for a while. A cousin of his."

"A Spaniard?"

"Yes, a paltry fellow. On account of his size, I mean: he looked more like a child than a man. Don Luisito, as he began to be known in Havana. For a time, it seemed there wasn't a dinner, dance, social gathering, or performance the three of them didn't attend together. Although, according to what I heard, for I saw nothing myself . . ."

She trailed off to take another sip.

"Where was I? Yes, according to what I heard, for I saw nothing with my own eyes," she went on, "it was she who fawned over the cousin. Laughing at his jokes, whispering in his ear, riding out with him in her trap whenever her husband was away on business. Tongues started to wag: Was their relationship indiscreet? Had she been seen coming and going from his room as she pleased? As you know, Don Mauro, people talk, even if what they say has no basis in fact. And, of course, he was the subject of as much gossip as she was."

Interesting, he reflected. *Interesting to know the rumors that were circulating in Havana about the woman who had thus far refused to cooperate with him. He cast a surreptitious glance at the wall clock. A quarter past four, and no news from her. It's still early,* he told himself. *Don't lose heart. Not yet.*

"So . . . what exactly did people say about him?"

The liquor seemed to have loosened Doña Caridad's tongue, and she spoke more freely now, with fewer pauses or attempts to ration the information. Although perhaps it wasn't the alcohol at all but merely the delight she took in discussing other people's affairs.

"They wondered: Was it true the cousin came over here to settle family scores? Was Don Gustavo implicated in some sordid affair and been forced to flee Spain all those years ago? Had he, in his youth, been in love with a woman who left him for someone else? Did he long to return to his mother country? Made-up stories for the most part, I suppose, don't you agree?"

"I suppose your supposition is correct," he conceded. *Worthy of the libretto of an operetta in the Teatro Tacón.*

"Until the cousin was no longer to be seen riding with her, or at social gatherings, and a few weeks later news came of his death. At their coffee plantation in the province of Las Villas, it was alleged."

"As a result of which they inherited his properties."

"Exactly."

"Any capital?"

"Not as far as I know. However, no sooner had they buried the fellow than she started to boast about their vast estates in Spain. Fine properties, she said. And a wine plantation."

"A vineyard, you say?"

Doña Caridad shrugged.

"Perhaps that's what they're called: I'm afraid I am unfamiliar with the names they give things in the mother country. In any case, to finish off—"

Just then one of the slave girls hurried in with what looked like a folded piece of paper for her mistress. Mauro Larrea sat up straight. Was this the message from Carola Gorostiza he had been waiting so impatiently for? *I accept to ally myself with you: Go straight to Señor Calafat and tell him yes.* He would have given the remaining fingers of his left land for this to have been her reply. But it wasn't.

"Alas, Señor Larrea, we will have to end our pleasant conversation there," said Doña Caridad, getting to her feet. "A family matter has arisen. A cousin of mine is about to give birth, and I must leave at once for Regla."

He rose to his feet also.

"Naturally, I shan't detain you a moment longer."

As they made to go their separate ways, she swung around.

"May I give you a piece of advice, Don Mauro?"

"Anything, coming from you," he replied, masking all trace of irony.

"Place your affections elsewhere. That woman isn't right for you."

He struggled to stifle a bitter laugh. His affections, she had said. His affections, for God's sake.

He spent the afternoon in his room, waiting in shirtsleeves, the shutters pulled to so that scarcely any light entered. First he wrote to Mariana and began by asking her about Nico. *Use your contacts, my child; you know people who travel to and from both continents. Find out all you can about him.* He went on to provide a detailed description of Havana, its inhabitants, streets, and flavors. He captured these images with pen on paper, keeping to himself the true cause of his anxiety and bewilderment, the thing that was undermining his integrity, turning his stomach, shaking the very foundations of his morality. Recalling his pregnant daughter, images of the little thirteen-year-old black girl impregnated by her master flashed through his mind. He thrust it from his thoughts and continued to write.

When he had finished the lengthy missive, he glanced at the clock. Five minutes to six. Still no word from the Gorostiza woman.

Afterward, he began composing a letter to his agent. He had intended to make it brief: a few general impressions, together with an outline of the two matters currently occupying his attention. One clean, the other soiled. One safe, the other risky. But the words wouldn't come: he was incapable of describing what he wanted to say without spelling it out word for word in terms he declined to use. *Dishonorable. Shameful. Inhumane.* He only succeeded in filling a couple of sheets with crossings out and inkblots. Finally he gave up. Then he set fire to the illegible pages using a tinder lighter before adding a postscript to his letter to Mariana. *Tell Elias everything is fine.*

He glanced once more at the clock. Twenty past seven. Still not a whisper from the Gorostiza woman.

It was getting dark when he pushed open the shutters and stepped out onto the balcony to finish his cigar. Shirt unbuttoned, he propped his elbows on the iron balustrade and contemplated the incessant hubbub below. Blacks and whites, whites and blacks, and every shade of skin color in between, coming from and going to a thousand different destinations, at all hours of the day and night, shouting, laughing, hawking their wares, uttering greetings and curses. *In a crazy city,* he reflected, *on a crazy island.*

Afterward he took a bath, dressing once more like a man of means. He bumped into two of his fellow guests, the Catalan businessman and the Dutch woman, who were leaving their rooms at the same time. They all descended the stairs together, although that evening, unlike them, Larrea did not make his way to the dining room.

CHAPTER NINETEEN

❧

The military band sounded the evening concert as a cannon blast from the Cabaña fortress announced the time: nine o'clock. La Plaza de Armas was teeming at that hour; half of Havana had turned out to enjoy the open-air music and the cool sea breeze. Some lounged on benches; others strolled among the borders and palm trees surrounding the statue of the unprepossessing King Ferdinand VII, perched on a plinth. Sitting inside the row of carriages circling the gardens, the city's most eligible young ladies were wooed by a procession of handsome gentleman admirers who flocked around the running boards.

Mauro Larrea leaned heavily against one of the columns of the Conde de Santovenia's palace, arms folded, a solemn expression on his face as the band launched tunes from operas and popular songs into the air. He was all too aware that at that very moment two of Calafat's partners were waving good-bye to their loved ones from the deck of the English Royal Mail steamship, bound for Buenos Aires, taking with them considerable sums of money and an extremely auspicious financial venture. A venture in which he himself could have participated but had slipped through his fingers forever.

Night had dropped suddenly like a black curtain, and the light from myriad candles flickered from the open balcony windows of the magnificent captain general's palace. With Santos Huesos by his side, Larrea continued to survey the scene distractedly, present yet absent, killing time as he stood propped against the stone pillar. A blind man approached selling tickets for a raffled pig. A young lad, head covered in scabs, offered to shine his boots, while another tried to sell him a knife. He shooed them away impatiently, and was starting to curse at being importuned by so many street urchins, when he felt a hand touch his right forearm.

Making to wrench himself free, he heard his name. He wheeled around to find himself face-to-face with a young mulatta.

"At last, Don Mauro, thank God!" she said, gasping for breath. "I've searched half of Havana for you."

Larrea recognized her instantly as the slender girl beating the carpets when he had stolen inside the Gorostiza residence.

"My mistress sent me: she wants to see you," the girl said, struggling to catch her breath. "There's a carriage waiting for you in the alleyway behind the Templete. The driver will take you to her."

Santos Huesos craned his neck as if to indicate to his master that he was ready. But when she saw his gesture, the girl stopped him short. She was tall and slender, with full lips and the longest eyelashes.

"My mistress asked that you go alone."

Perhaps there was still time. All Calafat needed was a signature. Confirmation, a written agreement. Possibly the ship hadn't yet weighed anchor and the Gorostiza woman had come to her senses.

"Where does she want to meet me?"

He had almost convinced himself that the girl would say the Caballería quay. Together with the old banker. Was it possible that she had finally agreed to the idea?

"How should I know, Don Mauro? That's the driver's job. I only know what Doña Carola told me."

The orchestra had struck up the first bars of Iradier's "La Paloma" when Larrea, elbowing his way through the throng, hurried toward the spot where the carriage was waiting for him.

To his dismay, the chosen meeting place couldn't have been less like a quayside from which a ship was about to set sail. Adjacent to the sacristy of the Cristo del Buen Viaje was a room where well-to-do ladies would go every Tuesday to sew and mend linen for the city's poor. Inside, lit by a tiny oil lamp and surrounded by shelves and chests filled with bolts of cloth, Carola Gorostiza was waiting for him.

He had scarcely put his head around the door when she hissed: "One of the servants told my husband of your visit this morning. That's why I sent a hired carriage for you and took another myself. I no longer trust my own shadow."

He responded by doffing his hat. He felt a stinging disappointment, but, summoning a vestige of pride, resolved not to let it show.

"Nor me, I presume."

"That goes without saying," she retorted. "However, at this stage of the game, I have no wish to rid myself of you. Nor you me."

He noticed she was clutching a small, dark object but couldn't make it out in the half-light.

"Have those friends of yours in the ice ship business left yet?" she asked with her customary sharpness.

"The refrigerated vessel."

"What does it matter? Answer me. Have they gone or not?"

He swallowed hard.

"I imagine so."

Carola Gorostiza gave a sardonic grin.

"Then you have only one card left to play. That other vessel carrying quite a different cargo."

Quaysides, rushed signatures, steamers sailing for the Río de la Plata—none of those things entered this woman's plans. She was right, the brigantine fitted with chains and shackles bound for the African coasts was his last card: the awful slave trade. Otherwise, without her capital he would be forced to make fresh plans. Once more, on his own, and penniless.

Even so, he resisted.

"I'm still skeptical."

He could see her right hand make darting movements in the light of the oil lamp. As if she were pinching and then releasing something, then pinching it again.

"The interested parties whom you met at the crockery store have all consented; the only one who hasn't is you. However, according to my sources, another prospective investor by the name of Agustín Vivancos has come forward overnight—in case you doubt my word. He owns a pharmacy on Calle de la Merced. Should you fail to respond, he is keen to take your place."

They fell silent as the clatter of carriage wheels on the cobblestones outside reached them through the closed window. Neither spoke until the noise diminished, before dying away altogether.

"Forgive me for saying so, Señora, but I find your behavior greatly disconcerting." He took a resolute step toward her. "At first you showed no interest in investing your money, and now, suddenly, you seem to be in a terrible hurry."

"Remember that it was you who put the idea into my head."

"That's true. But if you don't mind satisfying my curiosity, why are you persisting in this, and why act with such haste?"

A look of disdain on her face, she took a step toward him as well. At last Mauro Larrea could see what it was she had clasped in her hand: a pincushion used by the ladies who came there to make clothes for the poor, into which she had been mechanically stabbing the same pin, over and over again.

"For two reasons, Señor Larrea. Two very important reasons. The first concerns the business itself. Or should I say, those involved. Señor Novás's eldest daughter is a good friend of mine, and I trust her implicitly. I feel safer knowing my money will be in the hands of someone close to me, someone who will keep me informed about how the operation is going, if for some reason you decide to disappear. Someone, so to speak, in the family. Had I become involved in your ice ship, on the other hand, I would have been a woman alone among shrewd businessmen familiar with the world of finance, about which I understand little. Men who would never treat me as an equal."

Although there was some sense in what she said, he supposed that she was lying. In any case, he preferred not to consider whether or not to believe her.

"And the second reason?"

"The second reason, my friend, is of a far more intimate nature."

She paused, and for a few seconds he thought she would remain silent. He was mistaken.

"Are you married, Señor Larrea?"

"I was."

Another carriage rattled over the cobblestones, passing more swiftly this time.

"Then you will agree that marriage is a complex alliance that brings both joy and bitterness ... and occasionally it becomes a game of power. Your proposal set me thinking, and I came to the conclusion that if I had more money I might achieve greater power in my own marriage."

Greater power? Whatever for? he was on the verge of saying. But he stopped short, recalling Doña Caridad's words earlier that afternoon: Carola Gorostiza's keenness to please her husband's cousin who had come over from Spain; the strange triangle they formed; the woman on the other side of the ocean who had stolen Gustavo Zayas's heart, then abandoned him for another; a thousand past conflicts. He preferred to curb his curiosity. Questioning her would require reciprocity, and he was unwilling to reveal anything about himself. In the meantime, she was moving closer to him, stretching the limits of what was seemly.

The flounces of her skirts brushed between Larrea's legs. He was aware of her breasts pressed up against him. He could feel her breath.

"You placed temptation in my path," she said, her voice trembling. "Offering to make my inheritance grow without my having to lift a finger. I dislike men who leave a woman dangling."

And I dislike women who lead men on the way you do, he thought, but refrained from saying. Instead, without breaking their close proximity, he asked in a hushed, solemn voice, "Tell me honestly, Carola, have you no misgivings about the nature of this despicable trade?"

She tilted her head slowly then drew her lips close to his ear. Her dark hair brushed his cheek as she whispered her reply.

"If I ever experience remorse, my dear, I shall take the matter up with my confessor."

He stepped back a few paces, detaching himself from her female charms.

"For God's sake, leave the moralizing to the religious fanatics and Freemasons," Carola Gorostiza went on with vehemence. "Conscience won't fill your coffers, and you need money as much as I do. Withdraw enough of our funds to cover our joint share in the venture, then, at eleven o'clock tomorrow morning, walk into Novás's store as if you were going to buy something. I've decided to tell him about my part in this, and I'll be waiting for you there."

At that, she threw the pincushion onto the table and snuffed out the oil lamp. Afterward, without a word, she picked up the shawl from the back of her chair, placed it over her head, and left.

He stood staring into the darkness, amid shelves piled with sheets and bolts of fabric. He waited long enough to be sure their paths wouldn't cross. Slipping out behind the church, he confirmed that no carriage was waiting for him before heading down Calle de la Amargura toward his lodgings, overwhelmed by a feeling of unease.

He entered the darkened house, which was immersed in a sepulchral silence. Everyone was asleep and, unusually, Santos Huesos wasn't waiting for him either in the hallway or the courtyard. He started along the dim corridor but turned on his heel before he reached his room. Careful not to make a sound as he went into the dining room, he felt his way around the furniture until he found what he was looking for. Then he seized the neck of the liquor carafe and made off with it.

 ❧

He lay asleep facedown, diagonally across the bed, arms and legs akimbo, left hand dangling over the edge of the mattress, fingers brushing the tiled floor. He felt a slight pressure; someone was squeezing his ankle.

He awoke with a jolt, sat up startled, his head feeling like lead. Beneath the raised mosquito net, in the faint light filtering through the open balcony doors, he made out a familiar face.

"Is anything the matter, lad?"

"No."

"What do you mean, '*No*,' Santos?" he muttered. "You wake me up . . . at . . . what's the time?"

"Five o'clock in the morning; nearly daybreak."

"You wake me up at five in the morning, you dolt, and expect me to believe nothing is the matter."

"Don't get involved, *patrón.*"

It took a while for him to understand what he was hearing.

"Don't get involved," he heard his servant say again.

He ran his fingers through his hair, bemused.

"So, I'm not the only one who drank too much, or what?"

"They are human beings. Like you. Like me. They sweat, eat, think, fornicate. They get toothache, they mourn their dead."

He made a huge effort to summon a few dim memories from the previous night. He vaguely recalled last seeing Santos Huesos in Plaza de Armas, when the crowd began to sing the opening verses of "La Paloma" to the strains of the military band. Santos Huesos had been standing shoulder to shoulder with the slender mulatta girl with the generous smile.

"Has Doña Carola's slave girl been turning your head? Did she start gossiping the moment I went to meet her mistress?" Did—"

"The slave girl has a name. She's called Trinidad. They all have names, *patrón*."

He spoke in the same old voice. Serene, melodious. But resolute.

"Do you remember when we used to go down in the mines? You made us work our hearts out. You were hard when you had to be, yet always fair. You never treated us like animals. We were free to stay or leave as we wished."

Sitting up in bed, Mauro Larrea buried his face in his hands, trying to regain some clarity. His voice sounded cavernous.

"We're in Havana, damn it, not in the Real de Catorce mines. Those days are long gone; we have other problems now."

"Neither your men nor your children would want you to do what you're thinking of doing."

From beneath the mosquito netting, he saw Santos Huesos's figure slip out of the bedroom. Larrea slumped back on the bed as soon as he heard him close the door softly. He lay there until long past dawn but didn't fall asleep. Befuddled and numbed by the drink he had filched from Doña Caridad to take the edge off his disquiet, he couldn't decide whether the Chichimec Indian's presence in his room had been a grotesque dream or a depressing reality. He lay there for what seemed like an eternity, an acid taste in his mouth and a vague anguish churning his insides.

Don't think about it, you fool, don't think about it, he repeated to himself silently as he washed and dressed, then attempted to alleviate his diabolical hangover with cups of black coffee. There was no sign of Santos Huesos having returned. Nor did his friend Andrade's voice come to his aid.

It was almost ten o'clock when, nursing a splitting headache, he left his lodgings to face the city's daily hubbub. All he had to do was withdraw the money and sign the relevant receipt, and that would be that. A simple operation. Quick. Painless. *Don't think about it, brother, don't give it another thought.*

His attention was so utterly focused in one direction that, upon entering the courtyard, he nearly fell flat on his face. He cursed rudely as his foot came up against an unexpected object. This turned out to be a young black woman, who instinctively let out a shrill cry.

She was sitting propped against the column of the open gate, one breast protruding through her white blouse. Before the toe of Larrea's boot had struck her thigh, she had been innocently nursing her baby swathed in a cotton rag. Clutching at the wall to steady himself, his hand flat against the whitewashed surface, Mauro looked down.

A firm, round breast loomed up at him. Attached to it, a tiny mouth sucking at a nipple. And all at once, confronted by this simple image of a young mother with dark skin nursing a child, all those thoughts he had been desperately trying to thrust from his mind overwhelmed him with the force of a river bursting its banks. His hands extracting Nicolás from his wife Elvira's bleeding body; his hands on Mariana's belly the night of his departure from Mexico, sensing the new, unborn child. The skinny little slave girl violated by her aging master while she was cutting sugarcane; the baby daughter she had brought into the world when she was only thirteen, who was subsequently prized from her as one might peel away the skin of a fruit. Life wrenched asunder. Flesh and blood, breathing souls. Lives that burst forth amid agonizing screams and vanished on a precarious, fragile thread; lives that arrived bearing solace in the face of despair, healing rifts, bringing into the world a certainty that could not be bought or sold. Human life, undeniable life.

"Good morning, Larrea."

Calafat's voice greeted him from the far side of the courtyard, interrupting his musings. Doubtless the banker had come down to his office after breakfast and seen him there.

Larrea responded by standing up straight and raising his arm. As if to say, *I have nothing to say, I want nothing.* Calafat looked at him and pursed his lips.

"Really?"

He gestured silently with his chin. *Yes.* Then he wheeled around and disappeared into the crowded street.

He found his room exactly as when he had left; the maids had not yet been in to clean it. His rumpled bedsheets were half strewn across the floor, his dirty clothes sat in a pile, the ashtray was full, and the carafe, containing only a thimbleful of liquor, lay upturned beneath the bedside table. He slipped off his linen jacket, loosened his cravat, and closed the shutters. Then, leaving everything as it was, he sat down to wait.

At ten thirty, he heard the clock on the customs building strike the half hour. Eleven o'clock, eleven thirty. The light outside shone more brightly amid the gloom, projecting slender, horizontal lines on the walls. Finally, toward midday, he heard footsteps, shouting, shrieking. A commotion was drawing closer. Banging, creaking, doors slamming, as if a tornado were wreaking havoc inside the building. Until, without anyone bothering to knock, his door flew open.

"Wretch. No-good son of a whore! You're a coward and a traitor!"

"You can withdraw your money from Calafat's bank whenever you wish," he said impassively.

He'd had plenty of time to foresee how she would react.

"I've been waiting for you," she shouted. "I gave Novás my word you would come!"

Doña Caridad limped in after her, issuing a torrent of apologies. Four or five slaves followed behind, jostling each other in the doorway. Infected by her mistress's rage, the little bichon barked as though possessed by the hounds of Hell.

Ahead of them all, Carola Gorostiza filled her lungs with air and spewed her final warning:

"You haven't heard the last of me, Mauro Larrea; make no mistake about that."

CHAPTER TWENTY

༄

Later that evening Mauro returned to El Louvre Café, perhaps to avoid dwelling on recent events. Or to take the edge off his loneliness amid the crowd.

Weaving around the tables nearest the entrance, occupied by youths and swellheads, he made his way to the restaurant at the rear. With its luxuriant palms and enormous mirrors multiplying the number of diners, the room had a lively atmosphere. He ordered grilled red snapper, accompanied once again by French wine. Dispensing with dessert, he finished his meal with a coffee Cuban-style: strong, concentrated, with a hint of brown sugar to take away the bitterness. He had been lying to Doña Caridad the day before when he said his stomach couldn't take so much coffee. On the contrary, the thick dark liquid was about the only thing that had sustained him since his arrival.

While enjoying his fish, he had noticed several newcomers making their way up the broad staircase at the far end of the restaurant.

"Are there more tables upstairs?" he asked the waiter when he settled the bill.

"All the tables you could wish for, Señor."

The card games ombre and monte bank were currently all the rage, and the upstairs room at the Louvre was no exception. Although it was still relatively early, a couple of games were already under way. At a corner table a lone domino player slammed down his tiles, while from another came the rattle of dice. But Mauro Larrea's eyes were drawn toward an area at the back illuminated by hanging lamps.

Beneath them stood three billiard tables. Only one of them was occupied, by two men halfheartedly launching shots—Spaniards, he guessed, from their thick suits and formal manner as well as their accent, harsher and more clipped than that of the New World inhabitants.

He strolled over to one of the empty tables, running his hand thoughtfully over the polished wooden edge. Picking up a billiard ball, he pressed the cold ivory in his hand, felt its heft, then let it roll. Unhurriedly, savoring each moment, he plucked one of the cues from its stand. An indescribable feeling of well-being washed over him, like a comforting caress after a bad dream, perhaps the only taste of serenity he had had since disembarking in Havana.

As he surveyed the sea of green baize, he found himself finally confronting something he knew, something over which he could exercise his will and his mastery. All of a sudden, he was transported back to places that had disappeared in the recesses of his memory: the turbulent, menacing evenings in the mining camps, all those afternoons spent in filthy dives swarming with rowdy miners with blackened nails, desperately searching for the mother lode, a stroke of luck in the form of a seam that would take the sting out of poverty, unlock the door to a future free of the pangs of hunger. Dozens, hundreds, thousands of billiard games in dimly lit bars, playing on until dawn, with friends he had left behind along the way, with enemies who had become brothers, men who one fateful day would be swallowed up by the earth, or by some tragedy they were unable to overcome. Hard, terrible, devastating times. Even so, how he missed them now. At least back then he had a clear-cut reason for getting out of bed each morning.

He gripped the cue firmly and leaned over the table, extending his left arm to its full reach as he readied the shot. So far removed from the world he knew, frustrated and uncertain as he never thought he would be, for an instant Mauro Larrea rediscovered the man he had once been.

His carom was so cleanly executed that his compatriots at the neighboring table instantly stopped talking and stood their cues on the floor. Without introducing himself or learning their names and their professions, he played a first game against them. As the night wore on, they were replaced by other men who were more or less seasoned, keen to see how they measured up to the newcomer. He proceeded to win game after game as the room began filling up with people. Soon there was scarcely a free seat at any of the upstairs tables, and the smoke and voices rose to the rafters, spilling out from the high windows overlooking the Parque Central.

He was cueing up for his next shot on the white, concentrated on calculating the precise force with which he needed to hit the red ball resting against the cushion at the far end of the table, when something, he didn't know what, distracted him. A sudden movement, an unexpected comment. Or perhaps the simple intuition that the order of things had been disrupted. Without altering his position, he glanced up, his eyes straying beyond the edge of the table. And then he saw him.

He realized instantly that, unlike the other spectators, Gustavo Zayas wasn't merely enjoying his performance but was boring into his skin with his blue-eyed gaze.

With apparent calm, he slid the cue between the circle formed by his fingers, striking the ball with a loud crack. Then he stood erect, checked the time, and realized he had been playing for three hours. Eliciting a few murmurs of disappointment from the crowd, he replaced the cue in the stand with the intention of calling it an evening.

"Permit me to buy you a drink," he heard a voice behind him say.

Naturally. He accepted Carola Gorostiza's husband's unexpected invitation with a simple nod. *What the hell do you want with me?* he thought as the two of them made their way through the crowded room. *What tales has your wife been telling you?*

He accepted the offer of a brandy and requested a pitcher of water, which he downed in three glassfuls, suddenly aware of how thirsty he had been. He realized his cravat had come loose and his clothes were drenched in sweat, but his disheveled hair and glassy eyes were visible only to others. Zayas's appearance, by contrast, was immaculate, his hair neatly combed as always, his clothes and manner exquisite. Beyond that, he remained impenetrable.

"We met at Casilda Barrón's ball, do you remember?"

They were seated in two armchairs before a balcony that opened onto the Cuban night. Larrea contemplated Zayas for a few seconds before replying: the man had a look of sullenness on his habitually tense face. *For God's sake, man, what's ailing you?* he wanted to ask. But instead he replied: "I remember perfectly."

Their opening conversation was interrupted by several men approaching to congratulate Larrea on his excellent game; one recalled having seen him at the ball in El Cerro, another at the theater. They asked his name, where he was from—Spain? Yes, well, no, yes—and offered him cigars. They invited him to their salons and gaming tables, and despite the trivial nature of the banter that followed, Larrea began to feel that in the eyes of the world he was at last somebody again.

Gorostiza's brother-in-law remained attentive and vigilant as he sat, legs crossed, though he scarcely uttered a word.

"It was noble of Señor Zayas to allow you to steal the limelight this evening," declared one of those present, a customs agent if Larrea recalled correctly.

He raised his glass. *What?*

"Such expertise with a cue must run in the blood with you Spaniards. God alone knows why we Creoles haven't been blessed with it."

There was a burst of laughter, and Mauro Larrea halfheartedly joined in. Then another voice explained:

"Ever since he arrived in Havana all those years ago, our friend here has remained unrivaled at the billiard table."

All eyes turned toward Zayas, the best player in town, who had been chivalrous enough to allow an upstart to shine in his own territory.

Tread carefully, brother. Tread carefully, his agent's voice exploded in his brain.

He felt like yelling back at him, *But where the hell were you when I was desperate for your advice about that loathsome slave trader?*

Andrade was insistent: *Calm down, Mauro, don't rise to the bait. In this decadent city, gambling is a means of achieving one's designs. Tonight you have made a name for yourself, as well as contacts, and this will bring opportunities. Have a little patience, compadre, just a little.*

His friend's wise counsel came too late. A fresh wave of euphoria was already coursing through Mauro's veins. His easy triumphs over those nameless opponents had restored a shred of self-confidence, which in these wretched circumstances was like a balm. He was pleased that they had admired his game; that for a few solitary hours he had ceased to be a lost, invisible soul; that, albeit fleetingly, he felt once more like a man whom people respected and appreciated.

And yet something elusive had been lacking. There had been no fever in his eyes, no throbbing in his temples: tension had not seized him in the gut like a hungry coyote. He would not have slammed his fist into the wall had he lost, or howled like a banshee had he won.

But now, upon discovering that the husband of the woman who had refused to help him was the best billiard player in Havana, he felt the old fire stir in his belly. In the old days, that fire had made him try his luck blindly, to take on precarious business ventures or tough men twice his age with infinitely more money and experience.

As though borne on the sea breeze coming through the open windows, he felt the soul of the young miner he had once been—intuitive, dogged, bold—seep into his bones once more.

You didn't invite me for a drink to tell me how well I play, you bastard, he wanted to tell Zayas. *I know there's something more: you've heard something about me that displeases you, whether or not it's true.*

Zayas then spoke up.

"Would you excuse us, gentlemen?"

When they were finally alone, a waiter topped up their glasses and Larrea turned toward the balcony to get a breath of fresh air, running his fingers through his unruly hair.

"Go ahead then, speak your mind," he told Zayas.

"Keep away from my wife."

He nearly burst into laughter. *What kind of insinuations, hogwash, and lies has Carola Gorostiza been feeding her husband?*

"Listen, my friend, I've no idea what stories you've—"

"Let's settle the matter with a wager," Zayas declared impassively.

Don't you dare, he heard Andrade yell inside his head. *Explain to him, tell him the truth, disentangle yourself. You must stop this, you lunatic, before it's too late.* But his agent's voice was growing dimmer as a surge of adrenaline began coursing through his body.

He took a last draw on his cigar before tossing the butt in an arc through the balcony window. Leaning forward in his chair, he drew his face slowly closer to the supposed cuckold.

"What are the stakes?"

CHAPTER TWENTY-ONE

❧

The moment it grew light, he sent Santos Huesos to investigate.

"A neighborhood down by the bay, full of bad people, *patrón*," he proclaimed on his return. "That's El Manglar. And La Chucha is a black woman, old as the hills, with a gold tooth. She runs a business that is half brothel, half tavern. The roughest, rowdiest characters from the outskirts go there along with the most illustrious men in Havana. To drink rum, beer, and contraband bourbon. To dance if they have the opportunity, and sleep with whores of every color, or gamble away their money until dawn. That's what I found out."

Zayas had told him to be at El Manglar the following evening at midnight. "You and me. At La Chucha's place. A game of billiards. If I win, you agree never to see my wife again; you leave her alone for good."

"And if you lose?" Larrea had asked with a hint of bravado.

Carola Gorostiza's husband fixed him with his pale blue eyes.

"I'll leave. Go back to Spain for good, and she will remain in Havana. I'll leave the field open to you: you can be lovers for all the world to see, or do as you please. You'll never hear from me again."

Holy Mother of God.

Had Mauro Larrea not been inside so many of the wretched bars that sprang up around the mines, Zayas's proposal would have struck him as the deranged bluster of a man consumed by misplaced jealousy, or the ravings of a poor devil who had lost his wits. But among gamblers accustomed to playing for high stakes, whether in Mexico, Cuba, or in the furnaces of Hell itself, however outlandish the proposal made by the man opposite him, no one would have doubted his sincerity. He had seen even stranger bids placed on a table during a heated card game or a cockfight. Family fortunes, silver mines with rich deposits, an entire year's earnings wagered on a single card . . . In a bar he had once seen a desperate father surrender his teenage daughter's virginity without any qualms. He had witnessed many such things during countless nights of carousing. That was why Zayas's challenge, however bizarre, did not take him aback.

What amazed him was Carola Gorostiza's ability to deceive her husband without ruffling a single black hair on her carefully coiffed head. Ernesto's sister had revealed herself to be at once shrewd, deceitful, manipulative, and perverse. *Your wife has led you to believe that I am courting her*, he had wanted to tell Gustavo Zayas the night before. *That you are standing in my way, when in fact she is the one who is deceiving you, my friend. And as a result of this lie, which you appear to have swallowed whole, you are proposing a game of billiards, which I intend to accept. I will take up your challenge even though I never had anything to do with that creature who's your wife, nor would I should I live to be a hundred.*

If that's true, Andrade would have raged, *then why the devil are you picking up the gauntlet thrown down by this foolish fellow?* Larrea, however, had managed to muzzle his agent's voice in advance to prevent it from intruding on his conscience. For reasons he himself couldn't understand, he had decided to play along with this twisted game, and had no intention of backing down.

That was why, the first thing the next morning, even before going down to breakfast, he had sent Santos Huesos out to gather information about El Manglar and La Chucha. Three hours later he had his answer. El Manglar was a swampy area inhabited by lowlifes, and La Chucha was a former prostitute who now owned this legendary den.

He lunched frugally at Doña Caridad's guesthouse. As luck would have it, she did not eat with them that day. She had likely remained in Regla with her niece, who had just given birth. In any event, he was relieved she wasn't there, since he was in no mood for her chatter or her prying. After coffee had been served, he shut himself in his room, pre-occupied, contemplating what awaited him that night. What style of game would Gustavo Zayas play? What exactly had his wife told him? What would happen if he won, or if he lost?

When he perceived that Havana was abuzz once more after the torpor of the postprandial siesta, he went out.

"Señor Larrea, a pleasure to see you again," Calafat greeted him when he arrived at the banker's offices. "Although I suspect that you haven't come to tell me how much you regret not having invested in our venture."

"I have other concerns today, Don Julián."

"Promising ones?"

"I don't know yet."

He took a seat at the familiar mahogany desk, then said bluntly: "I need to withdraw some funds. Don Gustavo Zayas has challenged me to a game of billiards. Although in theory there is no money at stake, I prefer to be prepared for any eventuality."

The old banker handed him a cigar before replying. As usual. The two men clipped them and lit them in silence. Also as usual.

"I heard all about it," Calafat declared after taking a first draw.

"I thought as much."

"Nothing remains a secret for long in this indiscreet Pearl of the Antilles, my dear friend," the banker added, with a hint of bitter irony.

"Normally, I would have heard about it in La Dominica while taking my midmorning coffee, or someone would have been sure to mention it over dominoes. But this time news traveled even faster: the first thing this morning some visitors came making inquiries about you. I've been expecting you ever since."

Larrea responded by taking a long draw on his cigar. *Sonofabitch Zayas. This is more serious than I thought.*

"As I understand it, this is an affair of the heart," the banker said.

"So he believes, although the reality is very different. However, before I explain, I'd like to know who was making inquiries about me and what they wanted to know."

"The answer is three of Zayas's friends wanting to know a bit of everything, including the state of your finances."

"And what did you tell them?"

"That it was a private matter between you and me."

"I thank you for that."

"You needn't: I was simply doing my job. Absolute confidentiality regarding our clients' affairs has been the cornerstone of this business ever since my grandfather left his native Mallorca and founded it at the turn of the century. Although there are times when I wonder whether we wouldn't have all been better off had he remained an accountant in the peaceful port of Palma instead of venturing to this profligate island in the tropics. But forgive my senile digressions, my friend, and let us return to the present. Tell me, Larrea, if this isn't an affair of the heart, then what the devil is behind this extraordinary challenge?"

Mauro weighed possible responses. He could tell a barefaced lie. Or simply disguise the facts a little, alter them to suit himself. Or he could be open with Calafat, tell the truth about himself. After a brief pause, he decided on the final option. And so, condensing the facts although concealing nothing, he described the tortuous journey he had made from prosperous miner to Carola Gorostiza's alleged lover. He spoke of the American Sachs, the Tres Lunas mine, Tadeo Carrús and his oaf of a son, the countess's money, Nico and his unknown whereabouts, the disastrous errand Ernesto Gorostiza had entrusted him with, the accursed sister, and finally Zayas's challenge.

"By the Virgen de la Cobre, my friend, you're proving to be every bit as hot-blooded as these crazy Caribbeans all around us."

You and Andrade would get along like a house on fire, you cautious old devil, Larrea thought, even as he surprised himself responding to Calafat's words with a bitter laugh. *What on earth do I have to laugh about?*

"Just so you know who your clients are, Don Julián."

Calafat clicked his tongue.

"Gambling is a serious business in Cuba, are you aware?"

"As it is everywhere."

"And, in the eyes of these impetuous islanders, what Zayas has challenged you to is a kind of duel. A duel to save his honor, fought not with swords or pistols but rather with billiard cues."

"I'm afraid so."

"However, there are a few details that concern me."

He drummed his fingers on the table as both men reflected in silence.

"No matter how brilliant a player he is," the old man went on, "it would be too risky, too reckless of him, to assume he will beat you."

"I have no idea how good he is, of course. But you're right: any contest at this level contains an element of risk. Billiards is . . ."

He paused for a few seconds, searching for the right words. Despite the countless times he had played in his life, he never had occasion to speculate about the game.

"Billiards is a game of skill and precision, brains and technique, but it isn't purely mathematics. There are other factors involved: a player's physique, his temperament, the setting. And, above all, his opponent."

"As for that, how well Zayas plays won't be known until tonight.

In the meantime, what troubles me is what might lie behind this challenge."

"I just told you: his wife has convinced him that I—"

Calafat shook his head emphatically.

"No, no, no. I mean, yes and no. Zayas's wife may have wished to punish you and at the same time make her husband jealous, possibly convincing Zayas that there's something going on between the two of you. But what intrigues me is something that goes beyond the mere rage of a cuckold, if you'll pardon the expression. Something favorable to him, which she has unwittingly placed in his lap."

"Forgive me, but I don't quite understand what you're aiming at."

"Let me explain. To my knowledge, Gustavo Zayas is no forlorn lamb who bleats the moment he can smell a wolf nearby. He's a smart, levelheaded fellow whose businesses haven't always done well; a man who seems somewhat tortured, perhaps as a result of something in his past or the woman he shares his life with; who knows? But he is neither a coward nor a braggart."

"I scarcely know the fellow, but that seems like a fair description."

"Well, let's suppose he loses tonight. Wouldn't that make it suspiciously easy for you and his wife to pursue the alleged relationship you are having, or intending to have? If he wins, nothing changes. But if he should lose, which is something he himself could bring about with little effort, he is promising to step aside and elegantly leave the way open for you two to enjoy a future full of happiness. Doesn't the whole thing strike you as a little odd?"

That scoundrel Zayas, thought Mauro. *The old fellow could be right.*

"Forgive me for being cynical," Calafat went on, "but I've been thinking this over all day, and it wouldn't surprise me if Gustavo Zayas simply wanted to rid himself of his difficult wife. After his friends left my office this morning, I sent out my spies, who came back with stories about a family estate in Spain."

"Yes, I heard something about an inheritance from a first cousin."

"A cousin who died at their coffee plantation shortly after he arrived, and who bequeathed them a substantial amount of land in Andalusia."

"Land, properties, vineyards, or some such."

"If you win tonight, his faithless wife will remain safely in the hands of her valiant Mexican lover. He will have washed his hands of her and be free to leave, to go back to the mother country or wherever he pleases. With no constraints or responsibilities, or any claimants making demands on him. And without his wife."

Too convoluted. Too risky by far. And yet, he thought, *perhaps somewhere amid all this farfetched nonsense there is a grain of truth.*

"What about the state of his finances?"

"Turbulent, I suspect. Rather like his marriage."

"Does he owe you money?"

"A small amount," replied Calafat discreetly. "Financial ups and downs appear to be the stuff of their marriage, as are quarrels, separations, and reconciliations. Despite his best efforts, Zayas seems unable to square his accounts, either on his plantation or in his marriage. And one has only to look at her attire to see that she spends money as if it grew on trees."

"I see."

"So," the old man summed up, "Zayas just needs to lose the game tonight in order to saddle you with his wife, thereby clearing the way for his honorable farewell to Cuba."

Intricate as it might sound, Calafat's theory wasn't entirely illogical.

"What a couple," the old man murmured, following his words with a curt laugh. "But don't let me to add to your worries, Larrea. My suspicions are doubtless the mere imaginings of an old fantasist. The real reason for this contest is probably the wounded pride of a husband whose wife has manipulated him in order to get his attention."

May the Lord hear you, Larrea was about to say, without much conviction, but once again deferred to the old man's conjectures.

"The only thing we can be sure of is that time is not on your side, my friend, so I suggest we focus on keeping one step ahead. Now, tell me—"

"You tell me something first."

The old man raised his hands in an expansive gesture. "Whatever you wish."

"Forgive my bluntness, Don Julián, but why do you appear so interested in this disagreeable business of mine, which is of no consequence to you?"

"Because of a simple question of logical procedure. We agree that Zayas sees this as a sort of duel, correct? In which case, as with any veritable duel, you will require a second. As the custodian of your assets, and in view of the fact that you're all alone on this island, I feel a moral obligation to assume that role."

This time Mauro's laughter was genuine. *So what you want is to look after me, you old rogue. At my age.*

"I thank you from the bottom of my heart, dear friend, but I'm perfectly capable of confronting an adversary at a billiard table without any help."

Instead of a smile, he glimpsed a serious grimace beneath Calafat's bushy whiskers.

"Allow me to explain, then: Gustavo Zayas is Gustavo Zayas, El Manglar is El Manglar, and La Chucha is La Chucha. I am a respected Cuban banker and you are a ruined Spaniard, washed up on these shores by the winds of fate. Need I say more?"

Larrea realized in a flash that Calafat was right. He was on shifting, possibly treacherous ground, and what the old man was proposing was as simple as it was wise.

"So be it, then. I'm grateful to you."

"Needless to say, an excellent game of billiards is a far more honest pursuit than the vile business of buying and selling wretched Africans."

But the sinister shadow of Novás and his vessel from Baltimore with its shackles, chains, and tears had momentarily vanished from Mauro Larrea's thoughts. Anxieties and speculations were jostling in his mind, while his blood started to fizz with excitement.

The old man stood up and went over to the windows to open the shutters. Thick, leaden clouds loomed in the evening sky. The heat that day had been suffocating, and the air had grown increasingly humid with each passing hour. The wind was still low, and not a single raindrop had fallen, yet the heavens threatened to open at any moment.

"A storm is brewing," Calafat muttered.

He became reimmersed in thought as the noise of wheels on cobblestones seeped in through the window along with the raucous cries of the carriage drivers and a myriad other sounds.

"Lose."

"I beg your pardon?"

"Let him win," declared Calafat, his gaze apparently fixed on the street outside.

Without stirring from his chair, Larrea contemplated the slight figure of the old man against the window and waited for him to continue.

"Confound Zayas. Make him think that his plans have gone up in smoke and suggest a return match. Then go for the jugular."

The suggestion struck him like a lightning bolt. Between the eyes, dazzling.

"He fully expects you to fight him tooth and nail," Calafat added, wheeling around. "Regardless of your alleged affair with his wife, he knows how much a resounding victory would help you establish your presence here in Havana, in this land of strong passions, where we worship heroes even if their glory lasts only a day."

Larrea recalled the sweet, electrifying sensations of the night before, like a naked woman's hand caressing his back beneath the sheets, when he had realized he was visible again, respected in the eyes of others. He felt alive and emboldened. The thought of no longer being a ghost, of becoming once more the man he had been, albeit by winning a simple game of billiards, was as alluring to him as a siren's song. Perhaps it was worth going through all this infernal nonsense just for that.

"The fact is, my boy, that by accepting Zayas's challenge you've already shown you have what it takes," Calafat exclaimed as he moved away from the window and approached him.

No one had referred to him as "my boy" for a very long time. He was used to being addressed as "patrón," "master," "sir." Mariana and Nicolás called him *padre*, in the formal Spanish way, never using the more affectionate term *papa*, which was customary in the New World that had become home to all three of them. But not for a long time had anyone called him "boy." And, despite his fall from grace, his unease, and his forty-seven years of intense living, the word did not displease him.

He glanced at the sober wall clock above the old man's grizzled head, and at the oil painting of the port in the bay of Mallorca, from which Calafat's cautious ancestors had embarked for the wild Caribbean. Twenty to eight: time to get ready. He slapped the arm of the chair with his palm before rising and picking up his hat.

Placing it on his head, he said: "Since I am to be your ward, why not pick me up and take me to dinner before the battle commences?"

Without awaiting a reply, he started toward the door.

"Mauro," he heard as he clasped the handle.

He turned around.

"I've heard people talking about how brilliantly you played at El Louvre. Prepare to live up to your reputation."

CHAPTER TWENTY-TWO

The light shower that was falling when they left the restaurant on Paseo del Prado had become a deluge by the time they reached El Manglar. The muddy paths had turned to sludge, and the violent gusts of wind swept away anything that wasn't tied down. The rage of the tropical seas was determined to triumph that night, causing dogs to howl, forcing boats to seek moorings at the quaysides, and denuding the city's streets of carriages, traps, and any other sign of human life.

The only light that greeted them as they ventured into the quagmire came from the yellowish glow of a few lanterns, scattered haphazardly, as if the hand of a madman had dropped them there at random. Had they visited the place on any other day at that hour, they would have found a mass of humanity strolling up and down among the alleys lined with low-roofed dwellings: whores with enticing smiles flaunting their naked flesh; bearded sailors whose boats had just docked; scroungers, braggarts, pimps, and cardsharps; young men from good families; cocky toughs carrying blades up their sleeves; ragamuffins on the lookout for cats or cigarette ends; ample-bosomed matrons frying pork rinds in their doorways. These were the types who inhabited El

Manglar from dusk until dawn. Yet, when Calafat's carriage rolled up outside La Chucha's, there wasn't a soul in sight.

At the tavern, however, they were expected. A large black man wrapped in an oilcloth cape and carrying a large umbrella came outside to usher them out of the carriage. A thick plank of wood had been laid on the ground to prevent them from sinking up to their ankles in the mud. Five steps and they were safely inside.

All those whom the wind and rain had driven off the streets of Havana that night seemed to have gathered at La Chucha's. Santos Huesos, whom they had sent on ahead, could not have been more accurate in his description of the establishment. It was a dive, halfway between a huge tavern and a bordello, judging from the look of the women there, who were drinking and carousing among the patrons with scant concern for modesty and decorum.

Larrea, however, had little interest in the locals or the whores just then. His chief focus was the matter that had brought him there.

"Foul weather we're having tonight, Señor Julián," he heard the stocky servant say with an extravagant guffaw as he closed the dripping umbrella.

Larrea noticed that the servant was quite old and was even taller than he was, despite the hunchback that was visible when he removed his oilskin.

"Foul and filthy, Horacio, foul and filthy," muttered Calafat, removing his top hat and shaking it at arm's length so that the water that had collected in the rim did not splash his shoes.

So, the old rogue is a regular, Larrea reflected as he imitated Calafat's gesture. *What if this whole thing is a trap, a clever ruse cooked up by Zayas and my supposed guardian? Calm down, stay focused,* he commanded himself. Just then, he sensed a familiar presence, like a shadow, appear beside him.

"Everything in order, lad?" he asked Santos Huesos, scarcely moving his lips.

"He arrived just now; he's upstairs."

At that instant, the fellow called Horacio addressed him with an exaggerated bow that only accentuated the hunch on his back.

"Welcome to our humble abode, Señor Larrea. La Chucha is waiting for you in the turquoise salon. Follow me, please."

"Has Zayas brought an entourage?" Larrea whispered to his servant as the giant led them through the crowd.

"Well, I'd say about six or seven."

That sly bastard, he was about to say, but thought it wiser to hold his tongue in case one of the patrons mistakenly thought he was referring to them: in such places, brawls and stabbings were as abundant as the liquor that flowed out of the barrels and down people's throats.

"I want you covering my back all night. I trust you've come well prepared."

"Don't doubt it for a minute, *patrón.*"

Calafat and Larrea followed Horacio up the wooden staircase while Santos Huesos took up the rear, a knife and pistol concealed beneath his poncho. They perceived no threat among the other patrons, who were minding their own business: a few solitary figures sat drowning their demons and memories in rum while others shared jugs of beer and engaged in raucous banter, or gambled at tables where cards, Spanish pesos, and gold coins changed hands swiftly; many more were wooing the whores, rudely thrusting their hands up skirts and down cleavages while the women crossed themselves fearfully with each fresh rumble of thunder. On a dais at the far end of the room, a quintet of mulatto musicians were tuning up. Although no one appeared to take any interest in them, Santos Huesos took up his position behind them with military precision.

On the upper floor they were confronted by a pair of splendid carved sabicú doors, which looked completely out of place but turned out to be a foretaste of what they would discover in the salon, decorated with blue silk wall coverings, which most of the time remained under lock and key, out of bounds to the riffraff below.

Eight men were waiting for them inside, accompanied by the hostess and some of the classier whores provocatively dressed. As was customary in that and every other city, all the men, Larrea included, wore pin-striped trousers and varying tones of gray frock coat, white shirts with starched collars, and silk cravats.

"Welcome to my humble home," La Chucha greeted them in a deep, velvety voice that was a little throaty but still attractive.

Her gold tooth shone. Sixty-five, seventy, seventy-five—it was impossible to tell how many years had accumulated on that visage crowned by a tight gray chignon. For many decades, her almond-shaped eyes the color of honey and her exotic, gazelle-like body had made her the most coveted whore on the island—or so Calafat had told him over dinner. He understood why when he saw, amid a mass of wrinkles, her still-exquisite bone structure and her beguiling eyes sparkling in the glow of the candlelight.

When time had robbed her of some of her regal splendor, the former slave and subsequent concubine of well-to-do gentlemen had proved herself both astute and farsighted, using her savings to set up her own business. She had inherited the furnishings that decorated the sumptuous, exotic room from a handful of gentlemen who had fallen for her charms. Either to settle a debt or, on more than one occasion, as a bequest after they died of a stroke between her thighs, they had provided her with a motley collection of brass candlesticks, Chinese earthenware pots, Philippine chests, ancestral portraits of paler, mustier, less attractive races than her own, cavernous armchairs, and gold-leaf-framed mirrors. These were all arranged with a supreme indifference to prevailing notions of good taste or aesthetic harmony.

"La Chucha opens her salon only on very special occasions," Calafat had told him. For example, when the sugarcane harvest was over and the wealthy planters arrived in Havana with their pockets full. When one of Her Majesty's warships docked in the port, or when she wished to present a fresh batch of young prostitutes from New Orleans. Or sometimes when a customer needed a neutral venue for a special event such as that night.

"A pleasure to see you again, Don Julián. You've been neglecting me," she greeted him, extending her dark hand to Calafat with a magnificent flourish. "And a pleasure to meet our guest," she added, appraising Larrea with an expert eye while keeping her comments discreetly to herself. Turning to the others, she said: "Well, gentlemen, I think we're all here."

The men nodded silently as one.

During the course of the exchanged greetings, the two men's eyes had not yet met. They did so the very instant La Chucha addressed them: "Don Gustavo, Señor Larrea, if you'd be so kind."

The rest of those present, suddenly aware of their secondary role, took a step backward. Now at last the two stood face-to-face like the adversaries they were to be. The murmur of voices stopped dead as though cut with a knife; the sound of heavy rain on the flooded path outside drifted in through the open balcony windows.

Zayas's watery gaze was as impenetrable as it had been the previous night in El Louvre. He exuded self-assurance. Tall, dignified, and elegant, his fine hair impeccably groomed and blue blood doubtless throbbing in his veins, he wore no jewelry or other accessories: no rings or tiepins, no visible fob. Like Larrea.

"Good evening, Señor Zayas," he said, proffering his hand.

Carola Gorostiza's husband returned the greeting with deliberate precision. *You're a cool bastard,* thought Larrea.

"I trust you don't mind, I've brought my own cues."

Mauro Larrea gave a curt nod.

"I can lend you one if you wish."

Another brief gesture, this time of refusal.

"I'll use one belonging to the house, if Doña Chucha has no objection."

She gave her consent with a nod before ushering them to the table at the far end of the room. Surprisingly fine for such a dive, Larrea noticed instantly. Full-size, no pockets, nice and smooth. Above it, an impressive bronze three-branch lamp was suspended from the ceiling by thick chains. Dotted about the floor were brass spittoons, and along the wall a neat row of carved wooden seats.

In one corner, beneath an oil painting of naked nymphs, was the cue stand. Larrea headed toward it while Zayas undid a leather sheath and removed a magnificent cue of polished wood with a leather shaft and his name carved on the butt. Larrea tried several of the house cues before selecting one with the correct weight and feel. Both men then applied chalk to the tips before dusting their palms with talcum powder to absorb any moisture. They avoided looking at one another, each immersed in what he was doing, like a pair of duelists loading their weapons.

Apart from a few details, the terms of the challenge scarcely needed any discussion; both men understood the rules of the game they were to play: carom, or three-cushion billiards. The stakes had been firmly agreed upon the night before.

All thoughts of the foolishness of this contest were banished from Larrea's mind. His worries seemed to vanish into thin air as though blown away by the storm that was still battering the dark night over El Manglar. His opponent's scheming wife faded into the mist, as did his distant and recent past, his beginnings, his hopes, and his troubled future. Everything evaporated from his brain like smoke; from then on he would be only arms and fingers, sharp eyes and taut muscles, calculations and precision.

When they signaled that they were ready, their companions as well as the whores fell silent once more, withdrawing to a discreet distance from the table. A reverential hush descended on the room, while from below arose the rhythms of a *contradanza* mixed with the clamor of customers' voices and the furious stamp of the dancers' feet on wooden floors.

Then La Chucha, with her honey-colored eyes and glittering tooth, took on the seriousness of a trial judge. As if, instead of in that bordello-cum-tavern in one of the seediest port areas of the colonial city, they were in an official chamber of the captain general's palace.

A gold doubloon tossed into the air decided who would cue off first. As it landed on her palm, the stately profile of the quintessentially Spanish Isabella II marked the opening of the game.

"Don Mauro Larrea, the first turn falls to you."

CHAPTER TWENTY-THREE

᠃

A s the balls sped across the table, bouncing off the cushions before striking one another with a soft click or a resounding crack,
the game soon turned into a tense battle in which neither side gave
any quarter. There were no errors or concessions in this spellbinding
contest between two men with clearly contrasting styles and characters.

Mauro Larrea had to acknowledge that Gustavo Zayas was good,
devilishly good. A little overconfident in his posture, yet his shots were
expertly dazzling, his technique magnificently calculated by that un-
fathomable mind, which showed nothing of what was simmering on
the inside.

For his part, Larrea played bold shots, precariously balanced between
solidity and fluidity, between what he could anticipate and what his intuition impelled him to do. The exquisite style of the one player was pit-
ted against the hybrid, mongrel game of the other, clearly revealing the
disparity between the schools each hailed from: genteel salons as opposed
to filthy dens that had arisen in the shadows of mines and sinkholes.
Orthodoxy and cold brainwork in contrast to rapt passion and pastiche.

Their physiques and temperaments were as different as their way
of playing. Zayas, sharp and icy, his blond hair impeccably combed

back from his receding hairline, seemed inscrutable behind his blue eyes and studied gestures. Mauro Larrea, on the other hand, seemed all too human. He leaned over the table casually, lined up with the cue, his chin nearly touching it. His thick head of hair grew increasingly disheveled, legs flexed nimbly, arms at full stretch as he gripped, aimed, and shot.

The scores mounted steadily as the night wore on, continually fluctuating as the two men pursued the game's objective: that the first to reach a hundred and fifty caroms would be the winner.

They stalked each other like a pair of hungry wolves, never more than a few points apart. Twenty-six to twenty-nine, hand on the wood, endless circling about the table, more chalking up. Seventy-two to seventy-three, more talcum powder applied to the hands, ivory clacking against ivory. Zayas surged ahead; Larrea languished; Zayas fell behind; Larrea regained ground. A hundred and five to a hundred and eight. The margin remained narrow until the final stretch.

Had Calafat not alerted Mauro Larrea beforehand, he would have continued, unstoppable, until victory was his. But when the moment came, he was instantly aware of it: behind the exhilarating game, his mind had remained vigilant, watching to see whether the banker's suspicions would be borne out. And so they were, for no sooner had Zayas marked up a hundred and forty caroms, having proven his mastery before God and man, than his game began almost imperceptibly to fall off. He made no obvious blunders but rather minute errors of precision at just the right moment: a risky shot he didn't quite manage to pull off, a ball that missed its target by a few millimeters.

Mauro Larrea then took a convincing four-point lead. Until, after scoring his hundred and forty-fifth carom, he began to introduce a few errors into his own game with the same subtlety as his opponent. A riposte that wasn't quite on target, a ball that fell short by a whisker, a spin that lacked enough force to succeed.

For the first time, when the scores were even at a hundred and forty-six, realizing that his opponent was also slowing his game, Gustavo Zayas started to perspire. Copiously, from his temples, brow, and chest. He dropped his chalk on the floor, cursed between gritted teeth, the anxiety showing in his eyes. Just as old Calafat had suspected, Larrea's unexpected behavior had put him off his stroke. He had just realized that his opponent had no intention of going along with his plans by allowing him to lose at his whim.

Tension hung in the air; barely a sound could be heard in the room apart from an occasional cough, rain splashing into the puddles outside, and the two players' movements. At three-twenty in the morning, with an excruciating one hundred and forty-nine caroms apiece, one shot away from victory, it was Mauro Larrea's turn to play.

He gripped the cue and leaned over the table. The cue slid firmly through the circle formed by his fingers, his left hand manifesting the consequences of the explosion at Las Tres Lunas. He measured, prepared, aimed. Then, poised to take the shot, he hesitated. The silence was palpable as, with unnerving deliberateness, Larrea stood up straight. His eyes remained fixed on the cue for a few seconds, then he looked up. Calafat was twisting the tips of his mustache; next to him, La Chucha was watching Larrea with her strange honey-colored eyes as her fingers clenched the hunchback's arm. A quartet of whores stood craning their necks and biting their nails while a few of Zayas's cronies wore gloomy, alarmed expressions. Beyond them, Larrea could see a mass of faces lining the walls: bearded, disheveled men, some with rings in their ears; faded trollops. Some had even climbed onto the furniture to get a better view.

It was then Mauro realized that not a soul remained downstairs. There was no longer any music and stamping feet below. No more fandangos or rumbas, tangos or congas. Even the stragglers had now climbed the stairs, passing unimpeded through the sabicú doors that marked the frontier between the two floors, between the barroom frequented by ordinary folk and the flamboyant gaming room reserved for those blessed by good fortune. Eager to know the outcome, they had all crowded together to watch the fierce contest between these two gentlemen.

Larrea finally grasped the cue again, leaned over, lined himself up, and played the shot. The white ball that could have ended in a triumph for him sped off, hitting the three obligatory cushions before traveling unwaveringly toward the two balls. It edged past the red one with only the width of a coin's edge between.

A deep murmur spread through the room. Now it was Zayas's turn.

Zayas, still perspiring freely, rubbed his hands with talcum powder. Then, focusing his attention on the baize, he took his time to think through his strategy, or possibly to contemplate the significance of these final shots. Never in a million years had he imagined that Mauro Larrea would deliberately resist winning; that he would refuse to keep Carola, reject the triumph that would have spread his fame throughout Havana like the early morning mist. Despite Zayas's unease, his shot was clean and effective. The spin he put on the ball caused it to bounce off the three selected cushions before supposedly veering toward the two other balls. However, gradually the pace diminished until the ball rolled to a halt, a hairbreadth from its destination.

The crowd gave a stifled roar of frustrated admiration. Faces grimaced as the tension mounted. The score remained even. It was Larrea's turn. He would have gone on playing until Christmas, or possibly Easter, determined not to surrender—or what amounted to the same thing: he refused to win. And so, once again, he found himself considering the angles, weighing up the options, second-guessing his opponent. Then, placing his hand on the cue, he twisted his body and leaned over the table. The shot was as accurate as he had hoped. Instead of tracing a triangle, the ball struck only two cushions. It should have hit a third but merely rolled alongside it before coming to a halt.

This time the howl from the audience could be heard by half of El Manglar. Whether they were white or black, rich or poor, merchants, sailors, drunkards, floozies, planters, petty criminals, good or bad folk. By now, everyone there had realized that the two men were vying with each other to lose. They couldn't give a good goddamn what obscure reasons lay behind this eccentric behavior. All they wanted to see was which man succeeded in imposing his will.

When the clock struck half past four, Zayas accepted the fact that he had nothing to gain from continuing this outrageous battle of wills. In his bid to engineer a defeat to suit his own interests, he hadn't reckoned on things turning out this way. This damned Mexican, or fellow countryman, or whatever he was, was driving him out of his mind. Larrea's neck veins were bulging like ropes, his shoulders threatening to burst through his shirt seams, his hair tousled as though by the devil himself. He exhibited the reckless play of someone accustomed to blindly skirting the edge of a cliff, seemingly prepared to go on fighting to his last breath and in the process turn the erstwhile king of the billiard table into the laughingstock of the island. Zayas realized with sudden force that the only reasonably dignified way out for himself was to win.

Twenty minutes and a few polished shots later, a burst of applause signaled the end of the game. Both men were showered with praise, while La Chucha and the faithful Horacio, hitherto rapt in their ringside seats, ejected the invading crowd from the turquoise room. Zayas's friends congratulated Larrea even though he had lost; the whores gathered around him. He winked at Santos Huesos, still on guard at the rear, and shot a knowing look at Calafat. *Good work, my boy,* the old man seemed to be saying beneath his bushy whiskers. For his part, Larrea raised his hand to his chest and lowered his head solemnly in a display of gratitude.

Then he approached one of the balcony windows, greedily inhaling the last of the night air. The rain had ceased, and the storm had moved on toward Florida or the Bahamian Cays, leaving behind the prelude to a clear dawn. Soon the cannon at the naval station would sound the break of day and the city gates would open. People living outside would enter to pursue their business, along with carts on their way to market. The port would become a hive of activity, stores would open for trade, traps and carriages would appear in the streets. A new day would break in Havana, and once more he would be staring into the abyss.

Gazing down from the balcony at the mud-choked paths, he watched the last patrons of the brothel disappear amid the shadows. He thought he should follow their example, take Calafat's carriage back to his lodgings, go to bed and rest. Or perhaps he could remain, ending up in bed with one of La Chucha's whores instead. Now freed from the tension of the game, he noticed some that were extremely enticing, with their plunging cleavages and wasp waists encased in tight corsets.

Either of those two options would undoubtedly have been the most sensible way to end that feverish night: sleeping alone in his room on Calle Mercaderes, or wrapped around a woman's warm body. Nonetheless, neither was to happen.

Turning his gaze back to the room, he could see Zayas still holding his cue as his friends circled around him chattering and laughing. Carola Gorostiza's husband gave the impression of someone fully engaged in the scene: responding to their flattery, occasionally joining in with the general laughter, or replying when posed a question. But Mauro Larrea knew that Zayas hadn't digested this defeat dressed up as victory, for a stake had been driven through the man's heart. And he also knew how to prize it out.

Approaching Zayas, he extended his hand.

"My congratulations and compliments. You've shown yourself to be an excellent opponent as well as a first-class player."

Zayas mumbled a few brief words of thanks.

"I concede that the matter between us has been resolved," Mauro added in hushed tones. "Please convey my respects to your wife."

He perceived Zayas's silent rage in the set grimace of his mouth.

"Unless, that is . . ."

Before finishing his sentence, he knew that Zayas would accept.

"Unless, that is, you wish to settle the score and play a real game."

CHAPTER TWENTY-FOUR

✦

E veryone except Calafat was surprised by the announcement of a
fresh contest. *Lose, put him off his stroke, and then ask him for the
chance to get even,* the banker had suggested that very afternoon in his
office. And when the opportunity arose, he thought to himself, *Why not?*

"Go and fetch La Chucha," he asked one of the girls, who had a
child's face and a fleshy body.

Within the blink of an eye, the madam had come back.

"Señor Zayas and I have agreed to play another game," Mauro announced impassively. As if, after the five-hour onslaught their bodies
had just withstood, this was the most normal thing in the world.

"Why, of course, gentlemen."

Her gold tooth shone like the El Morro lighthouse as she doled out
orders to her charges. Drinks for the guests, water and chunks of ice,
flasks of liquor. Sweep the floor, brush the baize, fetch more talcum
powder and clean white towels. Tidy up this mess, for the love of the
goddess Oshun.

"And if either of you gentlemen would like to freshen up before you
start, please follow me."

Mauro was shown into a bathroom with a large tub in the center surrounded by a series of bawdy frescoes: jolly shepherdesses with hiked-up skirts; unusually well-hung huntsmen; Peeping Toms behind trees, breeches down around their ankles; pretty maidens being penetrated by handsome youths; and other similar scenes captured by a painter with a clumsy hand and a lewd imagination.

"Good Lord, how outrageous . . ." he murmured sarcastically as he stood over a basin, naked from the waist up. The soap smelled of whores and violets: he used it to wash his hands, armpits, face, neck, and chin, which at that hour was in need of a good shave. He swilled out his mouth and spat vigorously, then ran his wet fingers through his hair in an effort to tame his unruly locks.

The water did him good, removing the grimy layer of sweat, talcum powder, smoke, and chalk from his skin. He felt refreshed. As he was rubbing his chest dry with a towel he heard a rap on the door.

"Do you fancy a little relaxation, Señor?" a beautiful mulatta inquired sweetly, gazing at his bare chest. The answer was no.

Over by the window, he shook out his wrinkled shirt streaked with stains, which hours before had been pristine white and stiff with starch. He was about to slip it on again, when there was another knock at the door. After he had given his permission, it opened to reveal not another of La Chucha's whores come to offer her charms, nor Horacio checking he had everything he needed.

"I need to speak to you."

It was Zayas, looking dapper again, a businesslike tone to his voice, and no pretense at cordiality. Larrea responded simply by gesturing for him to enter.

"I should like to make a wager with you."

Larrea slipped his right arm into the shirtsleeve.

"I thought as much," he replied.

"However, I wish to explain that at present I am short of ready cash."

And you think I'm not? he thought.

"In that case I suggest we cancel the game," said Larrea, pulling on the other empty sleeve. "No hard feelings; we just call it quits and go home."

"That isn't my intention: I aim to do everything in my power to beat you."

There was restraint in his voice, not swagger. Or at least that was Larrea's impression as he tucked in his shirttails.

"We'll have to see about that," he murmured dryly, apparently focused on what he was doing.

"But first, as I said, I'd like to explain my situation to you."

"Please go ahead."

"I'm in no position to wager any money. But I have an alternative proposition."

A cynical guffaw issued from Mauro Larrea's throat.

"Do you know something, Zayas? I'm not used to gambling with men as complicated as you. Where I come from, you place whatever you have on the table. And if you have nothing, you withdraw honorably and no harm is done. So be a good fellow, would you, and stop fooling with me?"

"I propose to wager some properties."

Larrea turned toward the mirror to straighten his necktie. *No mistake about it, you're a stubborn bastard.*

"In the south of Spain," Zayas went on. "What I am willing to put on the table is a house, a vineyard, and a completely equipped winery. In return I propose that you put up fifty thousand escudos. Needless to say, the total value of my properties far exceeds that sum."

Mauro Larrea gave a faint laugh tinged with bitterness. Zayas was willing to gamble away his cousin's entire legacy, the properties his wife had so proudly boasted of. *You might be a damned Spaniard, my friend,* he reflected, *but the tropical air has made you lose your wits.*

"A highly risky wager, wouldn't you say?"

"Extremely. But that's all I have," replied Zayas coldly.

Larrea wheeled around, still adjusting his shirt collar.

"I insist we forget the whole thing. We played a memorable game, which in theory you won, although you and I both know I was the true victor. We can cancel the second if you like, pretend I never suggested a return match. We'll each go our separate ways. Why force the situation?"

"My offer stands."

Larrea took a step forward. The roosters in El Manglar had begun crowing in their coops.

"Do you accept that I never had the slightest interest in taking your wife away from you?"

"Your determination not to win has convinced me of that."

"Are you aware that she has the money you so desperately need? She inherited it from her mother's estate. I brought it over myself from Mexico. Her brother is a close friend of mine. That's the only connection between us."

If Zayas was at all surprised by this avowal, he did not show it.

"I suspected as much. In any case, let us just say that my wife doesn't enter into my immediate plans. And neither do her private assets."

His words and tone of voice confirmed Calafat's theory: this fellow wanted to get as far away as he could from Cuba, his wife, and his past. And to do so, he was prepared to stake everything. If he won, he would keep his properties and have enough money to pursue his plan. If he lost, he would be tied to a woman he clearly didn't love for the rest of his life. Then Larrea recalled what Doña Caridad had said about Zayas's troubled past. The family matters his cousin had come to Cuba to resolve. The other woman, who in the end never became his.

"You know what you're doing . . ."

His shirt, although still somewhat wrinkled and soiled, looked halfway decent. Now he pulled up his suspenders.

"You wager fifty thousand escudos and I three properties. The first to reach a hundred caroms is the winner."

Larrea stood arms akimbo, a posture he had adopted often during a certain period of his life. When bargaining hard over the price of his silver, when fighting tooth and nail over a mining deposit or seam. He stood that way unconsciously now: bold, defiant.

In the Andalusian's eyes he contemplated the reflection of a pitiful slave ship; he saw Carola Gorostiza's rebuttal; the nights he slept on the ground surrounded by coyotes and Chinaco soldiers on his way to Veracruz; Calafat's respectable business proposition, lost to him forever now; and his aimless wanderings through the Havana streets mulling over his unease.

Larrea decided it was about time his accursed luck changed once and for all.

"How can I be sure your offer is genuine?"

A clamor of voices that had been awaiting his next move suddenly resounded in his head. Andrade, Úrsula, Mariana. *How can you play this madman for fifty thousand escudos when your own assets don't amount to even half that?* his agent wailed. *Surely you aren't so rash as to use a slice of my capital in such a gigantic folly, are you?* bawled the old countess, striking the wooden floor with her cane. *For God's sake, Father, think of Nico. Of what you once were. Of my unborn child,* Mariana pleaded.

What if I win? he defied them.

What the hell would you do with those properties in Spain, however much they are worth? the three of them assailed him as one.

I'd sell them, of course, and use the money to return to Mexico. To my home, my life. To you all.

"If you don't trust me, I suggest we find a witness."

"I'd like Don Julián Calafat to act as intermediary, to attest to your wager in writing, and to be the sole witness."

He spoke with absolute resolve, with the boldness that in the past had come naturally to him, at a time when he would have burst out laughing had anyone suggested he would end up gambling his future in a Cuban bordello.

Zayas went to speak with the old man, leaving him alone again, standing stock-still in the center of the washroom with the bawdy characters on the walls staring down at him entwined in their carnal pleasures. He knew then that there was no going back.

He was preparing to fasten his gray silk cravat when he paused. *What the hell . . .* he muttered between gritted teeth. In honor of his mining days, those endless games in filthy taverns where he had learned everything he knew about billiards, he unbuttoned his shirt collar and returned to the turquoise room.

Calafat and Zayas were conversing in hushed tones over by the balcony. Zayas's cronies were enjoying the company of the few whores who remained awake, while La Chucha and Horacio walked around the room straightening the last of the paintings knocked askew by the crowd.

"I hope my improper dress won't offend anyone."

All eyes turned toward him. *Remember it's nearly six in the morning and this is a whorehouse, after all. And we're about to play for our lives,* he wanted to add.

The two adversaries approached the table as Calafat removed his eternal cigar from beneath his bushy mustache.

"Ladies and gentlemen," he said. "The players have expressed the wish for this to be a private game. Only myself, the proprietress, and Horacio, who will act as an assistant, will remain, assuming that both parties concerned are in agreement."

The two men nodded, while Zayas's friends looked openly annoyed. However, accompanied by the girls, they soon left. Santos Huesos followed behind, not before exchanging a knowing glance with his *patrón.*

The splendid sabicú doors were closed and La Chucha filled their glasses with liquor.

"Is this a private match between the two of you, gentlemen, or may I place a bet?" she asked in a voice that was still alluring despite her age. The takings that night from her girls had been meager, and she was hoping to make something extra out of this impromptu development.

"I'll cover your costs, Chucha," Calafat replied. "Simply toss the coin when I say."

Then, adopting a formal tone, the old man related the terms of the wager.

"Fifty thousand escudos on the part of Mauro Larrea de las Fuentes, and on the part of his opponent, Don Gustavo Zayas Montalvo, properties comprising a town house, winery, and vineyard located in the illustrious Spanish municipality of Jerez de la Frontera. Do both parties agree to play a game of one hundred caroms for the aforementioned stake, witnessed on this day by Doña María de Jesús Salazar?"

The two men muttered their acceptance while the old brothel keeper raised her dark bony hand to her heart, declaring "Yes, sir" in a clear voice before crossing herself. She had lost count of the number of similar acts of folly she had seen during her long years in the business.

The first light of dawn was starting to filter through the balcony windows when the Spanish queen flew into the air once more. Zayas won the toss this time, and so began the game that would change both men's lives forever.

The tension of earlier that night turned to ferocity at dawn. The green baize was a battleground now, the game a brutal combat. Once again there were magnificent shots, hypnotic trajectories, impossible angles masterfully overcome, and sharp outbursts of fury.

During the first half of the game, the two men came out even. Larrea played with his shirtsleeves rolled up past his elbows, displaying his scars and the muscles that no longer split rocks, nor extracted silver, but were nonetheless evident when he lined up his shots. Gustavo Zayas, despite his habitual composure, soon cast off his frock coat. The soft light of dawn had given way to the sun's first harsh rays: both men were perspiring freely, pushing themselves to the limit. But that was the extent of what they had in common, so vast were the differences between them. Mauro Larrea remained impulsive, almost feral, in his boldness and tenacity. Zayas was once again full of precision, but without the earlier premeditated flourishes or elegance.

They went on making one feverish shot after the other, beneath the exhausted yet rapt gaze of Calafat. Horacio had closed the shutters and was fanning La Chucha, who was half-asleep in her armchair. And then, halfway through the contest, two hours after the madness of the return game had commenced, a breach began to open. After his fiftieth carom, Mauro Larrea started to take the lead; the gap was small to begin with, then gradually started to grow, like a crack in a fine wineglass. Fifty-one to fifty-three, fifty-two to fifty-six. By the time Larrea reached sixty, Zayas was trailing by seven points.

Perhaps with a couple of hours' sleep, a proper meal, or a few cups of coffee, the Andalusian might have been able to claw his way back. Or if his eyes weren't stinging, his arms cramping, his stomach seized with nausea. But the fact was, for one reason or another, he lost control of the situation. And seeing himself falling behind, his nerves started to get the better of him for the second time. He made a few poor shots in too much haste, his mouth set in a grimace. Simple blunders gave way to worrying mistakes. The gap widened.

"Pour me another drink, Horacio."

As though the liquor would somehow provide him with the necessary stimulus to increase his score.

"And one for you, Don Mauro?" asked the servant.

He had stopped fanning La Chucha now that she was fast asleep, her long black arms stretched by her sides, her head resting on a velvet cushion.

Larrea declined the drink, his eyes fixed on the tip of his cue. Zayas, on the other hand, gestured with his empty glass. The hunchback refilled it.

Perhaps he lacked the mental stamina, or was simply physically drained, but for some reason that Larrea would never understand, Gustavo Zayas started to drink heavily. In an attempt to incite himself to win, or so that he could blame the liquor for what was increasingly obvious would be his defeat. Three-quarters of an hour later, Zayas hurled his cue to the ground in rage. Placing his hands flat on the wall for support, his head sinking between his shoulders, he bent over and vomited into one of the brass spittoons.

This time no shouts or acclaim hailed Mauro Larrea's victory; the crowd was absent, as were the whores and his opponent's cronies. Nor had he any desire to express his joy: he was stiff all over, his ears were buzzing, his fingers numb, and his mind hazy, enveloped in a dense fog like the morning mist that rose from the sea.

A heartfelt clap on the shoulder from old Calafat brought him back to reality; he nearly cried out in pain.

"Congratulations, my boy."

He had begun to emerge from his grave.

A future now awaited him across the ocean.

Part III

❧

JEREZ DE LA FRONTERA

CHAPTER TWENTY-FIVE

The shutters evidently had not been used or oiled in quite some time, for the clasps refused to budge. Only through the efforts of two pairs of hands did they finally yield, accompanied by creaks and groans from the hinges. Sunlight flooded the room and the phantom-like shapes of the furniture took on a sudden clarity.

Mauro Larrea lifted one of the dust sheets: beneath was a sofa covered in faded scarlet satin. Under another sheet he found a wobbly rosewood table. At the far side of the room he saw a magnificent fireplace with the remains of its last fire. On the floor next to it lay a dead pigeon.

His were the only footsteps that resounded as he strode across the imposing room. After helping him with the balcony shutters, the notary's clerk took refuge in the doorway. Waiting.

"So nobody has been looking after the house for a long while now?" asked Larrea, without turning around. As he said this, he pulled off another sheet: sleeping beneath it was a broken armchair with walnut armrests.

"No one as far as I know, sir. Ever since Don Luis left, nobody has been here. But, anyway, the rot set in long before that."

He spoke unctuously, apparently submissive and not asking any direct questions, but at the same time unable to conceal the gnawing curiosity aroused by the task the notary had given him. *Angulo, go with Señor Larrea to Don Luis Montalvo's house on Calle de la Tornería. Then, if there's time, take him to the winery on Calle del Muro. I have two appointments I need to keep. I'll see you here at half past one.*

While the mansion's new owner was striding around it stone-faced, this Angulo fellow could hardly wait for the visit to be over so that he could escape to the stall where he bought lunch every day, to spread the news. In fact, in his mind he was already going through how best to phrase it to create the greatest impact. *A Spaniard who made his fortune in the Americas—an Indiano—is the new owner of the Runt's house.* That seemed a good way to put it. Or perhaps he should say first that the Runt was dead and then add that a newly returned Spaniard had taken over the house?

Whatever order he said it in, the two main points were the Runt and the Indiano. Runt because finally everyone in Jerez was going to learn what had happened to Luis Montalvo, possessor of the nickname and of the mansion: dead and buried in Cuba, that had been his fate. And the Indiano, because that was the label he had immediately pinned on this stranger with such an impressive physique who that same morning had stridden into the notary's office and announced that his name was Mauro Larrea, creating a ripple of interest in all those present.

While the skinny, haggard-looking Angulo was already silently celebrating the effect of the cannonade he was about to fire, the two men continued to explore room after room along the upper-floor gallery. Another couple of sparsely furnished sitting rooms; a spacious dining room with a table that could seat eighteen guests, but only half that number of chairs; a small, bare chapel, and a good handful of bedrooms with sunken mattresses. The slits in the shutters occasionally allowed in some feeble rays of sun, but the overriding sensation was one of gloom combined with an unpleasant smell of staleness and animal urine.

"I assume that the servants' quarters and storage space will be up in the attic, as usual," commented the clerk.

"I beg your pardon?"

"The attic," Angulo repeated, pointing up at the ceiling. "The garrets—the lofts."

The Tarifa tiles and Genoa marble decorating the courtyard were filthy. Some of the doors had come off their hinges, several of the windows were broken, and the yellow ocher around the doorways had long since peeled off. In one corner of the vast kitchen, a cat that had recently given birth hissed at them, obviously feeling her position was threatened as the empress of this sad room with its cold fireplaces, smoky ceilings, and empty pitchers.

How long has this place been falling into decline? Larrea asked himself as he made his way back through the courtyard, where climbing weeds wound their way up the columns. The overriding sensation was one of decay after so many years of abandonment.

"Would you like to go and see the winery now?" asked the clerk, with little enthusiasm.

Mauro Larrea took the fob watch out of his pocket and gave a last look around his new property. Two slender palm trees, a host of clay pots filled with aspidistras that had run wild, a fountain with no water, and a pair of battered wicker armchairs bore witness to the agreeable hours that the shade of this splendid courtyard must have offered its inhabitants in the distant past. Now beneath its stone arches his feet encountered only dried mud, withered leaves, and animal droppings. If he had been of a more melancholy disposition, he might have asked himself what had become of the past owners of this place: the children who ran around the courtyard, the adults who rested, loved one another, and argued and conversed in every room of this vast mansion.

But since sentimental questions of this nature were not his style, he simply noted that there was only half an hour until his appointment with the notary.

"If you don't mind, I prefer to leave the winery for later. I'll walk back to your office; there's no need for you to accompany me. Go back to your tasks; I can look after myself."

His powerful voice with its strange foreign accent persuaded Angulo not to insist. They said good-bye at the entrance, each anxious to regain his freedom. Larrea wanted to digest all he had just seen, and the scrawny clerk was desperate to run off to the tavern, where each day he poured out the news and gossip he had gleaned thanks to his position.

What this Angulo, with his wheezing breath and sly expression, could not even imagine was that Mauro Larrea, despite his booming voice and resolute bearing as a wealthy man from the old Spanish colonies, was deep down just as disconcerted as he was. A thousand doubts assailed the miner's mind as he stepped out once more into the autumnal atmosphere of Calle de la Tornería, but he uttered only one of them, a question aimed at himself that was the essence of all the others: *What the devil are you doing here, compadre?*

It was all legally his, he knew that. He had won it from Carola Gorostiza's husband in front of reliable witnesses when Gustavo Zayas decided to risk everything of his own free will and in his right mind. The obscure reasons for his doing so were none of Larrea's business, but the outcome was. By goodness, it was. That was what a wager meant in Spain, in the Antilles, and in independent Mexico, in the highest society and in the lowest brothel. There was a wager, a game, and sometimes you won and sometimes you lost. This time luck had been on his side. And yet, after inspecting the desolate mansion, a feeling of bitterness returned in the shape of vague silhouettes from the far side of the ocean: *Why were you so reckless, Gustavo Zayas? Why did you run the risk of never returning?*

Finding his way by instinct, he crossed a square lined with four palatial mansions, then went through the Seville gate and took Calle Larga into the heart of the town. *Stop moaning,* he told himself. *You're the legitimate heir, and the intrigues of the previous owners are all one to you. Concentrate on what you have just seen: even taking its present lamentable state into account, that mansion must be worth a good deal. What you have to do now is to get rid of it, along with all the rest of what you inherited, as quickly as possible. That's why you're here: to sell it off, pocket the money, and cross the Atlantic back to the other shore.*

He continued on his way to the notary's office along an avenue lined with orange trees. Hardly any carriages passed him by: thank heavens, he thought, remembering the dangerous swarms of them on the streets of Havana. Caught up as he was in his own reflections, he barely registered the quiet, prosperous life of the town, with its two confectioners, three tailors' shops, five barbers, many aristocratic façades, a couple of pharmacies, a hardware store, and a handful of stores selling shoes, hats, or foodstuffs. Strolling in among them were passersby of all kinds: elegant ladies, gentlemen dressed in the English style, babies with their maids, schoolchildren, and ordinary people on their way home for lunch. Compared to the crazy rhythm of the cities in the Americas from which he had come, Jerez was like a feather pillow, although it escaped his notice.

What he did notice was the smell: a persistent odor that drifted over the roofs and seeped in through the windows. A smell that was neither human nor animal and was nothing like the constant aroma of roasting corn on the streets of Mexico or the tang of the sea in Havana. It was strange, pleasant in its way, and distinctive. Immersed in it, Mauro Larrea reached Calle Lancería, which seemed to be a zone of business offices and negotiation, with constant comings and goings. The notary Don Senén Blanco was waiting for him, having finished his morning's commitments.

"Señor Larrea, allow me to invite you to lunch at the Victoria Inn. This is not the time of day to sit discussing serious topics on an empty stomach."

As they walked toward Calle Corredera, Larrea calculated the notary must be ten years his elder and a good few inches shorter. Wearing a fine-quality frock coat, he had graying sideburns and spoke with a southern Spanish accent that was not unlike those heard in the New World.

Although Don Senén did not seem as inquisitive as his clerk Angulo, inside him the same curiosity was bubbling away. He had also been taken aback on hearing that, thanks to a series of incongruous transactions, the former possessions of the Montalvo family were now the rightful property of this returned Spaniard. This was not the first and would certainly not be the last unexpected operation from beyond the seas that he was called upon to certify as a notary; all well and good. His burning interest lay elsewhere, and this made him eager for the stranger to explain how the devil these properties had fallen into his hands, how the last bearer of the Montalvo name had died in the Antilles, and any additional details the newcomer might care to supply.

The two men sat down at a table giving on to the street, but protected from the commotion of carts, animals, and humans by a white lace curtain that covered the bottom half of the windows. No sooner were they seated across from each other than a lad of twelve or thirteen in a waiter's uniform arrived with his hair slicked down thanks to a liberal application of water and cheap soap, and plunked two small glasses on the tablecloth. The glasses were taller than they were wide, with narrow rims. And, for the moment at least, empty. Next to them he placed a bottle without a label and a small china dish filled with olives.

Larrea unfolded his napkin and took a deep breath as if he had again become aware of something that had been bothering him but that he had not yet been able to identify.

"What is that smell, Don Senén?"

"It is wine, Señor Larrea," the notary replied, pointing to some dark barrels at the far end of the restaurant. "The smell of must, of wineries, wineskins: the smell of Jerez."

He poured out the wine.

"That was the livelihood of the family whose properties you now own. The Montalvo family were always wine producers, yes indeed."

Larrea nodded, staring down at the golden liquid as he extended his hand toward the glass stem. The notary observed the scar reaching to his wrist and the two fingers crushed in Las Tres Lunas mine, but asked no questions.

"And how did it happen that the place fell into ruin, Don Senén, if I may be so bold as to inquire?"

"Because of one of those dreadful things that often happen in families, my dear sir. Not only here in Andalusia but in the rest of Spain, and I suppose in the Americas as well. The great-great-grandfather, great-grandfather, and grandfather break their backs building up a business, and then a moment arrives when the chain is broken: their children lack the same determination or ambition, or a tragedy occurs, or the grandchildren go off the rails and start to ruin matters."

Fortunately for Larrea, at that moment another boy dressed in the same spotless jacket but slightly older than the first one came over, relieving Larrea of the opportunity to dwell on the image of his son Nicolás and the certainty that his own legacy would not even reach the second generation.

"Are you ready to order, Don Senén?" the waiter asked.

"Good and ready, Rafael. Tell us what there is."

The boy reeled off the menu loudly and swiftly. "To start with, there's bean soup with chestnuts, chickpeas with prawns, and noodle soup. For the main course, a choice as usual between meat and fish. Of four-legged animals we have basted roast beef and pork cutlets in sauce; of those that go cheep, there's pigeon with rice. From the water we have shad from the river Guadalete, marinated dogfish, and cod with paprika."

Larrea barely understood more than four or five words, partly because of the waiter's closed pronunciation and partly because never in his life had he heard of some of the choices on offer. What on earth were shad or dogfish?

While the notary was deciding for both of them with the confidence of a regular customer, Mauro Larrea raised the glass of wine to his lips. With its sharp taste in his mouth, he surveyed the wooden barrels and the noisy lunchtime bustle, and with no wish to judge but speaking only to his own soul he mused: *So this is Jerez.*

"I would have been more than glad to invite you back home, but every day three daughters and three sons-in-law sit at my table, and I hardly think that's the most conducive atmosphere to discuss your affairs with the requisite privacy."

"I can only thank you," Larrea replied. Anxious to hear what news the notary had, he spread out his hands and said, "I'm all ears."

"Well, let's see . . . I haven't had the time to examine the earlier wills thoroughly because Don Luis Montalvo received his inheritance almost twenty years ago, and we keep all those documents stored in another office. But in principle everything you have shown me appears to be perfectly in order. According to the documents you've brought, you become the owner of all the properties, which comprise a house, a vineyard, and a winery as transferred by Don Gustavo Zayas, who in turn inherited them on the death of Don Luis Montalvo, the last owner of the properties we are aware of in this town."

The notary seemed to have no problem raising and lowering the wineglass to his mouth as he continued his professional rigmarole in a monotone.

"An executor in Havana and another in the town of Santa Clara in

Las Villas Province," he continued, "both provide official confirmation of these two facts. And whatever is signed in Cuba, since it is territory belonging to the Spanish crown, is immediately valid in peninsular Spain."

As if to sign off on everything he had quoted from memory, the notary popped an olive into his mouth. Larrea took the opportunity to ask a question of his own.

"As I understand it, Luis Montalvo and Gustavo Zayas were first cousins?"

This had been confirmed in the banker Calafat's office in Havana by Gustavo Zayas's representative when he had appeared the morning after the game of billiards to ratify the wager. And that was what the surnames in the will that he presented appeared to corroborate: Luis Montalvo Aguilar and Gustavo Zayas Montalvo. As soon as this business had been settled, and with fortune still smiling on him, Larrea had booked two passages for Cádiz on the mailboat *Fernando el Católico,* at that time owned by the Spanish government. Two days later, accompanied by the old banker down to the port, he had embarked with Santos Huesos. Larrea heard nothing more about Carola Gorostiza or her husband. The lasting image he retained of Zayas was of him leaning against the wall as he vomited into a spittoon in La Chucha's gaming room, pouring out body and soul.

"Yes indeed. Luis Montalvo's father, also called Luis, and Gustavo Zayas's mother, María Fernanda, were brother and sister. There was another brother, Jacobo, the father of two girls, who also died years ago. Luis the father was the firstborn son of the great Don Matías Montalvo, the patriarch of the family, and he in turn also had two sons: Matías, who unfortunately for everyone died as a youngster, and Luisito. Luisito was the youngest of the cousins; following the death of his elder brother, he was left in charge of the flagships of the family clan: the palatial mansion, the legendary winery, and the vineyard. In short, the same family troubles since time began; you'll soon find out what kind of lineage you've just become related to, if you'll excuse my irony."

Here the notary paused for a moment to refill the wineglasses, then went on displaying his remarkable powers of memory.

"I see, Señor Larrea, that you're not turning your nose up at our wine. That's excellent . . . As I was saying, Gustavo Zayas is the son of María Fernanda, the third of Old Man Matías's children and the only female: when I was young I thought she was a truly beautiful woman, or at least that's how I remember it now. Apparently she did not inherit any properties, but she did have a not-inconsiderable dowry. However, she made a bad marriage—they say she had little luck with her husband, and in the end she left here—for Seville, if I'm not mistaken."

The arrival of their first courses brought his lengthy explanation to a halt. A delicious dish of chickpeas with prawns for the gentlemen, the waiter announced. So, to help the stranger, the waiter expounded on the ingredients: very fresh headless prawns, cooked with a little sliced pepper, garlic, onion, and some paprika. While he was revealing these culinary secrets, Rafael stared quite openly at the notary's guest to see if he could glean any information. He had already been asked about him at one or two tables. *Rafaelito, my lad, who is the gentleman seated with Don Senén? I don't know, Don Tomás, but he doesn't seem to be from hereabouts, because he talks very differently. How differently? Like people from Madrid talk? Who can say, Don Pascual, in all my damned life I've never been beyond Lebrija, but I would say no, that man comes from farther away. From the colonies, perhaps? It could be, Don Eulogio, it could well be. Just wait, Don Eusebio, Don Leoncio, Don Cecilio, let's see if I hear anything while I'm serving them. As soon as I do, I'll come and tell you.*

"In short, disregarding all these family questions and as I was saying, I see no problem in legalizing the change of ownership in the land register without delay so that everything passes into your name," the notary continued, oblivious to the other diners' curiosity. "However, and speaking now in a personal capacity, I must say, Señor Larrea, that I have noticed one detail in the document that attracted my attention."

Larrea took his time swallowing his food: he was in no hurry, because he could anticipate what was coming next.

"I see that this transaction was a bestowal rather than a purchase, because nowhere is there any indication of the amount you paid for the properties."

"Is there a problem with that?"

"None at all," replied Blanco evenly. "Simple curiosity on my part. It caught my eye because it's not something that is commonly done in these parts. It's extremely rare that there is no money involved when it comes to a transfer of property."

They returned the spoons to their plates; the only sounds were of silverware meeting china and voices from the nearby tables. Larrea knew he had no reason to explain anything, that the transfer was aboveboard and legal. And yet he preferred to justify himself. In his own way, so that word would get about.

"Well," he said, carefully aligning his cutlery on his plate. "Don Gustavo Zayas's in-laws are very closely linked to my family in Mexico. His brother-in-law and I are about to celebrate the wedding of his daughter and my son. That is why between the two of us we reached certain agreements, exchanges of property that, in view of the circumstances . . ."

It was impossible, faced with this polite Spanish gentleman and in the noble town of Jerez, to talk of the El Louvre Café and the rash challenge his fellow countryman Zayas had made, or that stormy night in the Manglar brothel, or that diabolical first game in front of a crowd of ragged onlookers. Nor could he mention the banker and his bushy mustache, the madame La Chucha and her air of an aged African queen, the extravagant bathroom with its walls painted with obscenities where the wager for the return match was agreed upon. Or the bitter contest that he ended up winning.

"To cut a long story short," said Larrea, staring straight at the notary, "let's just say we entered into a special private agreement."

"I understand . . ." muttered Don Senén, his mouth half-full. Even though he was not sure that he did. "Be that as it may, I insist it is none of my business to pry into the wishes of others. I simply register them. But, turning to another matter, and if I'm not being indiscreet, I should like to ask you another question."

"Ask away."

"Do you by chance have any idea what on earth Luis Montalvo was doing in Cuba? His disappearance was something that surprised everyone here; nobody knows for certain when he left or where he was headed. Simply one fine day nobody saw him anymore, and no one could say where he had gone."

"Did he live alone?"

"Completely alone, and he led, shall we say . . . a somewhat relaxed life."

"Relaxed in what way?"

At that moment the fish arrived, covered in breadcrumbs, its white flesh promising succulent flavor. The waiter again lingered a little longer than necessary to see if he could learn anything about where the stranger was from. But the notary paused discreetly until the disappointed lad turned his back on them and pulled a face at his curious customers.

"He was a strange fellow. He had a physical problem that prevented him growing little more than four and a half feet tall: he would have come up to your elbow, more or less. That was where the nickname 'Runt' came from. But far from letting his size embarrass him, he chose to compensate for this defect with an unbridled passion for the good life. Parties, women, going on sprees, singing and dancing . . . Luisito

Montalvo did *everything*," he said, with a hint of irony. "Without a father from shortly after his twentieth birthday, and with a sick mother whom I suspect he drove into her grave not long afterward, he began to throw away the fortune he inherited."

"So he never concerned himself with the vineyard or the winery?"

"Never, although he didn't sell them, either. Simply, to everyone's astonishment, he refused to have anything to do with them, and let them go to rack and ruin."

Larrea decided to mention the visit he had made to the Montalvo family mansion a few hours earlier.

"As I saw for myself, the family house is also in a deplorable state."

"Until the death of Doña Piedad, Luis's mother, the family residence, at least, was more or less kept up. But when he was left on his own, people came and went there as if they owned the place. Friends, whores, gamblers, rogues. It's said Luisito sold off cheaply everything of value: paintings, porcelain, rugs, cutlery, even his sainted mother's jewels . . ."

"It's true there's not much left," Larrea confirmed. Only a few pieces of furniture that must have been hard to remove, and that some kind hand had covered with dust sheets. From all that he was now learning about the wastrel Luis Montalvo, he doubted whether he would have taken a precaution like that.

"Word had it that El Cachulo, a Gypsy from Seville with a sharp eye and a ready tongue, would often pull his cart up outside the house, fill it with goods, and then sell them to the highest bidder."

This was not the first time Larrea had heard about fortunes squandered by the lack of forethought or the reckless passions of descendants. He knew of more than one case in the mines of Guanajuato and the Mexican capital; he was also sure there were many in the splendid city of Havana. But this was the first that affected him directly, and so he paid close attention.

"Poor Little Runt," murmured the notary, with a mixture of wry amusement and compassion. "It can't have been easy for him to match his physique with the role of the promising heir of such a good-looking family as the Montalvos. His grandparents were an imposing couple. Both of them were handsome and elegant; I can still remember them coming out of High Mass. The same is true of all the descendants I have come across: just look at the cousin who's married to the Englishman and is back here at the moment. I scarcely recall Gustavo, though."

"Tall, blue-eyed, fair-haired . . ." Larrea said unenthusiastically. "Good-looking, as you say."

And a strange fish, he would have liked to add, *not in his appearance or manners so much as in his behavior and ideas.* Prudently, though, he kept this to himself.

"Anyway, Señor Larrea, we are straying from the point. I believe you still haven't answered my question."

"I'm sorry, but what question was that, Don Senén?"

"A very simple one that half of Jerez is going to ask me as soon as I leave this table. What on earth was Luisito Montalvo doing in Cuba?"

Larrea had no need to lie when he responded: "To be frank, dear sir, I haven't the faintest idea."

CHAPTER TWENTY-SIX

╭❧

F urther scenes of desolation: that was what he found when after
lunch the notary took him to the winery on Calle del Muro. In
spite of this, and the fact that there was no time to go in, Larrea was
satisfied with what he saw: a sizable area surrounded by damp walls that
had once been white but were now flaking and covered in mold. Nor
did he have a chance to visit the vineyard, but from the details Don
Senén gave him it did not seem at all negligible in size or potential, so
there would be more money in his pocket once he sold them, and fewer
obstacles for his return.

"If you are sure, Señor Larrea, that you want to put all this on the
market at once, the first thing you will need to do is to determine the
current value of the properties," the notary told him as they were saying
good-bye. "I think that the most sensible thing would be to leave all
that to a land agent."

"Whoever you recommend."

"I'll find you one I trust completely."

"How long will it take you to have all the deeds drawn up?"

"Let's say by the day after tomorrow."

"I'll be back here in two days' time, then."

They had reached Plaza del Arenal, where Larrea's hired carriage was waiting. They shook hands.

"Thursday at eleven, then, with the deeds and the agent. Give my regards to my old friend's son. God rest his father's soul. I'm sure Don Antonio Fatou and his wife are treating you like a lord in their house."

Larrea was already settled inside the carriage and the horses' hooves had begun to ring on the cobbles as the wheels began to turn, when he heard the notary shout: "Although it might be more convenient for you to leave Cádiz and install yourself here while everything is sorted out. In Jerez."

Larrea continued on his way without replying, and yet Don Senén's suggestion remained with him the length of the journey to Puerto de Santa María as night was falling. He considered it again on board the steamer taking him across the dark waters of the tranquil bay. He even thought of asking the opinion of Antonio Fatou, Don Julian Calafat's agent in Cádiz, in whose splendid house on Calle de la Verónica he was staying. This latest link in a chain of prosperous merchants connected with the Americas for more than a century had turned out to be a warm man in his thirties. Over the years, his predecessors had received the clients and friends of the Calafat family as if they were their own, and this arrangement was admirably reciprocated in Havana. "Don't even think of looking for anywhere else to stay," Fatou had told Larrea as soon as he read his letter of introduction. "It will be an honor to have you as our guest for however long your affairs require. I insist."

"How did your trip to Jerez go, Don Mauro?" his host asked the next morning when the two of them were finally alone.

They had just breakfasted on hot chocolate and warm churros under the gaze of three generations of traders with the Indies that peered down at them from portraits on the dining room walls. Although there was nothing ostentatious, the room gave the impression of taste and money well spent: the Pickman china, the marquetry table, and the silver spoons engraved with the family's intertwined initials.

Fatou's young wife, Paulita, had excused herself to attend to some domestic chores, but probably withdrew discreetly simply to leave them to talk. She was scarcely more than twenty, and still had the plump cheeks of an adolescent, but was obviously anxious to fulfill her new role as mistress of the house with regard to this guest of such striking appearance and manners who was presently sleeping under her roof. *Another little churro, Don Mauro? Shall I ask them to heat some more chocolate? Another spoon of sugar? Is everything as you like it? Can I get you anything more?* She was completely different from Mariana, who was always so determined and sure of herself, and yet in some way she reminded Larrea of his daughter. A new wife, a new house, a new universe for a young woman.

A pair of curious, indiscreet maids peeped out of the kitchen to get a glimpse of the new guest for themselves. *Benancia is right, he's handsome,* one of them said, drying her hands on her apron. *Handsome and well-dressed,* they agreed behind the curtain. *From Havana? They say he came from Cuba, but Frasca heard the masters talking last night and caught something about Mexico as well. Heaven only knows, sweetheart, where these people get their good looks. That's what I say, dear child. Heaven only knows.*

Oblivious to the servants' whispering, the two men went on talking at the table.

"Everything is progressing, thank goodness," Larrea continued. "Don Senén Blanco, the notary you recommended, was extremely friendly and efficient. I'm going back tomorrow to complete the formalities and to meet the land agent he selects to take care of the sales."

He added a few more details and made some inconsequential remarks. For the moment that was all he wished to say.

"So am I to conclude that the idea of taking on the business yourself has not even crossed your mind?" asked Fatou.

For God's sake, what do you think a miner like me could do with a vineyard and wines? Larrea almost blurted out, but checked himself.

"I'm afraid I have urgent matters to attend to in Mexico. That's why I'm hoping to dispose of all the properties as quickly as I can."

He mentioned a couple of supposed pressing affairs, some obligations and dates. It was all pure invention in order not to reveal that the only real concerns waiting for him in Mexico were to meet the first of the wretched Carrús's deadlines and to drag his own son to the altar, if necessary by the scruff of his neck.

"I can see that, of course," Fatou agreed. "Even so, it's a shame, because at the moment the wine trade is enjoying great success. You wouldn't be the first to bring capital from overseas to invest in the business. Even my father, may he rest in peace, was tempted to buy a few acres, until he fell ill . . ."

"I can offer you mine at a good price," Larrea said lightheartedly.

"I'd be more than happy to buy them, but as I'm just taking over the reins of the family business I'm afraid it would be too risky. One day, perhaps."

The only thing that Mauro Larrea knew about wines was that he had enjoyed them with his meals when his economic situation had allowed it. However, he had nothing to do that morning but wait, and Fatou did not appear to be in any hurry, either. So he encouraged him to continue.

"Well, anyway, Don Antonio, would it be rude of me if I serve myself a little more of your excellent chocolate while you tell me how the wine business operates hereabouts?"

"On the contrary, it will be my pleasure, my dear friend. Allow me, please."

He refilled their cups, and the spoons clinked on the La Cartuja porcelain.

"Let me confess from the outset that even though we ourselves are not wine producers, the trade in Jerez wines is practically our lifesaver. The wines and the cargos of salt we ship are what keep us going. Things became complicated for us after our American colonies won their independence. With all due respect, my friend, your Mexican compatriots and their counterparts in South America dealt us a heavy blow with their desire for freedom."

Fatou's words were spoken in a tone of cheerful irony rather than with any bitterness. Larrea simply shrugged as if to say there was nothing to be done about it.

"Fortunately, however," the agent went on, "almost in parallel with the reduction in trade with our colonies, the wine business entered a splendid period. And exports to Europe, and in particular to England, are what are preventing the decline not only of our company but I would say of the province of Cádiz as a whole."

"And what is so splendid about the wine trade, if I may ask?"

"It's a long story. Let's see if I can summarize it for you. Until the end of the last century, what the Jerez vintners produced were simply young wines and must that were sent in their undeveloped state to the British ports. Wines that were not yet finished, if you follow me. Once they arrived, they were aged and blended by the local merchants to suit their clients' tastes. Some sweeter, others less so, some with more or less body, more or less strong. As you must know."

No, Larrea didn't have the faintest idea. But he hid the fact.

"But for several decades now," Fatou went on, "the wine business here has become far more dynamic and prosperous. Now the entire process is carried out here, at its point of origin: of course, this is where the vines grow, but now we also look after the vintages and prepare them according to the demands of our English clients. Nowadays the term 'wine producer' has a much broader meaning than before: it usually includes all the stages of the business, the ones previously carried out separately by the growers, the people who stored the wines, and the exporters. And we, from the port or from houses like this one, make sure that the barrels of wine reach their destination, to the representatives and agents of the Jerez firms in Perfidious Albion. Or wherever is necessary."

"So in that way most of the profit stays here."

"Exactly; it stays in this land, thank God."

Stupid Runt, thought Larrea as he took a sip of the already half-cold chocolate. *Why were you such a fool as to allow a business like that to go under?* As he was silently telling himself this, another equally silent voice piped up. Andrade: *Who are you to reproach that man for anything, when you risked your entire business on a single card with a gringo who crossed your path one day?* Larrea: *Who are you to scold me like that, Andrade?* Andrade: *I've only come to remind you of what you should never forget.* Larrea: *Well, just you forget me and let me find out what this wine business is all about.* Andrade: *Why, if you're not even going to get a sniff of it? I know, brother, I know. But if only you and I were young enough and had our former strength . . . If only we could start all over again . . .*

The phantom of his agent in Mexico vanished among the intricate moldings of the ceiling the moment Larrea replaced his cup on its saucer.

"So tell me, my friend, what commercial value are we talking about for this wine trade?"

"It represents more or less twenty percent of Spain's total exports. It spearheads our national economy."

Holy Mother of God. What a fool you were, Luis Montalvo. And you, Gustavo Zayas, the king of billiards in Havana. Why, after inheriting from your lunatic of a cousin, didn't you return at once to your homeland to restore the fortunes of your disastrous family legacy? Why did you insist on risking everything with me? Why did you try your luck in such a crazy manner? Fortunately, Fatou's great desire to explain shook him out of these reflections.

"In short, now that our former colonies are on their own and all we

Spaniards have left are the Antilles and the Philippines, what is saving
our ports and markets from going bankrupt is having been able to re-
direct our overseas trade toward England and Europe."

"I see . . ." muttered Larrea.

"Of course, if one day the children of Britannia stop drinking sherry
and we find winds of independence blowing in the Caribbean and the
Pacific as well, then the province of Cádiz and all of us within it will
sink without a trace. So here's to sherry, if only for that reason . . ." said
Fatou, raising his cup with an ironic smile.

Larrea copied him, with little enthusiasm.

Discreet coughs from the butler interrupted their toast. "Don Antonio, excuse me, but Don Alvaro Toledo is waiting for you in the
reception room," he announced. This brought their pleasant conversation to a close, and each of them went about his business. Fatou
went downstairs to catch up with the appointment he was late for. And
Mauro Larrea was left to fill the hours of waiting as best he could, and
to do battle once more against his feeling of unease.

He set off down Calle de la Verónica, accompanied by Santos Huesos. The mining Don Quixote and the Chichimec Sancho, with no
horse or donkey to ride. Just to see. And perhaps to think.

Ever since he had arrived in the Americas at the age of twenty-two
with two children and a couple of bundles of old clothes, the name of
this city had constantly resounded in his brain. Cádiz, the mythical city
of Cádiz, the far end of the umbilical cord that continued to unite the
New World with its enfeebled mother country even though nearly all
her infants had already turned their backs on her. Cádiz, from which
so much came, and to where less and less returned.

He had been constrained to journey to Mexico from Bordeaux,
since relations between the Spanish metropolis and its rebel former
colony were extremely tense, and in the years when Spain refused to
acknowledge Mexico's independence, maritime traffic was much easier

from the French ports. That was why Larrea never really knew what this legendary port—the southern gateway to the Americas—was like. And that windy autumn morning when the levanter blew in from Africa with spectacular gusts, when he could finally explore its nooks and crannies and get an overall view of it, up and down and from all sides, he did not recognize it. In his mind he had idealized Cádiz as a huge, bustling metropolis, but however hard he looked he could not find any trace of that.

Its population was three or four times smaller than Havana's, and it was infinitely less opulent than the ancient capital of the Aztecs. Surrounded by the sea, it was modest but charming, with its narrow streets, its houses all the same height, and the watchtowers from which ships entering the bay or departing for other continents could be seen. Without ostentation or brilliance; reserved, attractive, and manageable. *So this is Cádiz,* he told himself.

There was no lack of people thronging the streets, almost all of them walking and almost all the same skin color. Stopping unhurriedly to greet one another, exchange a few words, a message, or some gossip, or to complain of the treacherous wind raising the women's skirts and stealing papers and hats from the men. Negotiating, trading, settling their business. But this scene was nothing like the thunderous, uncontrollable din of the cities in the Americas. There was no trace of the tumult of Mexican Indians crying their wares or of the slaves hurrying through the pearl of the Antilles, carrying huge blocks of ice or sacks of coffee on their shoulders.

As he walked through Plaza de Isabel II and along Calle Nueva, he found no cafés as splendid as La Dominica or El Louvre. There was not even a tenth the number of carriages on Calle Ancha as on a similar street in Havana, nor any grand theaters like El Tacón. Nor could he see any monumental churches, or heraldic coats of arms, or palatial mansions similar to those of the sugar aristocracy in Cuba or the old miners of the Mexican viceroyalty. None of the squares could compare with the vast Zócalo he used to cross almost every day in his carriage before fortune turned her back on him. And the gentle Alameda leading down to the bay was nothing like the splendid paseos of Bucareli and the Prado, where Creoles from Mexico City and Havana enjoyed a ride in their carriages and landaus to see and be seen. No sign of the chaos of animals, people, and buildings filling the streets of the New World that he had so recently left behind. Spain was withdrawing into itself, and little remained of the glorious empire on which the sun never set. For good or ill, everybody was being forced to become the master of his own destiny. *So this is Cádiz,* he repeated to himself.

They went into a fried-fish stall to eat, and then walked down toward the sea. Nobody seemed surprised by the presence of a Mexican Indian with a lustrous head of hair alongside a foreign gentleman: they were more than accustomed to seeing people of a different color and way of speaking. As the gusts of wind ruffled the hair on both men, lifting the tails of Larrea's frock coat and Santos Huesos's colorful poncho, they stared at the ocean from the Banda del Vendaval. And Mauro Larrea finally thought he understood. How could he, a ruined miner, comprehend everything Cádiz was or had been: what had happened over the centuries on its streets and quays; what was discussed in its social circles or behind closed doors; what had been defended from its walls and bulwarks; what promises had been made in its churches; what courage it had shown in adverse times; or what cargo had been loaded and unloaded on ships that raced to the Indies and back, time and time again? What could he know about this city and this world if for decades he had not spoken or thought or even felt like a Spaniard, if his essence wherever he set his foot was that of a permanent foreigner, a pure ambiguity—an exile from two countries, the child of a double uprooting, not properly belonging anywhere, or with a place of his own to return to?

Evening was falling by the time he and Santos Huesos climbed back up the slope of Calle de la Verónica toward the Fatou family residence. They were greeted between the coughs of the ancient butler, Genaro, inherited by the young couple along with the house and business.

"Soon after you left this morning a lady came asking for you, Don Mauro. She called again after lunch, around three o'clock."'

Larrea frowned, at a loss, as the rickety old man held a silver platter out to him. On it was a simple card. White, spotless, distinguished.

MRS. SOL CLAYDON

29, CHESTER SQUARE, BELGRAVIA

LONDON

The last two lines had been firmly crossed out. Underneath, in handwriting, was a new address:

Plaza del Cabildo Viejo 5, Jerez

CHAPTER TWENTY-SEVEN

⟨◈⟩

As agreed, Larrea arrived at Don Senén's office at eleven in the morning. The notary proceeded to introduce the land agent Don Amador Zarco, an expert in assessing the value and transfer of farms and haciendas throughout the Jerez region. A large, middle-aged man built like a butcher, with plump fingers and a strong Andalusian accent, Don Amador was dressed like a well-off farm owner, with a wide-brimmed hat and a black sash around his waist.

After their mutual greetings and amid the sounds floating in from the noisy Calle Lancería, the agent proceeded to describe the properties in great detail and give his estimates of their worth. Forty-nine acres of vineyards with its ranch, wells, cisterns, and the corresponding equipment. A winery in Calle del Muro with its warehouse, offices, storerooms, and other facilities, not to mention hundreds of barrels—many but not all of them empty—a variety of tools and a cooper's workshop. A three-storied house on Calle de la Tornería with seventeen rooms, a main courtyard, another rear yard, servants' quarters, coach houses and stables, as well as other ancient buildings that he proceeded to describe in detail.

Mauro Larrea listened with all his attention and when, after a long, tedious list, Don Amador announced the estimated value of each of these properties, he almost thumped the table and let out a fierce whoop of joy. With that money he could cancel at a stroke at least two of the three installments of the debt he owed to Tadeo Carrús and celebrate his son Nico's wedding in style. Jerez was in a fervor thanks to its wine and its trade. Everyone had told him as much, and so he would be able to sell first the winery and then the vineyard, or the reverse, in no time at all. Or possibly the house first and then . . . in any case, he was about to emerge from the well and see the light.

While Larrea was savoring his good fortune, the notary and the land agent exchanged looks. The agent cleared his throat:

"Señor Larrea, there is one condition," he said, jerking the miner out of his daydreams, "which to some extent governs any further proceedings."

"And what might that be?"

His mind was racing. Was it that everything was in such a deplorable state that this would somewhat reduce the price of the properties? He didn't care: he was prepared to settle for less. Or perhaps that some of the goods would take longer than others to be sold? No matter, they could send him the final sum all in good time. He meanwhile would return to Mexico and take up the reins of his life where he had left them.

It was the notary who spoke next.

"Well, it is something we had not contemplated, something I discovered when we finally found a copy of the last wishes of Don Matías Montalvo, the grandfather of Don Luis and his cousin Don Gustavo Zayas. It is a clause in the will that the patriarch insisted on: the family properties were to be indivisible."

"Explain, would you?"

"Twenty years."

"What about twenty years?"

"By the irrevocable decision of the testator, twenty years must pass from the moment of his death before the main items of the inheritance can be split and put up for sale independently of each other."

Frowning, Larrea leaned uncomfortably forward in his chair.

"And how long will it be until this condition is met?"

"Eleven and a half months."

"Almost a year, then," Larrea said sourly.

"Not as long as that," retorted the agent, trying to sound positive.

"The way I interpret it," the notary continued, "is that this is a way of guaranteeing the continuity of everything built up by the deceased patriarch. *Testamentum est voluntatis nostrae iusta sententia de eo quod quis post mortem suam fieri velit.*"

Enough of your damned Latin! Larrea almost shouted. Instead, he clenched his fists and restrained himself as he waited for clarification.

"As the Romans put it, my friend: a will is the just expression of what one wishes to see done after one's death. Matías Montalvo's restrictive clause may not be very common, but it's not the first time I've seen something similar. It is usually stipulated in cases where the testator does not completely trust the heirs' commitment to continuity. And so this clause shows that the good old man did not exactly trust his own descendants."

"In short, that means . . ."

It was the land agent who made things clear, in his thick Andalusian accent.

"It means that everything has to be sold together: mansion, winery, and vineyard. Which, and I hope I am wrong in this, I don't think is going to be easy in the short term. These are good times in this region, and the wine trade attracts capital day and night, with people coming here from places that most people cannot even locate on a map. But with everything bundled up together like that, I'm not sure. There will be some who want a vineyard, but not a house or winery. Others who want the winery, but not a vineyard or house. And I know people who are looking for a house, but not vines or a winery."

"Be that as it may," the notary interrupted him, in an attempt to restore calm, "it's not such a long wait."

A year isn't a long wait? Larrea almost roared at him. *You have no idea what a year means at this point in my life. What do you know about my needs and obligations?* He only just managed to restrain himself.

"How about renting?" he asked, stroking the scar on his hand.

"Renting the properties? I'm afraid you won't be able to do that, either: it is also expressly forbidden in the will. Not sold or rented. If that had not been the case, Luisito Montalvo would have been sure to look for someone to rent the properties and so make money out of them. Don Matías was a farsighted man: he wanted to be sure that the jewels among his assets would stay as a *pro indiviso* lot. All or nothing."

There was a fierce intake of breath from Larrea, who was no longer hiding his frustration. Then he expelled all the air.

"Damn the old man," he said out loud, stroking his jaw.

"If it's any consolation, I very much doubt that Don Gustavo Zayas had any knowledge of that clause in the will when you two agreed on the transaction."

Through Larrea's mind flashed the memory of La Chucha's brothel and the ivory billiard balls shooting across the green baize as if possessed. The brutal shots he and Zayas had played, their fingers covered in talc and chalk. Their aching bodies, unshaven cheeks, and disheveled hair; their unbuttoned shirts, the sweat. He, too, doubted very much whether at a time like that his adversary had any thought of such legal technicalities.

"Anyway, Don Mauro," the land agent said, "if you so wish, I'll set about the task at once."

"What is your commission, my friend?"

"The normal figure is a tenth part."

"I'll give you fifteen percent if you can sort it out in a month."

The agent's jowls shook like a cow's udder.

"That seems very difficult to me, sir."

"And twenty if you're able to resolve it within two weeks."

The agent stroked his chin. Holy Mother of God! Larrea went still further.

"Or a quarter of the price if you can find me a purchaser before next Friday."

The land agent walked away, bemused. As he replaced his hat and started off down Calle Lancería, he remembered what he had been hearing for years about these returned Spaniards from the colonies. Sure of themselves, and resolute: that was what he had been told about them—those Indianos who had become millionaires overseas and who in recent years had made the return journey and were buying land and vineyards like someone buying lupine seeds to eat from the market.

"Hasn't the fellow just offered me the biggest commission in my life without so much as blinking?" he said out loud, bringing his great bulk to a stop in the middle of the street. Two women passing by looked at him as if he were raving, but he did not even notice. *This Larrea fellow is selling, not buying,* he reminded himself. But his attitude fit exactly all that he had heard: not just determined, but bold. He spat on the ground. *What a rogue that Indiano is,* he thought. With a touch of envy. Or admiration.

Oblivious to the land agent's reflections out in the street, Mauro Larrea and the notary continued signing documents and completing the final legal requirements. It was all over in half an hour.

"Are you going to decide to move to Jerez while all this is settled, my friend? Or are you thinking of staying on in Cádiz? Or perhaps returning to Mexico to await the outcome?"

"For the moment I'm not sure, Don Senén; this latest news has considerably upset my plans. I'll have to think closely about what best suits me. As soon as I decide anything definite, I'll let you know."

Santos Huesos was waiting for him in the office doorway. The two of them set off through the puddles that a light morning rain had brought. The rain had ceased as suddenly as it had begun. They walked past the Consistorio council building, through Plaza de la Yerba and Plaza de los Plateros, and finally started down the narrow Calle de la Tornería.

"Have you got the keys, lad?" he asked Santos Huesos.

"Of course, *patrón*."

"Then let's go to the house."

Neither of them had any real idea for what reason.

Unlike the previous day and his lengthy walk around Cádiz, when he had observed everything and tried to analyze it, on this occasion Larrea scarcely noticed his surroundings. He was looking inside himself. Trying to take in what the land agent and the notary had just told him. None of the whitewashed façades, the wrought-iron grilles, or the activities of the passersby interested him in the slightest. All that was consuming him was the thought that he had a fortune within his grasp but very little possibility of seizing it.

"Go and take a look," he said to Santos as he opened the studded wooden gate. "See if you can find somewhere for us to eat."

As he crossed the courtyard with its filthy tiles and withered leaves soaked by the rainwater from earlier that morning, he was again struck by the sense of decay. He walked slowly through all the rooms: first on the ground floor, then on the one above. The moldering main rooms; the inhospitable bedrooms. The tiny, bare chapel, as cold as the grave. No altar, no chalice, no wine decanter, no little bells.

He heard footsteps on the staircase behind him, and asked without turning around:

"Back already, my friend?"

His voice echoed through the empty mansion as he continued to consider the chapel. Not even a simple crucifix on the wall. All he could see was a bulky shape in one corner covered with a piece of cloth. Pulling it away, he found a small prayer stool underneath. Its maroon cloth was half eaten away by rats, and some of the crossbars had broken off. It was just about big enough for a small child to kneel on.

"My grandfather Matías had it made for my first Communion."

He spun around in consternation.

"What he never found out was that the night before that great day, my cousins, my sister, and I forced open the tabernacle and each of us ate four or five of the holy wafers. Delighted to meet you at last, Señor Larrea. Welcome to Jerez."

Her face was delicate and her whole appearance harmonious. Her big brown eyes were brimming with curiosity.

"Sol Claydon," she said, extending a gloved hand. "Although for part of my life I was also Soledad Montalvo. And this was my home."

CHAPTER TWENTY-EIGHT

❧

M auro Larrea was slow to react, searching for words that would not betray his feeling of being the intruder in the mansion.

She spoke before he could recover.

"I understand you are the new owner."

"Forgive me for not returning your visit, madam. I received your card yesterday, and . . ."

She raised her chin slightly, and that was enough to make any further excuses unnecessary. No need, she seemed to be saying.

"I had things to attend to in Cádiz; I simply wanted to pay my respects."

His mind was in turmoil. *My God, what the devil do you say to a woman in her position? A woman with blood ties to what you now possess thanks to a few diabolical games of billiards? Someone who peers so intently inside you to find out who you are and what on earth you are doing somewhere where you have no right to be.*

At a loss for words, he resorted to gestures, straightening his broad shoulders and sweeping his hat over his heart. And a nod of the head, a fleeting but unmistakable gesture of thanks to this beautiful being who had just made her appearance in his troubled noonday. *Where did you come from, and what are you after?* he would have liked to ask. *What do you want from me?*

She was wearing a short light-gray cloak. Underneath was a turquoise morning dress. Forty splendid years old, give or take a year, he calculated. A pair of kid gloves and hazel-colored hair drawn up in a neat chignon. A small hat with two elegant pheasant feathers artfully attached to one side. No jewelry that he could see.

"I hear you've come from the Americas."'

"You've been well informed."

"And apparently it was my first cousin Gustavo Zayas who transferred these properties into your name."

"They came to me through him, indeed."

They were now closer to one another, he having left the chapel, and she having finished climbing the stairs. The unwelcoming gallery, which in its days of former glory had seen the comings and goings of the Montalvo family, their friends, belongings, servants, and loved ones, was now the backdrop for this unlikely conversation between the new owner and the descendant of the previous ones.

"At a reasonable price?"

"Let's just say at one that was advantageous to my interests."

Sol Claydon allowed several seconds to go by, continuing to look straight at this man with his impressive frame and well-defined features who was standing before her in an attitude that was a mixture of respect and arrogance. He waited without reacting, struggling to ensure that beneath his apparent calm appearance she would not notice the profound uneasiness nagging at him.

"What about Luis?" she went on. "Did you also meet my cousin Luis?"

"Never," he replied as firmly as possible, so that she would not be in the slightest doubt that he had ever had anything to do with that man's journey to Cuba or his sad destiny there. He added: "His death occurred before I arrived in Havana, and so I can't offer any further details. I'm sorry."

At this, she turned her eyes from him and looked around her, at the peeling walls, the dirt, the desolation.

"What a shame you did not have the chance to see this in another time."

She gave a slight smile, a hint of bitter nostalgia apparent at the corners of her mouth.

"Ever since receiving the news the day before yesterday that a prosperous gentleman from the New World was the new owner of our estate, I've been unable to stop reflecting on what my role ought to be in this unexpected turn of events."

"We have only just finished going through all the documents; they are all legal and aboveboard," he said defensively. He sounded brusque, and was immediately sorry for it. He made an attempt to be more neutral: "If you wish, you can verify everything at Don Senén Blanco's office."

Now there was a hint of subtle irony to her half smile.

"Naturally, I have already done so."

Naturally. Or what were you thinking, you fool: that you were going to fleece her family and she was going to accept it on your say-so?

"What I was hoping," she went on, "was to find a way to add to this transfer, as one might call it, some kind of ceremonial note, however slight. And, if you like, to add a touch of humanity."

He had not the slightest idea of what she meant by this, but he nodded.

"Whatever you wish, madam, of course."

With a look steeped in melancholy she gazed once more at the dreadful state of what had once been her home. He took advantage to take a good look at her. Her grace, her poise, her equanimity.

"I'm not here to hold you to account, Señor Larrea. As you can imagine, this situation is far from pleasant for me, but I understand that it is perfectly legal and as such I must accept it."

He dipped his head again in recognition of her consideration.

"That being the case, and making the best of it that I can, as the last descendant of the unfortunate line of the Montalvos in Jerez, and before all memory of us is erased forever, I am here simply to symbolically lower our colors and to wish you all the best for the future."

"Thank you for your kindness, Señora Claydon. But you might possibly be interested to know that I have no intention of keeping these properties. I am only in Spain temporarily, in order to arrange their sale and then to leave once more."

"That is of no matter. However brief your stay may be, I don't think it would go amiss for you to learn something about those of us who lived under these roofs before darkness fell on us. Would you care to come with me?"

Without waiting for a reply, she set off determinedly for the main salon. He had no choice but to follow.

It must have been hard for the Runt to match his physique with that of a good-looking family like the Montalvos. That was what the notary had told him while they were eating at the Victoria Inn a couple of days earlier. This was confirmed by this attractive woman with her easy step and fine bones who moved so freely past the torn wall hangings. Mauro Larrea, the supposedly powerful and rich returned emigrant, found himself robbed of all ability to respond, and so simply listened in silence.

"It was here that the big parties, dances, and receptions were organized. Our grandparents' name days, the end of the wine harvest, our baptisms . . . There were carpets from Brussels and damask curtains, with a huge chandelier of crystal and bronze suspended from the ceiling. On that wall hung a Flemish tapestry with an extraordinary hunting scene, and there, between the window balconies, were some divine Venetian mirrors that my parents brought back from their honeymoon in Italy. They multiplied the light from the candles a hundredfold."

She walked around the dark salon without looking at him. Her voice was bewitching, an Andalusian cadence somewhat tempered by her frequent use of English. She went over to the fireplace, glancing down at the dead pigeon that was still there on the floor. Then she moved on to the dining room.

"When we were ten, we were allowed to sit at table with the adults. It was a great occasion, a kind of coming out in society for children. At this table the best vintages from our winery were drunk, and French wine, too, lots of champagne. At Christmas, Paca, the cook, would kill three turkeys, and after dinner Uncle Luis and my father would bring in some Gypsies with their guitars, tambourines, and castanets. They would sing carols for us and dance, and afterward they took away what was left from our feast."

She lifted the dust sheet from one of the few remaining chairs, then another, and a third, but could not find what she was looking for. She made a slight sound of annoyance.

"I wanted to show you our grandparents' chairs: I'd forgotten they'd gone, too. The arms were carved like a lion's claws: when I was really young they scared me stiff, but as I grew they began to fascinate me. During our wedding lunch, our grandparents let Edward and me sit in them. That was the only occasion they did not occupy their customary seats."

The name of her husband was what least interested Mauro about her at that moment, and so it quickly slipped his mind. Instead he was taking in all the scraps and images of a bygone age that she evoked as they went from room to room. She dismissed the bedrooms and the smaller rooms with a few insignificant remarks, until they came back to the part of the gallery where they had first met. She went into the last room. It was completely bare and gave no clue as to what it had once been.

"And this was the game room. Our favorite place. Señor Larrea, do you have a game room in your house in . . . ?"

There were three seconds of silence before he completed the sentence.

"In Mexico. My home is in Mexico City. And, yes, it might be said that I have a game room there, too."

At least I did, he thought. *Now it is teetering on the brink, and however incredible it might seem, it depends on this house of yours whether I keep or lose it.*

"And what games do you play there?" she asked pleasantly.

"A bit of everything."

"Billiards, for example?"

He hid his suspicions beneath a false casualness.

"Yes, madam. We also play billiards."

"In here we used to have a magnificent mahogany table," she said, standing in the center of the room and stretching out her slender silk-swathed arms. "My father and my uncles used to play superb games that often lasted all night. My grandmother was like a harpy when she saw his friends coming downstairs in the early morning, disheveled after a night's entertainment."

Long journeys to Italy, celebrations with Gypsies and guitars, games of billiards with friends until the early hours. Larrea was beginning to understand old Don Matías's determination to keep his descendants on a tight rein after his death.

"As we became a little older," Soledad went on, "grandfather took on a billiard teacher for my cousins. He was a rather eccentric Frenchman who was a real master. My sister Inés and I would slip in to watch them: it was far more interesting than sitting and doing embroidery for the orphans in the foundling hospital, as they used to try to make us do."

So that's where your skill came from, Zayas, Larrea thought, recalling the way his opponent had played: the complicated shots, the subtle ricochets. And under the scrutiny of this pair of eyes trying to penetrate his armor as a solid, wealthy miner from far away, he found it impossible to say nothing.

"I had the occasion to play your cousin Gustavo at billiards in Havana."

As a dark, leaden cloud obscures the sun, Soledad Montalvo's eyes suddenly seemed to darken.

"Is that so?" she said, her voice icy.

"One night. Two games."

She took several steps toward the door, as though she had not heard him or wished to put an end to this particular conversation. All of a sudden she stopped and turned to face him.

"He was always the best player of all. I don't know if he told you, but he never lived permanently in Jerez. When they married, his parents—my uncle and aunt—set up house in Seville, but he spent long periods here with us: Christmas, Easter, the wine harvest. He always dreamt of coming here: to him, this was paradise. Then he left for good, and I haven't heard anything of him for the past two decades."

She paused a few moments before asking: "How is he?"

Ruined. Tormented. Unhappy, without a doubt. Tied to a ghastly woman he doesn't love. And I've done my bit to push him even further under. Larrea could have said all this to her, but instead he bit his tongue.

"Well, I suppose," he lied instead. "We did not meet very often, except on social occasions. We only played billiards together once. After that . . . after that we were involved in a few business matters, and for a variety of reasons we ended up carrying out the operation that led to these properties passing into my hands."

He had tried to be as vague as possible without sounding false; convincing without giving anything away. Since he had been so imprecise, he was expecting her to come back with the awkward questions for which he had no answer. About one cousin or the other, possibly even about the woman with whom they had formed a triangle in Luis's final days.

However, Sol Claydon's curiosity led her in another direction.

"And who won those games?"

Even though he was trying with all his might to keep it silent, he finally heard inside his head the voice he had not wanted to hear. *Don't be such a fool! Keep your mouth shut! Change the conversation right now; don't go there, Mauro, don't go there.* And silently he replied: *Be quiet, Elias, let me share with this woman the only wretched triumph I've had in a very long time. Can't you see that, despite her polite attention, to her I'm nothing more than an upstart, a usurper? Let me show her a little pride, brother. It's all I have left; don't make me swallow that as well.*

"I did."

He tried to protect himself. So that Soledad Montalvo would not continue trying to find out about his unfortunate rival, he immediately asked another question.

"Was your cousin Luis also a billiards enthusiast?"

Her face took on a nostalgic look.

"It was impossible for him. He was always a small, weak child, a tiny little thing. And from about the age of eleven or twelve, he ceased to grow altogether. He was seen by doctors all over Spain; they even took him to Berlin to be examined by a supposedly miracle-working specialist. They tortured the poor child: iron calipers, leather thongs to hang him by his feet. But no one could find the cause or the cure."

She ended in almost a whisper: "I can still hardly believe that Little Runt is dead."

Little Runt, she called him, the vivid popular expression from the region contrasting with her usual cosmopolitan sophistication. When she mentioned Luis, all the coldness she had shown when talking about Gustavo suddenly became tenderness, as if the two cousins represented opposite poles in her affections.

"According to what I heard from the notary," said Larrea, "nobody knew he was in Cuba. Or that he had passed away."

She smiled once more, again with that hint of irony on her lips.

"Those who needed to know did."

She fell silent, staring straight at him as though weighing up if it was worth continuing to satisfy the curiosity of a stranger.

"The only people who knew were his doctor and I," she finally conceded. "We heard the news of his death a few weeks ago, when Dr. Ysasi received a letter from Gustavo. We were still waiting to receive the death certificate to announce his passing and to organize the funeral."

"I'm sorry to have been the one to bring everything to a head so quickly."

She shrugged graciously, as if to say, *What can one do?*

Don't go any further, you idiot. Don't even think it. These peremptory warnings whipped through his brain, but he quickly sidestepped them.

"Or perhaps your cousin was intending to come to Jerez to bring the news himself."

Sol Claydon's brown eyes opened as big as saucers. She asked incredulously: "Was that truly his intention?"

"I believe he was considering it, although in the end he rejected the idea."

What emerged from her throat was almost a sob.

"Gustavo back in Jerez, my goodness . . ."

There was noise from down below. Santos Huesos had just returned. With that sixth sense of his that led him to detect any tense situation from leagues away, he immediately realized his master was not alone and stole away again.

By then, however, Sol Claydon had recovered her aplomb.

"Well, these are unfortunate family questions I won't bore you with any further, Señor Larrea," she said. The friendly tone had returned to her voice. "I think I've taken up far too much of your time; as I said when I arrived, my only wish was to welcome you here. And possibly, deep down, to renew my acquaintance with my past in this house before bidding it a final good-bye."

She hesitated, as if unsure whether or not to continue.

"Do you know that for years we thought my daughters would be Luis's heirs? That was what was in his original will."

So he changed his will at the last moment, did he? Damn and blast him. Why? An unexpected change that favored Gustavo Zayas and Carola Gorostiza. And, by extension, him. A cold sweat trickled down his back. *Cut loose, my friend. Step away; keep out of it. That crazy sister of your son's future father-in-law has already got you into enough trouble.*

Trying to disguise his confusion, Larrea replied in all sincerity: "I hadn't the faintest idea."

"Well, I'm afraid that is how it is."

Had Sol Claydon been a different kind of woman, she might possibly have aroused at least a hint of compassion amid his wariness. But the last of the Montalvos was not the sort to provoke pity. That was why she gave him no time to react.

"I have four of them, you know. The eldest is nineteen, the youngest has just turned eleven. They're half-English, half-Spanish."

This was followed by a brief pause, and then another question that, like most of the others, caught him off guard.

"Do you have children, Mauro?"

She had called him by his first name, and something stirred inside him. It had been a long time since any woman had penetrated his intimate world in this way. Far too long.

He swallowed.

"Two."

"And a wife? Is there a Señora Larrea waiting for you somewhere?"

"Not for many years now."

"I'm truly sorry. My husband is English. We used to live in London, but we have always been coming and going to Jerez, and we decided to settle here almost two months ago. I trust you will do us the honor of dining with us one of these days."

With this vague invitation that concluded nothing and committed her to nothing, she turned to go. As she approached the broad staircase that had once been one of the treasures of the mansion, she glanced with distaste at the crust of dirt on the banister. Seeing the state it was in, she decided not to risk touching the wood. She started down without leaning on it, raising her skirt so that her feet would not get caught in her petticoats or step in the mess on the wet marble.

In three bounds he was beside her.

"Be careful. Hold on to me."

He crooked his right elbow, and she clung to it without false modesty. Although there were several layers of clothing between them, he could sense her heartbeat and her skin. Then, stirred by something that had no name or trace in his memory, the miner laid his huge, disfigured left hand on the glove of Sol Claydon, of Soledad Montalvo, of the woman she was now and the child she had been. As if wanting to emphasize his support to avoid any untoward fall. Or as though trying to guarantee that, despite having robbed her daughters of their legacy and having turned their lives upside down, this disturbing individual who had come from across the ocean, this man who looked like some opportunistic migrant and spoke in only half-truths, was someone she could put her trust in.

They descended the stairs arm-in-arm, step after step, without a word. Separated by the worlds they inhabited and by their own interests, joined by the proximity of their bodies.

At the bottom, she moved away from him and murmured her thanks. He replied with a hoarse "Don't mention it."

As he studied her slender back and the way her skirts swept the tiles of the threshold on her way out, Mauro Larrea was certain that this luminous woman's soul must harbor dark shadows. And a twinge in his stomach gave him a sense of foreboding that he himself had now become one of those shadows.

He lost sight of her when she turned into Calle de la Tornería. It was only then that he realized the hand he had held hers in was still clenched, as though reluctant to let go of her.

CHAPTER TWENTY-NINE

❧

That night, Mauro Larrea returned to the Fatou family house in Cádiz. The following day, while conversing with his hosts at the dinner table, with ancestors staring down at them from the walls, churros on the table, and thick chocolate steaming in cups from the new bride's dowry, Larrea informed them that he had decided to install himself in Jerez.

"I think that's the most sensible idea; it will be easier for me to negotiate with any potential purchasers from there, and to look after all the matters arising from the transaction."

"But tell us, Don Mauro, if it's not being rude," said Paulita hesitantly, "is the place you're going to move into in a proper state? Because if there's anything you need . . ." She paused to look across at her husband, as if seeking his support.

"Of course you have only to ask," he finished on her behalf. "Utensils, furniture—anything you think we could help you with. We have plenty of everything in our storehouses. The unfortunate deaths of various members of the family in recent years have obliged us to close three houses."

It would have been so easy to say yes, to accept the young couple's offer, fill a couple of carts to the brim with solid armchairs and mat-tresses, china cabinets, screens, and wardrobes, which would make his new home a little more comfortable. But it seemed wiser not to build bridges or create more commitments than were strictly necessary.

"I thank you with all my heart, but I think I've imposed myself on you quite enough already."

Before he had returned to Cádiz, Larrea had instructed Santos Hue-sos to remain behind in the mansion on Calle de la Tornería. "Manage this well, my lad," he told him, handing him money before leaving. Their passages from Havana had already cost him a large part of his scant capital, and so they had to be careful about what they spent.

"Go out at first light to see what you can find to spruce up a pair of rooms there for us to live in; we'll keep the others locked. Find people to clean the place up, buy only the minimum, and see which remaining articles from the previous owners we can still use."

"I don't want to contradict you, *patrón*, but are you sure that you and I are going to live here?"

"What's wrong, Santos Huesos? It seems to me you've become very fussy. Where did you grow up, if not in the mountains of San Miguelito? And me, in a wretched forge. Have you forgotten the nights we spent sleeping on the ground with bonfires at Real de Catorce? And, more recently, the journey we made with those Chinaco soldiers from Mexico City to Veracruz? Get a move on and stop complaining; you sound like an old maid on her way to morning Mass."

"I've no wish to speak of what is none of my business, Don Mauro, but what are people going to think when they discover you're living in this ruin? They all believe you're a Mexican silver millionaire."

An extravagant millionaire come from overseas, that was exactly what Larrea had intended his façade to be. But what did their opinion of him matter if he intended to return whence he came as soon as he had sold everything? Nobody in that town would ever hear of him again.

In spite of his denials, Fatou's wife could not resist fulfilling her domestic role. That was how she had seen her mother and mother-in-law behave in their lifetimes, and she wanted to do likewise in her own household now that she was married. No doubt this was the first opportunity she had found to show herself a good hostess to such a prepossessing guest. And so, in midmorning, while Larrea was gathering up the last of his things and closing his trunks, wondering for the umpteenth time whether this move was a mistake or not, Paulita knocked timidly at his bedroom door.

"Forgive the intrusion, Don Mauro, but I've taken the liberty of preparing a few sets of bed linen and a few other little things to help you be more comfortable. You can return them when you come back to Cádiz to board ship again. If as you say your new home has been shut up for a long time, even if it has everything you need in it, doubtless it will be damp and musty."

God bless you, child, he was on the point of saying.

"Since you've gone to all the trouble, it would be very impolite of me not to accept your kindness. I promise to return it all to you in perfect condition."

He heard discreet little coughs from the butler, Genaro, behind him.

"Forgive me for interrupting you, Señorita. Don Antoñito has asked me to give this to Don Mauro."

"Don Antonio and Señora, not Señorita, Genaro," the young woman whispered, correcting the old man for what must have been the hundredth time. "Now we are Don Antonio and Señora: How often do I have to tell you?"

Too many years had gone by for him to change his ways, the old servant must have thought, although he did not seem greatly troubled: he had seen them both since their birth. Ignoring the innocent spouse, he handed their guest a small bundle covered in stamps from Havana. The neat handwriting was Calafat's.

"I'll leave you with your correspondence. I don't want to detain you any longer," said Paulita. She would have liked to list everything she was intending to lend him, so that he could see how carefully she had chosen. Four sets of linen sheets, half a dozen cotton towels, two embroidered muslin tablecloths, all of them perfumed with camphor and rosemary. In addition, several woolen blankets from Grazalema, white wax candles and some oil lamps, and . . .

By the time she had gone over the list in her mind, she was still out in the corridor and he had barricaded himself in his room. As there was no paper-knife at hand, he tore the bundle open with his teeth. This was urgent. He needed to know if the news came directly from the old banker in Havana and whether, as they had agreed, he had also sent news of his family in Mexico. Fortunately, there was plenty of both.

He began with Andrade's letter, anxious to know what he had found out about Nicolás's whereabouts. Yes, he had been found. In Paris, of course. The miner felt a surge of relief. Mariana will tell you the details, he read. There followed an update on his own disastrous financial position and a summary of events in the country he had left behind. His debts were more or less under control, but apart from the mansion on San Felipe Neri, which was hanging by a thread, there was nothing left of his once ample wealth. Mexico for its part was still bubbling like a cauldron: the guerrillas fighting Juárez were still causing trouble, while Liberals and Conservatives could not make peace. Wherever Andrade went, Larrea's friends and acquaintances asked after him: in the Café del Progreso, coming out of Mass at La Profesa, or during events at the Coliseo. Andrade assured all and sundry that his affairs abroad were flourishing. "No one suspects anything, but sort something out as quickly as possible, Mauro, by all that's holy. The Gorostiza family is still planning the wedding, even if your boy doesn't seem to know when he's coming back. He'll be sure to do so as soon as what little money he has left runs out. Luckily or not, we can't send him even a paltry amount." He ended with a "God bless you, brother" and a postscript: "For the moment I haven't heard a thing from Tadeo and Dimas Carrús."

Larrea then read the lengthy missive from Mariana with all the details about Nico. A brother of a friend's fiancé had bumped into him in Paris. This was in the early hours during a soirée in Place des Vosges, at the home of a Chilean lady with a somewhat loose reputation. He was surrounded by other whelps from the newly independent American republics, with several glasses of champagne inside him and pretty uncertain regarding his return to Mexico. He thought of going back shortly, he had said. Or perhaps not. Larrea almost crumpled the letter in disgust. *Brainless idiot, dissolute wretch,* he growled. *With that Gorostiza girl pining for you. Calm down, you fool,* he told himself. *At least we've found him and he is in one piece.* Even if, as his agent had noted, by now he must have little money left to go on living the high life. Which meant he would have no choice but to return to Mexico, where the wolves lay in wait for him. He preferred not to dwell on it, but carried on reading his daughter's letter. It was full of juicy titbits: the baby was still growing inside her, if it was a boy it was to be called Alonso, and her mother-in-law insisted it should be called Úrsula if it was a girl. She felt more pregnant every day, and spent all her time eating cakes in syrup and peanut bars. Once he had finished, Larrea looked at the date; a swift calculation made his stomach clench: by now his daughter, Mariana, must be about to give birth.

Finally it was Calafat's turn. The banker had sent him something that had arrived on the day after his departure from Havana from a town in the interior: Luis Montalvo's Spanish identity document and the death and burial certificates from the main parish of Villa Clara. *The very documents she is expecting,* he thought, remembering what Sol Claydon had said. Suddenly through his mind flashed her beautiful face and her easy manner. Her subtle irony, her elegant self-possession, her back when she walked away from him. *Keep on reading; don't get sidetracked,* he told himself. Although there were no details of these documents' origin, the banker appeared to have no doubt they were genuine. It was Gustavo Zayas himself who had forwarded them from Las Villas Province, where his coffee plantation was. And although this was not written anywhere, they were addressed not to Gustavo Zayas's own cousin or the doctor in Jerez whom she had mentioned but to Mauro Larrea. In case he needed to justify the facts they contained, wrote the old man. Or to pass them on to whoever it might concern.

∽

He left Cádiz at first light the next morning; his two trunks and the chest of linen went with him. The pouch with the countess's money stayed behind with Fatou for safekeeping.

When he reached Jerez, he noticed that the entrance and the court-yard to the house looked much cleaner than before.

"Santos Huesos, as soon as we get back to Mexico I'm going to ride to the hills of Potosí to ask your father for your hand in marriage."

The Chicimec Indian laughed to himself.

"All it took was to spread a few small coins around, *patrón.*"

The grime had diminished somewhat in the courtyard, on the stair-case, and on the gallery tiles; the floors in the main rooms had been swept and washed. The few pieces of furniture previously scattered throughout the rooms and attic had been brought together in what was once the game room to make a space that was more or less inhabitable.

"Should we bring in your trunks, then?"

"Better leave them all afternoon by the front entrance for everyone passing by to see. That way they will all think we have lots of baggage; we don't want anyone to know this is all we have."

And so the opulent leather trunks with their bronze borders and clasps were in full view of anybody who cared to come and peer through the wide-open gates. Until evening, when between the two of them they carried the trunks up to the first floor.

Thanks to the bed linen lent by sweet little Paulita, they slept soundly on their first night in the house. Larrea was awakened at dawn by a cockerel in a nearby yard. The bells of San Marcos brought him out of bed. Santos Huesos had already filled half a wineskin with water for him to wash in the yard behind the house, then served him breakfast in the room where the billiard table had once stood.

"I swear on my children you're worth your weight in gold, you rogue."

His servant smiled without a word as his master devoured the meal, not once asking where the bread and milk had come from, or the heavy earthenware crockery, which was colorful if rather chipped. Larrea ate slowly: he knew that after his breakfast there was no way he could postpone what had been on his mind since the day before. Unable to decide, he took a coin and left the decision to chance.

"Which hand, lad?" he said, putting them both behind his back.

"It'll be the same whatever I choose, I suppose."

"Come on, which one?"

"The right hand, then."

Larrea opened his empty hand, unsure if this was good or bad news.

If Santos had chosen the left one, where the coin was, that would have meant Larrea went to Sol Claydon's house to share with her the documents concerning her cousin Luis Montalvo. He had been considering this ever since he received the package from Calafat. After all, she was in Jerez and was, if not his legal heir, then at least his moral inheritor. The Little Runt, she had called him. And yet again he recalled her face and voice, her long arms as they stretched out to show him where the billiard table had been, the light touch of her hand, her narrow waist and harmonious way of walking as she took her leave. *Stop this nonsense, you idiot,* he roared silently to his conscience. But his servant had chosen his right hand. *So you keep the documents to yourself. Everyone here already knows that the cousin is dead; the notary Don Senén has all the proof he needs. Keep them even if you have no idea why or what for.*

"Santos, my boy"—Larrea jumped up from his chair—"I'll leave you to finish things here while I go and sort out some business in town."

His first trip to the winery had been in a carriage, accompanied by the notary. Now, on foot and in a strange place, it proved complicated to find. The old Arab quarter of Jerez with its tangle of narrow alleyways was a devilish labyrinth; the imposing mansions of the local aristocracy with their coats of arms stood alongside far more ordinary houses in a strange architectural jumble. On a couple of occasions he had to retrace his steps; more than once he stopped to ask a passerby, until finally he arrived at the winery on Calle del Muro. More than thirty yards of wall on a corner, crying out for a coat of whitewash. By the side of the wooden entrance gates, two old men were sitting on a stone bench.

"God be with you," said one of them.

"We've been expecting the master for several days now."

Between the two of them they could count fewer than eight teeth and more than a hundred and fifty years of age. They had weather-beaten, leathery faces, with lines that were more like furrows. Struggling to their feet, they removed their battered hats and bowed respectfully to him.

"A very good day to you, gentlemen."

"We heard you have taken over Don Matías's properties, and here we are, ready to serve you in any way."

"Well, the truth is, I don't know . . ."

"We can show you the winery and tell you everything you need to know."

How courteous these people from Jerez are, thought Larrea. *Sometimes they take the form of beautiful ladies; at others, skinny bodies on the edge of the grave, like these two.*

"Have you ever worked here?" he asked, extending his hand to both of them. The mere contact with the rough, calloused hands of the old men told him the answer was yes.

"Your servant here was the storeman for thirty-six years, and my relative here a few years longer. His name is Marcelino Cañada, and he's as deaf as a post. You'd do best to talk to me: Severiano Pontones, at your service."

They both wore rope sandals worn down by the cobbled streets, and rough cotton trousers with a broad black sash around the waist.

"Mauro Larrea, pleased to meet you. I've brought the key with me."

"There's no need, sir; all you have to do is push."

It only took a good shove with his shoulder for the wooden gate to give way, revealing a big rectangular space bordered with acacia trees. At the far end stood a building with a pitched roof. High and sober, it must have been completely white in its day, when it was whitewashed once a year. Now the bottom half was stained with black, moldy patches.

"Here on this side is where the offices are. That was where they did the accounts and the correspondence," said the deaf old man, raising his voice and pointing to the left of the building.

Three strides brought Larrea close. He peered in through a window, but all he could see were cobwebs and grime.

"They made off with all the furniture years ago."

"What did you say?"

"I'm telling the new master that they made off with the furniture years ago!"

"By the Virgin, it's been years . . ."

"And this was Don Matías's office. And the administrator's."

"This was the reception room for visitors and buyers."

"And behind is the barrel workshop."

"What was that?"

"The workshop, Marcelino, the workshop!"

Larrea kept on walking, ignoring their shouting, and soon came to the main building. Although it looked shut, he guessed that the big door would give way as easily as the gate onto the street.

He leaned the weight of the left side of his body against it and pushed.

Stillness. Rest. And a silence in the dark interior that made him shudder. That was his first impression when he stepped inside. A cathedral ceiling with exposed wooden beams, a beaten-earth floor, the light filtered by rush curtains hanging at the windows. And the smell. That smell. The aroma of wine that floated through the streets of Jerez and was multiplied a hundredfold in here.

Four naves communicated with one another thanks to arches and stylized columns. In front of him the floor was covered with hundreds of dark wooden casks piled up in three rows.

Orderly, dark, serene.

Behind him, as if in a token of respect, the old storemen fell silent.

CHAPTER THIRTY

L arrea went to attend to the rest of his business in a confused state, his eyes and nostrils still filled with the winery. Bewildered, disorientated by the sensation.

His steps took him next to Don Senén Blanco's office, to inform him that he had decided to settle in Jerez while he was waiting to sell. After that he again made his way along the narrow Calle de la Tornería. Back home.

"There was a visit for us, *patrón*."

Santos handed him something that he had been half expecting: an envelope with a blue wax seal on the back. Inside was a brief message written in small, firm handwriting on thick ivory paper. The Claydons had the honor of inviting him to dinner the following evening.

"Was it she who came?"

"She sent a maid, a foreign woman."

That evening they shut the street gates so that no one would see him roll up his sleeves and share the workload with his servant as they continued to make the mansion look more respectable. Bare-armed, and with the strength that in earlier days they had employed to descend mine shafts and penetrate along underground galleries, they now pulled up grass and weeds, tidied and fixed tiles on the walls and roof. They were covered in dirt and scratches. They cursed, blasphemed, spat. Until the sun set and there was nothing else for it but to stop.

The next morning was spent at the same task. It was impossible to tell how long their stay would be, and so they might as well fix up the house. At the same time, working with his hands and brute force as he once had to mine silver in the depths of the earth, Mauro Larrea kept his mind busy and let the hours pass by.

Night had already fallen by the time he left for Cabildo Viejo Square. It was also known as the Plaza de los Escribanos, because every morning this was where scriveners sat under awnings to attend to complainants and plaintiffs, mothers of the soldiery and lovers—anyone who needed to put in black-and-white whatever was coursing through their minds and hearts. Before that, with the last of the daylight, Larrea had scrubbed himself clean with one of the bergamot soaps that Mariana had added to his luggage, and then shaved in a cracked mirror that Santos Huesos had found in one of the attics. He dressed in his best evening wear, and even fished a bottle of Macassar oil out of one of the trunks and spread it generously over his thick hair. It had been a long time since he had taken such care over his appearance. *Go easy, you idiot,* he reproached himself when he realized why he was doing all this.

At this time of day, the handsome façades that embellished the square—the Renaissance town council building, the Gothic San Dionisio church, and the imposing private mansions—were deep in shadow, and the bustling activity in the streets had already begun to ease off. In Mexico, Mauro Larrea would never have dreamt of attending a dinner on foot. He always used to arrive in his carriage with his coachman, Laureano, dressed up in showy livery and the mares in their finest harnesses. Now he was striding down the winding streets of the old Arab quarter, feeling the effects of all his hard work in his aching muscles and with his hands deep in his pockets. Smelling the wine in the air, avoiding stray dogs and puddles, caught up in this alien world. And yet he was far from feeling ill at ease.

In spite of arriving at the appointed hour, it was a long while before someone answered his raps on the splendid bronze door knocker. A stiff, bald butler finally appeared and ushered him in. He walked across a fine marble-encrusted compass rose decorating the hallway. "Good evening, sir, please do come in," the man said to him in English as he accompanied him to a room on the right of the central courtyard. Unlike his open yard in Mexico and in the house where he was staying in Jerez, this was a veranda covered by a glass roof.

Once the butler had left, nobody came to greet him. It must be some foreign custom, he thought to himself. No other servant appeared, nor could he hear any of the domestics scurrying about that usually preceded a dinner. Nor was there the sound of footsteps from the family's four daughters.

Accompanied by the loud ticking of a magnificent clock over the lighted fireplace, Larrea decided to take a good look at the habitat of the last of the Montalvos. The oil paintings and watercolors decorating the walls. The heavy drapes, the vases filled with fresh flowers on their alabaster plinths. The thick carpets, the portraits, the oil lamps. More than ten minutes had gone by before at last he heard her steps in the hall and saw her enter the room, giving off a busy, energetic air as she arranged the folds of her skirt, trying to smile and sound natural.

"I'm sure you must be thinking that we are completely rude in this house. I beg you to forgive us."

He was so distracted and caught up by her whirlwind appearance that for a few moments his mind could not take in anything else. She was wearing a green velvet evening gown that exposed her attractive if somewhat bony shoulders, was gathered in at the waist, and had a neckline just high enough not to undermine her elegance.

"And, above all, I must ask you to excuse my husband. Some unexpected business has meant he had to leave Jerez. I'm extremely sorry, but he won't be able to join us this evening."

He was on the verge of saying "I'm not sorry, my dear; not sorry in the least." Probably her husband was an interesting man. Well traveled, educated, distinguished. And rich. The complete English gentleman. But even so . . .

He decided to be polite, however.

"If that's the case, perhaps you prefer to cancel the dinner. There will be another opportunity."

"Not in the slightest, not at all, I won't hear of it . . ." Sol Claydon insisted. She paused for an instant, as if realizing she needed to calm down. It was plain she had been caught up in something else and found it hard to readjust. Perhaps it was the demands on her time in her husband's absence, or some adolescent problem with one of her daughters, or a slight disagreement with her staff . . .

"Our cook would never forgive me," she added. "We brought her with us from London and as yet she has had little chance to demonstrate her skills for any guests."

"In that case . . ."

"Besides, if you're thinking you might be bored spending an evening alone with me, I should tell you that we will have company."

Larrea could not tell if there was any hint of irony in her words. He had no time to dwell on this, though, because at that moment, even though he had not heard any knock on the front door, another person entered the room.

"Ah, at last, Manuel, my dear."

Her greeting betrayed a sense of relief that did not go unnoticed by Larrea.

"Dr. Manuel Ysasi is our doctor, an old and cherished friend of the family, as were his father and grandfather before him. He is the one who attends to all our ailments. And Mauro Larrea, as I have already told you, my dear, is—"

He preferred to anticipate her.

"The intruder who has turned up from across the sea. A pleasure to meet you."

"I'm delighted to meet you at last; I've heard all about you."

And I'm delighted as well, thought Mauro as he extended his hand to him. *You were the Runt's doctor and the only person to whom Zayas sent news of his death from Cuba. To you, and not to the two men's cousin, Soledad. I wonder why.*

A smartly uniformed maid came in with an aperitif tray. Their conversation remained inconsequential but gradually became less formal: Dr. Ysasi, a slight figure with a black beard, was addressed as Manuel, while the other two settled on Mauro for the Mexican miner. What do you think of Jerez? How long are you thinking of staying? What is life like in the independent New World?—empty questions that received insubstantial replies until the butler announced dinner was served in his best English.

"Thank you, Palmer," Soledad replied in English, in the firm tone of the mistress of the house. She added in a low voice in Spanish: "It's costing him a great effort to learn our language."

They crossed the ample hallway and climbed the stairs to the first-floor dining room. The walls were lined with chinoiserie paper, and the furniture was Chippendale. Ten chairs surrounded the table, which was covered in a linen cloth, with two slender candlesticks and places laid for three.

The servants began to scurry behind their backs. Wine was served in cut-glass decanters with silver mouths and handles as the different courses, the conversation, and impressions began to flow.

"And now, to accompany the poultry," their hostess said at one point, "what the finest palates in Jerez would recommend would be a good amontillado. But my husband had wanted to try something else from our cellar. I hope you like this burgundy."

She raised her glass delicately; the candlelight brought out deep-red glints from the wine, which she and the doctor contemplated admiringly. Larrea on the other hand took advantage to study her once more without attracting attention. Her bare shoulders contrasting with the moss-colored velvet of her dress. Her long neck and sharp collarbones. Her high cheeks and smooth skin.

"Romanée-Conti," she went on, unaware of his scrutiny. "It's our favorite. After extremely lengthy negotiations, four years ago Edward became their sole representative in England. It's something that honors us and makes us proud."

The two men tried the wine, and both praised its body and aroma.

"Magnificent," Larrea said sincerely. "And since we're on the subject, Señora Claydon . . ."

"Sol, please."

"Since we're on the subject, Sol . . . As I understand it, and I beg you to forgive my curiosity and my ignorance, your current business is not exactly producing wine as your family used to do but selling wine that others make?"

Before responding, she placed her glass on the tablecloth and waited while the carved slices of meat were served. Then she raised her enchanting voice. To him.

"That is more or less the case. My husband, Edward, is what is known in English as a wine merchant, which has little to do with the idea of a merchant we have in Spain. He does not usually sell wines directly for consumption. He is . . . let's call him an agent, a *marchand*. An importer with international connections who looks for—and, I have to say, generally finds—excellent vintages in different countries and makes sure they arrive in England in the best possible condition.

Port, madeira, clarets from Bordeaux. He also represents several French growers, mostly from Champagne, Cognac, and the Burgundy region."

"As well, of course," the doctor broke in without a qualm, "as making sure that our sherry reaches the Thames. That is how he came to marry our lady from Jerez."

"Or why the lady from Jerez married an English wine merchant," Soledad retorted, playfully and with a touch of irony, "to increase the fame of our solera. And now, Mauro, your turn to answer a question: Please tell us what apart from the property transactions has brought you here. If it's not being indiscreet, what exactly do you do?"

For the umpteenth time, he repeated his story, trying to sound both convincing and truthful. Mexico's internal tensions and the friction with European countries, his interest in diversifying his business—all the senseless patter he had been concocting ever since his daughter's eccentric mother-in-law had provided him with a ridiculous argument that to his great surprise seemed to make sense to anyone hearing it.

"And before you decided to make your way outside Mexico, what did you do there?"

They were still enjoying the pheasant with chestnuts and the splendid wine, dabbing their lips with the linen napkins and conversing quite naturally. The white wax candles were slowly burning down, and the husband was not mentioned again. The fire continued to crackle in the hearth, and the evening rolled pleasantly on. Perhaps for that reason, because of the fleeting sensation of well-being Mauro Larrea had not felt in his bones for such a long time, and even though he could anticipate that what he was about to say would send his distant agent into a rage, Larrea chose not to hold back.

"In reality, I was never anything more than a miner on whom fortune smiled at a certain point in life."

Sol Claydon's fork remained poised between plate and mouth. After a couple of seconds, she deposited it once more on the Crown Derby china as if it were too heavy for her to be able to concentrate. Now the two sides of the new owner of her family's inheritance fitted together. On the one hand, the impeccable evening tails he was wearing now, and the elegant frock coat she had first seen him in, his determined way of buying and selling, his worldly manners and tastes. On the other, those broad, square shoulders of his, the strong arms that had supported her as she went down the stairs, the big, weather-beaten hands bearing the marks of his adventures . . . his intensely masculine presence.

"A mining entrepreneur, I suppose you mean," said Dr. Ysasi. "One of those who risk their money in excavations."

"Yes, in recent years. But before that I was toughened up deep in silver mines, smashing rocks in the darkness, sweating blood six days a week to earn a miserable pittance."

There, I've said it now, compadre, he told his agent mentally. *Now if you wish you can shout at me all you like. But I had to let it out: now that my present is one big lie, you have to understand that I want to tell the truth about my past at least.*

From across the ocean, Andrade made no reply.

"That's very interesting," said the doctor, sounding sincere.

"Our dear Manuel here is quite a liberal, Mauro, a freethinker. He flirts dangerously with socialism. I'm sure he won't leave you in peace until he's heard all about you."

When the desserts arrived, they were still conversing in a lively vein, skirting around the awkward details that had brought him to Jerez: Gustavo Zayas, Little Runt's death, his shady deal. "*Charlotte russe à la vanille*, our cook's specialty," announced Soledad. To go with it, the sweetness of a Pedro Ximénez wine that seemed as dense and dark as ebony. Afterward they moved to the library: further relaxed conversation while they savored the aromatic coffee, glasses of Armagnac, pistachio Turkish delight, and magnificent cigars from the Philippines, which she offered them from a small carved box.

"Please do feel free to smoke."

Mauro was surprised that she had to give her permission until he realized he had not seen a single woman with a cigar or cigarette in her mouth since his arrival in Spain. Nothing could be further from the situation in Mexico and Havana, where females smoked tobacco as much as men, and with equal enjoyment.

"Tell us about your children, Mauro," she said.

He touched on the subject briefly as they sat in comfortable armchairs surrounded by leather-bound books in glass cabinets. About the child Mariana would soon be giving birth to, about Nico's stay in Europe and his imminent marriage.

"It's hard when they're so far away, isn't it? Even if it's more convenient for them, at least in our case. That's something you're spared, Manuel, being such a confirmed bachelor."

"So are your daughters still in England?" asked Larrea, allowing the doctor no chance to comment. Now the pieces were falling into place, and he could better understand the strange quiet in the house.

"That's right. The two younger ones are at a Catholic boarding school in Surrey, and the two elder ones are being looked after by good friends in Chelsea, in London. As you can imagine, they were desperate not to give up all the attractions of a big city: the balls, the functions, their first suitors."

"How are they getting on with Spanish, by the way?" asked Dr. Ysasi.

"I must confess to my shame that Brianda and Estela are dreadful at it. They find it impossible to pronounce the rolling *R*'s, and to distinguish between *tú* and *usted*. It was easier with the older ones, Marina and Lucrecia, because I spent more time with them and took very seriously the idea that my children should not lose a large part of their identity. And yet, with the younger two . . . well, things have changed, and I'm afraid they are more moved by 'Rule, Britannia!' than by Andalusian songs. They're much more the daughters of Queen Victoria than of our Spanish Reina Isabel."

All three of them laughed. The clock struck eleven and the doctor suggested he and Larrea should leave.

"It's time for us to allow our hostess to get some rest, don't you think, Mauro?"

Sol and Larrea descended the staircase side by side, this time without touching. The butler brought their things; as the master of the house was absent, Sol accompanied them almost as far as the front entrance. She held out her hand in farewell; he merely brushed it with his lips. As he touched and felt her skin, a shudder ran through his body.

"It has been a very pleasant evening."

Out of the corner of his eye he saw Dr. Ysasi busy with his own affairs: he picked up his Gladstone bag and donned the cape Palmer was holding out. The butler said a few incomprehensible words to him and the doctor nodded, listening closely.

"The pleasure was all mine. I hope we can repeat it once Edward gets back. Although before then, perhaps . . . I believe you haven't been out to La Templanza yet, have you?"

Templanza . . . didn't that mean temperance? Yes, that was what he needed, loads of temperance. But he doubted whether she was referring to the cardinal virtue that he had been so sadly lacking for so long. He raised an inquisitive eyebrow.

"La Templanza, our vineyard," she clarified. "Or, rather, the vineyard you now own."

"I'm sorry, I wasn't aware the vineyard had a name."

"As mines do, I suppose."

"That's true, we usually baptize mines with a name as well."

"Well, the same happens here. Would you allow me to accompany you to what once belonged to our family, so that you can get to know it? We can go in my carriage. Would tomorrow morning at ten suit you?"

At this she lowered her voice, and it was then that Mauro Larrea suddenly realized that the French wines, the Russian dessert, the lack of indiscreet questions, the Manila tobacco, and, above all, the enchantment that oozed from every pore of this woman's body all came at a price.

"I need to ask you something in private."

CHAPTER THIRTY-ONE

"Are gentlemen from the Americas accustomed to retiring early, or would you accept a last drink with me?"

The gates of the Claydon house had just swung shut behind them, and it was Manuel Ysasi who made this invitation when they were out in the street.

"I'd like nothing better."

The doctor had turned out to be an excellent conversationalist, intelligent and pleasant. And Larrea needed another drink to help digest Soledad Montalvo's parting words, which were still ringing in his ears. A woman who needed a favor. Yet again.

They crossed Calle Algarve, then walked along Calle Larga toward the Puerta de Sevilla.

"I hope you don't mind walking. I inherited an old phaeton from my father for nighttime emergencies or if I ever have to visit some farm laborer's cottage, but I normally get around on foot."

"On the contrary, my friend."

"I must warn you that there is no great amount of nightlife here. Despite the economic boom, Jerez is still a small city that retains a lot of the Moorish town it once was. Only some forty thousand of us live here, even though we have enough wineries to derail a train: more than five hundred of them at the last count. As I suppose you already know, the great majority of the population lives either directly or indirectly from wine."

"And they live well, from what I can see," said Larrea, pointing out some of the magnificent family mansions lining the road.

"That depends on whether fortune has smiled on you or not. Just ask the hired hands in the vineyards and big estates. They work from dawn till dusk for next to nothing, eat miserable soups made with black bread, water, and only a few drops of oil, and sleep on stone benches until they return to their toil at first light."

"Don't forget, I've already been warned of your socialist sympathies, my friend," said Larrea. The doctor accepted his irony with good grace.

"To be frank, there is a lot that's positive here, too; I've no wish at all to leave you with a bad impression. For example, as you can see, we have the benefit of gas street lighting, and the mayor has announced that we are about to receive running water from the springs of Tempul. We also have a railway that is used above all to transport wine barrels down to the bay, a good number of elementary schools, and a secondary school. We even have a regional economic society plagued with eminent men, and a more-than-decent hospital. And the former town hall, next to Sol Montalvo's mansion, has recently been converted into a library. There is a lot of work in the vineyards, and above all in the wineries: warehousemen, foremen, coopers . . ."

Mauro Larrea could not help but notice that Ysasi called Sol Claydon by her maiden name, even though according to English law a woman lost the right to use it the moment she said "I do" at the altar. *Sol Montalvo*, he had said; without meaning to, he was showing what a close, long-standing friendship he had with her.

They continued chatting as they passed the last poor souls still out on the streets. A bootblack, an old woman as bent as a hook who offered them matches and cigarette papers, four or five shady characters. The doors of the stalls, cafés, and inns in the center of the city were all closed; most of the locals were already safely at home sitting around a warm brazier full of coals. At that moment a night watchman with a sharpened stick and an oil lamp greeted them with a Hail Mary from beneath his heavy brown cape.

"As you can see, we even have armed patrols at night."

"That doesn't seem like a poor outcome, by heavens."

"The problem is not Jerez, Mauro; here to some extent we are privileged. The problem is what a disaster Spain is. Luckily, almost all you former colonies are now independent from us."

Larrea had no intention of getting involved in any political arguments with the good doctor; his interest lay in another direction. He had already heard enough generalizations about the town; now was the moment to focus on his own particular concerns. From the wide mouth of the funnel to the narrow neck. He interrupted his newfound friend.

"Can you clear something up for me, Manuel, if it's no trouble? I suppose that the successful activity of the wine producers has had a lot to do with all this progress, hasn't it?"

"Obviously. Jerez has always been a town of land laborers and winegrowers, but it was the emergence of larger wineries and the increased capital in the last few decades that has given rise to the current prosperity. These new wine producers are having the region's centuries-old landowners for breakfast, if you'll pardon the expression. The ones who have owned land, palaces, and noble titles since the Middle Ages are now in full retreat from the energy and economic might of this new class. They are offering them matrimonial alliances with their children and all other kinds of pacts. The Montalvo family, in fact, was to a certain extent an example of how these two distinct worlds could end up amalgamating."

That's where I wanted to get to, thought Larrea, secretly pleased with himself. *To that complicated family that blind destiny has somehow linked me with. To the clan of that woman who has just invited me to dinner and deployed all her charms and enchantment only to then pull out a stiletto and run me through, heaven knows for what reason. Speak, Doctor, tell me all about them.*

But it was not to be, at least not for the moment. They had left Calle Larga behind and were not far from Larrea's new residence.

"See? Here's another example of our city's dynamic growth: the Casino Jerezano."

In front of them rose an imposing baroque construction with vast windows and airy closed-in bays. In the center was a magnificent red-and-white marble doorway flanked with Solomonic columns and topped by a superb open balcony.

They stood beneath the stars for a few moments, admiring the façade.

"Impressive, isn't it? You should know, though, that it's only being rented until the new club premises are finished. This is the former palace of the Marquis of Montana. The poor man only managed to enjoy it for seven years before he died."

"Are we going in here, then?"

"Some other day. For now I want to take you somewhere that is both similar and different at the same time."

They set off toward the Calle del Duque de la Victoria, which everyone in Jerez still called Calle Porvera because it followed the line of the old wall of that name.

"The members of the Casino Jerezano Club we have just left behind are from the petty and middle bourgeoisie; they often have interesting talks and are active in the cultural sphere. But there is another club that welcomes those with large fortunes and the high bourgeoisie, the titans who trade with half the world, the real aristocracy of wine with names like Garvey, Domecq, González, Gordon, Williams, Lassaletta, Loustau, or Misa. There are even a few Ysasis among them, though not from my branch of the family. More or less fifty families altogether."

"A lot of them sound foreign . . ."

"Some are French in origin, but most prominent are those of British ancestry. Some people call them the 'sherry royalty.' Sherry is what they call our wines from Jerez outside Spain. And there have also been legendary men who, like you, are Indianos. Pemartín and Apezechea, for example, are repatriated Spaniards, although unfortunately they are both dead now."

An Indiano—what a label they had given him. Although possibly it was not a bad disguise beneath which he could hide his truth from the world.

"Here we are, dear Mauro," announced the doctor at last, coming to a halt outside another magnificent building. "The Isabel II Club, the wealthiest, most exclusive club in Jerez. As the name indicates, it's monarchic and patriotic through and through, but at the same time it is very anglophile in its tastes and customs. It's almost like one of the London clubs."

"And is it this select group to which a man with your ideas belongs, Doctor?" the Mexican miner asked slyly.

Ysasi chuckled as he let the other man go in ahead of him.

"I look after the health of every one of them, and of their numerous offspring, and so it makes sense for them to treat me as one of them. As if I were selling barrels of wine even to the pope in Rome. And, of course, it goes without saying that if you yourself, Mauro, took it upon yourself to revive the Montalvo business, you'd be welcome, too."

"I'm afraid my plans are directed elsewhere, my dear friend," muttered Larrea, stepping inside.

There was not the slightest trace of the hectic nighttime noise he was used to from cafés in Mexico and Havana. Instead a relaxed atmosphere reigned among leather armchairs and carpeted floors. Groups chatting, Spanish and English newspapers scattered on the tables, a few quiet games of cards, the last cups of coffee. Naturally, only men; there was not the slightest trace of femininity.

There was a pleasant smell of wood polished with carnauba wax, expensive tobacco, and foreign colognes. The two men sat beneath a large mirror, and it was not long before a waiter came over.

"Brandy?" the doctor suggested.

"Perfect."

"Let me surprise you."

He ordered something that Larrea did not catch. The waiter nodded and soon returned to fill two glasses from a bottle without a label. They sniffed the bouquet first, then tasted it. First there was an intense aroma, and then it was smooth on the palate. They swirled the contents slowly around the glass and gazed at the caramel-colored liquid in the candlelight.

"It's not exactly Edward Claydon's Armagnac."

"But it's not bad, either. Is it French as well?"

The doctor smiled mischievously.

"Not at all. It's from Jerez, a completely local product. Produced in a winery not three hundred yards from here."

"Don't make fun of me, Doctor."'

"I'm not, I promise you. It's brandy aged in the same oak barrels that held the wine. Some enterprising wine merchants are already starting to put it on the market. They say they found the recipe by pure chance, when an order from The Netherlands was left unpaid and it aged without ever being sold. I personally think that must be just one more legend and that it was more than just a fluke."

"I think it is a fine drink, whatever its origin."

"Some people are starting to call it Spanish cognac, although I bet the Frenchies aren't that keen on the name."

They sipped their drinks again.

"Why did Luis Montalvo let everything go to rack and ruin, Manuel?"

Perhaps it was the warmth of the brandy that made him express his curiosity so openly. Or the trust he already felt toward this slender doctor with his jet-black beard and liberal ideas. Larrea had already asked the same question of the good-natured notary the day they met, but his answer had been vague. And at his first meeting with Sol Claydon, she had rushed him almost at a gallop through a nostalgic tour of her clan's splendor, and yet had been careful not to supply any details. Maybe the family doctor, a more scientific and Cartesian sort, could help him grasp once and for all the soul of the Montalvos.

Ysasi needed to take another sip of brandy before replying.

"Because he never considered himself worthy of his inheritance."

Larrea was still trying to take this in when an elderly gentleman appeared behind them. He looked very distinguished, with a curly graying beard that reached halfway down his chest.

"A very good evening to you, gentlemen."

"Good evening, Don José María," the doctor greeted him. "Allow me to introduce—"

He could not finish his sentence.

"Welcome to our club, Señor Larrea."

"Don José María Wilkinson," Ysasi said, apparently not surprised that the newcomer already knew the miner's name. "He is the club's chairman as well as being one of the most renowned wine producers in Jerez."

"And the number one devotee of the excellent medical care our dear doctor here offers."

As the object of this compliment acknowledged it with a brief nod of the head, Señor Wilkinson concentrated his attention on Larrea.

"We have already heard of you and your links to the properties Don Matías Montalvo used to own."

Despite his surname, this Wilkinson spoke without trace of an English accent. Larrea reacted to his words in the same way as the doctor, with a brief nod. He preferred not to add anything more about his intentions. Not even the gunpowder that Tadeo Carrús had threatened to use to blow up his house on San Felipe Neri would have spread as quickly as news did in this town.

"Although I understand your intention is not to stay, do feel free to use our facilities for however long you remain in Jerez."

Larrea thanked him formally for the kind offer. He thought this would bring the interruption to an end, but the chairman seemed in no hurry to leave the two men alone.

"And if at any time you change your mind and decide to revive the vineyard and the winery, count on us for whatever you need—and, believe me, I speak on behalf of all our members. Don Matías was one of the founders of this club, and so, in memory of him and his family, nothing would please us more than to see someone restore glory to the enterprise he and his predecessors created with such determination and heart."

"As you'll find out, Mauro, these wine merchants are a race apart," Manuel Ysasi added. "They compete fiercely for markets, and yet they help and defend each other, they meet socially, and they even marry each other's children. Don't dismiss his promise: it's no empty gesture; it's a real offer of a helping hand."

As if I had nothing more urgent to do than to devote myself to getting mixed up in a ruined business, thought Larrea. Fortunately, Wilkinson insisted no further.

"At any rate, and so that you won't leave Jerez without getting to know us, I'll ask our member and friend Fernández de Villavicencio to arrange an invitation to the ball he gives annually in his Alcázar palace. Every year we celebrate a significant event that concerns one of us. On this occasion it will be in honor of the Claydons, now that they have returned. Soledad, the wife—"

"Is the granddaughter of Don Matías Montalvo: I know," Larrea finished for him.

"I see you have already met. Excellent. As I said, my dear Señor Larrea, we trust we shall see you there together with the doctor."

As soon as the wine producer and his bushy beard had retired, Ysasi refilled their glasses.

"I'm sure you and I will make an excellent couple at the ball, Mauro. What do you prefer, the polka or the polonaise?"

Larrea's loud laugh made several heads turn.

"For God's sake, stop talking nonsense and continue telling me about the Montalvos. Let's see if I can understand that family once and for all, dammit."

"I no longer remember where we had got to, so allow me paint you a picture in broad brushstrokes. The Montalvos always seemed immortal. Rich, good-looking, entertaining. All of them blessed by good fortune, even little Luisito, with all his limitations: he was the family's eternal child. Loved, pampered, literally wrapped in cotton wool. He was the youngest of the cousins. That, as well as his physical condition, meant he never once imagined he would be the heir of the great Don Matías's fortune. Sometimes, though, life surprises us with its ricochets and sends us off in a different direction when we least expect it."

You don't say, my friend.

Unaware of the miner's thoughts, the doctor went on: "But a decline in their fortunes seemed inevitable as soon as one got to know Don Matías's successors, Luis and Jacobo—the fathers of Luisito and Soledad."

"The ones who invited Gypsies to Christmas dinners and played billiards until dawn?"

The doctor gave a hearty laugh.

"Sol told you that, did she? That was the two brothers' outward reputation: the one their children, nephews, and nieces, and those of us who were their friends, all adored. They were outrageously sociable and uniquely fine-looking; amusing, elegant, witty, generous. There was little more than a year between them and they were alike as two peas in a pod—physically and temperamentally. The shame was that, in addition to these virtues, they also had some less laudable characteristics: they were spendthrifts, slackers, gamblers, womanizers. They were irresponsible, and their heads were filled with sawdust. Don Matías never managed to bring them into line, whereas he was as upright and honest a man as you could wish to find. The grandson of someone from the Cantabrian mountains who had made his way as a shopkeeper in Chiclana, where his father grew up selling dried beans, chickpeas, rice, and cheap wines behind a counter. Do you know where Cantabria is? It's in the north of the country, and they came south from there . . ."

"They also reached Mexico."

"You'll know, then, what kind of person I'm talking about: tenacious, hardworking men who came from nothing and started their own businesses. Some of them, like Don Matías's grandfather, invested what they earned in vines and prospered. Once the family was settled in Jerez, with solid capital and his business on a sure footing, his heir asked on his son Matías's behalf for the hand in marriage of Elisa Osorio, the daughter of the ruined Marquis of Benaocaz, a young Jerez beauty with a lineage as noble as her estate was poor. And so, as has become very common in these parts in recent years, nobility was allied to finance, as I've already explained."

"The prosperous wine bourgeoisie marrying into the impoverished local aristocracy, is that right?"

"Exactly. I see you've already learned a lot, my friend. Another glass?"

"Why not?" said Larrea, sliding his glass across the marble tabletop. And ten more if need be, if only Ysasi carried on talking.

"To sum up: Don Matías followed in his predecessors' footsteps. He worked his fingers to the bone, used his foresight and intelligence to multiply his investments and capital a hundredfold. But he made one huge mistake."

"He neglected his children," Larrea concluded. And Nico's shadow flitted through his mind.

"That's right. He was so obsessed with increasing his wealth that they escaped his control. By the time Don Matías realized this, they were both like stray bullets shooting off in directions it was impossible to correct. His wife, Doña Elisa, pinned her hopes on marrying them to two young women from prominent families, but they had neither dowries nor character to bring to their marriages. Luis and Jacobo never had houses of their own: to the end of their days they went on living in the mansion on Calle de la Tornería where you are currently staying. And it was pretty much the same with the daughter, the beautiful María Fernanda: a disastrous marriage with Andrés Zayas, one of her brothers' friends from Seville whose pockets were empty but who lived the high life."

Go slowly, Ysasi, slowly. Gustavo Zayas and his affairs will require more time. Let's do things in order and leave him until later. Fortunately, the doctor drank another sip of brandy and then took up the story again at the point Larrea was wishing for.

"Well, eventually, having given up on his sons, Don Matías began to put his trust in the third generation. In the firstborn of his firstborn, to be precise, who was also called Matías—Matí. Despite being the son of a well-known rake, he appeared to be made of sterner stuff. As good-looking and friendly as his father, but with a great deal more brains. From an early age he liked to accompany his grandfather to the winery. He spoke English because he had been at school in England; he knew all the workmen by name and was starting to understand the secrets of the trade."

"I suppose he was also your friend."

At this, the doctor raised his glass toward the ceiling with a melancholy smile, as if making a toast to someone no longer in the land of the living.

"Yes, my good friend Matí. In fact, we were as thick as thieves from infancy: we were more or less the same age, give or take a year, and I spent all my time with them. Matí and Luisito, the two brothers. Gustavo, too, whenever he came here from Seville. Inés and Soledad. I grew up without a mother and was an only child, and so either I was accompanying my grandfather to attend to Doña Elisa's aches and pains, or my father to deal with any other health problems in the family. I used to stay to have lunch, dinner, even to sleep. If I counted the hours of my childhood and youth I spent with the Montalvos, they would be far more than in my own house. Until it all began to fall apart."

This time it was Mauro Larrea who picked up the bottle and poured them two more glasses. When he lifted the bottle, he saw they had already drunk more than half.

"Exactly two days after Sol and Edward Clayton's wedding."

Ysasi fell silent, as if mentally traveling back in time.

"It was during a hunt in Coto de Doñana: a terrible accident. Either due to carelessness or simply a dark twist of fate, Matí ended up with a lead bullet in his stomach, and there was nothing anyone could do for him."

By all that's holy, a son killed with his guts hanging out in the first flush of youth. Larrea thought of Nico, of Mariana, and choked. He would have liked to ask for more details, if it really was an accident, or if someone was guilty, but the doctor, with his tongue loosened by the brandy and also perhaps from nostalgia, continued to pour out his memories:

"I'm not saying it all came crashing down at once, as if the family had been hit by one of those French time bombs, but following Matí the grandson's burial, things started to slide toward a catastrophe. His father, Luis, became a complete hypochondriac. His uncle, Luis's brother Jacobo, continued burning the candle at both ends, but only halfheartedly. Don Matías, the grandfather, aged as if crushed beneath a hundred-pound stone, and the women in the family shut themselves in to say the rosary and to occupy themselves entirely with their ailments."

"What about you and the younger generation?"

"To cut a long story short, let's just say we already had our paths marked out. As they had planned, Sol settled in London with Edward and started her own family; she used to come back to Jerez from time to time, but less and less often. For his part, Gustavo embarked for Cuba, and after that we heard very little from him. Sol's sister Inés became a nun in a cloistered Augustinian order. I went on studying at the Faculty of Medical Sciences in Cádiz, then completed my qualifications in Madrid. In other words, our group disintegrated. And while Jerez prospered, that paradise where we grew up believing we were protected from the whole world gradually vanished."

"And little Luis was the only one who stayed."

"At first, following Matí's death, Luisito was sent to the Naval College in Seville, but he soon returned, and he was the only one to witness the family's fall. He ended up burying all the older generation, one after the other. Fortunately or unfortunately for Runt, they did not take long to start passing away. And when after a number of years he was left all alone . . . well, I think you know . . ."

They were the last to leave the club that night. As they passed through the Puerta de Sevilla no one else was in sight. Ysasi insisted on accompanying him back to the mansion. When they reached it, he looked up at its façade as if wanting to take it all in.

"When Luisito left for Cuba, I think he was well aware that there would never be a way back."

"What do you mean, Manuel?"

"Luis Montalvo was dying, and he knew it. He was aware the end was near."

CHAPTER THIRTY-TWO

჻

"I was thinking of coming in my phaeton, as I said, but when I saw what a magnificent day it was, I changed my mind."

Soledad spoke without dismounting from her horse. She was sheathed in an exquisite black riding habit that, despite its masculine air, only served to make her look even more attractive. A short jacket with a narrow waist, a white high-collared shirt, an ample skirt to allow her to move freely, a top hat with a small veil over her pinned-back hair. She was tall, straight-backed, imposing. Next to her, a lad was holding the bridle of another splendid mount. For him, he presumed.

They left Jerez behind, taking byroads, tracks, and paths under the midmorning sun as they headed for La Templanza, across bright hills filled with silence and fresh air. Hundreds if not thousands of vines were planted in row upon row, twisting in upon themselves, with no leaves or fruit, anchored to the ground. She told him that this kind of white, porous earth was known as *albariza*.

"In autumn the vines look dead, their stocks are dried-out, they've lost their color. But they're only sleeping, taking a rest. Gathering the strength that will rise from their roots. Gaining nourishment to bring forth new life."

They rode side by side as they conversed. Soledad did most of the talking.

"They're not just planted haphazardly," she continued. "The vines need the blessing of the winds, the alternation of the sea breezes from the west and the dry, eastern ones. Looking after them is a complicated art."

Riding at a slow trot, they had reached what she called the "house of vines." It, too, was in a precarious state. They dismounted and allowed their horses to rest.

"You see? Our vines—or, more precisely, your vines—have had nobody caring for them for years, and now just look."

It was true. Dried leaves curled up on the branches, shriveled-up shoots.

She was speaking without looking at him, with one hand shading her eyes as she scanned the horizon. He gazed again at her delicate neck and the line of her molasses-colored hair. Some strands had slipped out of her bun during the ride and shone in the near-noonday sun.

"When we were children we loved coming here for the grape harvest. We often persuaded the adults to let us stay and sleep. At night we would steal out to the beds of straw where the grapes were left to dry so that we could listen to the laborers talking and singing."

It would have been polite of the miner to show more interest in the story she was telling him. In fact, he was intrigued to learn about vines and grapes, everything that grew aboveground that he knew nothing about. But he could not forget that Sol Claydon had brought him out of Jerez for another reason. And since he sensed he wasn't going to like it, he wanted to hear what it was as soon as possible.

"The harvest is usually at the beginning of September," she went on, "when the temperature starts to ease off. But it's the vine itself that establishes the time: its height, its foliage, and even its fragrance will indicate when the grapes are ripe. Sometimes the vintners wait until the moon is in the fourth quarter, because they think that's when the fruit will be softer and sweeter. Or if there's been rain, the harvesting is postponed so that the roots can fill with the cold again—that's the white dust that gathers on them—because it helps speed up the fermentation later on. If the moment isn't well chosen, the wine will be of lower quality. If the grapes are harvested too early, the wine will be weak; if the moment is right, they'll turn out robust, strong, full-bodied."

She stood there, a striking image in her riding habit, with the light and the land enveloping her. She sounded nostalgic but also showed an evident wealth of knowledge about all that surrounded them. As well as a covert wish to delay for as long as possible her real intentions.

"Apart from all the hard work at the grape harvest, even at quieter moments such as later in autumn there was always activity around here. The surveyor, the caretaker, the laborers . . . My friends in London always laugh when I tell them vines are looked after with almost as much care as English rose gardens."

She walked over to the front door of the house but did not even touch it.

"My goodness, what a state it's in . . ." she murmured. "Could you try opening it?"

He did the same as with the winery, putting his shoulder to it. Inside, it smelled of desolation. Empty rooms, no water pitchers in their store, the larder empty of food. But this time Soledad didn't get carried away by memories; only a pair of old, worn-out straw-bottomed chairs caught her attention.

She went over and picked up one of them, intending to bring it with her.

"Leave it, you'll get dirty."

Mauro Larrea picked up both the chairs and carried them out into the sunshine. Dusting them off with his handkerchief, he placed them against the front wall, facing the vast area of bare vines. Two humble low chairs with fraying canes where once upon a time the hired hands must have sat beneath the stars after their long hours of toil, or the caretaker and his wife rested and chatted, or the children of the house on those magical nights perfumed with the smell of recently picked grapes that Soledad Montalvo remembered so well. Chairs that were witness to simple lives, to the relentless passage of time and the seasons in their eternal round. Now, incongruously, the two of them were occupying the chairs, with their fine clothes, their complicated lives, and their air of people who had little to do with the earth and its demands.

She raised her face to the sky, eyes shut tight.

"In London they'd think I was a lunatic if they saw me in Saint James's or Hyde Park sitting out in the sun like this."

A dove was cooing, the rusty weathervane squeaked on the rooftop, and they prolonged for a few moments longer the unreal sensation of peace. But Mauro Larrea knew that, beneath this apparent calm, beneath the temperance that lent its name to the vineyard and behind which she was pretending to shelter, something was stirring. This disconcerting woman who only a few days before had slipped into his life had not brought him to this isolated spot to talk about the grape harvests of her childhood or asked him to bring out the chairs so that they could sit together admiring the countryside's calm beauty.

"When are you going to tell me what you want from me?"

She didn't shift her posture or open her eyes. She simply sat there, allowing the rays of the autumn sun to caress her skin.

"Have you ever been completely wrong about an important decision in your life, Mauro?"

"I'm afraid I have."

"One that dragged other people into it, put them at risk?"

"That, too."

"And how far would you go to correct that mistake?"

"Up to now, I've crossed an ocean and arrived in Jerez."

"Then I hope you'll understand me."

She lowered her face and turned her slender figure toward him.

"I need you to pretend to be my cousin Luisito."

At any other moment, Mauro Larrea's immediate reaction would have been a rude remark or a bitter guffaw. But out there, in the midst of the silence of the parched land and bare vines, he immediately realized that her plea was not some extravagant whim but something she had carefully considered. He hid his bewilderment and let her go on.

"A while ago," Soledad said, "I did something I shouldn't have, something that the persons affected never knew about. Let's say I carried out some inappropriate commercial transactions."

She gazed out toward the horizon again, shielding herself from his intrigued look.

"I don't think it's necessary to go into details. I only want you to know I did it in an attempt to protect my daughters, and to some extent myself."

She appeared to have collected her thoughts and pushed back a lock of escaped hair.

"I was aware of the risk I was running, but I was confident that if in the unlikely event that now unfortunately seems to have transpired, I could count on Luisito. What I didn't count on was that by then Luisito would no longer be with us."

Inappropriate commercial transactions, she had said. And she was asking for his help. Here was another woman he didn't know trying to convince him to go behind her husband's back. Havana, Carola Gorostiza, the garden at her friend Casilda Barrón's mansion in El Cerro. A proud figure dressed in bright yellow seated in her carriage with the sea swaying gently in a bay filled with sailing boats, brigantines, and schooners. After that dreadful experience, he could have only one answer.

"I'm very sorry to have to say this, Soledad, but I don't think I'm the right person."

Her response came quick as a flash. Obviously she had already prepared it.

"Before you refuse, bear in mind that in return I am in a position to help you. I have many contacts in the wine market throughout Europe. I can find you a much more reliable buyer than those that flabby old agent Zarco is likely to come up with. And without the exorbitant commission you offered him."

He twisted his mouth. So she was already well aware of his movements.

"I see that news flies."

"In no time at all."

"Be that as it may, I must insist that it's impossible for me to agree to what you're asking. Over many years, life has taught me that it's best for everyone to settle their own affairs, with no one else getting involved."

She raised her hand as a shield once more and scanned the chalky hills, pausing before her next sally. Larrea peered down at the white dust and scuffed it with his foot, not wanting to think. Then he stroked the scar on his hand. Above their heads the rusty weathervane creaked as it changed direction.

"I am not unaware, Mauro, that you, too, have a somewhat shady past."

He stifled a hoarse, bitter laugh.

"Is that why you invited me last night, to size me up?"

"Partly. I've also been investigating here and there."

"And what did you discover?"

"Very little, to be honest. But enough to raise some doubts in my mind."

"About what?"

"About you and your circumstances. What, for example, is a rich Mexican silver miner doing so far from his concerns, working to fix the tiles on an abandoned mansion at the far ends of the earth?"

Another guttural laugh remained stuck in his throat.

"Have you sent someone to spy on me?"

"Naturally," she admitted, arranging the hem of her skirt to avoid its getting too dusty. Or possibly pretending to do so. "That's how I know you are willing to live like a savage, with no furniture and with a leaky roof, until you manage to sell at any price properties for which you never paid a penny."

That damned notary. *When and where did you blab all this, Senén Blanco,* the miner muttered to himself. *Or damned notary clerk,* he thought, remembering Angulo, the unctuous employee who had taken him to the mansion on Calle de la Tornería for the first time. He tried to keep his voice calm.

"Forgive me being so frank, Señora Claydon, but I believe my personal affairs are none of your business."

In order to reestablish a distance between them, he had used her married name again. When she stopped gazing at the horizon and turned toward him once more, he could see she was clear-minded and determined.

"I'm still trying to take in the fact that we no longer own a single stone or cask or sad vine stock of what was once our great family fortune. Allow me at least a legitimate right to curiosity: that of trying to find out who the person really is that has ended up possessing what we once had and fancifully thought we would be able to keep. Anyway, I beg you not to see my inquiries as a gratuitous invasion of your private affairs. I am also keeping a close eye on you for a selfish reason: I need you."

"Why me? You don't know me; I suppose you have other friends. Someone closer, more trustworthy."

"I could say that it's for a sentimental reason: the legacy of the Montalvos is now in your hands. That creates a bond between us and in some way makes you Luisito's heir. Does that convince you?"

"I'd prefer a more honest explanation, if it's not too much to ask."

There was a sudden gust of wind. White dust spiraled from the chalky earth, and a few strands of her hair came loose once more. Then the English wine merchant's wife gave her second reason, the real one, without looking at him, her eyes fixed on the vines, the immense sky, or empty space.

"What if I tell you I'm desperate and you appeared out of the blue at the most crucial moment? Because I realize that you'll disappear as soon as your fortunes change, and so when the wind starts to blow against me once more, I'll find it too hard to trace you."

An elusive exile, a fleeting shadow, he thought with a stab of bitterness. *That's what cursed fate has turned you into, compadre. Into a mere coatrack on which to hang a dead man's name or to be clung to by any beautiful woman willing to hide her disloyalty from her husband.*

Unaware of his thoughts and determined at least for him to hear her out, Soledad went on outlining her plans.

"It would only mean pretending to be my cousin temporarily to a lawyer from London who speaks no Spanish."

"You know as well as I do this isn't some pantomime. Here in Spain, in your England, or in the Americas, it is out-and-out fraud."

"You would only have to be polite, perhaps offer him a glass of amontillado, allow him to verify you are who you say you are and reply in the affirmative when he asks."

"When he asks what?"

"If over the past few months you have carried out a series of transactions with Edward Claydon. Some transfers of shares and properties."

"And did your cousin really do that?"

"The truth is, I did it all. I counterfeited the documents, the accounts, and the signatures of both of them: of Luis and of my husband. Then I put part of the shares and properties in the names of my own daughters. The rest, though, is still in the name of my deceased cousin."

A question shot through his mind. *For the love of God, what kind of woman are you, Soledad Montalvo?* She, however, did not appear to be affected: she must be more than accustomed to living with all this on her conscience.

"The lawyer must be on his way; in fact, I think he'll be here very soon. There's someone in London who is questioning the authenticity of the transactions and is sending him to check. He's accompanied by our administrator, someone I trust wholeheartedly, and whose discretion I can rely on."

"What about your husband?"

"He knows absolutely nothing, and believe me when I tell you that's the best for all concerned. He's going to be out of Jerez for a few days on business. I don't intend him to find out anything."

By the time they left La Templanza the sky was less friendly, with clouds brewing, while the breeze continued to stir up white dust devils among the vines. They rode back in tense silence until they entered the town once more. Both of them were relieved to hear the rattle of carriages on the cobbles, the cries of the dairymen, and here and there a snatch of song behind a barred window from an anonymous girl busy with her chores.

When they entered the Claydon stable Mauro Larrea did not wait for the groom but leapt from his horse and helped Soledad dismount. With her hand in his just as before.

"Please at least consider it" were her last words before she admitted defeat. As though to underscore them, her steed gave a loud neigh.

His only reply was to touch the brim of his hat. Then he turned around and walked off.

CHAPTER THIRTY-THREE

e was still irritated as he pushed open the wooden door to the mansion, determined to put an end to Soledad Montalvo's crazy scheme before she could get her hopes up in any way. He would go to his bedroom, collect the documents from her cousin Luisito that Calafat had sent from Cuba, then return to her house and put a stop to everything.

He went into the austere room, furnished with the bare minimum: a brass bed with a sunken mattress, an armchair propped against a wall, a wardrobe with a door missing. His trunks stood in one corner.

Hastily, he undid the clasps on one of them and rummaged inside, but could not find what he was looking for. He did not bother to close it again but opened the other one, tossing on the floor all the absurd domestic items that the attentive Paulita Fatou had lent him from Cádiz. Embroidered napkins flew through the air, and so did linen sheets. A satin bedspread, for heaven's sake! Finally he found what he was looking for at the bottom of the trunk.

Stuffing the papers between his frock coat and his chest, in less than ten minutes he was alongside the San Dionisio church, staring at the entrance to the Claydon mansion beyond the scriveners' colorful stalls and the passersby crowding the square. A few moments later, he raised the heavy bronze door knocker.

Palmer, the butler, opened much more quickly than on the previous evening. Even before the door had fully opened, he was anxiously ushering Larrea inside. A glance was enough to show him that everything was exactly as he remembered it, although now it was bathed in the sunlight filtering through the glass roof over the courtyard. The compass rose was still in the floor, the leafy plants in their Oriental tubs.

He had no time to take anything else in: as if she had been on the alert for any call from the entrance, he saw Soledad coming to meet him. She was still in her riding habit, looking slender and gracious; all she had removed was her hat. But from the few feet that separated them, he noted a profound change in her: her face was ashen, her eyes terror-stricken. She held her long neck stiffly, and her skin was as pale as if the blood were no longer flowing through her body. Something was threatening her as if she were an animal at bay: a beautiful roe deer about to be hit by a gunshot, an elegant chestnut mare set on by coyotes in the middle of the night.

The look they exchanged was magnetic.

Voices could be heard behind the half-open door she had just appeared through. Stern men's voices. Foreigners. A faint murmur emerged from her mouth:

"Edward's son's lawyer came sooner than I expected. He's here already."

All of a sudden, from somewhere deep inside, Mauro Larrea felt an irrational urge to clutch her to him. To feel her warm body against his chest, bury his face in her hair, whisper in her ear. *Whatever happens, Soledad, everything is going to be all right,* he wanted to tell her. But inside his head, with the insistence of the sledgehammer he had so often used to smash at minerals deep in the mines, a single word was repeated over and over. *No. No. No.*

He took two steps toward her, and then three and four.

"I can see this isn't a good moment for us to talk. I'd better go."

Her only response was a look of utter anguish. Sol Claydon was not accustomed to begging for favors. He knew she would never ask any. But the words her lips could not pronounce were obvious from the despair in her eyes. *Help me, Mauro,* they seemed to be shouting. Or that is what he understood.

All his caution and doubts, his strict determination to stay within the bounds of good sense and not allow himself to be swept away—all of it dissolved like a pinch of salt in boiling water.

Putting his hand on the curve of her waist, he forced her to turn around and head back toward the room she had just left. Two words emerged from his mouth:

"Let's go."

The men inside fell silent when they saw the couple come in. Solid, sure of themselves, striding confidently. Or so it seemed.

"Gentlemen, a good day to you. My name is Luis Montalvo and I believe you wish to speak to me."

He walked straight up to them and extended his hand forcefully. The same hand he had used to conclude deals and agreements when he was transferring tons of silver; the one he had used to introduce himself to the cream of Mexican society and to sign contracts with a whole series of zeros on the right-hand side. The hand of the influential man he had once been, and which from now on he would pretend still to be. Except that now he was about to do so using the bogus identity of a dead man.

The meeting took place in a room he had not seen on his previous visit: an office or study, possibly the place where on other occasions the master of the house conducted his business. Now, however, there was no one sitting in the leather chair behind the desk: all those present were close to the door, gathered at a round table strewn with documents.

The two men standing there introduced themselves without entirely managing to conceal their astonishment at his sudden appearance. Soledad immediately repeated their names and their positions so that Mauro would know who he was dealing with. Mr. Jonathan Wells, the lawyer representing Alan Claydon, and Mr. Andrew Gaskin, administrator of the family firm Claydon & Claydon. She simply mentioned the name of the third person, a young, inexperienced clerk who rose from his seat and nodded politely before sitting down once more.

Briefly recalling their conversation in La Templanza, Mauro Larrea deduced that the first of these men—in his forties, fair-haired, lanky, and with bushy sideburns—was what might be called his adversary. The second—shorter, with less hair, and nearing fifty—was his ally. The Alan Claydon whom Sol had mentioned a moment earlier must be her husband's absent son. There was someone in London who questioned the authenticity of the transactions, she had told him out among the vines. It was clear now whom she meant by that. And his lawyer was present to defend his interests.

Both these gentlemen were dressed with some elegance: fine cloth frock coats, gold fob watches, shiny boots. *What do you want from her? What risk is she running? How do you intend to punish her?*—he would have liked to ask all this of the fair-haired Englishman. While these questions were going through his mind, Soledad, who had miraculously recovered her composure, began to speak in a rapid mixture of Spanish and English.

"Don Luis Montalvo," she said, gripping his forearm with feigned assurance, "is my first cousin. As I believe you are aware, my maiden name is also Montalvo. Our fathers were brothers."

A dense silence descended on the room.

"And to prove it," he added, forcing himself not to react to the contact with her, "allow me to . . ."

He slowly raised his right hand to his heart, crushing the cloth of his frock coat. The unmistakable sound of crumpled paper could be heard. He slipped his fingers into the inside pocket. The tips brushed against the folded-up documents he had taken from the trunk: the ones Calafat had sent him from Cuba. While the others observed him in bewilderment, he felt their weight. The thickest must be the death and burial certificates: they had to stay where they were. The thinner one, which was no more than a single folded sheet, was the identity document that allowed Runt to travel to the Antilles.

He had been planning to hand over both documents to Soledad as proof of his refusal to get mixed up in her problems. And yet now her anguish had completely undermined his determination. As four pairs of eyes looked on in astonishment, he gently took the document between his thumb and first finger and slowly, very slowly, removed it from its hiding place.

"In order for there to be no uncertainties, and for my identity to be proven beyond all doubt, please read and verify this."

He handed the document straight to the English lawyer. Even though he did not understand a word of what was written on it, the lawyer studied it closely and then showed it to the clerk for him to copy in his flowery handwriting. Don Luis Montalvo Aguilar, born in Jerez de la Frontera, residing in Calle de la Tornería, the son of Don Luis and Doña Piedad . . .

Silence reigned in the room as they all looked on closely. Once the clerk had finished copying the document, the legal representative passed it to the administrator. He folded the paper and returned it to its supposed owner without a word. During all this time, Sol scarcely dared breathe.

"Very well, gentlemen," said the bogus Luis Montalvo. "Now I am entirely at your disposition."

Sol translated his words into English, then invited them all to sit around the table, as though realizing that this part of the conversation could take a long time. "Would you like something to drink?" she asked, pointing to a side table well stocked with liquor, a splendid silver samovar, and sweetmeats. After all the men declined, she served herself a cup of tea.

There ensued a whole series of questions, many of them direct and probing. The lawyer was obviously well prepared. Do you confirm that you met with Mr. Edward Claydon on such and such a day . . . ? Do you affirm that you know . . . ? Are you aware of having signed . . . ? Do you admit having received . . . ? Surreptitiously, hidden among the phrases she translated into Spanish, Sol gave Mauro tiny clues as to what he should reply. As they improvised, an almost organic complicity grew up between the two of them. This was so seamless and convincing it was as if they had spent their whole lives together pulling handkerchiefs out of a top hat.

Mauro fended off the attacks with aplomb while the clerk painstakingly wrote down all his replies with a goose quill pen. *Yes, sir, you are correct. Yes, sir, I ratify that point. You are quite right, sir, that's exactly how it was.* He even allowed himself to embellish his answers with a few minor inventions of his own. *Yes, sir, I remember that day perfectly. How could I not recall that detail? Of course I do.*

There were tense silences between each question. All that could be heard was the scrape of the quill across the sheets of paper and the background noises entering the window from the busy square outside. At one point the administrator served himself a cup of tea from the samovar. Sol left hers practically untouched, while the lawyer, the clerk, and the supposed cousin did not so much as moisten their lips. The questions often concerned Sol as well; she replied with unshakable equanimity, straight-backed, her voice calm, her hands on the table. During the gaps in the questioning, Mauro fixed his attention on them: on the slim wrists emerging from the lace cuffs peeping out from her riding habit; on her tapering fingers adorned with only two rings on the ring finger of her left hand. A superb single diamond ring and a gold band. Her engagement and weddings rings, he guessed. Her wedding to a man to whom on a certain day in the past she had vowed love and loyalty, and whom she was now deceiving by stealing his fortune from him little by little. And he himself was helping her do it.

Almost three hours had gone by before it was all over. Sol Claydon and the fake Luis Montalvo emerged from it unscathed, completely in control after having shown at all times an impenetrable self-assurance. No one could have guessed that they had just walked blindfolded along the edge of a precipice.

The lawyer and his clerk began to gather their papers. Mauro Larrea played with the other man's identity document between his fingers. Standing by one of the windows, the administrator and Sol quietly exchanged a few words in English.

They said good-bye: the older administrator warmly, the younger lawyer with polite coldness. The clerk simply bobbed his head once more. Sol accompanied them to the entrance hall while Mauro remained in the study, trying to recover his composure, as yet unable to get everything into perspective and still less to judge the consequences he could face for what had just taken place. All he saw with any clarity was that Soledad Montalvo had cleverly and systematically been transferring into her cousin's name shares, properties, and assets from her husband's business until he had been practically fleeced.

While the voices of the departing Englishmen could still be heard in the distance, Andrade's far-off howl somehow slipped into his mind. *You've just become the greatest idiot in the universe, compadre. May God forgive you.* In order not to have to respond, Mauro got up, poured himself a glass of brandy from a decanter, and gulped half of it down at once. Just at that moment, Soledad reappeared.

She closed the door and leaned back against it. Then she raised her hands to her mouth, completely covering it to stifle a huge cry of relief. And like that, with the bottom half of her face covered, their eyes were fixed in an endless gaze, until finally he lifted his glass as a tribute to the brilliant performance they had put on.

Eventually she moved away from the door and came toward him.

"I have no words to express how grateful I am."

"I trust that from now on everything will be better."

"Do you know what I would like to do now, if it weren't completely inappropriate?"

To embrace him, burst out laughing, give him one long, endless kiss. Or at least, that is how he interpreted what she was longing to do. In a vain attempt to disguise the rush of warmth surging inside him, he downed the rest of the brandy.

In the end, however, what the deceitful wife of the rich wine merchant did was to repress her desires and behave with moderation. As if copying the name of the vineyard, Soledad Montalvo recovered her temperate disposition and kept her emotions under control.

"I still have a long way to go, Mauro. This was only one battle in the lengthy war against my husband's eldest son. But I would never have won it without you."

CHAPTER THIRTY-FOUR

D ay had dawned no more than half an hour earlier, and Mauro was already finished tying his cravat and was about to don his blue frock coat. Unable to sleep, he had decided to spend the day in Cádiz. He needed to get away, to put some distance between them. To think.

Santos Huesos poked his head around the door.

"There's someone to see you at the entrance, *patrón.*"

"Who?"

"It's better if you come."

What if it were Zarco, the land agent? A stab of anxiety helped spur him on down the stairs.

He was mistaken: it was a couple he did not recognize. Obviously humble and of uncertain age: anywhere between sixty and the end of life. Skinny as rakes, the skin on their faces and hands furrowed by many years of hard work. The woman was wearing rough petticoats and a brown cloth shawl, and had her white hair done up in a bun. The man had on a pair of homespun cotton trousers with a woolen sash around his waist. On seeing Mauro, they both dipped their heads as a mark of respect.

"A good day to you. What may I do for you?"

With strong Andalusian accents, they introduced themselves as former servants at the mansion. They said they had come to pay their respects to the new owner. A tear ran down the old woman's wrinkled cheek as she spoke of the deceased Luisito Montalvo. Then she wiped her nose.

"We're also here to see if we can help the young master in any way."

Larrea guessed they must be referring to him. A "young master" at the age of forty-seven. But on that misty morning he had no desire to laugh.

"Thank you, but the fact is I am here only for a short time; I do not intend to stay any longer than necessary."

"That's no problem: just as we arrived, we can go away again on the breeze whenever you wish. Angustias here is a wonderful cook, and I do whatever I am told to, Your Honor. Our children are off our hands, and it's always good to have something to add to the pot."

Larrea rubbed his chin thoughtfully. It meant more expenditure and less intimacy. But it was true they could do with somebody to wash their clothes and prepare some food other than the hunks of meat Santos Huesos roasted on a fire in a corner of the rear courtyard, as if they were still in the Mexican mountains or in one of the old mining camps. Somebody to see who was coming or looking in from the street, and who could give them a hand to do up this ruin of a house. *You live like a savage,* Sol Claydon had told him. And she wasn't far wrong.

"Well, now, Santos, what do you think?" he said, raising his voice to talk over his shoulder. His servant was nowhere to be seen, but Larrea knew he was somewhere close by, listening like a shadow from some corner or other.

"Well, I suppose we could do with a little bit of help, *patrón.*"

Larrea thought it over for a few more moments.

"All right, you can stay. You'll receive your orders from this man, Santos Huesos Quevedo Calderón," he said, slapping the shoulder of his servant, who had appeared as if by magic. "He'll tell you what there is to be done."

The newcomers—Angustias and Simón—lowered their heads again as a token of gratitude. They glanced out of the corners of their eyes at the Chicimeca Indian. Although they could not appreciate the irony of his literary surnames, they realized this was the first time in their lives that they had ever seen an Indian, observing his long hair, poncho, and ever-ready knife. *And, to top it all,* the husband muttered under his breath, *he is going to give us orders.*

Mauro Larrea walked off toward El Ejido and entered the station from Plaza de la Madre de Dios; he had decided to travel by train. In Mexico, despite many plans and concessions, the railway was not yet a reality. In Cuba it did exist, especially to transport sugar from the plantations in the countryside to the coast, from where it could be shipped to the rest of the world. However, during his brief stay on the island, he had not had occasion to travel in this new invention. As a result, at any other stage of his life, this short voyage of discovery would have filled his mind with ideas as he avidly sniffed out a profitable opportunity to introduce it in the New World. On that morning, though, all he did was observe the comings and goings of the not-very-numerous passengers, and the infinitely greater number of wine barrels being transported from the Jerez cellars to the sea.

Ensconced in a first-class carriage, he reached the port of Trocadero, and from there traveled to the city of Cádiz on a steamship. The railroad was said to be only the third to exist in Spain, and it was five years since it had opened, with its four locomotives hauling freight wagons and passengers. The arrival of this important sign of progress was celebrated in Jerez with a great official act in the station, and a good handful of popular celebrations as well: musical bands in the bullfight arena, cockfights organized in the streets, a performance of Verdi's *Il Trovatore* in the theater, and two thousand loaves of bread distributed to the poor of the town. On that day, even in the prison and the lunatic asylum they had a feast.

The first thing Mauro did when he reached Cádiz was to dispatch his mail. In fits and starts, he had managed to write to Mariana and Andrade. He wrote to his daughter with a knot in his stomach as he recalled that Elvira had lost her life as a result of childbirth. He wished Mariana strength and courage to bring her baby into the world. To his agent, he wrote what as usual were no more than half-truths: *I'm on the brink of a wonderful transaction that will put an end to all our problems, I'll be back soon, we'll pay Tadeo Carrús in time, we'll see Nico married in style, we'll get things back to normal.*

After that, he wandered through the streets of the city: from the quays to the Puerta de la Caleta, from the cathedral to Parque Genovés. All the time he was turning over and over in his mind what he did and did not want to think about: the reckless way in which, egged on by Sol Claydon, he had broken all the most elementary rules of common sense and legality.

He bought writing paper at a printer's in Calle del Sacramento, and ate cuttlefish with potatoes that he was served in a store on the Plazuela del Carbón. He washed it down with two glasses of pale dry wine, sniffing it beforehand in the way he had seen the notary, the doctor, and even Soledad herself do. The sharp smell brought back memories of the deserted, silent Montalvo winery, the creaking sound of the rusty weathervane on the roof of the house of vines out at La Templanza. He recalled the silhouette of a disconcerting woman sitting beside him in an old straw-bottomed chair, staring at an ocean of white earth and tangled vines as she impassively proposed to him the most outlandish of all the extraordinary things that life had thrown at him. *You damned idiot,* he growled to himself as he dropped a few coins on the counter. Then he went outside again and breathed in a lungful of sea air.

The distance he had put between Jerez and Cádiz had been of little use: his mind was still troubled and his questions still went unanswered. Tired of wandering around aimlessly, he made up his mind to return, but first proposed to visit Antonio Fatou in his house on Calle de la Verónica to round off the day by exchanging words with another human being.

"My dear Mauro," his affable young host greeted him as soon as he heard of his arrival, "what a pleasure to see you here with us again. And what a coincidence."

Mauro frowned. A coincidence? Nothing that happened to him of late had been by pure chance. Seeing his reaction, Fatou took it as a query and hastened to offer him an explanation.

"In fact, Genaro told me only a little while ago that someone had been here asking after you. Another lady, apparently." He was about to nod his head knowingly, as if to say *How lucky you are to have so many ladies pursuing you,* but the stern frown on Mauro Larrea's face led him to change his mind.

"The same one who was here before?"

"I haven't the slightest idea. Wait, and we'll find out."

The ancient butler came wearily into the office, racked with coughs as usual.

"Don Antonio says someone came looking for me, Genaro. Tell me about her, please."

"A lady, Don Mauro. She left not an hour ago."

Larrea repeated his question: "The same one as the last time?"

"I don't think so."

"Did she leave her card?"

"She wouldn't hear of it, even though I asked her."

"Did she at least offer her name or say what she wanted with me?"

"Not a word."

"Did you give her my new address?"

"No, sir, because I don't know it and master Antonio was not here."

Lacking any further information, Fatou sent the butler back to his duties, telling him to have two cups of coffee brought. The two men talked briefly about nothing in particular until the miner, calculating the time he would need to take the steamer and then the train back to Jerez, said good-bye.

He had only taken a dozen steps along Calle de la Verónica when he decided to return. This time, however, he did not go into the offices looking for their owner but slipped inside the gate, where he found the person he wanted.

"I forgot to ask you, Genaro . . ." he said, plunging his hand into his frock coat pocket and pulling out a splendid Vueltabajo cigar. "That lady who came asking for me: What was she like, exactly?"

Before the old man could open his mouth, the cigar, from the box that Calafat had given Larrea before he embarked in Havana, was already lying snug in the butler's piqué vest.

"A good-looking woman she was, sir. Elegant and with jet-black hair."

"How did she speak?"

"Differently."

His hacking cough silenced him for a few seconds until finally he was able to add: "For my part, I think she came from the Americas, like you, or somewhere of the sort."

Larrea strode down to the quay intending to cross to Trocadero as soon as possible, but he was too late: he came to a halt, breathing heavily, and with hands on hips watched as a boat sailed off, catching the last of the sunlight. "Goddamned rotten luck," he said, not caring if anybody heard him. It might have been a trick his own fantasy was playing on him, but among the passengers on the deck of the steamer he thought he made out a familiar silhouette seated on a small trunk.

He took the next steamer; by the time he reached Jerez, night had fallen. No sooner were his footsteps resounding in the entrance of the mansion on Calle de la Tornería than he called out gruffly: "Santos!"

"At your orders, *patrón*," replied his servant from some dark corner among the arcades on the first-floor gallery.

"Did we have another visit?"

"Well, I'd be inclined to say we did, Don Mauro."

Finding out his new address would not have been particularly difficult for anyone: after all, his appearance as a returned Indiano fallen from the skies and his link to Luisito Montalvo had made of him the most newsworthy thing to have happened in Jerez in recent days.

"Spit it out, then."

But his servant's answer was not what he had been expecting.

"The fat old man who is in charge of the sale wants to see you tomorrow morning. In the Café de la Paz on Calle Larga. At ten o'clock."

Larrea felt as if he were receiving another blow to the stomach.

"What else did he say?"

"That was all, but I think that maybe he's already found us a buyer."

⁓

By the time Mauro Larrea saw the land agent's bulky body coming toward him, he had already read *El Guadalete* from start to finish, had allowed a painstaking bootblack to shine his shoes, and was on his third coffee of the morning. Once again he had risen at first light, pondering what Amador Zarco might have to say, and unable to dismiss from his mind the worrying image that had persisted ever since the previous evening in Cádiz: the sight of a figure moving away from him on a steamship across the waves of the bay.

"A good day to you, the Lord be praised, Don Mauro." The newcomer immediately dropped his hat onto a nearby chair and sat opposite the miner.

"Pleased to see you," was Larrea's curt response.

"Today seems rather cooler, doesn't it? As the saying goes: from All Souls to Christmas, winter comes to pass. Although, as my poor mother, peace be with her, used to remark, you shouldn't pay too much attention to sayings."

Mauro drummed his fingers on the marble tabletop to convey to the other man to get on with it once and for all. Faced with his obvious impatience, the portly agent no longer beat about the bush.

"I don't want to celebrate too soon, but we may just be in luck and have something interesting in view."

At that precise moment they were interrupted by a young waiter.

"Here's your special coffee, Don Amador."

He placed a bottle alongside the cup.

"God bless you, my boy." The lad had hardly turned away from them when the agent continued: "Some people from Madrid have already half promised to make a big purchase in Sanlúcar. They've been looking around here for a couple of months now."

While he was talking, Zarco took the cork from the bottle and, to Mauro's amazement, poured a splash into his coffee.

"It's brandy, not wine," Zarco pointed out.

Mauro waved his hand impatiently. *You can ruin your coffee however you see fit, my friend. But now do me the favor of getting on with it.*

"I've tempted them with your properties, and they have taken the bait."

"How many of them are there?"

The small porcelain cup was almost hidden between Zarco's pudgy fingers as he raised it to his mouth. He emptied it in one swallow.

"Two of them: one who's putting up the money and the other who is his adviser. In other words, someone who's stinking rich and his secretary," he said, replacing his cup on its saucer. "They haven't the faintest idea about vineyards or wine, but they do know that the market is growing by the day and are willing to invest."

He looked at Mauro appealingly.

"It's not going to be easy, I can tell you that now. They've almost committed themselves to the other agreement, and there's no lack of offers, and so in the remote possibility that your properties should interest them, they're bound to drive a hard bargain. But we lose nothing by trying, don't you think?"

Amador Zarco had nothing more to say, and fell silent because there wasn't much more he knew. His commission was still at 20 percent, and so he was just as eager as Larrea was to make the sale quickly and advantageously.

They left the café together after agreeing to meet again as soon as Zarco found out when the interested parties would reach Jerez. As they were saying their farewells in the doorway, Mauro Larrea spied Santos Huesos among the passersby on Calle Larga.

Seeing him in the distance, this was possibly the first time he realized how incongruous his faithful servant looked in this part of Andalusia, where there was no shortage of dark skins from exposure to the sun or from several centuries of the presence of the Moors. But nobody there had the Mexican Indian's bronze-colored skin, or his dark, shoulder-length hair, or his build. No one dressed like him, either, with a scarf knotted around his head under his hat, and his ever-present brightly colored poncho. He had been with Larrea for fifteen years, ever since he was a lanky, bright youngster who slipped through the galleries of the mines as agilely as a snake.

Larrea finished saying good-bye to the land agent. Momentarily concerned at what news his servant might be bringing, he stood and waited for him to approach.

"What's the problem, Santos?"

"Someone is looking for you."

He took a deep, anxious breath, looking from side to side. The daily bustle of people and the sound of their voices. The house fronts, the orange trees. Jerez.

"A lady you know?"

"Well, yes and no," Santos replied, handing him a small envelope.

On this occasion, perhaps due to haste, it had no seal. Recognizing the handwriting, Mauro tore it open. *I beg you to come to my residence as quickly as possible.* Instead of a signature, two initials: S. C.

Sol Claydon wanted to see him urgently. *What did you expect, you idiot, that your recklessness would have no consequences? That your mistake would go unpunished?* Amid the morning hubbub he could not tell whether the furious voice of recrimination was his agent Andrade's or his own.

"Fine, Santos, I've got the message. But you must remain alert, because we might be getting another visit. If we do, make the person wait in the courtyard—don't let them into the house. And don't take a single chair out; they're to wait, that's all."

With that, he strode off, but paused as he came to the beginning of Calle Lancería. He remembered he had something pending, something that with everything that had been going on in recent days had slipped his mind. And despite Soledad's urgent plea, he decided to resolve it at once. It would take him no time at all, and it was better to get it over and done with to avoid any more serious problems.

He looked around and saw the half-open door of a narrow apartment building. He peered inside: no one in sight. For the time it would take him, this would do. He stopped a young boy, pointed out the notary Don Senén Blanco's office, and gave him a coin and instructions. Three minutes later Angulo, the gossipy clerk who had first taken him to the mansion on Calle de la Tornería, still wearing his percaline cuffs, stepped curiously into the dark entrance where Mauro was waiting for him.

It was Sol herself who, without realizing it, had put Mauro on guard. It was from the notary's office that the news had leaked out that he had taken over the Montalvo family's properties without any money being involved, and that there was something not entirely transparent about the transaction. Mauro knew Don Senén Blanco was the sort of honest man who was no blabbermouth. This led him to suspect the source that everything came from. And that was why he was now about to act.

First he pushed the clerk up against the tiles in the doorway, and then came the warning.

"If you breathe another word about me or my affairs, the next time I'll split you in two."

He grasped him by the neck and at once all the blood in the poor devil's body rushed to his face.

"Is that clear, you louse?"

When the only reply was a stifled gurgle, Mauro banged his head against the wall and squeezed his throat even tighter.

"Are you sure you understood?"

A trail of saliva emerged from the clerk's terrified mouth, and a faint squeak that seemed to say "Yes."

"All right, let's make sure we don't need to meet again."

He left the clerk with his body slumped as if he was about to collapse to the ground, braying like a donkey. Before he had time to react, Mauro was out in the street, adjusting his shirt cuffs and winking at the astonished young boy.

This time there was no need for Palmer to open the door: Soledad was waiting for him. He again experienced the same indescribable sensation that made his skin tingle ever since he had first met her. She was wearing a cherry-colored dress; her harmonious features were once more clouded by worry.

"I'm truly sorry for disturbing you again, Mauro, but I think we have another problem."

Another problem, she said. Not the same one as two days earlier, prolonged, multiplied, entangled, or resolved. Another, different problem. And she had said *we have.* In the plural. As if it was no longer a problem of hers that she needed help with but something linked from the outset to them both.

Without another word, she shepherded him toward the reception room where he had waited for her on the first evening.

"Go in, please."

The sofa that had on that occasion been empty was now occupied. By a woman. Lying stretched out, with two cushions under her head, and a face as pale as wax. Her black hair hanging loose, dressed entirely in black, and with a plunging neckline that a skinny young mulatta was constantly fanning.

He heard a murmur behind him.

"You know who she is, don't you?"

He answered without turning: "I'm very much afraid I do."

"She arrived only an hour ago. She is unwell. I've sent for Manuel Ysasi."

"Did she say anything?"

"She only managed to mutter that she was the wife of my cousin Gustavo. Everything else was incomprehensible."

The two of them continued to stare at the ottoman. He was a step in front, with Sol Claydon behind him, whispering in his ear.

"She also mentioned your name. Several times."

His alarm mingled with the agitation he felt at sensing the warmth emanating from her and her voice so close to him.

"She mentioned my name—and what else?"

"Disconnected phrases, words here and there. Everything jumbled up, not making sense. As far as I could understand, something about a wager."

CHAPTER THIRTY-FIVE

⁂

D r. Ysasi took her pulse, pressed her stomach, and placed two fingers on the side of her neck. Then he examined her mouth and the pupils of her eyes.

"Nothing to worry about. She is dehydrated and exhausted: common symptoms following a long sea voyage."

Taking a vial of laudanum out of his bag, he asked them to prepare a drink of squeezed lemon with three teaspoons of sugar. Next he turned his attention to the young slave, following the same procedure. He had told them to close the thick curtains, and the room was enveloped in a gloom that contrasted strongly with the morning sunlight flooding the square outside. The miner and their hostess watched the doctor going about his business from a distance, both of them still standing, a preoccupied expression on their faces.

"She only needs to rest," the doctor concluded.

Mauro Larrea turned toward Soledad and whispered in her ear: "We have to get her out of here."

She nodded her head slowly in agreement.

"I suppose all this has to do with Luis's inheritance."

"Undoubtedly. And that doesn't suit either of us."

"Done," announced the doctor, unaware of the conversation going on between them. "It would be best not to move her for now; let her rest on the sofa. And as for this little one," he added, pointing to the young slave, "give her something to eat. She's famished."

Soledad rang a little bell, and one of the maids appeared. She was English, like all the domestic servants. After giving her the relevant orders, Soledad sent her off to the kitchen with the mulatta in her charge.

"Unfortunately, Edward is still not here, and I would prefer not to remain on my own with her. Would it be too much trouble for you two to stay to lunch with me?"

The most sensible thing, thought Mauro Larrea, would be to leave on the spot and give himself time to think what to do next. Although she was now resting calmly, he was sure that Zayas's spouse had disembarked in Spain at the eye of a menacing tropical storm: he was only too well aware what she was capable of. She would let her tongue run away with her to anyone willing to listen, twist what had happened, make public the extravagant way in which the Jerez properties had slipped through her husband's fingers. She was even capable of attempting some legal means to lay her claim to the goods won in the wager. And even though without a doubt nothing would return to Zayas, because the law would end up supporting Mauro, she would achieve something the miner could not tolerate: get him tangled up in lawsuits and disputes, delay his plans, and thwart his most urgent intentions. Time was racing against him: he had already used up two of the four months he had agreed to with Tadeo Carrús. He had to find a way to frustrate this Mexican woman's intentions. To neutralize her.

He glanced at Soledad as she was gazing at the crumpled figure on the sofa, an expression of concern on her face. If Zayas's wife began to move her pieces, he would not be the only one compromised: if she started investigating what had happened to Luis Montalvo's properties, Soledad would be dragged down as well.

"I willingly accept your invitation, dear Sol," Dr. Ysasi proclaimed as he was gathering his equipment and putting it away in his bag. "I'm far more attracted by the skills of your cook than by those of my old Sagrario, who rarely ventures beyond her habitual stews. First, though, allow me to wash my hands."

Despite the fact that warning voices were colliding inside his head, Mauro Larrea's mouth betrayed him: "I'll join you, too."

The doctor left the room, leaving the pair of them enveloped in the strange midday light blocked by the heavy velvet curtains. They stood there both contemplating the supine body of the newcomer. Several moments of apparent calm went by, during which one could almost hear their brains whirring as they sifted information and pieced it together.

She was the first to speak.

"Why is she so anxious to find you?"

He knew there was no point in continuing to lie.

"Probably because she does not agree with the manner in which Gustavo Zayas and I settled on the transfer of his cousin Luisito's properties."

"And is there in fact any reason for her to be dissatisfied?"

He also knew he would have to explain things fully.

"That depends on whether someone can accept that her husband wagered his inheritance on a game of billiards."

❧

The dishes and wines were excellent yet again, the china splendid, the glasses equally fine. But the cordial atmosphere of the first evening had entirely evaporated.

Even though he knew he did not have to justify himself to anyone, Mauro kept to his decision to be sincere this once at least. After all, Soledad had already confided her underhanded maneuvers to him. And the good doctor would not harm him in any way.

"Look, I'm no gambler or unscrupulous opportunist but simply someone dedicated to his own affairs who suddenly found everything had gone wrong. And while I was trying to reestablish myself, without any effort from me, I was presented with a situation that ended up greatly in my favor. And the person who created that situation was Carola Gorostiza, who obliged her husband to act."

Neither Manuel Ysasi nor Soledad asked him any other direct question, but their curiosity floated silently in the air like the wings of some majestic bird.

Mauro hesitated over how much to say, how much to keep quiet, how far he should go. It was all too confused, too unlikely. The money Ernesto Gorostiza sent to his sister, his desperate search in Havana for a good business deal, the refrigerated ship, the shameful matter of the slave trafficking. It was all too murky for them to be able to digest over their luncheon. He decided to sum up everything as concisely as possible.

"She led her husband to believe she had a romantic liaison with me."

Soledad's fish knife remained hovering in the air above the sea bass on her plate.

"As a result, he challenged me," Mauro continued. "To a kind of reckless duel on a green baize table with wooden cues and ivory balls."

"So now she's come to call you to account, or to try to invalidate what you won."

"I imagine so. And even knowing her the way I believe I do, it wouldn't surprise me if she also wants to discover if Luisito Montalvo owned anything more. After all, he made Gustavo his only heir in a perfectly legal fashion."

"In that, at least, she'll come away empty-handed, because poor Little Runt didn't have a penny left to his name."

Hearing the doctor affirm this, both Mauro Larrea and Soledad raised their forks to their mouths, looked down at the same time, and together chewed on mouthfuls of fish more slowly than necessary. It was as if, together with the white, tender flesh of the sea bass, they also wished to masticate their unease. In the end, she was the one to speak.

"In fact, Manuel, it may well be that Luisito, without being aware of it, did own more than he thought."

When she went on to give him brief details of the astounding things she had done, the doctor's jaw dropped. Concealment, counterfeit signatures, illicit ruses. Not to mention the indispensable part Mauro Larrea had played in a sublime impersonation of Luis Montalvo for the benefit of an English lawyer.

"The devil take you, I don't know which of you is being more reckless: the miner who makes off with someone else's fortune thanks to a crazy wager, or the faithful, distinguished spouse who has stripped her own family business bare."

"There are things that go beyond what we judge we can control," said Sol, finally raising her calm eyes. "Situations that push one to the end of our tether. I'd have been only too happy to continue with my comfortable life in London with my four lovely daughters, my affairs under control, and my busy social life. I would never have thought of committing the slightest fault had Edward's son Alan not decided to attack us."

However disconcerting this affirmation, neither of the men dared interrupt her.

"He tricked his father into making him a partner in the business behind my back. He made absolutely disastrous decisions without consulting him, deceived him, and prepared the way once and for all for my daughters and me to be left in an extremely weak position the day that Edward was no longer there."

This time it was not wine she raised to her lips but a large glass of water, perhaps to help dilute the mixture of anger and sadness that had inflamed her face.

"My husband has very serious problems, Mauro. The fact that nobody has seen him since we moved here is not due to unavoidable business trips or inconvenient headaches; those are nothing but excuses I am careful to spread. Unfortunately, it is something far more complicated. And as long as he is in no fit condition to take measures that will ward off the attacks his eldest son is making against the 'little southern Gypsies,' as he scornfully calls my daughters and me, the responsibility for protecting us lies in my hands. And so I had no other choice than to act."

"But, for heaven's sake, you didn't have to break the law in the way you did, Sol . . ." said Ysasi.

"I took the only course open to me, dear Doctor. I destroyed the business from within—in the only way I knew."

A loud bang brought their conversation to an abrupt close. It was as though something heavy had fallen to the floor or hit a wall somewhere in the house. The glasses on the table trembled slightly, and the glass droplets on the chandelier banged against each other, producing a gentle tinkling sound. Soledad and Mauro made to stand up at once, but Dr. Ysasi restrained them.

"I'll see to it."

He strode swiftly out of the dining room.

It could have been Carola Gorostiza, thought Mauro; perhaps she had fallen trying to get up. Or possibly it was only a problem with the servants: perhaps a maid had stumbled. Sol tried to make light of it.

"Don't worry, I'm sure it was nothing."

Placing her knife and fork on her plate, she gave him a devastated look.

"Everything is getting out of hand; it's all getting worse and worse . . ."

Mauro searched in his mind but could think of no adequate reply.

"Don't you find there are days when you want the world to stop, Mauro? For it to stop spinning and give us some respite? To leave us immobile as statues, like mere posts in the ground, so that we wouldn't have to think, or decide, or sort things out? So that the wolves would stop baring their fangs at us?"

Of course there were days like that in his life. Loads of them in recent times. To look no further, at that precise moment he would have given all he had once possessed to continue sharing this lunch with her for all eternity. Seated on his left, the two of them alone in this dining room with its chinoiserie wallpaper, contemplating her harmonious face with the high cheekbones, the way her collarbones were framed by her dress. He resisted the temptation to stretch out his arm and seize her hand as he had done the first day they had met, then grasp it firmly and tell her not to worry, that he was at her side, that everything would soon be over, and in a good way. Asking himself why, at his age and with all his experience, just when he thought nothing more would ever surprise him, he suddenly felt this vertigo.

Since it was impossible for him to share these sensations with her, he set off on a different tack.

"Did you hear anything more from the English lawyer?"

"Only that he is in Gibraltar. For the moment he hasn't returned to London."

"Is that a worry?"

"I've no idea," she admitted. "I really don't know. Possibly not: it could be has hasn't been able to find a passage on any P&O steamer heading for Southampton, or perhaps he has other business apart from mine that is keeping him here."

"Or . . . ?"

"Or he could be waiting for someone."

"Your husband's son, for example?"

"I don't know that, either. I only wish I did, and could confirm to you that everything is progressing as it should be, and that our farce has succeeded. The fact is, though, that with every day that goes by, my doubts only grow."

"Let's wait and see," he said without conviction. "Right now we have to face another problem."

The roast pullet they had been served after the sea bass had grown cold on their plates. They had both lost their appetite, but not the need to carry on talking.

"Do you think Gustavo could have agreed to his wife's mad decision to come here on her own from Cuba?"

"I doubt it. She might even have arranged it so that he knew nothing. She probably invented something: a trip to Mexico, or heaven knows what."

He sensed that she wanted to ask him something but did not know how to put it into words. She raised her glass to her lips, as if to give herself strength.

"Tell me, Mauro, what state was my cousin in?"

"Personally, or in his business affairs?"

She hesitated. Took another sip of wine.

"Both."

Mauro Larrea observed how cold Soledad seemed toward Zayas, and the controlled distance she kept at any mention of his name. This time, however, he assumed she wanted to know about his personal feelings.

"Believe me if I tell you I hardly had anything to do with him, but my impression was that he was leagues away from being even moderately happy."

The servants cleared away the dishes they had barely touched, served dessert, and withdrew.

"And you must also believe me when I say that there was never any romantic relationship between Carola Gorostiza and myself."

She dipped her chin slightly in acknowledgment.

"Although it is true that we do have another kind of relationship."

"My goodness," she murmured. From her tone, it was plain that this admission did not exactly please her, but she concealed her feelings behind a spoonful of crème brûlée.

"Her brother is a friend of mine in Mexico and will soon become someone close to my family. His daughter is about to be wed to my son, Nicolás."

"My goodness," she repeated, this time less sourly.

"That is how I met her when I arrived in Havana: her brother Ernesto entrusted me with some money for her. That was why I contacted her, and everything else followed from that."

"And what is this lady like when she hasn't taken it into her head to collapse?"

Sol appeared to have recovered some of the sparkle in her doe's eyes, and a touch of the subtle irony that usually guided her conversation.

"Arrogant. Haughty. Cold. Impudent. And I can think of a few other adjectives that I will keep to myself out of politeness."

"Do you know she spent these last years writing to Luisito, insisting time and again that he cross the ocean and visit them? She described the splendid life they had in Havana, the great coffee plantation they owned, the immense satisfaction Gustavo would feel on seeing him again after so many years, and how often she had imagined what their beloved Spanish cousin would be like. She even seemed, if you'll forgive my being rude, to be leading him on. Gustavo probably never told his wife about poor Little Runt's physical limitations."

"Don't worry about being rude; I'm convinced you're not mistaken. But how do you know about all this?"

"From the letters signed by her that I keep in my writing desk drawer. I took them from Luisito's house with the rest of his personal belongings before you moved in."

So it was Carola Gorostiza who dragged Luis Montalvo to Cuba, knowing full well he was a bachelor who owned several properties but had no descendants and was a blood relative of her husband. And doubtless that was why she schemed, persevered, and did not give up until she had him draw up a new will that cut out his nieces and left his first cousin Gustavo as his only heir, even though he had not seen or heard from him for two decades. Clever Carola Gorostiza. Clever and tenacious.

They were interrupted when the doctor came back in.

"Everything is as it should be," he said, taking his seat.

Soledad closed her eyes for a moment and nodded, comprehending what Manuel Ysasi meant without any need for words. Mauro Larrea looked at both of them in turn. All of a sudden the trust he had gained during the lunch and previous days seemed to crumble as he felt he was left out of their complicity. *What are they hiding from me? What do they want to keep me away from? What is going on with your husband, Soledad? Why are you so distant from Gustavo? And what on earth am I doing in the midst of you all?*

Oblivious to what the miner was thinking, the doctor resumed his meal and the conversation. There was nothing Mauro could do but defer his suspicions.

"I've looked in on our lady friend and given her a generous dose of chloral hydrate so that she stays sedated. She won't wake for several hours now, but even so, I think you need to consider what you intend to do with her."

Throw her to the bottom of an abandoned mine, the miner would have liked to tell him.

"Send her back where she came from" was what he in fact said. "How long do you think it will be until she is in a fit state to undertake the return journey?"

"I don't think it will take her long to recover."

"However that may be, the crucial thing right now is to get her out of this house and keep her out of circulation."

Silence spread over the dining room table as the three of them pondered a solution. Sending her on her own to Cádiz to wait for a ship would be too risky. Keeping her in the ruinous mansion on Calle de la Tornería was out of the question. Lodging her in some public hostelry was even more unthinkable.

Until Sol Claydon came up with her proposal, a suggestion that crashed like a stone thrown at a windowpane.

CHAPTER THIRTY-SIX

❧

They debated the pros and cons over cups of black coffee in the library.

"I don't think you realize what a huge blunder you're making."

"Do we have any other choice?"

"What about trying to talk to her calmly, to get her to consider what she's doing?"

"And tell her what?" Sol broke in exasperatedly. "Are we to sweet-talk her so that she is kind enough to go back to Havana and get out of our way? Persuade her gently that she should leave us in peace?"

Leaping from her seat like an enraged cat, she took four or five aimless steps and then turned to face the two men once more.

"Or shall we tell her that in the name of Luis Montalvo, just waiting to be inherited by her and Gustavo as soon as they carry out the necessary steps, there are stocks and shares worth several hundred thousand pounds sterling? What if we also reveal to her that this money belongs to my family, saved from the clutches of my daughters' stepbrother thanks to my murkiest, most despicable machinations?"

Her cheeks were flushed, her eyes flashing. She took another few steps, her long skirt brushing the flowery arabesques of the carpet, until she was standing next to the armchair where Mauro Larrea was seated with his legs crossed, observing her.

"Or shall we tell her that this gentleman here is so fine and generous that he will forgive her husband his considerable gambling debts so that she can enjoy her fleeting visit to the mother country? That he is going to return for nothing the properties that that idiotic, cowardly, and irresponsible cousin of mine chose to wager on a night of billiards?"

Consciously or not, voluntarily or involuntarily, to emphasize her words she had rested her right hand on Mauro's shoulder. Far from withdrawing it as her indignation grew, when she was asking the second question full of disdain for Zayas her fingers only dug more deeply into it, almost passing through the cloth of his frock coat close to his neck, sending an irrepressible surge of desire shooting though the miner's insides.

"Besides, Manuel, it's Gustavo we're talking about. Our dearly beloved Gustavo. Don't forget that."

Even with Sol clutching his shoulder, and his unexpected reaction that shook him body and soul, he was aware of the bitter sarcasm in this last remark. "Our dearly beloved Gustavo," she had said. And in her words, as was the case whenever that cousin was mentioned, there was not the slightest trace of warmth.

Manuel Ysasi responded resignedly.

"Well, in that case, and even though I'm still convinced that keeping her against her will is a huge mistake, I suppose you leave me no other option."

"Does that mean you agree to have her in your house?"

She lifted her hand from Mauro's shoulder to gesture toward the doctor. He felt suddenly bereft.

"I hope you both understand that if this affair ever gets out in Jerez, I risk losing most of my patients. And I don't have a prosperous wine business or silver mines to fall back on; I live from my work, and then only when I manage to get paid."

"Don't be such a pessimist, Manuel, my dear," Sol said with a hint of mischief. "We're not going to abduct anybody. We're merely going to offer a few days' free hospitality to a not-entirely-welcome guest."

"And I'll personally make sure I take her to Cádiz and put her on board ship just as soon as you decide she is well enough to travel," Mauro concluded. "In fact, I'll try to find out promptly what day the next steamer for the Antilles is leaving."

Ysasi brought the conversation to a close with dark irony.

"I stopped believing in the intervention of a wonderful supreme being in our humble earthly affairs a long time ago, but may God have mercy on us if anything goes wrong with this crazy plan."

~

They installed her in the doctor's residence on Calle Francos, in the old house he had inherited from his father, who in turn had inherited it from his grandfather. Ysasi lived there surrounded by the same furniture and the same maidservant who had served his family for three generations. They chose a bedroom at the back, overlooking a yard for animals, with a narrow window that was conveniently far from any neighboring dwelling. They put the slave Trinidad in the adjoining room so that she could attend to all Doña Carola's needs. Soledad gave instructions to Sagrario, the aged maid. Chicken broth and omelets, lamb sweetbreads, lots of jugs of fresh water, frequent changes of her sheets and chamber pots, and a categorical rejection of any attempt she made to leave.

Santos Huesos took charge of the key and stood guard at the end of the corridor.

"What if she causes trouble, *patrón*, and the doctor isn't here?"

"Send the old woman to look for me."

Then he gestured briefly toward the Indian's right hip: the place where he always kept his knife. After waiting for the others to return to the lower floor, he made himself clear:

"If she goes too far, calm her down. Just a little."

As soon as everything was settled, Sol announced she would be on her way. Doubtless she was needed for her husband's complex problems, the ones Mauro was still in the dark about. Or perhaps she simply had no strength left to continue the fight.

Sagrario, the age-weary maid, appeared, dragging her feet and limping slightly. She brought Sol's cloak, her gloves, and the elegant hat with ostrich feathers: an outfit better suited to the sophisticated streets of the West End of London than for crossing the narrow streets of Jerez in the middle of the night.

Her carriage was waiting outside, and Mauro accompanied her to the front entrance.

"So you will find out about the next sailings for Cuba?"

"It will be the first thing I do tomorrow morning."

There was hardly any light in the strip between the house and the street; the weak light of a candle distorted their features.

"Let's hope that it all comes to an end soon," she said, slipping on her gloves. Just to say something, without making any great effort to show she was convinced it would.

That it all would come to an end soon. Everything: a huge, bottomless sack that could fit a thousand of their own and other people's problems. They would need more than their fair share of good fortune for all these to be tossed into the air and come out intact.

"We'll do our best to make sure it does." And then, to disguise the lack of conviction he also felt, he added: "Do you know that this very morning I learned that there could be some possible buyers for your family's properties?"

"You don't say."

Impossible for her to convey any less enthusiasm.

"People from Madrid. They've almost agreed on a purchase elsewhere, but are willing to consider my offer as well."

"Especially if you're offering an advantageous price."

"I fear I may have no other choice."

Standing in the semidarkness with her back to the Triana tiles of Ysasi's old family house, her hat and gloves already arranged, and the cloak around her fine shoulders, she gave him a tired half smile.

"You're in a hurry to get back to Mexico, aren't you?"

"I'm afraid so."

"You have your home awaiting you, your children and friends . . . and possibly a woman, too."

He could just as easily have replied yes as no, and neither would have been a lie. *Yes, of course: my splendid colonial palace on Calle San Felipe Neri awaits me, as does my lovely daughter, Mariana, by now a young mother; and of course my young pup, Nicolás, on the verge of becoming linked to the highest society in Mexico as soon as he returns from Paris; so, too, do my many powerful and prosperous friends, and more than one beautiful woman who has always shown herself willing to share her bed and her heart with me.* Or: *No, of course not* could also have been his answer. *Actually, there is very little awaiting me back there. The deeds to my house are in the hands of a usurer who is choking the life out of me with his inflexible time limits. My daughter has her own life, and my son is a dunderhead who will end up doing whatever suits him. I have gagged my friend Andrade, who is my brother and my conscience, so that he can't shout at me for being such a half-wit. And as for women, not one of those who has passed through my life at some point or other ever succeeded in attracting, moving, or perturbing me one percent, Soledad Montalvo, as much—ever since that cloudy midday in your family's dilapidated mansion—as you have attracted, moved, and perturbed me.*

What he finally said was a lot less detailed and emotional, far more neutral: "That is where I ought to be."

"Are you sure?"

He looked at her in confusion, knitting his thick eyebrows.

"Life sweeps us along, Mauro. It took hold of me when I was young and dropped me in a huge, cold city, to live in an alien world. Twenty years later, when I had already adapted to that universe, circumstances have brought me back here. Unforeseen winds sometimes chart the paths we take, and at other times our return journey. Often it is not worth fighting against them."

Raising a gloved hand, she pressed it to his lips to prevent him from contradicting her.

CHAPTER THIRTY-SEVEN

⁓

A clinking of glasses and bottles; the hubbub of relaxed voices and the strumming of a guitar. About a dozen and a half men and only three women. Three Gypsies. One of them, very young and skinny, was absorbed in rolling cigarettes, while a second, livelier-looking girl was allowing an elegant gentleman to flirt with her, though without any great interest. The third, with half-closed eyes and a face as wrinkled as a Malaga raisin, seemed to be dozing as she leaned back against the wall.

Almost nobody there was as well dressed or as refined as the doctor and Mauro Larrea, but the arrival of the two men in the bar in the San Miguel district did not seem to surprise the other clients. Quite the opposite: several called out "A good evening to you" as the two crossed the threshold. *God grant us a good night, Doctor and friend. A pleasure to see you here again, Don Manué.*

After a frugal meal at the doctor's bachelor residence, they had checked that Carola Gorostiza was still asleep, that the young mulatta was resting next door, and that Santos Huesos was at the ready in the passageway for what he hoped would be a calm night. Reassured that nothing untoward would happen until the next morning at least, Manuel Ysasi suggested they go out to get some fresh air.

"Did you read my mind, Doctor?"

"You're already acquainted with where high society entertains itself. What would you say to me taking you to see the other Jerez?"

That was how they had ended up in this tavern on Plaza de la Cruz Vieja, in a district that in the distant past had been a neighborhood outside the walls but now formed part of the south of the city.

They sat at one of the empty tables on benches that had been dragged into the area lit by oil lamps. Behind the nearby counter was a wide shelf filled with bottles and casks of wine. A serious-looking youth less than twenty years old was drying dishes silently while casting melancholy glances at the young, skinny Gypsy girl. She meanwhile went on rolling cigarettes without once raising her eyes from her task.

The youth, evidently the bar owner's son, came over, quickly bringing two narrow glasses filled with an amber-colored liquid; they had not needed to order.

"How is your father, my lad?"

"Huh, so-so. He can't seem to get better."

"Tell him to come and see me on Monday. And to carry on with the mustard poultices and inhale from a bowl with pine needles in it."

"Whatever you say, Don Manuel."

The boy had scarcely left their table when a young man with bushy sideburns and dark eyes came up to their table.

"Two more noggins for the doctor and his companion, Tomás. Today I've got the coin to pay."

"Forget it, Raimundo, forget it . . ." the doctor protested.

"What d'you mean, Don Manué, with all I owe you?"

The stranger turned to Mauro.

"I owe my boy's life to this man, my friend, if you didn't know it. Yes, he saved the life of my kid, he did. He was sick, very sick . . ."

At that instant, a woman wearing rope sandals and wrapped in a coarse cotton shawl rushed into the bar. Peering anxiously left and right, she finally discovered the person she was looking for. She reached them in three hasty strides.

"Oh, Don Manué, Don Manué . . . Come to my house a moment to see my Ambrosio, for the love of God, no more than a moment, I swear . . ." she insisted in a panic. "My neighbor just told me she saw you heading this way so I've come looking for you, Doctor; he's dying on me. He seemed fine this afternoon, quiet as could be, when something came over him . . ." She sank her clawlike fingers into the doctor's hand and pulled. "Come and take a look for a moment, Don Manué, for the love of God, he's just across the way from here, right next to the church . . ."

"It was a bad idea bringing you here, Mauro," the doctor growled, freeing his hand. "Will you excuse me for a quarter of an hour?"

He hardly had time to say "Of course" before Manuel Ysasi was wrapping his cloak around his shoulders and following the agitated woman to the door. After placing two more glasses of wine on their table, the bar owner's son returned to his task, still casting forlorn glances at the young Gypsy girl. The man with the bushy sideburns returned to the group at the back of the room, where one person was still strumming a guitar, another was clapping his hands, while a third began softly launching into a song about ill-fated love.

Mauro was almost glad to be left alone to enjoy the wine without having to talk to anyone. No need to pretend or lie.

The respite did not last long.

"I hear you've taken over Little Runt's house."

He was so caught up in holding up the glass and contemplating the mahogany-colored wine as it swirled around the glass that he had not seen the old Gypsy woman approach carrying a straw-bottomed chair. Without asking or waiting for permission, she sat down at the table diagonally opposite him. From close up she appeared even more ancient, as though her face were a piece of leather scored with a knife.

She had thin, oily hair drawn back in a small chignon. From her ears dangled a long pair of gold and coral earrings that pulled her earlobes down to her jawline.

"And that Don Luisito has croaked. That's what I've been told, may God take him to His bosom. Even though he was so small, he used to like having a good time, although lately he didn't seem in the mood for it. He used to come down this way a lot. Sometimes on his own, or with friends, or with Don Matí. He was a good man, Little Runt was, one of the best," she said solemnly. And, to emphasize her words, she made a cross with a bony thumb on an equally grimy and twisted forefinger, and kissed it with a sound like a cupping glass.

Mauro found it hard to follow her: she had no teeth, spoke in a hoarse voice, and used expressions he had never heard in Mexico.

"Will you buy me a drink, kind sir, and I'll read from your palm what is going to happen with your wealth and your future?"

At any other time he would have shooed the woman away without a second thought. *Leave me in peace, get away. Please, go,* he would have said. Or possibly even without the *please.* That was what he had very often done in Mexico with those beggars who offered to read the secrets of his soul in exchange for a penny, and with the women who stopped him on the streets of Havana with cigars in their mouths, determined to tell his fortune in coconuts or shells.

But perhaps the fault that night lay with the strong, mellow sherry that was already warming his insides, or the day full of shocks he had just had, or the confused sensations that had recently been tearing at his body with the fury of fighting cocks. Whatever the case, this time he accepted. "Go on, then," he said, holding out his hand toward her. "Let's see what you can see in my blasted future."

"My, what an incredible hand this is, my child. You've got more scratches on it than a day laborer after the wine harvest. It's going to be very hard to read your fortune there."

"So leave it, then." He immediately regretted having given way to such a stupid idea.

"No, sir, no. Even if they're hidden by many scars, I can see many things here . . ."

"All right, go on."

From the back of the room could still be heard a quiet clapping of hands, the guitar, and a voice following the flamenco rhythm with verses complaining of love's betrayals and revenge.

"I can see you have known many things in life that were cut in half."

She was not wrong there. The father he never knew, a trader passing through his village who didn't even bequeath him his name. Abandoned by his own mother when he was still very young, left in the care of a grandfather, a man of few words and emotions who always missed his Basque country homeland and never got used to the dry Castilian plains. His marriage to Elvira, the flight to the Americas, his eventual ruin—all of these at some moment or other had been crucial breaks in his life. There was little continuity: the Gypsy woman was on the right track. Although that was not so different, he imagined, from the fate of a lot of human beings with the same number of years behind them. The old trickster had probably repeated the same phrase hundreds of times.

"I also see there is something you have your hands on now, and if you aren't careful, you'll lose that, too."

What if she means that the Montalvo mansion and the other properties will slip through my fingers? he imagined. *And what if that break was thanks to a sizable quantity of gold ounces?*

"And is it also written that this thing I have my hands on is going to be taken from me by some gentlemen from Madrid?" he asked somewhat disdainfully, thinking of the possible purchasers.

"That an old woman like me cannot know, my love. I can only say you need to use your noodle wisely," she said, raising a crooked finger to her temple, "because as I see here, possibly you're going to have doubts. And you know how the saying goes in Andalusia: a sardine that the cat takes away won't return to your dish someday."

Mauro almost burst out laughing at this sublime piece of reasoning.

"Very good, old woman. Now I can see my future as clear as day," he said, trying to bring this fortune-telling session to a close.

"Just one moment, good sir, one moment. There's something here that's glowing hot. But for that I'll first need to wet my whistle. Come on, Tomás, my boy, give your grandmother here a glass of your best brew. On this gentleman, isn't that right?"

She didn't even wait for the youth to place the glass on the table but grabbed it from him and gulped it down. Then she lowered her voice and spoke seriously and soberly.

"A spider has you in its web, fine sir."

"I don't understand you."

"You're crazy about a female. But as you well know, she isn't free."

Mauro frowned but said nothing. Nothing.

"You see?" she said, running her scabbed finger across his outstretched palm. "It says so clearly here. Here, between these three lines, is the triangle. And before long, someone is going to leave it. By fire or by water, I see someone departing."

That's only too obvious, you old witch, he was about to mutter as he pulled his hand violently away with a mixture of irritation and puzzlement. For days now in his mind's eye he had seen himself on board a ship heading for Veracruz; he had no need of being reminded of it. With the Atlantic spray and breeze on his face, watching from the deck of a steamship as the white, luminous outline of Cádiz grew smaller and smaller in the distance until it was no more than a dot beyond the waves. Leaving behind this ancient Spain, this Jerez that had led him in such an unexpected way to relive sensations buried deep in his memory. Starting out again on the return journey: returning to his world, his life. Alone, as always. Returning to a world where nothing now would ever be the same.

"And there's one last thing I want to tell you, sir. Just one little thing I can see right here . . ."

At that moment the door to the tavern flew open and Ysasi reentered.

"Well, now, Rosario, what's going on here? I'm only away for ten minutes or so and here you are bamboozling my friend with your nonsense. Tomás, your father's going to give you a good thrashing when he gets over his whooping cough and discovers you've been allowing this old Gypsy woman in here night after night. C'mon, you old crone, leave us in peace and be off to bed with you. And take your granddaughters with you; this is no time of night for the three of you to be lounging about here."

The old woman obeyed without a word of protest; there were few with more authority among these people than the black-bearded doctor who out of pure altruism attended to all their aches and pains.

"I'm truly sorry I had to abandon you."

Mauro waved away the apology as if he were also trying to dismiss the echo of the Gypsy's voice. They immediately returned to their wine and their conversation. Another two glasses and talk of this San Miguel district and those around it. The Gorostiza woman's convalescence; *Another two, please, Tomás.* And, finally, where everything led. Soledad.

"You may think, quite rightly, that I'm butting in where I'm not wanted, but there's something I need to know to complete the picture of all the pieces that are floating around in my head."

"For good or ill, Mauro, you're already up to your neck in the lives of the Montalvos and their dependents. So ask away."

"What exactly is going on with her husband?"

The doctor took a deep breath, puffing out his cheeks in a way that lent his angular face a very different expression. Then he blew out the air, taking the time he needed to order what he wanted to say.

"At first it was thought that what he had was nothing more than fits of melancholy: the illness that lodges in the mind and lashes out in a way that paralyzes the will. Bouts of sadness, bursts of baseless anguish that lead to dejection and despair."

So that was what it was all about: imbalances of the mind and temperament. The miner was beginning to understand. And to put two and two together.

"So that's why she says that his own son betrayed him, taking advantage of his weakness to act in the family business against the interests of Soledad and her daughters," Mauro noted.

"I suppose so. Of course, in a normal situation I am absolutely convinced Edward would never have acted in any way that could harm them." He smiled with a hint of nostalgia. "I've rarely seen a man so devoted to his wife as he used to be."

By now the tavern was full to the rafters. A second guitar had joined the earlier quiet one, and they were both being played with more enthusiasm. The subdued songs they had heard on their arrival had given way to a riotous mixture of hands clapping, guitars, voices, and stamping feet that made the whole tavern shake.

"I can remember him on the day of the wedding," Ysasi continued unperturbed, completely accustomed to all the noise, "with that aristocratic Norman air he used to have. Always so tall, so fair, so straight-backed. Suddenly there he was in the La Colegiata church, his usual elegance redoubled, receiving congratulations and awaiting the arrival of our Sol."

If Mauro Larrea had known what jealousy was, if he had ever felt it in his bones, he would have immediately recognized the feeling from the stab of some blind pain that passed through him as he imagined a radiant Soledad Montalvo saying *I do, for richer or poorer, in sickness and in health,* at the high altar. *Idiot,* his conscience whispered to him, *you're turning into a sentimental imbecile.* And he could sense his agent Andrade laughing out loud at him on the other side of the ocean.

"The fact was that on that sunny morning in early October no one could have suspected that scarcely two days later the grandson Matías, Luisito's older brother, would die, and everything would begin to fall apart."

"And did no one care that she left Jerez? That a stranger was carrying her off to London, that—"

"Edward, a stranger? No, no; perhaps I didn't express myself properly, or perhaps I forget sometimes that you are unaware of details I take for granted. Edward Clayton was almost like one of the family; he was very close to them. He was the representative of the family business in England, Don Matías's right-hand man for the export of his sherry."

Something did not quite fit: there was something not quite right about the image of this good-looking young man Mauro had just been imagining walking down the main aisle of La Colegiata to the sounds of the organ, with the beautiful Soledad on his arm, and the patriarch of the family's solid commercial business. That was why, until he had the answer, he preferred not to interrupt the doctor.

"For more than a decade he had been spending long periods in Jerez, and always stayed with the family. Back in those days he had nothing to do with Sol, or . . . or with Inés."

"Inés is the sister who became a nun, isn't she?"

Ysasi nodded, then repeated the name: "Inés, that's right." Nothing more. Mauro tried to fit all the pieces together in his mind, but not even a chisel would have enabled him to do so. From the back of the room, more clapping, more singing, more sublime flamenco and stamping feet.

"Well, my friend, I suppose that's life."

"What's life, Doctor?"

"That with age we begin an irreversible decline."

"But whose age are we talking about? Forgive me, but I'm becoming more and more lost."

The doctor clicked his tongue, flapped his hand resignedly, and banged the wineglass on the table with a thud.

"Forgive me, Mauro. It's the fault of me and the wine; I thought you knew."

"Knew what?"

"That Edward Claydon is almost thirty years older than his wife."

CHAPTER THIRTY-EIGHT

He had recently woken and was in the kitchen, his hair disheveled as if he had been fighting all the devil's cohorts, and dressed only in a pair of trousers and a shirt open to the waist. He was trying to light the fire to heat some coffee, when he heard someone coming in from the yard at the back of the mansion. It was Angustias and Simón, the aged servant couple. He had had little opportunity to bump into them, but the house was grateful for their presence. The yard and staircase were cleaner, the rooms more livable despite their poor condition, his freshly washed white shirts were hung out on a line to dry and then appeared miraculously impeccable in the wardrobe. And at whatever time he arrived, there was always some warmth left in the hearth and something to eat laid out on a worktop.

The dense clouds of the early morning had not yet lifted, and the chill and darkness had not left the kitchen, when he heard the couple wishing, "God grant us a good day."

"Look what we've brought you, young master," said the woman. "My middle son hunted it yesterday. Look how beautiful it is."

She raised a dead gray-furred rabbit by its hind legs.

"Are you going to have lunch here today, Don Mauro? Or if not, I can leave it for your dinner, because I was thinking of stewing it with garlic."

"I've no idea what I will do for lunch, and don't worry about dinner, because I won't be here."

The invitation that the chairman of the social club had mentioned a few days earlier had not taken long to arrive. A ball at the Alcázar palace, the residence of the Fernández de Villavicencio family, the Dukes of San Lorenzo. In honor of the Claydons, as the invitation said. A dignified but friendly gathering that would include all the cream of Jerez society. He could turn the invitation down if he wished; nothing and no one was obliging him to go. But, possibly out of deference, possibly out of curiosity toward this unknown world of landowners and thoroughbred wine producers whom he barely knew, he accepted.

"Well, I'll leave it in a pot on the stove, and you do as you wish."

"Where's the Indian?" her husband broke in.

"That *Indian* has a name, Simón," his wife reproached him. "He's called Santos Huesos, if you don't remember. And he's better than an apostle, even if he has hair as long as Christ on the Cross and skin of a different color."

"He didn't spend the night here," Mauro said. "He has things I need him to attend to elsewhere." He did not go into details. As it was, he simply asked: "Could you prepare me a big pot of strong coffee, Angustias?"

"I was about to do so; you don't even have to ask. And once I've done that, I'll start skinning the rabbit: you'll see how delicious I make it. Poor little Don Luisito used to lick his fingers whenever I made it: I put in garlic, a splash of wine, and a bay leaf. Then I used to serve it to him with croutons . . ."

He left her to her culinary reminiscences and went out to wash in the courtyard, a towel over his shoulder.

"Wait for me to heat you some water, Don Mauro, or you'll catch pneumonia!"

By then he had already plunged his head into the freezing dawn water.

He had woken with a start early that morning, even though it had been very late by the time he came home, with the sherry and the noise of the flamenco guitars and clapping still resounding in his brain. *This is not going to be an easy day*, he thought, thinking of the Gorostiza woman. He dried off the streams of water running down his chest. Better get started as soon as possible.

The bells of San Marcos were ringing for nine o'clock Mass when he left the mansion, his hair still damp, on his way to Calle Francos. Manuel Ysasi was already at his door packing a stethoscope into his bag as he prepared to do his rounds.

"How was the night?"

"I heard nothing until I opened my eyes around seven. According to your servant, our guest complained a lot, but I've just been up to examine her, and apart from having the temper of a wildcat, she is fine. Although she doesn't think much of you, to judge by the insults she dedicated to you."

They exchanged a few more words by the door, then said goodbye. The doctor was headed for Cádiz on professional business that he quickly explained, without Mauro taking it in at all. His mind was elsewhere as he made ready to confront the tropical storm from Havana.

When he heard Mauro call, Santos Huesos came out of the room next to Carola Gorostiza's, followed like a shadow by the skinny mulatta. The same one she had left him with in the Plaza de Armas in Havana the night of retreat when her mistress asked to see him in that church, he recalled. But this was no time to call up scattered memories from the far side of the ocean; what was most urgent now was to work out what on earth he was going to do with that woman.

"Don't worry yourself, *patrón*, she's quiet now."

"What was she complaining about?"

"She got a little upset when she woke up this morning and saw she couldn't get out of the bedroom, but it passed."

"Did you have to go in and talk to her?"

"Well yes, I did."

"Did she recognize you?"

"Well, now, of course, Don Mauro. She remembered seeing me at your side in Havana. And if you intend to ask if she wanted to know about you, the answer is yes, she did, *patrón*. But all I told her was that you were very busy and probably couldn't come to see her today."

"How does she look?"

"I think there's not much wrong with her health. But with that foul character of hers, I don't know how she's going to take being kept a prisoner."

"Has she eaten?"

At that moment Sagrario, the aged servant woman, came limping along the corridor toward them.

"What's that, young master? She was hungrier than a jailbird in La Carraca Jail."

"Did she go back to sleep?"

"No, sir." The person who responded was the sweet Trinidad, silent until now behind Santos Huesos's back. "I've got her looking pretty as a picture; all I need to do now is her hair. She's almost ready to go out."

"Ready to go nowhere," growled the miner as he walked toward the room at the end. "The key, Santos," he said, holding out his hand.

Two turns of the lock and in he went.

She was on her feet waiting for him, having heard his voice on the other side of the door. Furious, as he expected.

"What were you thinking, you imbecile! Do me the favor of letting me out of here this instant!"

She did not seem to look unwell despite the contrast between this modest room and her magenta gown, crowned by her magnificent black hair that reached halfway down her back.

"I'm afraid that won't be possible for a few days. Then I'll take you to Cádiz and put you on a ship back to Havana."

"Don't even think it!"

"To come here from Cuba was complete madness, Señora Gorostiza. I beg you to reconsider your behavior and to stay calm for a few days. Your departure will be arranged before too long."

"Be aware that I have no intention of leaving this city until I have recovered every last inch of land that belongs to me. So you can stop sending me Indians and quacks, and let's settle our business once and for all."

Mauro took a deep breath, trying to retain his composure.

"There is nothing to settle. Everything took place as your husband and I agreed. It is all aboveboard and ratified in legal deeds. Your efforts to recover what you have lost make no sense, Señora. Think it over and accept it."

She stared straight at him with those sly black eyes of hers. From her mouth issued a sound like a rattlesnake, as though a bitter, dry cough had got stuck somewhere inside her.

"You don't understand a thing, Larrea; not a thing."

He raised his hands in a weary gesture.

"Truly, I understand nothing. Neither about your schemes nor what you are trying to achieve. And by now I couldn't care less. The only thing I know is that you have no reason to be here."

"I need to see Soledad."

"Are you referring to Señora Claydon?"

"To my husband's cousin, who is the cause of all this."

What was the point of continuing with her ravings? There was no sense to them.

"I don't believe she shares your interest; I advise you to forget her."

Now she did laugh out loud, with a sarcastic ring to her voice.

"Or has she made a fool of you, too? Is that it?"

Stay calm, brother, Mauro told himself. *Don't play along with her; don't let her ensnare you.*

"Be aware that I intend to report you to the authorities."

"If you need anything, let my servant know."

"And that I will inform my brother of your behavior."

"Try to rest and conserve your energy: as you know, crossing the Atlantic can be stormy."

Seeing Mauro Larrea turn and head for the door with the intention of leaving her locked in, her indignation flared into anger, and she tried to fling herself on him. To stop him, slap him, show him her fury. He protected himself with an outstretched arm.

"Be careful," he warned her sternly. "That's enough."

"I want to see Soledad!" she screamed.

He grasped the doorknob as if he had not heard her.

"I'll be back when I can."

"After being at the root of all my husband's woes, won't that evil woman even come to speak with me?"

He did not know what to make of this disconcerting statement; nor did he think it worthwhile bothering to outline the details that contradicted her accusation. That it was her own machinations that had robbed Sol's daughters of their future inheritance, for example; that it was her ruses that had led her cousin Luis Montalvo, a poor, wretched, worn-out devil, to abandon the world he knew to go to die in a foreign land. Soledad had more to reproach her with than the other way around. But Mauro had no wish to go into all that, either.

"I think you are becoming delirious, Señora; you need to get more rest," he advised her, with one foot in the corridor.

"You're not going to get free of me."

"Please be so good as to behave."

Her last shriek echoed through the quickly closed door, accompanied by the sound of her fist beating furiously on the wood.

"You are a contemptible man, Larrea! The son of a whore, a . . . a . . ."

He did not even hear her final insults; his mind was already racing with other matters.

৯

Two thousand six hundred sovereigns for a cabin, or one thousand seven hundred and fifty on board deck: that was what it was going to cost him to send the Gorostiza woman back to Havana. And with the slave alongside her, it would be twice that much. He had just been informed of this in a travel bureau on Calle Algarve, which he had left cursing his ill luck at not only having to work out how to get rid of her troublesome presence but at this unexpected bite out of his meager capital.

Five days later the mailboat *Reina de los Angeles* was to set sail from Cádiz. He was given a leaflet showing that the ship would call at Las Palmas, San Juan de Puerto Rico, Santo Domingo, and Santiago de Cuba. Four or five weeks at sea, maybe six, depending as you know on the winds, they told him. He was so anxious to be rid of her that he was tempted to reserve the passages there and then, but reason prevailed. *Wait, compadre, at least a day,* he convinced himself. *See what happens today, and tomorrow morning you can settle things,* he told himself. From that point on, until the intentions of the people from Madrid became clear, what he had wanted to avoid at all costs would become inevitable: dipping into the money from his daughter's mother-in-law, not in order to invest it in profitable schemes as she had wished, but to enable him to stay afloat.

"Mauro?"

All the apparently solid reasoning and calculations piling up in his mind came crashing down like a house of cards. All it took was the presence of Sol Montalvo behind him in Plaza de la Yerba, walking gracefully toward him under the bare trees and the leaden skies of that gloomy autumn morning, in her lavender-colored cloak and her inquiring look as she headed for Calle Francos.

"Have you seen her?"

He gave her a brief summary, leaving out some of the details, as they stood facing each other in the middle of the tiny square filled with the hustle and bustle of open stores and people going about their daily business.

"At any rate, I think I should like to talk to her. After all, she is my cousin's wife."

"You'd do better to avoid it."

She shook her head.

"There's something I need to know."

He went straight to the point.

"What?"

"About Luisito." She looked down at the ground, strewn with dirty, trampled leaves, then said in a low voice: "What his last days were like. What happened when he met Gustavo again."

All around them the morning was filled with activity. Souls crossing on the way to Plaza de los Plateros or Plaza del Arenal; bodies stepping out of the way of carriages, greeting one another, and stopping for a few moments to ask after the health of a relative or to complain about the bad weather. Two distinguished-looking ladies came toward them, bursting the invisible bubble of melancholy she had momentarily become enveloped in. *Soledad my dear, what a pleasure to see you. How are your daughters? How is Edward? I can't tell you how sorry I am about the loss of Luis; you must tell us when the funeral is. We'll see each other in the Alcázar at the Fernández de Villavicencio's mansion, won't we? Delighted to meet you, Señor Larrea. A pleasure. Until tonight, then, a pleasure.*

"Nothing good would come of it, believe me," said Mauro, returning to their conversation as soon as the two ladies were out of sight.

Now it was an extremely respectable-looking elderly gentleman who interrupted them. Fresh greetings, fresh condolences, a flirtatious remark. *Until tonight, my dear. An honor, Señor Larrea.*

Perhaps these encounters were not so much inconvenient interruptions as warning signs: Do not continue in that direction. The thought crossed the miner's mind, and it seemed as though that was how Soledad saw it, too, because she immediately changed the topic of conversation and her tone.

"Manuel has told me you've been invited to the ball. He doesn't know if he will be coming, as he has some medical appointments in Cádiz. How do you intend to get there?"

"I haven't the slightest idea," he said frankly.

"Come to my house, then we can go together in my carriage."

Two seconds silence. Three.

"What about your husband?"

"He's still away."

He knew she was lying. Now that he was finally aware of the wine merchant's age and many complications, he surmised that it would be hard for him to remain away from his wife's side.

And she knew he was aware of this. But neither of them gave the game away.

"I shall be there, then, if you consider it convenient, dressed to the hilt as an opulent returned Indiano."

Soledad's expression changed at last, and he felt a kind of ridiculous, childish satisfaction at having succeeded in making her smile despite all the storm clouds. *What a dolt!* bellowed Andrade. Or Mauro's conscience. *Why don't you two leave me in peace? Get out of here!*

"And so that you won't ever again reproach me for living like a savage, you should also know that I have engaged servants."

"That's good."

"An elderly couple who have already worked for your family."

"Angustias and Simón? Why, what a coincidence. And are you pleased with them? Angustias was the daughter of Paca, my grandparents' old cook. Both of them were expert."

"That's what she boasts. Today in fact she was going to make me—"

She interrupted him gaily: "You don't mean to say that Angustias is going to cook her legendary rabbit with garlic for you?"

He was on the point of asking her how the devil she knew that, when a sudden flash of intuition silenced him. *Of course she knew, you idiot! Why wouldn't she?* Sol Claydon knew that the servant couple would come to his new residence because she herself had made sure of it: she was the one who had decided they should help restore her family's dilapidated mansion so that he could live there with a modicum of comfort; she was the one who told Angustias to prepare him hot food and wash his clothes, and who made sure that the old woman would get on with Santos Huesos. Soledad Montalvo knew all this and more because, for the first time in his life, this experienced, determined miner, toughened by a thousand battles, had come up against a woman who, looking after her own interests and needs, was always three steps ahead of him.

CHAPTER THIRTY-NINE

◈

The afternoon threatened rain.
"Santos!"

His cry was still echoing around the walls when Mauro remembered there was no point calling him: his servant was still on guard outside Carola Gorostiza's room.

He had just been searching in one of his trunks for an umbrella he could not find. Any other day he would not have minded getting wet if the skies did open, but not this particular one. His presence at the Alcázar palace accompanying Sol Claydon was going to seem strange enough as it was without him turning up soaking wet.

He thought about asking Angustias or Simón and was on the way to the kitchen, when he changed his mind. Perhaps there might be an umbrella up in one of the attics. One of Little Runt's or someone else's. Santos Huesos and he had already been up there to bring down the few pieces of furniture and other household objects they now lived among, from the old woolen mattresses they slept on to the clay candlesticks holding the tapers that lit their gloomy nights. Maybe he would find it; it cost nothing to try.

He rummaged through the old wardrobes and chests of drawers

in rooms where the faded brown walls showed the passage of time: a lack of warmth and whitewash. Still visible amid the flaking paint were dirty handprints, stains, small holes, and hundreds of patches of damp; there were even some clumsy drawings scribbled with a piece of charcoal or a sharp instrument: the end of a key, the edge of a stone. *God is salvation,* read some letters in a spot that must once have been the head of a bed. "Mother," said another inscription in a clumsy, almost illegible hand. At the end of a low passageway, behind the door to a room where a pair of cribs and a wooden horse with a moth-eaten mane were sleeping the sleep of the just, Mauro discovered another drawing. At a height somewhere between his elbow and shoulder, and about two hand spans in size. A heart.

Some instinct led him to crouch down and take a closer look: like an animal that is not pursuing any prey but intuitively stretches out its neck and pricks up its ears when its sense of smell detects a possible quarry nearby. Perhaps it was the hunch that a little maid enamored of a young, skinny laborer would never have drawn this symbol with such precision; perhaps it was the refined, incongruous substance used to paint it: ink or possibly even oil paint. For whatever reason, Mauro bent to peer as closely as possible.

The heart was pierced by an arrow, wounded by an adolescent love. At both ends of the arrow he could make out some letters. The capitals were big and firmly drawn, the smaller letters neat and concise. The name that the letters formed to the left, above the feathers of the arrow, began with a *G*. To the right, by the tip, the other name began with an *S*. *G* for *Gustavo*, *S* for *Soledad*.

He scarcely had time to take in this innocent but disturbing discovery when the sound of Angustias shouting from down below made him straighten up. She was calling out to him anxiously.

"I couldn't find you anywhere, master! How could I possibly imagine you'd be poking around up there!" she said with relief when she saw him come running down the stairs from the least respectable part of the mansion.

She did not even give him the chance to ask why she was looking for him so urgently.

"There's a man at the entrance for you," she announced. "It looks as if he came in a hurry, but yours truly here can't understand a word he's saying, and Simón has gone off to the blacksmith's to look for a picklock, so please could you come, Don Mauro and see what the poor fellow wants?"

Something must have happened in Calle Francos, he thought as he rushed along the gallery and leapt down the splendid marble staircase. The Gorostiza woman must have been up to mischief. Santos Huesos didn't want to leave her on her own, and so he's sent somebody to warn me.

But the person waiting for him came from another direction.

"Señor Larrea come Claydon house immediately please" was how Palmer the butler greeted him in execrable Spanish. "Milord and milady have problem. Doctor Ysasi not be in town. You come quick."

Larrea frowned. *Milady*, the man had said. And *milord* as well. As he had suspected, Edward Claydon was not away on a business trip but was under the same roof as his wife.

"What is the problem, Palmer?"

"Son of milord here."

So Alan Claydon had appeared. That made matters even more complicated.

As they walked along, the butler briefly explained the situation in a few almost incomprehensible words. "They held in bedroom of Señor Claydon. Son not allow out. Door locked inside. Friends of son wait study."

They went in by the back entrance, through the gateway he and Soledad had ridden through after she, with the excuse of showing him La Templanza, had somehow inveigled him into her life in a way there was no going back on now. In the kitchen they came across a matronly-looking cook and two maids, all three of them more English than five o'clock tea. They all looked worried and ill at ease.

The background to the current situation needed no explanation: Soledad's stepson had decided not to send representatives but to act on his own behalf. And not exactly in a friendly fashion. This being the case, Mauro Larrea was faced with two options. The first was to wait patiently for everything to sort itself out on its own. To wait until Alan Claydon, son of the master of the house's first marriage, decided of his own free will to stop harassing his father and his wife, opened the door to the room on the upper floor in which he was keeping the couple locked, and, together with the two friends he had probably arrived with from Gibraltar, climbed back into his carriage and left along the road by which he had come. And then, once all this was resolved—and as always behind the back of her husband—he could offer Sol a hand-kerchief to dry any tears she might have shed. Or a shoulder on which to comfort her dismay.

That was the first and probably the more sensible solution.

The second was quite different. Doubtless a far less rational one. Much riskier. This was the one he chose.

"Number 27, Calle Francos. Santos Huesos. Go and tell him to come at once."

This order was the first of his decisions and was aimed at one of the maids. The next instruction was to the butler.

"Explain exactly where they are and in what situation."

"Top floor. Bedroom. Son locked door inside. Two windows back courtyard. Son arrive before noon, mistress out. Came back near one clock, son not allow her leave. No food. No drink. Nothing for milord. Few word apart shout milady. Also blows."

"Show me the windows."

They both walked stealthily out into the backyard, while the two women stayed in the kitchen. Staying close to the walls to avoid being seen from above, they looked up at the openings on the upper floors. Almost all of them were quite small and barred, incongruous, one would have thought, with the place where the prosperous owner of this prosperous residence chose to sleep. But this was no time to wonder why Edward Claydon occupied one of these doubtless less-than-opulent back rooms. Nor to wonder whether or not his wife shared the same sheets with him each night, although this was the next question that presented itself unbidden in Larrea's mind. *Concentrate,* he told himself as he continued to gaze up at the second floor of the house. *Study it closely and work out how on earth you're going to manage to get up there.*

"Where does that one lead to?" he asked, pointing to a small window without bars. It was narrow but big enough for him to clamber through. If he could only climb up to it.

Palmer rubbed his arms energetically as if washing them. Larrea deduced he meant it was a bathroom.

"Close to the bedroom?"

The butler silently pressed his two hands together. Next to it, he seemed to be indicating.

"Is there a connecting door?"

The response was a nod of the head.

"Open or closed?"

"Closed."

Damned bad luck, he was on the point of saying. But before he could, the butler had taken from his belt a hoop from which hung more than a dozen jangling keys. He unhooked one of them and handed it to Larrea. Hardly even glancing at him, the miner stuffed it in his pocket.

He looked up for places that offered handholds. A windowsill, a cornice, a protruding edge: anything he could grab hold of. "Here, take this," he said, untying his cravat. There was no time to lose: the skies were still leaden, and night was drawing nigh. It might well rain, which would make things even worse.

As Mauro removed his frock coat and waistcoat he quickly made a plan of action, just as he had so often done in the past when he was drilling the ground in search of seams of silver in its bowels. Except that now he was aboveground, heading vertically with almost nothing to support him. "This is what I'm going to do," he explained as he removed his stiff collar and cuff links. In fact, he was not particularly concerned whether or not the butler knew what he was intending to do, but saying it out loud seemed to him to make more plausible the procedure he was unable to draw on paper. "I'm going to climb up here. Then, if I can, I'll aim over there," he said, busily rolling up his sleeves. "After that, I'll try to reach that part up on the far side." As he spoke, he pointed to the wall. Palmer agreed without a word. In some distant corner of Mauro's brain, his agent Andrade moved his lips as if he were trying desperately to shout something at him, but his words did not reach the miner.

After he removed all his unnecessary clothing, the two essentials he had taken before running to the Claydon house were revealed: his Colt Walker revolver and his Mexican knife with its bone hilt; he had carried them with him through half a lifetime, and this wasn't the moment to leave them behind.

"Son of milord not good for family. But be careful, sir," muttered the butler when he saw these weapons. Despite his apparently phlegmatic appearance, his words betrayed an undercurrent of concern.

Mauro almost fell three times. The first would probably only have led to a cracked rib without any great repercussions; the second could have snapped a leg. And the third, the result of a miscalculation some fifteen feet up in the air in the encroaching darkness, would have bashed his head in. He managed to avoid all three accidents by a whisker. In between these three near misses, and despite his strong, supple efforts, he scraped the skin off his hands, stabbed himself in the thigh on a projecting iron bar, and grazed his back on an overhanging gutter. Nonetheless, he made it. Once he reached the window, he smashed the glass with his fist, stuck in his hand to turn the handle, squeezed through the frame, and wriggled in.

He glanced quickly around the room: a large bathtub of veined marble, a porcelain toilet, and two or three towels folded on a chair. Nothing else: no mirrors, no cosmetics or toiletries. An austere, excessively bare room. Almost hospital-like. A single door on the right-hand side: locked, as the butler had foreseen. Mauro would gladly have looked for some water to refresh his throat and clean off the dirt and blood on his hands. But, realizing that time was not on his side, he contented himself with rubbing his torn and bruised hands on his trouser legs.

He had not the faintest idea of the scene that might confront him, but he preferred not to lose a second: the smashing glass could have been heard on the other side of the partition. Without any further delay, he slipped the key into the lock, turned it, and kicked the door wide open.

The room was illuminated only by the dying light of day seeping in through the open curtains. No candles, no oil lamps. But even in this semidarkness he could make out the room and its occupants.

Soledad was standing up. She was wearing the same attire he had seen her in that morning, but her hair was bedraggled, and the sleeves and collar were unbuttoned. Since she did not have the proper clothes to protect her from the evening chill, she was wearing a man's mohair scarf around her shoulders.

Mauro's rapid inspection also revealed a man with a pale skin and straw-colored hair. Around mid- to late thirties, with a blond beard and prominent sideburns, jacketless, and with an undone cravat. He gave the impression of having been lounging on a divan around which were strewn dozens of sheets of paper. When he heard the door suddenly burst open he had obviously leapt up to confront this intruder with torn clothing, bloody hands, and the look of someone not wishing to treat him in any kindly fashion.

"Who the hell are you?" he roared in English.

The miner had no need of a translator to understand.

"Mauro . . ." whispered Soledad.

The third man, husband and father respectively, was nowhere to be seen, but his presence could be sensed behind a wide wooden screen that created a parallel space of which Mauro Larrea could see only the foot of a bed as he heard a stream of incomprehensible words.

By now on his feet, Claydon's son seemed to hesitate whether to challenge him or not. He was tall and stocky but not muscular. Mauro had imagined him much younger, perhaps the same age as Nicolás, but his adulthood fitted his father's age. His astonished face reflected a mixture of rage and incredulity.

"Who the hell is he?" he shouted, this time to his stepmother.

Before she could decide whether to reply or not, Mauro Larrea asked her, "Does he speak Spanish?"

"Hardly at all."

"Does he have a weapon?"

As he asked her these questions, he kept his eyes on her stepson. Soledad was tense, on the alert.

"He has a cane with an ivory top close at hand."

"Tell him to throw it on the floor near me."

When she transmitted this message in English, his response was a nervous laugh. Seeing his reluctance to obey, the miner decided to take action. Four strides and he was standing before the man. With a fifth step, he grasped him by the collar and pushed him against the wall.

"How is your husband?"

"Relatively calm. And fortunately he has no idea what is going on."

"And what does this scoundrel want?"

He stared fixedly into the man's bemused face and continued to press against his chest.

"He doesn't seem to know that someone replaced Luisito, but now he is after all the rest: everything in our daughters' names as well as what I have deposited in a safe place he does not know of. He is also trying to disqualify his father and have me sidelined."

Mauro had still not looked at her but continued holding the Englishman, who was growing redder and redder. From his mouth came phrases Mauro couldn't understand and had no wish to.

"Is that what all those documents are for?" asked Mauro, jerking his chin in the direction of the papers strewn at the foot of the divan.

"He was demanding I sign them before he let me out."

"Did he succeed?"

"Not one bit."

In spite of the dramatic scene, he almost smiled. Soledad Montalvo was tough. Tough as teak.

"Let's get this over with, then. What do you want me to do with him?"

"Wait."

A few moments later he could feel Sol's body practically pressed up against him. Her hands were at his waist, her fingers feeling for something. He held his breath as she explored the leather sheath on his left side, sensing her fingers on his body. He swallowed hard and let her carry on.

"Do you know how Angustias skins rabbits, Mauro?"

He took her sudden question as an instruction: he swiftly pulled her stepson away from the wall and stepped behind him. He grabbed his arms and pushed his chest toward Sol. Claydon tried to wriggle free but was being held so firmly, he almost dislocated a shoulder. Howling with pain, he finally seemed to realize what was going on and decided it would be best not to move.

The Mexican knife that Soledad had taken from Mauro's sheath was now threatening his crotch. Then slowly, very slowly, she began to run it up his body.

"First she ties their hind legs and hangs them from an iron hook. Then she slits their skin. From top to bottom, like this."

Claydon broke out in a sweat. The blade slid smoothly over his clothes. Inch by inch. Over his genitals. His groin. His belly. Calmly, without haste. His muscles straining, the miner watched silently as she wielded the knife.

"When we were little, we used to take turns helping her," she said hoarsely. "It was disgusting and fascinating at the same time."

She still had strands of hair dangling loose; the sleeves of her dress were unbuttoned from the elbow; her shawl had fallen to the floor, and her eyes glinted in the semidarkness. By now the blade was traveling slowly upward over her stepson's stomach, reaching the sternum and then his unprotected throat, pressing against the pale white flesh.

"He never accepted me at his father's side; I was always a hindrance."

Pinioned and still sweating profusely, the Englishman closed his eyes. The steel tip seemed to pierce his Adam's apple.

"And as my girls were born, I was increasingly in the way."

The knife explored his jawbone. Left to right, right to left, like a barber giving someone a crazy shave. Then Soledad spoke harshly.

"This cretin doesn't deserve any better treatment than a rabbit, but to avoid any further problems we had best let him go."

She underscored her words by drawing the blade lightly over his cheek, just above his beard. Like someone running their nail over a sheet of paper. A trace of blood appeared.

"Are you sure?"

"I'm sure," she said, holding the weapon out to Mauro. She did this daintily, as though rather than a hunting knife she were handing him a malachite letter opener. The Englishman was still struggling for breath.

Soledad gave her daughters' half brother one last scornful look. Then spat in his face. Fear and astonishment prevented him from reacting: her saliva made it hard for him to see out of his right eye. It mixed in his fair beard with his own sweat and the trickle of blood from his cut cheek. His befuddled brain tried to come to terms with all that had happened in the last five minutes in a room where he had been in complete control for more than five hours. Who was this wild animal who had kicked the door down and then almost broken his arms, and why was his father's wife on such good terms with him?

At that instant the sound of someone treading on the broken glass in the adjoining bathroom could be heard.

"Come in, Santos: you've arrived just in time," said Mauro, raising his voice even before he could see him. He pushed the Englishman away from him like someone disposing of an evil-smelling bundle. Claydon stumbled against a small table, almost knocking it over, and fell over it. He had difficulty regaining his balance and began to furiously rub his aching wrists.

Santos Huesos stepped in the room, ready for his orders.

"Keep him in here and be ready to take him out any minute," Mauro instructed him. He picked up the Englishman's cane and threw it to his servant. "I'm going down to see to his friends."

By this time Soledad had gone over to the screen separating her husband from the rest of the room. Behind it, she checked that the row did not appear to have caused him any upset: a monotonous, unintelligible stream of words was still issuing from the mouth of someone who must once have been a good-looking, lively, and energetic man.

"Fortunately, before this scoundrel locked us in, I was able to give him three times the usual dose of his medicine," she said without turning around. "I always carry it with me; I inject him through a hollow needle. It's the only way to keep him calm. And then only sometimes."

Mauro watched her from the doorway in the darkness, wiping the sweat from his face with a sleeve.

She went on: "The wretch took everything from his father, and more. With the advance on his inheritance he set himself up in the Cape Colony and started his own wine business. It always had its ups and downs, which we helped him over with our own money. Until the day he ruined it once and for all and then, hearing of Edward's condition, decided to quit Africa and return to England to rob us of what his father and then I had managed to build up over the years."

With one hand still on the edge of the screen, Sol turned to face them.

"The specialists seem never to agree on a diagnosis. Some of them call it a psychic disorder, others a collapse of his faculties, still others moral dementia . . ."

"And what do you call it?"

"Madness, pure and simple. A mind lost in the mists of unreason."

CHAPTER FORTY

᪽

H alf an hour later, an English carriage crossed the streets of Jerez, heading south toward the Bay of Cádiz and the Gibraltar countryside, flanked by a man on horseback. When they had climbed La Alcubilla hill and the last lights of the town had disappeared, the rider galloped in front of the carriage, forcing the driver to stop. Without dismounting, he opened the left-hand door and heard his servant's voice from inside.

"All's well here, *patrón.*"

Santos Huesos handed him back the pistol he had used to keep the passengers quiet during their journey. From the saddle of the Claydons' chestnut mare, Mauro Larrea bent down so that the three men in the carriage could see his face. The two companions had turned out to be a skinny English friend and a man from Gibraltar with an impenetrable accent. Tired of waiting for hours, both of them had drunk more than their fair share of the house owner's liquor, and were half-intoxicated and clumsy in their movements. They had not put up the slightest objection when the miner had ordered them to leave the house and wait in the carriage. Doubtless they were relieved to see an end to the tedious family business in which they had been so unnecessarily involved.

The stepson, however, proved a different matter. Having recovered from his initial shock at the confrontation in the bedroom, he had become defiant again. Now, recognizing in the darkness the features of this strange intruder who had ruined all his plans, he challenged him directly.

Mauro could not comprehend a word of it, but the man was obviously outraged and fuming, shouting at the top of his voice.

"Damn and blast it, Santos, can you understand anything this rogue is saying?"

"Not a word."

"What are we waiting for, then? Let's shut him up!"

The two men sprang into action as one. Mauro Larrea cocked his revolver and pressed it against the Englishman's pale temple. Santos Huesos grabbed him by the hand. Fearful of what might happen, the other two held their breath.

First came the sound of a bone breaking, then the howl of pain.

"The other one as well, don't you think?"

"I guess so. We don't want him to go on cursing us, do we?"

There was a second snapping sound, and the stepson howled again. When his cry died away, there was no further show of bravado or defiant gestures, only a quiet moaning like that of a stuck pig gradually running out of breath.

The revolver was returned to its owner's waist, and Santos Huesos climbed up behind his master on the back of the horse. Mauro Larrea gave the carriage driver a signal to resume the journey, though he realized this might not be the end of the matter. Two broken thumbs were a powerful reason not to try anything again, but he knew that someone like Alan Claydon, either in person or through others, would always be back.

Mauro made a stop at Calle Francos to make sure everything was as it should be and to drop off Santos Huesos. The doctor had not yet returned from Cádiz, Carola Gorostiza had been calm the whole evening, and the maid Sagrario was beating eggs in the kitchen with Trinidad's help. It took Mauro no time at all to reach the Claydon house on Plaza del Cabildo Viejo.

Soledad was seated in the study, wearing the same crumpled dress, the sleeves unbuttoned and the neckline awry, her hair still tousled. She was staring into the fire when Palmer led him into a room he had not entered before. There were no embroidery frames or easels on which to paint charming dawn landscapes; there were few feminine touches or ornaments in a room dominated by ledgers, binders, and piles of documents tied with red ribbons. Inkpots, pens, and blotters took the place that any other lady of her social position would have filled with porcelain cupids or shepherds. Sheets of paper and boxes of correspondence were piled up rather than romantic novels or old issues of fashion magazines. Four oval portraits of beautiful young girls with similar features to their mother were practically the only concession to everyday reality.

"Thank you," she sighed.

Don't mention it; it was nothing. No effort at all. He could have uttered any of these clichés but preferred not to be so hypocritical. Yes, of course it had taken a great effort. And there had been a cost. Not simply the rash climb that had almost ended in him breaking his neck, or the unpleasant confrontation with such a despicable creature. Not even the fact that he had been obliged to threaten that villain at gunpoint, or for giving Santos Huesos such a cruel order without his voice trembling. What had most perturbed him—what was like a dagger being driven into him—was something else less immediate and obvious but far more wounding: the unshakable solidity of the relationship between Soledad and Edward Claydon; the certainty that, whatever the circumstances, there existed between them a titanic and invulnerable alliance.

Without waiting to be invited, filthy and disheveled as he was, he removed the stopper from a bottle on a nearby tray, served himself a large glass, and went to sit in a chair like hers. He then referred to what, judging from this particular room in which she was receiving him, he guessed she wished to convey to him.

"So you are the one who runs the business now."

She nodded, still staring into the fire, surrounded by this array of work items and paraphernalia that seemed as though they belonged in a bookkeeper or lawyer's office.

"I started to get involved when Edward displayed the first symptoms, shortly after I became pregnant with our youngest daughter, Estela. Apparently in his family there was a tendency toward . . . let's call it eccentricity. And as soon as he realized he might have inherited this in its worst possible form, he took it upon himself to teach me all I needed to know to run things when he was no longer able to do so."

Absentmindedly she began to play with the glass stopper.

"By then I had been living for more than a decade in London, dedicated to my daughters and living a busy social life. At first it had cost me the earth to adapt, as you can imagine. Finding myself so far from Jerez, from my family, from this southern land and its light. You can't imagine how often I wept under those gray skies, regretting my departure, only wishing I could return. Sometimes I even thought of escaping—of flinging a few things in a case and stealing on board one of those sherry boats that left every day for Cádiz to load up with barrels of wine."

The crackling fire seemed to echo the sad laugh Soledad gave as she recalled the crazy notion that went through her mind during those bittersweet days of her youth.

"But it's not hard to give in to the temptations of a metropolis with three million inhabitants when you have all the necessary contacts, more than enough money, and a husband attentive to your every whim.

And so I became acclimatized in every sense, and started to frequent soirees, went shopping, became a regular at masquerades and tearooms, as if my existence was an endless carousel of frivolity."

Soledad stood up and went over to the window. She looked out at the almost deserted square lit by a handful of gas lamps, although perhaps she could see no further than her own memories. She was still holding the glass stopper, feeling its edges as she went on.

"Until one day Edward suggested I go with him on one of his trips to Burgundy. There, as we were visiting the vineyards of the Côte de Beaune, he told me I should prepare myself for what was inexorably drawing near. No more frivolity: the moment had arrived to face the cruelest, harshest reality. Either I took the reins or we went under. Fortunately, at first his crises occurred only infrequently. That meant he could help me learn the rudiments of the business, get to know its secrets and all those involved. As his condition grew worse, I started pulling the strings in the shadows. For seven years now, everything has been in my hands. And that's how it could have continued had it not been for . . ."

"Had it not been for the return of your stepson."

"While I was in Portugal concluding the purchase of a large shipment of port, and once again concealing my husband's absence with a thousand excuses, Alan took advantage of my trip. He saw Edward, who was not in his right mind and could not remember that his son had already received a substantial inheritance or suspect what the consequences of this new move would be. Alan managed to persuade him to sign documents that made him a partner in our firm and gave him a considerable number of rights and privileges. From that point on, as you already know, I had no choice but to start to take precautions. And when things became really murky and Edward's mental health deteriorated irreversibly, I decided to come home."

She was still at the window. He had risen to his feet and was standing next to her. Their faces were reflected in the glass. Shoulder to shoulder, both of them grave looking, close to one another and yet worlds apart.

"I mistakenly believed that Jerez would be the best refuge, a safe haven where I would feel protected. I thought I could radically reorganize the business from here: I would do without the European suppliers and concentrate exclusively on exporting sherry while I kept Edward sheltered from all attacks. I began taking drastic measures: I would have nothing more to do with the clarets from Bordeaux, marsala from Sicily, wines from Burgundy and the Moselle, or champagnes. I wanted to go back to what had been the essence of the business right from the start: sherry. This is a splendid moment for our wines in England. Demand is increasing spectacularly, and prices are going up correspondingly. The outlook couldn't be more promising."

She fell silent for a few seconds, as if to order her thoughts. Then she went on.

"I even thought about exploiting La Templanza again, and my family's winery, and so become both a wine producer and a supplier. Of course, naïvely it never crossed my mind that my daughters would not in the end inherit that legacy when my cousin Luisito died. I arranged for my daughters to go to boarding schools for the time being and to stay with friends, with the intention of soon bringing them back over here. I closed up our house in Belgravia and began my return journey. But I was wrong. I could not foresee just how far Alan would go."

They were still gazing at each other's reflections in the windowpane. A light rain had started to fall.

"Why are you telling me all this, Soledad?"

"So that you will be aware of all my lights and shadows before we each go our separate ways. I don't know exactly what Edward's and my future will be, but I have to decide at once. The only conclusion I have reached this evening is that we cannot continue like this, with Alan threatening us with lawyers or with his own presence. That could lead to a public scandal and to his father's mental health deteriorating still further. It was stupid of me to think that this would be a solution."

"What are you going to do then? Return to London?"

"Not at all: that would leave us completely at his mercy. I was considering what to do when you arrived. We could perhaps seek temporary refuge in Malta. A great friend of ours is a high-ranking naval officer stationed at Valletta. It would be relatively easy to travel there by sea, and we would have military protection that Alan would not dare to flout. Or we could set sail for Bordeaux and then hide in some distant château in Médoc. Over the years, our contacts in the wine trade there have become firm friends. Possibly we could even . . ." She paused for a few moments, took a deep breath, then went on: "Whatever the case, Mauro, what I want to do now is to stop involving you once and for all in our sordid family business. You have already done enough for us, and I don't want our affairs to complicate yours. I'm sorry I suggested you think again about putting the properties up for sale; that was a mistake. I naïvely thought that . . . if you stayed and got them going again . . . Well, anyway, by now it's all the same. The only thing I wished you to know is that we will be leaving shortly. And it would also be wise for you to disappear before too long."

Better that way. Better for everyone. Each of them going his or her own way: the unexpected outcome of a destiny neither of them had sought, but to which life's unpredictable twists and turns had driven them.

Only his own reflection remained as Sol moved away from the window.

"And now life goes on. We'll have to hurry or we'll be late for the ball."

He stared at her incredulously.

"Are you sure?"

"Even though I'll have to justify Edward's absence with yet another excuse, the ball is in our honor. Among the guests will be almost all the wine producers who have been our family friends: those who attended my wedding and those who went to my relatives' funerals. I can't be so rude as not to put in an appearance. For old times' sake and for the return of the prodigal daughter, even if they can have no idea of how disastrous my decision to come back has been."

She glanced at the clock over the mantelpiece.

"We are supposed to be there in a little more than an hour. It would be best if I picked you up."

CHAPTER FORTY-ONE

❧

A soft rain was falling. The coachman clicked his tongue and cracked his whip. The horses immediately set off again. Soledad was waiting for him inside the carriage, wearing a dark blue cloak edged with ermine, her pale neck standing out from the fur, her eyes shining in the darkness. Distinguished and graceful as ever; the dark clouds kept at bay in a face cleverly dusted with *poudre d'amour*, her anxiety disguised with a seductive fragrance of bergamot. In control of the situation, sure of herself once more. Or forcing herself to muster the courage to give the appearance this was the case.

"Won't it seem odd for the person being honored in this way to turn up with an anonymous new arrival?"

She laughed with a hint of sarcasm, her long diamond earrings dancing in the darkness as they caught the light from a gas lamp.

"You're hardly anonymous by now, are you? Hardly anybody will not know who you are, where you come from, and what you are doing here. Everyone is aware of how we are linked because of our former properties, and they will all recognize that someone of Edward's age can have a sudden health problem: that at least is the rumor I intend to spread right and left. Besides, these wine producers of ours are men of the world. They're quite accustomed to putting up with the eccentric behavior of foreigners. And, despite our origins, at this stage in our lives that is what both you and I mainly are."

The façade of the baroque Alcázar palace glittered in the light of the torches placed in iron rings on either side of the main entrance. Since they were almost the last to arrive, everybody turned as one to look at them. The expatriate granddaughter of the great Matías Montalvo, spectacular in the Prussian-blue gown that became visible when she slipped off her fur cloak; the returned Indiano in his immaculate evening tails who looked every inch the prosperous New World businessman now back in the mother country.

Not even in their wildest imagination could any of the guests have thought that this slender lady with a cosmopolitan air, whose hand and cheeks were now being kissed and who was smiling back as she received compliments, praise, and congratulations, had only a few hours earlier run a hunting knife over the cowering body of her husband's son. Or that, beneath his spotless gloves, the prosperous miner with the foreign accent and graying hair had his hands bandaged because they had been so badly grazed when he climbed like a lizard up the vertical face of a wall.

There were greetings and compliments in a refined, friendly atmosphere. *Soledad, my dear, how wonderful it is to have you back among us; Señor Larrea, such an honor to receive you in Jerez.* More smiles and praise and compliments. If anyone wondered what on earth the last descendant of the old clan was doing in the company of this upstart stranger who had mysteriously ended up owning the family properties, they concealed it with perfect decorum.

Beneath three magnificent brass chandeliers, the ballroom contained almost all the wine-producing oligarchy and the local landowning aristocracy. Their figures were multiplied in the sumptuous gilded mirrors lining the walls. The satins, silks, and velvets worn by the ladies shimmered in the candlelight, and an abundance of discreet but eloquent jewelry was on display. Among the men, carefully trimmed beards, formal attire, fragrances from Atkinsons of Old Bond Street, and a fair scattering of medals. In short, sober luxury that avoided ostentation: less opulent than in Mexico, less exuberant than in Havana, but nonetheless giving the impression of nobility, money, good taste, and sophistication.

A quintet played waltzes by Strauss and Lanner, galops, and mazurkas that the dancers marked by stamping their feet. The owners of the palace greeted them; Soledad was soon invited to dance, and just then José María Wilkinson, the chairman of the social club, came over and spoke to Mauro in a friendly manner.

"Come with me, my friend, let me introduce you."

Mauro engaged in conversation with a succession of elegant gentlemen whose names were redolent of wine: González, Domecq, Loustau, Gordon, Permatín, Lassaleta, Garvey . . . For the umpteenth time, Mauro rolled out his sincere lies and half-truths. The political complexities that had supposedly led him to quit the fledgling Mexican republic, the opportunities the mother country offered to the uprooted children now returning from her insurgent colonies, their pockets allegedly stuffed with money, and an endless series of similarly realistic-sounding nonsense. Everyone was extremely courteous toward him, engaging him in fluid talk: asking him questions, answering his queries, explaining, offering him his first insights into this world of white, chalky earth, vineyards, and wineries.

Until, after more than two hours of circulating independently of each other, Soledad caught up with him in the group of men among whom he was being entertained.

"I'm sure our guest is enjoying your conversation immensely, dear friends, but I fear that if I don't take him away this instant he will not be able to claim the dance I promised him."

Of course, dear Sol, several of the men said. *We won't detain him any longer; please, Señor Larrea; forgive us, dear Soledad, of course you must, for heaven's sake.*

"My father would not have missed a single polonaise on a day like today. And as a true daughter of Jacobo Montalvo, I have to live up to his reputation: a complete fool when it came to business, and an expert on the dance floor, as I'm sure you all so fondly remember."

Well-meaning laughter greeted this tribute to her parent, although none of them appeared to notice the irony in her words.

Perhaps it was the warm reception he had received from the wine producers that led Mauro to relax and to push to a corner of his mind the violent incidents of earlier that day. Or possibly yet again it was the attraction of Soledad, that mixture of charm and dignity she had shown through all the storms and shipwrecks of her life. Whatever the reason, the moment they took to the dance floor, everything vanished for Mauro Larrea as if a magician had sent an ace of hearts up in smoke: the thorny problems that constantly pounded in his brain, the existence of the contemptible stepson, the music enveloping him. All of this seemed to disappear as soon as he put his arm around Soledad's waist and felt the light touch of her long arm on his back. He could have stayed like that, feeling her body against his, his chin almost caressing the bare skin of her shoulder as he inhaled her perfume, with no thought for the commotion of the previous hours or the troubled future awaiting him. Unconcerned that this might be the first and last time they danced together; not caring to remember that she was preparing to leave in order to protect a husband lost in the mists of dementia, someone she had perhaps never loved passionately but to whom she would go on being loyal until his dying day.

As is often the case with this kind of dreamy state, it was something prosaic and immediate that brought him back to reality. Manuel Ysasi, dressed in his street clothes rather than in formal attire, was watching them with an anxious look from one of the ballroom's tall open doors, waiting for either of them to spot him. It might have been Soledad who first noticed him, or Mauro himself. Whoever it was, they both met his gaze as they continued to whirl around to the rhythm of a dance that suddenly seemed endless. The message he was conveying from a distance was clear, and only needed a few discreet gestures: *Something serious has happened; we need to talk.* As soon as he was certain they had understood, the doctor vanished.

Half an hour and many excuses and inescapable farewells later, the two of them left the palace under a large umbrella and climbed into the Claydon carriage. Dr. Ysasi was waiting impatiently inside.

"I don't know who is crazier, poor Edward or you two."

Mauro's muscles tensed; Soledad raised her chin defiantly. But neither of them said a word as the carriage began to move off. By silent, mutual agreement they let the doctor continue.

"A few hours ago I was coming around the bay on my way back from Cádiz. I stopped for supper at an inn some way before Las Cruces, a little more than a league from Jerez. That was where I found him, together with a couple of associates."

There was no need for the doctor to spell out the name of Alan Claydon for them to realize who he was talking about.

"But you don't know each other," Sol protested.

"That's true. We had only seen each other once on the day of your wedding, when I was no more than a medical student and he was a spoiled adolescent as furious at his father's new marriage as a calf being weaned. But he does bear somewhat of a resemblance to Edward. And he speaks English. And his friends were calling him by his name as well as mentioning you several times. So I didn't have to be a genius to guess what was going on."

"Did you introduce yourself?" asked Soledad.

"Not by my name or my relationship with you, but I had no choice but to do so as a doctor, given the sad state he was in."

Soledad looked at him inquisitively, while Mauro cleared his throat.

"Some heartless brute had broken both his thumbs."

"Good Lord . . ." Soledad's voice sounded strained as it emerged from the furs at her throat.

The miner turned his face to peer out of the right-hand window, as if he were much more interested in the gloomy night outside than in the matter being discussed inside the coach.

"He also had a knife cut on his cheek. Fortunately only a superficial one. But obviously done with evil intent."

This time she was the one who suddenly averted her gaze to the night outside. Seated opposite them, the doctor had no difficulty interpreting their reactions.

"You two have behaved like irresponsible barbarians. You have pretended a dead man was alive in front of a lawyer; you inveigled me into keeping that Gorostiza woman prisoner in my own house; and now you've mistreated Edward's son."

"Impersonating Luisito has had no further consequences," Soledad insisted, still gazing out of the window.

"Carola Gorostiza will soon be embarking for Havana in the same state she arrived in," added Mauro.

"And as for Alan, with a bit of luck, by tomorrow morning he'll be in Gibraltar."

"With a bit of luck, tomorrow morning you two will be able to avoid going to Belén jail and will only have to go explain yourselves to the civil guard."

Hearing this dire prediction, they both turned back to gaze at him.

"Alan Claydon has no intention of returning to Gibraltar. After I had put splints on his thumbs at the inn, he asked me for the name and address of his country's representative in Jerez. I told him I didn't know, but that wasn't true: I do know who the vice-consul is, and where he lives. I also know that your stepson's intention is to find him, explain the facts, and seek his support in bringing criminal charges against you, Sol."

"She had nothing to do with that attack," the miner interjected.

"That's not the main problem, although it's true that our friend from Gibraltar did mention an Indian—your servant, I suppose, Mauro—and a violent man on horseback whom I suppose would be you. But as things stand, that's the least of our worries."

They both looked at him questioningly.

At that moment, the coach drew up outside the house in Plaza del Cabildo Viejo. The sound of the wheels and the horses' hooves ceased and Ysasi lowered his voice to a whisper.

"What Edward's son is alleging is that his father, a British subject suffering from serious health problems, is being detained against his will in a foreign country by his own wife and her supposed lover. And to resolve this, he intends to call for urgent diplomatic action and the intervention of his country's authorities from Gibraltar. His associates left for the Rock tonight in a mule cart to inform the appropriate officials as swiftly as possible. He himself has stayed on at the inn, aiming to return here tomorrow morning. He is furious and seems ready to implicate the whole world. He's determined this won't end here."

"But . . . this can't be . . . it goes beyond . . . this . . ."

Soledad's indignation was so great, she could not immediately find the words to express it. Her fury threatened to explode beyond the coach's dark interior.

"I'll go myself to talk to the vice-consul first thing in the morning," she said. "I don't know him personally, except for the fact that he has not been in the post long, but I'll go to see him and clear everything up. I'll . . ."

"Sol, listen," her friend said, trying to calm her.

"I'll explain in detail everything that has happened today. Alan's arrival and his . . . his . . ."

"Sol, listen to me," the doctor insisted, desperately trying to make her see reason.

"And then . . . then . . ."

It was at this point that Mauro Larrea, seated beside her, turned and grasped her firmly by the wrists. Although this was no longer the sensual contact of the ball, or the caress of skin against skin, something again stirred deep inside him when he felt her delicate bones between his fingers and their eyes met once more in the darkness.

"And then nothing. Calm down and pay attention to Manuel, please."

Soledad swallowed as if she were forcing down shards of glass, in a frantic attempt to regain her composure.

"For now you shouldn't speak to anyone, because you're too closely involved," said Ysasi. "We have to think how we can approach the vice-consul more subtly, more indirectly."

"We could try to stop Claydon from coming back to Jerez," Mauro suggested.

"But definitely not using the methods you've already tried, Larrea," the doctor said resolutely. "I don't know how these things are settled between Mexican miners or elsewhere in that legendary New World you've come from, but that's not how things are done here. Here, decent people don't deal with their adversaries by pressing a gun to their head or by ordering their servants to become bone breakers."

Mauro raised his right hand. *That's enough,* he implied. *Message understood, compadre, I don't need any more sermons.* It was then that he realized it was a long time since he had heard his agent Andrade's voice in his conscience, and he suddenly saw why. Dr. Ysasi, speaking to him as a friend in the familiar way he used for the whole Montalvo family, had taken over Andrade's role of telling him how to stay on the straight and narrow. Whether or not he took his advice was another matter.

"But, Manuel," Soledad insisted, "you can explain to whoever is necessary that that's not the way things are . . ."

"I can clinically confirm the state of Edward's mental health. I can swear to all and sundry that you have always tried to protect him, and that for years you have been concerned day and night with his welfare. I can also testify that I have seen with my own eyes how his son has played dirty tricks on both of you, how he has sucked money out of you like a leech, how he has never had any regard for you and has taken advantage of his father's mental condition to carry out a whole series of financial abuses. But my testimony would be worthless. Given my friendship with you, I am discredited from the start in this matter."

The doctor's argument could not have been more convincing. But it didn't end there.

"And as for the alleged sentimental link between you two," he continued, "I can also swear by all that's holy that this man is not your lover, despite the fact that the Montalvo family properties have passed obscurely into his hands. But the fact is that all Jerez has seen you arrive and leave the Alcázar palace together. They have seen you dance together in perfect harmony and seen how well you get on. And dozens of others, people in the street, have seen over the past few days how you two have been going in and out of each other's homes with complete freedom. If anybody should wish to give an evil twist to things, there would be more than enough evidence. Some people would no doubt maintain that you have blatantly trampled on the norms of decent behavior between an honest family woman and an unattached stranger."

"For the love of God, Manuel, it's not as though—"

"I'm not making any moral judgment on the way you behave, but the fact is this isn't a big capital like London, Sol. Or like Mexico City or Havana, Mauro. Jerez is a small town in the south of Spain. It is Roman Catholic to the core, a place where certain kinds of public behavior can be hard to accept and can lead to unfortunate consequences. And you ought to know that as well as I do."

Yet again the doctor's argument was undeniable, however hard it was for them to accept. Shielded by being outsiders and protected by the comforting feeling that they were not part of local life, they had both felt free to behave as they saw fit in their desperate efforts to resolve their own problems. And although they were both certain they had not taken a single socially reprehensible step as far as their relationship was concerned, it was true that appearances suggested otherwise.

"I'm really afraid that it is just the two of you facing the abyss," the doctor added. "And that being so, the sooner we decide what to do, the better."

A dense silence fell over the three of them. They were still seated in the carriage, talking in low voices outside the main entrance to the house, while a quiet rain ran down its windows. Sol buried her head in her hands as if pressing her slender fingers against it could help her brain function more readily. Ysasi was still frowning intently. Mauro Larrea soon broke the silence.

"Without proof there is no crime. The first thing we must do is to get Señor Claydon out of this house and keep him somewhere that no one would ever suspect."

CHAPTER FORTY-TWO

❧

They had been shut in the library for some time, trying unsuccessfully to come up with a sensible plan. The pendulum clock showed ten minutes past two in the morning. The ever-present bottle of liquor was half-empty.

"I think it's a completely crazy proposal."

This was Ysasi's reaction to a suggestion from Soledad.

The idea of the safe place they could transfer her husband to had suddenly occurred to her. She immediately blurted it out with the same mixture of fear and euphoria as if she had found a cure for polio. The doctor's rejection of it was stern, definitive. Leaning against the mantelpiece as he downed his third glass of brandy, the miner simply listened.

"Nobody would ever dream of thinking Edward was in a convent," Sol insisted.

"The problem isn't the convent as such."

Ysasi had gotten up from his armchair and was pacing the room with unsteady steps.

"Then what is it?"

"The problem is your sister, Inés. You know that as well as I do."

Her lack of an answer confirmed his supposition. Normally so rational, articulate, and reasonable, the doctor now turned his narrow back on them, caught up in his own thoughts. Soledad went over and laid her hand on his shoulder.

"It's been more than twenty years, Manuel. We have no other way out, we have to try it."

His silence only led her to insist still further.

"Perhaps she'll come around and accept it."

"Out of Christian piety?" the doctor said sarcastically.

"For Edward. And for you and me. For what we all once meant to her."

"I very much doubt it. She didn't even wish to meet your daughters when they were born."

"Yes she did."

Ysasi turned, a look of surprise on his face.

"You always told me she would never allow you to see her."

"That's true. But as soon as I brought them back to Spain a few months after I gave birth, I took them in my arms each time to the convent church."

The miner noticed that for the first time Soledad, always so dignified and sure of herself, could not prevent her voice from quavering.

"I used to sit on my own with each of them in front of the images of Saint Rita de Cascia and the Infant Jesus in his silver manger. And I'm sure that from some corner of that empty church she saw and heard me."

Several intense moments went by, in which like a couple of snails they withdrew into themselves to struggle with a whole host of unhappy memories. Something told Mauro that their thoughts about the sister and friend they shared went far beyond that of a pious young girl who one fine day took the veil in order to serve the Lord.

The doctor was the first to poke his head out again.

"She would never even give us the chance to ask her."

Combining scraps and fragments of their dialogue with a few details he had heard in recent days in Jerez, Mauro Larrea tried to imagine the situation. But he found it impossible. He lacked facts, elements, clear ideas, that would allow him to understand exactly what at some point in the remote past had happened between Inés Montalvo and her family, and why she never wanted to know anything more about them once she had entered the convent. However, this was no time to amuse himself playing guessing games, or to ask for precise explanations of something that really did not concern him. What was needed was swift action, the pressing need to find a solution. That is what led him to interject: "What if I were the one to ask her?"

≈

He strode along dark streets narrow as knives, still in his tails, with a top hat and cape. The rain had ceased, but the ground was still full of puddles that he sometimes managed to avoid, and sometimes not. He was wide-awake, concentrating so as not to get distracted among the balconies with their wrought-iron bars and straw mats used for shutters. He could not allow himself the slightest deviation: there was not a minute to lose.

The whole of Jerez was asleep when three o'clock rang out from the tower of the La Colegiata church. By then, he had almost reached Plaza Ponce de León. He recognized the church by its window that Ysasi and Soledad had described for him. Renaissance architecture, they told him. And extremely beautiful, she had added. But there was no time to appreciate these details: all that interested him in this ancient work of art was that it marked the end of his journey. Now all he had to do was find the door to the Santa María de Gracia convent, where the sisters of the cloistered Augustinian order spent their time in prayer and meditation sheltered from the fickle world outside.

He found the door down a narrow side alleyway and pounded on it with his fist. Nothing. He tried again. Again nothing. And then, as the clouds suddenly cleared from around the moon, he saw a rope dangling to his right. A rope that made a bell ring inside the building. He tugged on it and a few moments later someone came scurrying to the door, drew back a bolt, and opened a tiny, barred window without allowing themselves to be seen.

"Hail Mary, full of grace."

His voice rang out harshly in the bare night.

"Conceived without sin," responded a frightened, sleepy voice from the other side of the door.

"I need to talk urgently to Mother Constanza. It's a grave family matter. Either you tell her to come out at once, or in ten minutes I'll start ringing the bell, and will not stop until I've woken the whole neighborhood."

The window slid shut at once, the bolt was drawn back across it, and he was left awaiting the result of his threat. Wrapped in his cape on this dark, starless night, he was finally able to pause and consider the extraordinary circumstances that had led him to come and disturb the peace of a handful of innocent nuns instead of being tucked up in his bed like any honest person. He still did not know how much truth there was in the recriminations the doctor had made against Soledad and him regarding their closeness in public and the ostentatious way they had displayed their friendship. *Quite possibly he is right*, thought the miner. And now their attitude was being used against them, and threatened to have their enemies going for their throats.

While he was pondering this, he heard the bolt being drawn back again.

"What can we do for you?"

The voice sounded calm and yet firm. He could catch no glimpse of a face.

"We need to speak, Sister."

"Mother. Reverend Mother, if you please."

This brief exchange was sufficient for Mauro to realize that the woman he would have to negotiate with was far from being an innocent mendicant nun devoted to saying her prayers and making cream tarts for the greater glory of God. He would need to be careful: this was a struggle between equals.

"Of course: Reverend Mother, that's right. Forgive my stupidity. However, I beg you to hear me out."

"About what?"

"About your family."

"I have no family but the Lord God and this community."

"You know as well as I do that isn't true."

The silence of the deserted alleyway was so complete that the only noise came from their breathing on either side of the narrow slit.

"Who has sent you: my cousin Luisito?"

"Your cousin has passed away."

He waited for her to react by asking a question about how or when Little Runt had died. Or for her at least to murmur a "May he rest in peace." When she did neither, he ventured to say: "I've come on behalf of your sister, Soledad. Her husband is in critical condition."

Tell her I'm begging her to help me, that I'm doing so in memory of our parents and our cousins, for everything that we once shared, that we once were . . . Sol had given him this message squeezing his hands as tightly as she could as she tried to hold back her tears. And even if it was the last thing he ever did, he was determined to deliver her plea.

"I find it hard to see how I could do anything for them, as they live outside our borders."

"Not anymore. They have been back in Jerez for some time now."

Again the only response was several moments of intense silence. Mauro went on.

"They need somewhere to shelter him. He is sick, and somebody is trying to take advantage of his weakness."

"From what affliction does he suffer?"

"A profound mental disorder."

He's crazy! he was tempted to shout at her. *And his wife is desperate. Help them, for God's sake.*

"I'm afraid that this humble servant of the Lord can do little about that. In our convent we only care for the anxieties and tribulations of the spirit faced with the Almighty."

"It will only be for a few days."

"There is no lack of inns in this town."

"Look here, Señora . . ."

"Reverend Mother," she reminded him again, sharply.

"Look here, Reverend Mother," he went on, trying to stay patient. "I know you have had nothing to do with your family for many years now, and I am not one to get involved in whatever matters may have separated you, or to beg you to put them aside. I'm only a poor sinner who knows little about religion and how to follow its teachings, but I still remember what my parish priest preached in my childhood about what it meant to be a good Christian. And among the fourteen good works—and correct me if my memory fails me—there were questions such as looking after the sick, feeding the hungry, giving the thirsty drink, giving shelter to the pilgrim . . ."

The whispered reply was as sharp as a dagger.

"I don't need an impious Indiano to come here in the middle of the night and give me a lesson on the gifts of mercy."

His reply, in a hoarse murmur, was even more cutting.

"I am only asking you, if you are not disposed to help your brother-in-law as the Inés Montalvo you once were, that you at least consider it as a damned duty corresponding to your present condition as a servant of God."

"The Lord forgive me if I say you're a heretic and a blasphemer."

"You are quite right, Señora, to say that I have sinned more than enough for my soul to end up burning in the fires of Hell. But so will yours if you refuse your help to those so in need of it at this moment."

The slit in front of him slammed shut with a thud that echoed all the way down the alleyway. Mauro did not move: something told him that this was not the end of the matter. A few minutes later his suspicions were confirmed when he heard the timid young voice that had first attended him.

"Reverend Mother Constanza is waiting for you at the doorway to the garden behind the house."

As soon as they met at the spot indicated, the two of them began to walk quickly along together. Glancing at her out of the corner of his eye, Mauro calculated she was more or less the same height as Soledad, but beneath her habit and wimple it was impossible for him to tell if there were any other similarities between them.

"I beg you to forgive my rude manner, Reverend Mother, but unfortunately the situation is extremely urgent."

Contrary to Sol's habitual readiness to talk, the former Inés Montalvo did not seem inclined to say a word to the irreverent miner. Even so, he thought it best to explain his own role in the matter. The fact that she said nothing did not necessarily mean she was not willing to listen.

"Allow me to introduce myself as the new owner of your family's properties. To cut a long story short, your cousin, Luis Montalvo, at his death in Cuba, bequeathed them to your other cousin, Gustavo, who has lived on that island for many years. And they passed from Gustavo to me."

He left out the details of exactly how this change of ownership had occurred. In fact, faced with the nun's stubborn silence, he decided to say nothing more as they advanced through the night down dark streets still filled with puddles, their capes billowing as they strode along. When they finally reached the front entrance to the Claydon residence, she was the one who finally relieved the tension with an order.

"I wish to see the sick person on my own. Kindly inform anyone concerned of this."

Mauro Larrea went on into the house in search of Soledad and the doctor. Mother Constanza stood waiting sternly in the darkness on the compass rose in the vestibule.

"She refuses to see you both," he told Soledad and Manuel straight out. "But she agreed: she'll take him in."

Bewilderment was painted on their faces in gloomy shades. Then two tears slid down Soledad's cheeks, enough to break Mauro's heart. He turned to look at the doctor but could not see his face. Ysasi preferred to turn his back on him and what he had just heard.

Despite this, they obeyed the instructions. They kept their mouths closed and made sure all the doors were shut. Palmer, the butler, was the only person to accompany the nun to Edward's bedroom.

She spent three-quarters of an hour on her own with the wine merchant, by the light from a single candle. Nobody knew if they talked or communicated in some other way. Perhaps Edward Claydon did not come around from sleep or madness for even a moment. Or possibly he did, and in this dark figure who appeared at his bedside in the middle of the night and knelt down to weep and pray, the tormented mind of the elderly Englishman fleetingly glimpsed the beautiful, slender-waisted young girl with long chestnut plaits that Inés Montalvo had once been, before she had shaved her head and withdrawn from the world. Back in the days when the mansion on Calle de la Tornería was full of friends, laughter, and hopes for the future that were to shrivel and disappear like paper burnt in a flame.

Meanwhile, in the library, as the fire died in the hearth and none of them thought to replenish it, each struggled with his own phantoms

as best he could. When at last they saw the imposing figure of Mother
Constanza in the doorway, they rose to their feet as one.

"In the name of our Lord and for the good of his soul, I agree to
lodge him in a cell in our convent. We must leave at once; we need to
have him installed before lauds."

Neither Soledad nor the doctor could find a word to say. They had
both been struck dumb at the sight of this solemn, distant figure in
her black habit. At first neither of them could mentally connect the
beloved little girl of their memories and this daunting nun who was
gazing at them with reddened, sorrowful eyes from beneath her forbid-
ding wimple.

Her first decision was that no one was to accompany them.

"We are going to the house of God, not to an inn."

Her harsh tone immediately dampened any impulse the others
might have had to try to approach her.

Mauro Larrea watched the three of them from a discreet position
in the most dimly lit corner of the library, smoking his cigar as he
leaned against an alabaster pedestal. When finally he was able to make
out the nun's features in the half-light, it was hard for him to make
any comparison between the two sisters: it was almost impossible to
separate their features from everything that enveloped them. Soledad
was framed by her lustrous head of hair, drawn up in a tight chignon,
and by the sumptuous midnight-blue ball gown she was still wearing,
which left her shoulders, neckline, collarbones, arms, and back bare:
tempting areas of firm flesh and seductive skin. Around Inés, by contrast, there were only yards of rough black wool and a few patches of
white cloth covering her throat and forehead. On the one hand, all the
care and attention of a woman of the world; on the other, the indelible
marks of years of reclusion and meditation. This was all that he was
able to gather, because the encounter lasted barely a minute.

Soledad was unable to retrain herself.

"Inés, I beg you, wait: Let's talk for a moment at least . . ."

Unbending, the nun turned on her heel and walked away.

The house then came to life as preparations were made. Now that he had succeeded in his task of convincing Mother Constanza, Mauro Larrea remained on the sidelines, standing swathed in the smoke from his cigar while the others quickly resolved all the essential practical matters. He felt like an intruder in these intimate comings and goings, the instructions and silences of this foreign clan, and yet he knew he could not leave. There were still important questions to be answered.

At length, the sounds of horses and the wheels of the family coach could be heard rending the silence of the deserted square. Shortly afterward, Soledad and Manuel came back into the library. The weight of desolation hung heavily on them. Sol could barely hold back her tears, and raised her clenched hand to her mouth in an attempt to recover her composure. The doctor looked as tense and tormented as a starving wolf on a windy, dust-filled night.

"We have to decide what to do about the vice-consul."

Mauro Larrea's words sounded stern and tactless—insolent, even—given the delicate situation the other two found themselves in. But they produced the desired effect: it helped bring them back to reality, to finish swallowing the bitter taste that had stuck in their throats at seeing Soledad's vulnerable husband and Manuel's friend being handed over in the early hours to the care of a severe servant of the Church, someone in whom they had been unable to glimpse even the slightest sign of the young girl who had once been so close to them.

"If Claydon's son is determined to return to Jerez, he's bound to be here soon," Mauro added. "Let's say he gets here by ten o'clock and then spends an hour desperately trying to find someone who half understands what he's saying, and tells him who his compatriot the vice-consul is, where he lives, and makes his way there. By then it will be eleven or half past eleven at most. So that is all the time we have."

"I'll have talked to the vice-consul by then. Manuel has told me who he is: Charles Peter Gordon, a Scotsman who lives in Plaza del Mercado. He's a member of the Gordon clan and must have known my family. He might even have been a friend of my grandfather or my father . . ."

"I've also told you that it's not a good idea."

Manuel Ysasi interrupted her with this note of caution, but Sol paid no heed.

"I'll go early and explain everything to him. I'll tell him Edward is in Seville or . . . or in Madrid, or for all I know that he's gone to the spa at Gigonza. Or, better still, that he had to go back to London on urgent business. I'll warn him what to expect from Alan and trust that he'll have more faith in me than in him."

"*Excusatio non petita, accusatio manifiesta,* I insist," the doctor said. "It makes no sense to defend yourself from something no one has yet accused you of. I think it's unwise, Sol."

Like a beautiful animal at bay, she turned her eyes to Mauro. *Help me; don't let me be caught,* she was pleading silently. Yet again.

"I'm sorry, Soledad, but I think it's time to put a stop to this nonsense."

Don't betray me, Mauro. Not you.

The look she gave him burnt deep inside like a pair of the red-hot pincers that his grandfather had taught him to use in the old smithy where he grew up. Yet he had to counter this somehow, and to do so he was left with only one weapon: to appear as cold as ice.

"The doctor is right."

The appearance of Palmer distracted their attention. Mauro was infinitely relieved when Soledad's eyes ceased desperately begging him for help. *Coward,* he reproached himself.

She stood up suddenly and rushed over to the butler, questioning him in English. Palmer gave brief replies, and although he remained as phlegmatic as ever, his exhaustion was plain to see. *Everything is fine. The master arrived safely and is now within the convent walls.* Still anguished, Sol told him in an almost unintelligible whisper that he could go. To wish him good night at this ungodly hour would have seemed like a joke in poor taste.

"Come to my house early in the morning, Mauro, to see how Gustavo's wife has fared overnight. I'll leave at first light to find Edward's son before she gets up," Ysasi concluded. "I'll try to explain the truth to him, and we'll see what he decides to do. I would only ask you, for your own good, to stay out of this: things are poisonous enough as it is. And now I believe it's time for all of us to try to get some rest. Let's see if sleep can bring a little calm to our poor minds."

CHAPTER FORTY-THREE

When Mauro Larrea emerged into Plaza del Cabildo Viejo, another gray day was dawning. The nearby doorways were just starting to open, and the first morning smells were wafting from the kitchens. A few early risers were already in the streets: a milkman with his old mule loaded down with clay pitchers; a priest in his cassock, biretta, and cape on his way to first Mass; young domestic maids, little more than girls, heading sleepy-eyed for the wealthy mansions to start their day's toil. Almost all of them turned to look at him: it was an uncommon sight to see such a man in evening dress at the hour when the cocks had grown tired of crowing and the city was beginning to wake up. He quickened his step in response, and because urgency was snapping at his heels.

Upon reaching his house, he washed up with cold water out in the yard and proceeded to shave. After smoothing down his hair, unkempt from the intense, emotion-filled night, he donned his town clothes: twill trousers, spotless white shirt with an impeccably tied cravat, a nut-colored frock coat. By the time he came down, there was a heavenly smell wafting from the kitchen.

"As soon as I arrived I realized the master had got up early," said

Angustias by way of a greeting. "So I've prepared breakfast in case you have to leave in a hurry."

He was on the point of seizing her face in his hands and bestowing a kiss on her dark brow, weathered by the sun in the fields, the passage of the years, and her sorrows. Instead, all he said was: "God bless you, woman." He was as hungry as a wolf, but had not even stopped to think he would do well to line his stomach before he set out again.

"I'll bring it up straightaway, Don Mauro."

"By no means."

He ate in the kitchen, hardly bothering to sit down, devouring three fried eggs with bacon, several generous slices of still-warm bread, and two huge bowls of milk with a splash of coffee. His mouth still half-full, he grunted a farewell and started off again without even replying to her inquiry as to whether he would be back at lunchtime.

I only hope so, he thought as he crossed the court. If only by then everything had been settled, the doctor had come to an arrangement with Claydon's son, and everything had returned to some semblance of normality. Perhaps not, he reflected. Nothing would return to normal in his life, because it had never been normal since he arrived in Jerez. Not since Soledad Montalvo had crossed his path, not since he had agreed to enter her world, each of them with his own motives. She, out of the demands of necessity, and he . . . He preferred not to label his feelings: What good would it do? He decided to shake off these thoughts in the same way as half an hour earlier he had shaken off the cold water to dry himself: without thinking about it, almost brusquely. Better for him to concentrate on matters at hand; the morning was advancing rapidly and there were urgent questions to resolve.

The door to the house on Calle Francos was ajar. So, too, was the wrought-iron gate separating the entrance from the courtyard. Mauro stepped cautiously inside. As he did so, he heard it. A commotion, noises, shouting. A sharp cry, then further confused screams.

He ran up the steps three at a time, then strode along the gallery. It was a chaotic but eloquent scene. Two disheveled females screaming at each other. Neither of them saw him coming: it was his loud voice that made them both turn their heads toward him.

The old woman, Sagrario, took a step backward, revealing the slave, Trinidad, bathed in tears. Panic and astonishment mingled in their faces when they saw him approach.

Behind them was an open door. The door to Carola Gorostiza's room, wide-open.

"Don Mauro, it wasn't me—" the servant began.

He cut her short.

"Where is she?"

Their two mouths seemed to be saying something, but neither of them dared utter it out loud.

"Where is she?" Although he tried not to sound too harsh, he could not help it.

At length the old servant spoke again, in a frightened whisper.

"We don't know."

"What about my servant?"

He turned to the slave.

"Where has your mistress gone, girl?" he growled.

She was still crying, her hair in disarray and her arms flailing. But she did not reply. Seizing her by the shoulders, he repeated the question increasingly harshly until she was more terrified than distressed.

"I don't know, sir. How would I know that?"

Stay calm, brother, he told himself. *You need to know what happened and you're not going to get anywhere by scaring this poor child and the old woman. Think of your own children and calm down.* He gulped in what seemed like all the air in the entire corridor, then breathed it all out once more. The most important thing, he reminded himself, was that Carola Gorostiza had escaped. And that, if Santos Huesos had not managed to find her yet, most likely by now she was roaming the streets, creating even more problems for him.

"Let's see if we can all cool down so that I can figure out what happened."

The two heads nodded respectfully.

"Trinidad, please calm down. Nothing is going to happen. We'll find her, and in a few days' time the two of you will be heading back to Havana, going home. And in four or five weeks you'll be strolling around Plaza Vieja again. But first you have to help me, all right?"

Her only reply was a jumble of unintelligible sounds.

"I don't understand you, my girl."

She was still sobbing and gasping for breath, which made it impossible for him to make out her words. In the end it was the old servant Sagrario who explained.

"She doesn't want to go back with her mistress, Don Mauro. She says she won't be dragged back to Cuba with her. That what she wants is to stay here with Santos Huesos."

A thought flashed through Mauro's mind. *Santos Huesos, you rogue, what have you been putting into this poor creature's head?*

"We can discuss that all in good time," he said, making a supreme effort not to lose his temper again. "But now I need to know exactly what happened. When and how she managed to get out of the room, what she took with her, if anyone has the remotest idea of where she could have gone."

The old maidservant limped forward.

"This is how it was, sir. Don Manuel left at first light without even sleeping in his bed; he must have had some medical emergency. The fact is that when I got up I went straight to the kitchen and then stepped out to get some coals for the fire. When I came back, I saw the street door was open, but I thought that the doctor must have been in such haste he didn't close it properly. So then I made breakfast for our guest, but when I went to take it up to her, I saw she had flown away like a bird."

"And you, Trinidad, where were you while all this was going on?"

Her sobs, which by now had abated to some extent, returned with renewed force.

"Where were you, Trinidad?" he repeated.

None of them had realized that Santos Huesos, as stealthy as ever, had come back and was walking along the corridor toward them. When he reached the far end, he was the one who answered.

"In the room next door, *patrón*," he said, almost out of breath.

And Trinidad finally said something comprehensible: "With him, in bed."

Scandalized at hearing that she had been in the room with Santos Huesos, the old woman crossed herself. Mauro Larrea's furious glance conveyed everything he would have said to his servant if he had been able to freely unburden himself. *God's blood, you villain, you two spent the night rolling around between the sheets like mad things while that Gorostiza woman escaped at the worst possible moment.*

"At midnight I took the key to my mistress's bedroom from his pocket and when he wasn't looking I opened the bedroom door," Trinidad blurted out. "Then I put it back without him noticing. As soon as she heard the doctor leave this morning, she waited awhile and then went after him."

Santos Huesos's unexpected arrival appeared to have calmed her. Having the man with whom she had shared her body, whispers, and secrets had renewed her courage.

"Don't blame him, sir, because I'm the only guilty one."

Tears came into her eyes again, but this time they were different.

"My mistress promised me," she said in her lilting Caribbean accent, ". . . that if I got the key for her she would give me my freedom certificate so that I'd no longer be a slave and could go wherever I liked with him. But that if I didn't, when we got back to Cuba she'd send me to the coffee plantation, where she herself would tie me to the capstan and have the overseer flog me with twenty-five lashes."

Enough. For the moment, that was all he needed to know. Sagrario, horrified at this sinister threat, put her arm around the girl's shoulders to comfort her. Still catching his breath after his run, Santos Huesos did not lower his gaze, acknowledging in silence the colossal mistake he had made.

No point insisting on what could not be altered, thought Larrea.

"Come on, lad," he said. "Let's go and look for her; you and I can talk some other time. Let's be off without losing another second."

When they were out in the street, the first thing Mauro did was to send his servant to Plaza del Cabildo Viejo to inform Sol, just in case it had occurred to her cousin's wife to go there. She had said Sol was the cause of all the misfortunes in her marriage. And in his mind's eye he saw once again the heart scratched into the wall in his house. The *G* for *Gustavo.* The *S* for *Soledad.*

Next, he hired a carriage to take him to visit guesthouses and inns, just in case Carola Gorostiza had taken it into her head to rent a room while she was deciding what to do next. He tried the places in Calle Corredera, the Calle de Doña Blanca, and Plaza del Arenal, but none of them had any news of her. As he rushed from one to another, he also went into the notary's office on Calle Lancería, hoping to be able to put out a feeler that could reach where he could not go. "An old female friend who's just arrived from Cuba has got lost, Don Senén," he lied to the notary. "She's rather disturbed, and is capable of saying the most complete nonsense. If by any chance you come across her, for heaven's sake, keep her with you and let me know."

He was about to leave when his gaze fell upon the nosy clerk with whom he had had that rather extraordinary meeting a few days earlier. The poor fellow was trying to pretend he was not there, head buried in a leather-bound tome as he furiously scribbled something to escape the threat from the Mexican miner. Mauro came to a halt in front of his desk and said something to him that the others could not hear but was clear enough: Come outside at once.

"Find a way to get out of your obligations here. You must scour the town for any person in authority to whom someone could present a formal or informal complaint. Or anyplace where someone could say too much to a person in power, if you follow me. Whether they are civilians, military officers, or churchmen."

His stomach churning, the clerk simply muttered, "Whatever you say, sir."

"Find out if a lady going by the name of Carola Gorostiza de Zayas has been in any of these places and whether she said anything about me. If the answer is no, put a guard on every door to watch if she appears later. I don't care if they are a crippled beggar or an army officer, just so long as they keep their eyes open and if necessary stop an elegant lady with jet-black hair and an accent from abroad."

"Yes, yes, yes . . ." stammered poor skinny Angulo, twisting his fingers nervously.

"If you find her, there's three silver sovereigns in it for you. If on the other hand I hear that any word of this has got out, I'll send my servant to pull out your wisdom teeth. And I wouldn't trust the instrument he chooses for that kind of surgery."

He turned his back on the clerk, and left. Santos Huesos was waiting for him on the street corner.

"Let's go back to Calle de la Tornería; it's unlikely, but perhaps she decided to go there."

Angustias and Simón said neither of them had seen any lady of that description.

"Go out and look for her, will you? And if you find her, do your best to bring her here, even if you have to drag her. Then keep her shut up in the kitchen for me. If she puts up a fight, threaten her with a poker so that she doesn't leave."

Abandoning their carriage at the start of Calle Larga, they continued their search among lines of orange trees and the busy morning activity. Taking each side of the street, they entered shops, grocery stores, and cafés. Nothing. Larrea thought he glimpsed her in a gray skirt turning a corner, then in a black hat, and again in the silhouette of a woman in a short brown cloak leaving a shoe shop. But none of these was her. Where on earth could that blasted woman have gone?

He consulted his watch. Twenty minutes to eleven. *Quick, back to Dr. Ysasi's house. By now he must have returned from the inn with news of Alan Claydon.*

To his bewilderment, there was no carriage visible outside the house. Neither the doctor's aged phaeton, nor the English carriage that had brought Soledad's stepson to Jerez: no one had arrived yet. He checked the time again: the morning was advancing with the implacable beat of a military charge. The doctor was missing and the Mexican woman had still not appeared.

"You asked in Plaza del Arenal whether anyone hired a carriage, didn't you?"

"While you were looking in the taverns, *patrón.*"

"And?"

"And nothing."

"Of course. Where would that lunatic go on her own, without her slave or her baggage, and without settling the questions she thinks we still have to sort out?"

"Well I'm inclined to think yes, she did."

"Yes, she did what?"

"That the lady has flown from Jerez. That she's more scared of you than if she'd seen a ghost, as they say in these parts. To my mind, she's done everything she can to put some distance between you, so that she can deal with things more safely from there."

Santos could be right. Why not? Carola Gorostiza knew that in Jerez he was bound to find her sooner or later. She had nowhere to hide there, she didn't know anyone linked to Cuba, and it was only a small town. She also knew that, as soon as he found her, he would shut her in again. And not for anything in the world was she willing to let that happen.

"Let's go to the railway station."

When they arrived, there was just one train in the station, and it was already empty.

Only one of the passengers who had got off the train was still on the platform. A young man surrounded by trunks. Tall, lithe, handsome, his hair tousled, and dressed with all the elegance of a great capital. Half hidden behind a sallow-skinned employee who only reached to his shoulders, he was listening intently to the man's instructions.

"Santos, swear on your mother's grave that I'm not also losing what little reason is left to me."

"You're still in your right mind as far as I can tell, Don Mauro. For now, at least."

"Well, then, do you see what I see?"

"With these eyes that one day will be eaten by worms, *patrón*: at this very moment I am looking at the boy Nicolás."

CHAPTER FORTY-FOUR

❧

Their embrace was heartfelt. Nicolás, the cause of so many sleepless nights over his childhood measles and scarlet fever, the creator of such problems and such laughter, as unpredictable as a revolver in the hands of a blind man, was standing there on the station platform in Jerez.

Questions came gushing out from both their mouths. Where? When? How? Then they hugged each other again. There was a knot in the pit of Mauro Larrea's stomach. *So you're alive, you young devil. Safe and sound, and grown into a man.* A feeling of infinite relief swept over his body.

"How did you find me, you scoundrel?"

"This planet is growing smaller all the time, Father. You wouldn't believe how many discoveries there are. Daguerreotypes, the telegraph . . ."

Santos Huesos gave the boy of the family another huge hug, then set about organizing the two porters who started to load the young man's copious baggage.

"Don't give me all that nonsense, Nico. We can talk later about how you got away from Lens and the awkward position you left me in with Rousset."

"When I was in Paris," replied Nicolás, neatly sidestepping his father's implied threat, "one evening I was invited to a residence on Boulevard des Italiens. It was a reunion of Mexican patriots who had fled like chickens from Juárez's regime and were now plotting, surrounded by Houbigant perfume and bottles of chilled champagne. Just think of that."

"Concentrate, my boy."

"There I met some of your old friends: Ferrán López del Olmo, the owner of that big printer's on Calle de los Donceles, and Germán Carrillo, who was traveling in Europe with his two young children."

Mauro frowned.

"And did they know where I was?"

"No, but they told me that our commercial attaché had informed them that if they ever ran into me, there was a letter waiting for me at the embassy."

"A letter from Elias, I imagine."

"That's right."

"And when you ran out of money, you went to collect it. Except that you were disappointed: there wasn't much money along with it."

By now they had left the platform and were heading for their carriage.

"Not only did he ask me to perform financial magic with what little he sent," Nicolás confirmed, "but he also ordered me not to even think of returning to Mexico before you arrived. He told me you were settling some business in the mother country, and that if I wanted news of you I should contact someone called Fatou in Cádiz."

"Contact him by letter, I suppose, is what Andrade meant. I don't think he would ever imagine you coming here yourself."

"But that's what I preferred to do. Since I couldn't pay for a decent passage, I embarked at Le Havre in a coal boat that called in at Cádiz and here I am."

Mauro glanced at him out of the corner of his eye as they walked and talked. Conflicting feelings between heart and head overwhelmed him. On the one hand, he was immensely relieved to have alongside him someone who had been a fragile little tadpole but was now a self-confident twenty-year-old with cosmopolitan airs and an astonishing savoir faire. On the other, his son's untimely arrival upset the precarious balance that had existed until that moment. And as things stood that morning, the worst of it was that he had not the faintest idea what to do with him.

Nico jolted him out of his thoughts with a hearty slap on his shoulder.

"We need to have a long talk, Monsieur Larrea."

Despite the jocular tone, his father detected a note of unexpected seriousness.

"You have to tell me what on earth you are doing in this far corner of the Old World," he went on. "And there are things about me that I'd like you to know as well."

Of course they had to talk. But at the right time.

"Naturally, but, for now, accompany Santos and get settled. I'll take another carriage and go sort out something I need to deal with. We'll meet again as soon as I possibly can."

He left his son protesting behind his back.

"To Calle Francos," he told the driver of the first carriage he came across outside the station.

Nothing had changed in the scene outside Ysasi's house. No vehicles apart from a rag-and-bone man's cart and two water sellers' mules. He looked at the time: twenty past twelve. Too late for the doctor not to have returned, with or without the Englishman. *Something must have gone wrong,* he muttered to himself.

He renewed his search for the Gorostiza woman, in case in the end she had not left Jerez. "Take a turn in that direction," he instructed the driver. "Now down here; then turn this way, carry straight on, stop, wait, go on, stop again." His imagination played tricks on him once more: he thought he saw her coming out of the San Miguel church, then going into San Marcos, then coming down the steps at La Colegiata. But no: not a sign of her, alive or dead.

The person he did see as he drove past the stall on Calle de la Pescadería was the notary clerk. A fine drizzle was falling that soaked everyone, but Angulo was waiting at the corner of Plaza del Arenal where he thought the Mexican miner might eventually appear. A shake of his head was enough for Mauro to understand without having to descend from his carriage. Nothing for now. The gossipy clerk's searches had yielded nothing as yet. "Drive on," Mauro told the coachman.

His next destination was Plaza del Cabildo Viejo. To his surprise, he found the studded doorway wide-open. He leapt from the carriage before the horse had even come to a standstill. *What the devil is going on?* he wondered.

Palmer came out to meet him with his undertaker's air. Before he could say anything in his tortuous Spanish, Dr. Ysasi came rushing up behind him. He appeared utterly disconsolate.

"I've just arrived and now I'm off again. It was all in vain. Edward's son obviously changed his mind. He left the inn before daybreak, heading south, according to the owner."

Mauro preferred to stifle the curses that rose to his lips.

"I rode several leagues without catching up with him," the doctor continued. "All I can tell is that for some reason he changed his plans and decided not to come back to Jerez. Not for the moment, at least."

"It seems that misfortune really never does come alone."

"Sol has just told me: Gustavo's wife has flown the coop. I'm going there now."

Mauro wanted to give him the details, but the doctor interrupted him.

"Go into the study at once."

Rather than ask why, Mauro knitted his brow. The explanation was not long in coming.

"Your potential buyers have arrived."

"The ones Zarco mentioned?"

"We ran into them in the entrance, and to judge from their expressions they're not exactly pleased to be here. But you must have offered Zarco a fat slice for being your intermediary, because he's capable of going without bacon for a month rather than allowing his clients to go back to Madrid without seeing you. And our beloved Soledad has no intention of letting them leave until she knows you're here."

The stepson, disappeared. The Mexican woman, flown the coop. Nicolás, dropped from heaven in the middle of the railway station. And now his possible saviors—the only ones who might be able to help him return to Mexico—had been dragged in at the worst possible moment. *My God, sometimes life is such a treacherous bitch.*

"Each of us has to cover a flank," said Ysasi. And despite his lack of religious beliefs, he added: "And may God help us."

Three men were waiting for Mauro in the same reception room where a few days earlier he had pretended to be the deceased Little Runt. Except that on this occasion they were not foreigners but Spaniards. One, the agent from Jerez; the other two were from Madrid. Or at least that was where they had come from and where they were in a hurry to return: two obviously distinguished gentlemen who rose to greet him with the required courtesy. The lord and his minion, it seemed to Mauro: one who put up the money and sought advice; the other who offered him that advice and made suggestions. Zarco had no need to get up, because he was already standing, his face red and his jowls flopping down over his shirt front.

In the middle of the three men stood Soledad. Calm, mistress of the scene, radiant in an ice-gray taffeta dress. Like a fairground magician, she had somehow managed to make all signs of fatigue and tension disappear from her face. Unlike during her meeting with the Englishmen, her look was no longer that of a cornered beast. Now she showed only a steely determination. Heaven only knew what she was telling them.

"Here you are at last, Señor Larrea. Fortunately you have arrived at the perfect moment, just when I have finished explaining to Señor Perales and Señor Galiano the characteristics of the properties we have on offer."

She spoke firmly, assuredly, almost professionally. The cause of and accomplice in his most reckless mistakes, the woman who by merely coming close sent uncontrollable primal waves through his body; the loyal wife, protector, and guide of a man who was not him—this woman had given way to a new Soledad Montalvo that Mauro Larrea as yet did not know. The one who bought, sold, negotiated, and competed as an equal in a male world of finance and transactions. This exclusively masculine world into which she had been thrown willy-nilly and in which, driven by a naked instinct for survival, she had learned to navigate with all the agility of a trapeze artist who is aware that sometimes one has to work without a safety net.

As if she had any real wish to help these strangers lay their hands on what she had always thought would be hers! thought Mauro as he exchanged formal greetings without any real enthusiasm. "Charmed, I'm sure. Welcome."

"To fill you in, Señor Larrea, I have just told these gentlemen about the magnificent acres we possess in the Macharnudo area for the cultivation of vines. I have also detailed for them the various features of the mansion that would be part and parcel of any sale. And now it is time for us to be on our way."

"Where to?" he asked with a barely perceptible gesture that she immediately understood.

"We are going to show them the winery, the origin until a few years ago of our famous soleras that were so appreciated in international commerce. Be so kind as to follow us, would you, gentlemen?"

While Zarco was exchanging a few words with the potential buyers on their way to the door, Mauro seized her by the elbow and forced her to come to a halt for a moment. As he leaned down to whisper in her ear, he was yet again assailed by her perfume and the beguiling warmth of her skin.

"Gustavo's wife has still not appeared," he muttered between clenched teeth.

"All the more reason, then," she murmured, scarcely moving her lips.

"Reason for what?"

"For you to take these two imbeciles for all they're worth, so that you and I can get out of here before everything comes crashing down."

CHAPTER FORTY-FIVE

⟡

They descended from their carriages next to the large wall surrounding the winery, a wall that had once gleamed with whitewash but was now, thanks to long years of neglect, a mixture of brown and gray-green, and almost black in some parts. Mauro Larrea opened the main gate the same way as he had on the previous occasion, by giving it a hefty shove. The rusty hinges creaked and allowed them to enter into the big central courtyard festooned with acacias. It was raining again; Soledad and the purchasers from Madrid were sheltered beneath large umbrellas, while the rotund Zarco and he had only their hats to ward it off. Mauro was tempted to offer Soledad his arm to keep her from slipping on the greasy cobbles, but refrained from doing so. Better to keep up the façade of a cold business relationship that she had chosen to display. Better for her to stay in control.

It was not long since he had first visited the place escorted by the two old cellarmen, on a sunlit day far less ominous than this one, but to him it seemed like an eternity. Apart from that, everything was the same. The tall vines that had provided shade on distant summer days now looked bare and sad; the bougainvilleas had no flowers; the clay pots were all empty. The cracked roof tiles were like gutters, sending the rainwater gushing down.

If Soledad was affected in any way by this contact with the ruins of her splendid past, she was careful to disguise it. Wrapped in her cloak, her head covered by an astrakhan-trimmed hood, she concentrated on pointing out details and reeling off figures such as the dimensions and area precisely and in a firm tone of voice. She gave only relevant information and avoided any sentimental shadows from the past. "Take a good look, gentlemen, at how splendidly it is designed, and the excellent materials used for its construction. How easy, how simple, it would be to restore it to its former glory."

She took out a hoop of old keys from beneath her cloak. "Would you please open the doors for us," she told the land agent. They entered dark offices Mauro had never seen before, but through which she moved as though in her element. The "writing rooms," she called them, the offices where employees in eyeshades and protective cuffs once carried out all the daily administrative tasks. All that was left were the remains of a few yellowing, trampled-on invoices. The now-decrepit reception room, where a couple of rickety chairs had been pushed against a wall; the offices for higher-ranking employees, where not a single pane of glass remained in the windows; and, finally, the patriarch's own room, the legendary Don Matías's private fiefdom, now no more than an evil-smelling den. No sign of the silver inkstand or the glass-fronted bookcases or the magnificent mahogany desk with its leather top. All that was left was desolation and dirt.

"With a few thousand sovereigns, it could be restored to its previous state in less than no time. But the important part comes next."

She pointed to more buildings at the far end of the property. The washing room, the barrel workshop, the tasting room, she explained, walking on. She led them to the tall building on the far side of the central courtyard, the main facility Mauro had been shown by the aged cellarmen. It was just as lofty and imposing as he remembered, with its imposing cathedral ceiling, but with less light due to the rain. The smell, however, was identical: dampness, wood, wine.

"As I suppose you will have appreciated," Soledad added from the doorway, pushing back her hood, "the winery is constructed facing the Atlantic, in order to make use of the winds and the benefits of the sea breezes. They are what in good measure enable our wines to be robust and clean—the winds, and the patience and knowledge of those caring for the vines. Come with me, please."

They all followed her as her voice echoed from the arches and walls.

"As you can see, the design of the building is essentially uncompli-cated. An architectural simplicity passed down through the ages. Al-ways higher than the surrounding ground, with a pitched roof to lessen the effects of the sun, and thick walls to retain the coolness."

Now they were walking slowly through the aisles between the barrels stored in racks three or four high, from where the wine was decanted from top to bottom to give it consistency. "These are our magnificent soleras," she said. Removing one of the large cork plugs, she sniffed the aroma with her eyes closed, then replaced it.

"In these oak barrels the miracle we call the 'bloom' takes place: a natural veil of tiny microorganisms that covers the wine and protects it, nourishes it, and gives it body. It's thanks to this bloom that the wine acquires the qualities that were known by the Romans as the five *F*'s: *fortitia*, *formosa*, *fragrantia*, *frigida*, and *frisca*. In other words, strength, beauty, fragrance, freshness, and age."

While the four men paid close attention to the words and move-ments of the only woman in the group, the water from their capes and umbrellas was creating small puddles on the yellow earthen floor.

"However, I suspect you have had enough of hearing me carry on in this way; I'm sure everyone has tried to sell you their wineries as the best. So now, gentlemen, the moment has come for us to concentrate on what really matters: offers and opportunities. What we are able to offer you, and what you wish to get out of it."

To the once distinguished young Andalusian girl Soledad Montalvo, brought up dressed in lace, with English nannies and Mass every Sunday morning, as well as to the refined, cosmopolitan Sol Claydon, used to shopping at Fortnum & Mason, going to opening nights at West End theaters and Mayfair salons, was now added yet another personality. That of the consummate businesswoman and tough negotiator, the faithful disciple of her wine merchant husband and her astute grandfather, the inheritor of the soul of the ancient Phoenicians who three thousand years earlier had brought the first vine stocks from the far side of the Mediterranean to these lands that they called Xera, and that over the centuries became known as Jerez.

Her voice became even more commanding.

"We are aware that for several weeks now you have been visiting vineyards and wineries in Chiclana, Sanlúcar, and El Puerto de Santa María, and that you've been even as far as El Condado. We also know you are seriously considering several offers that, because the prices are lower than ours, could at first sight seem more attractive. But allow me to tell you, gentlemen, how mistaken you are."

The two possible buyers from Madrid could not hide their astonishment. Zarco started to sweat. And the miner kept his feelings under tight control to avoid showing his amazement at the mixture of courage and impertinence he was witnessing: the unwavering self-belief of someone able to display the pride of a class or caste that combined immensely different yet complementary qualities. Tradition and initiative, elegance and lack of fear, pride in belonging and wings to fly: the spirit of the legendary Jerez wine producers, whose essence Mauro was only now beginning to properly appreciate.

"I have no doubt that, given the interest you appear to have in making an entry into the world of wine, you will have been making inquiries and have learned how complicated the last link in the chain can be. The first: becoming producers, which you can achieve by buying good vines and ensuring that the laborers harvest them properly. The second: becoming wine stockists, which will not be hard, either, if you manage to find an excellent winery, a good foreman, and capable, willing workers. But the third stage, exporting your wines, is without a shadow of a doubt the most uncertain of all for you, for obvious reasons. However, we are in a position to make that difficult leap easy for you: we can offer you instant access to the most prized sales networks outside this country."

Mauro went on studying her, five steps behind the others with his arms folded and legs apart, observing her hands, fluttering with easy eloquence; her lips as they offered guarantees and concessions with astonishing assurance, the whole time including him in the "we" she used. My goodness, she had them eating out of her hand: you only had to look at them to see that the effect on this Señor Perales and his secretary was devastating. They whispered in each other's ears, cleared their throats, glanced surreptitiously at one another, nudged their elbows. The buttons on Zarco's jacket were threatening to burst at the mere thought of the juicy commission he would pocket if the señora were able to squeeze a little harder.

"We are fully aware that the price of our properties is a high one. I regret to inform you, however, that it is also nonnegotiable: we are not going to drop it by even half of one percent."

If he had not trusted her blindly, Mauro's guffaw at this would have resonated from the walls and the high whitewashed arches and bounced off the hundreds of barrels. *Has your husband's lunacy affected you, too, dear Soledad?* he could have asked her. He of course would have been more than willing to lower the price, to consider any offer, and to make various concessions in order to lay his hands on a good sum of money and get out of there. But as the stubborn bargainer that he, too, had once been in his glory days, he immediately recognized the sheer audacity of her proposal. And so he stayed silent.

"Contacts, agents, importers, distributors, merchants. I myself represent one of the foremost houses in London: Claydon & Claydon of Regent Street. We study every detail of the demand, and are at each moment aware of the fluctuations in prices, tastes, and quality. And we are prepared to place all this expertise at your disposal. The thriving British market is growing by the day, its expansion seems unstoppable, and Spanish wines now account for forty percent of their market. However, there are extremely powerful rivals who are constantly fighting for their share. As ever, port wines from Portugal, tokays from Hungary, German hocks and Moselle wines—even wines from the New World—are increasingly becoming available in the British Isles. Not forgetting, of course, the legendary and ever-active winegrowers from the many regions of France. The competition, my friends, is ferocious. And even more so for any newcomers to this fascinating, gloriously complex universe."

None of them dared breathe a word. Soledad soon came to the conclusion of her performance.

"You already know the price we are asking, thanks to our agent here. Think it over and decide, gentlemen. And now, if you'll excuse me, I have a few other urgent matters to attend to this midday."

To sleep a few hours after one of the saddest nights in my life, for example. To discover how my poor husband is, enclosed in his convent cell. To find a runaway Mexican woman married to someone who during part of my life occupied an important place in my heart. To anticipate the next move by a perverse stepson determined to strip me of all I have achieved after long years of struggle. Soledad Montalvo could have told them all this as she walked between the rows of barrels toward the exit. Instead she simply left behind a trail of silence and an overwhelming sense of emptiness.

Mauro Larrea extended his hand to the purchasers.

"I have nothing to add, gentlemen; it's all been said already. If you wish to get in touch, you know where to find us."

As he headed for the door to catch up with Soledad, Mauro was gripped by a feeling of unease as sharp as the claws of a hungry wildcat. *Why do you find it so hard to rejoice, you wretch? You're a step away from getting everything you wanted so much, of reaching all your goals, and yet you aren't salivating like a ravenous dog over a piece of fresh meat.*

A hissing sound forced him out of these reflections. Unsettled, he turned his head to left and right. Only a few feet away, half hidden among the big, dark barrels, he glimpsed an unexpected presence.

"What the blazes are you doing here, Nico?" he asked in astonishment.

"Killing time until my father decides whether or not he can pay me some attention."

Touché. The reception he had given his son after so long apart had not been exactly welcoming. But circumstances were threatening to engulf him, as in the past the fetid waters at the bottom of Las Tres Lunas mine had done, when a sudden flood had been on the verge of making an orphan of the boy who was now accusing him of paternal neglect. Or as when Tadeo Carrús had given him a cruel time limit of four months, half of which had already gone by.

"I'm really sorry, truly I am, but things grew complicated in the most unfortunate way. Give me a day—just one day—to sort it all out. Then the two of us can sit down placidly and talk things over at leisure. I have to tell you things that concern you and it would be better to do so calmly."

"I suppose there is no alternative. And in the meantime," said Nicolás, apparently recovering his habitual good humor, "I have to admit that I find this new turn in your life fascinating. That old woman, Angustias, told me you were now the owner of a winery, and so I came here out of curiosity, with no idea you were about. Then I saw you all inside and didn't want to interrupt."

"You used your brain: it wasn't the right moment."

"That's precisely what I wanted to say to you."

"What?"

"That you should use your brain."

Mauro could not help grinning sarcastically. His son advising him not to be an ass: that really was the world turned upside down.

"I don't know what you're talking about, Nico."

They were walking slowly side by side across the courtyard. A light rain was still falling. Anyone seeing them from the back, the side, or the front would have noticed that they were the same height and equally handsome. The father more solid and well built. The son more agile, willowy. Both of them good-looking in their way.

"Don't lose them."

"I still don't understand."

"Neither this winery nor that woman."

CHAPTER FORTY-SIX

༄

After witnessing Soledad Montalvo's performance, a change came over Nicolás. As if endowed with a sudden spontaneous common sense, he realized this was not the moment to demand attention for himself. And so, to everyone's surprise, he suddenly announced he had urgent letters to write. He was lying, of course; he simply wanted to leave the way clear for his father to finish off what he had to do, whatever it was that bothered him and had transformed him into a completely different man from the one who had bid him good-bye in the San Felipe Neri mansion a few months earlier.

For his part, the miner suspected his son was up to something, something he had not yet even hinted at but was the real reason for his coming to Jerez. Something that he knew would bring even more problems. That was why he had chosen not to ask Nico anything, to postpone this encounter with the inevitable and not add to the worries already afflicting him.

They both kept up the pretense, like accomplices. Nico stayed at the mansion on Calle de la Tornería, while Mauro Larrea went first to Calle Francos, where to his dismay he found there was still no trace of the Gorostiza woman, and then flew to the only place in the world that he really wanted to be.

Soledad received him in a state of great irritation because her sister, Inés, had refused to permit her to see her own husband. *This is a place for contemplation and prayer, not a spa with sulfur baths,* she had protested, without allowing herself to be seen when Soledad went on to the convent from the winery. *He is fine and is at peace, with a novice taking care of him at all times.* That was all.

Sol had taken refuge once more in her study, that den from which, Mauro now knew, she pulled the strings of the Claydon business in the shadows. Although the hands on the clocks showed that only seventeen hours had elapsed, time seemed to have leapt forward since the first time Mauro Larrea had entered that room—since, standing at the window the previous night, she had announced her decision to leave Jerez and the dark clouds of this noontide when neither of them, weary, frustrated, and confused, could see so much as a chink of light at the end of any of the tunnels opening so gloomily before them.

"I've just told the servants to start packing. There's no point waiting any longer."

Then, as though driven by the same haste she had instilled in her staff, she herself began to organize the piles on her desk as she talked. He watched from a few feet away as she folded sheets scrawled with notes, sorted through letters in various languages, and quickly glanced at other papers before tearing them up. Her activity matched the fury she felt inside. She was getting ready to leave for good. She was slipping away from him.

"God only knows where that wretch of a stepson of mine and my cousin's wife have gone," she added without pausing in her task. "All I'm sure of is that, sooner rather than later, he is going to bare his fangs at us again, and that we need to be gone before he does."

To avoid troubling his soul at the thought of what the world would be like when he could no longer see her every day, Mauro Larrea simply asked: "To Malta, then?"

Her reply was a shake of the head as she continued ruthlessly tearing up sheets of paper full of figures.

"No, to Portugal. Gaia, close to Porto. I think that's the easiest to reach by sea from Cádiz and to be relatively near to home and the girls." She paused for a moment, then added in a lower voice. "Nearer to London, I mean." She went on more animatedly: "Friends from the wine trade will take us in. They're English, too. There are strong bonds between us; they'd do anything for Edward. It's a port of call for almost all the British ships, so it won't take us long to find passages. Only Palmer and one of the maidservants will go with us; we'll manage. While I finish organizing everything, and just in case Alan should reappear, I'll stay here quietly and leave Edward in the hands of Inés."

A whole host of questions were whirling around the miner's brain, but the most recent events had been so tangled, so demanding of time and attention, that he had not had a moment's pause to sort them out. Perhaps now, with just the two of them so uncertain of their future, in the gray light of this room where nobody had even bothered to light a lamp while outside the drizzle continued to fall on a square empty of stalls, clerks, and customers—perhaps now was the moment to put his doubts to her.

"Why is your sister acting this way? What does she have against her past, against you?"

Without waiting for her invitation, he settled in the same armchair he had sat in the night before. With this informality, he seemed to be saying: *Come and sit beside me, Soledad. Stop pouring your anger into tearing up bits of paper. Come here and talk to me.*

She stared blankly in front of her for a few moments, her hands still full of documents, trying to find an adequate response. Then she threw the papers onto the still-cluttered desk and, as if she had read his mind, came over to him.

"I've been trying for twenty years to properly describe her attitude, and still haven't succeeded," she said, sitting in the armchair opposite him. "Resentment, perhaps?" she wondered, crossing her legs beneath her Piedmont silk skirt. "Rancor? Or simply a painful disappointment? A huge, bitter disappointment that I sense will never end."

She fell silent again for a few seconds, as though trying to find the best way to put this into words.

"She thinks we left her on her own at the very worst moment, following our cousin Matí's funeral. Manuel went back to his medical studies in Cádiz; I left with Edward to start my life as a newly married woman; Gustavo ended up in the Americas. Inés was left alone as our elders slid inexorably into decline. Our grandmother, my mother, and the aunts with their eternal mourning, laudanum, and gloomy rosaries. Grandfather eaten away by illness. Uncle Luis, Matí and Luisito's father, sunk in a deep well of sorrow from which he never emerged, and our wastrel father, Jacobo, increasingly lost with each passing day in the slums and bawdy houses."

"What about Luis, the Runt?"

"At first they sent him to a boarding school in Seville. He was only fifteen but barely looked more than ten. He was profoundly affected by his elder brother's death; he went into a deep depression and took ages to recover. And so Inés was the only one who at first seemed destined to remain in the midst of that hell, living with a troop of the living dead. She begged us to help, but none of us listened, and we all fled. From the desolation, the ruin of our family. From the bitter end to our youth. And Inés, who until then had not shown any particular pious vocation, chose to shut herself away in a convent rather than to have to put up with it all."

It certainly was a sad panorama, he reflected, without taking his eyes from her. The life of a promising young man cut off in his prime, and as a consequence a whole clan was left in a state of profound despair. Sad indeed, but something still bothered him: he did not see this as being sufficiently devastating to have provoked a collective tragedy on such a scale. Perhaps it was for this reason, because the story she had told was not sufficiently convincing, and both of them knew it, that following a few further moments of silence she decided to reveal more.

"What did Manuel tell you happened during that hunting party to Doñana?" she asked, pressing the tips of her fingers under her chin.

"That it was an accident."

"An anonymous shot that went astray?"

"I think that's what I recall."

"What you know is the story we invented, the one we always tell other people. The truth is that the shot that killed Matí did not come from some unknown gun but from one of ours." She paused and swallowed hard. "From Gustavo's, in fact."

In his mind's eye, Mauro caught a fleeting glimpse of his rival's blue eyes. The ones he'd seen in El Louvre Café. The ones in La Chucha's place. Impenetrable, hermetic, as though filled with clear water turned to stone. *So that was the weight on you, my friend,* he said to himself. For the first time he felt a hint of somber compassion for his adversary.

"It was his sense of guilt that made him leave for the Americas," Sol went on. "No one ever said the word *killer* but we all thought it. Gustavo killed Matí, and so our grandfather gave him a considerable sum in hard cash and ordered him to go away and disappear from our lives. To the Indies or to Hell. For him almost to cease to exist."

His reckless wager, Calafat's intuition, the sound of the ivory balls as they caromed off each other on the green baize during the devilish game they became caught up in. Everything was starting to make sense.

Soledad's voice jolted him out of Havana and back to Jerez.

"But there was already tension in the air. We were inseparable as children, but we had grown up and were moving apart. In that eternal domestic paradise in which we lived, we had naïvely promised to be united and faithful to one another forever. From when we were little, a gaggle of innocent builders of dreams, we created the perfect structure: Inés and Manuel would marry; Gustavo would be my husband. Matí never took part in those fantasies of ours, but as the older cousin he was in charge, and so we decided we would find him a beautiful young lady who wouldn't cause us any problems. And Luisito, Little Runt, would stay unmarried at our side as a faithful ally. We would all remain the best of friends, have loads of children, and the doors of our shared house would always be open for anyone wishing to see our never-ending happiness."

"Until reality decided otherwise," Mauro prompted.

Her mouth twisted in a mixture of irony and bitterness. Outside, the rain continued to trickle down the windowpanes.

"Until grandfather Matías began to plan a very different future for us. And before we even realized that there was a world outside full of men and women with whom we might eventually share our lives, he changed all the pieces on the board."

Mauro Larrea recalled what Ysasi had told him in the tavern. The generational transfer.

At that moment the little maid with the sallow face came into the study carrying a tray of snacks. She laid it down next to them: cuts of cold meat on a linen cloth, small sandwiches, a bottle, two cut-glass wineglasses. She spoke a few words in English, but he only managed to catch "Mister Palmer" and guessed that this was the butler's idea when he saw that lunchtime had come and gone without anyone going near the dining room. The maid then pointed to an oil lamp with a deco-rated screen on one of the tables. She must have asked her mistress if she wanted it lit to provide some light in the gloomy room. The reply was a decisive "No, thank you."

They paid no attention to the food, either. Soledad had pushed open the door to her past, and there was no place there for the sherry or the duck breasts on the tray. At most this was an opportunity to chew over a kind of bitter nostalgia and share it with the man listening to her.

"Our grandfather set his sights on his grandchildren. That meant he worked out a sophisticated scheme, part of which included marrying off one of us girls to his English agent. That was intended to secure part of his business: the wine exports. He didn't care that Inés and I were then seventeen and sixteen, or that Edward was older than our own father and had an almost adolescent son. Nor was grandfather concerned that neither of us could understand at first why all of a sudden this friend of the family whom we had known since we were little girls started to bring us Gunter's marmalade from London, invited us to stroll along the Alameda Vieja, and insisted we read Keats's melancholy odes to improve our English pronunciation. Edward obviously was not against the idea. And so I ended up, not yet eighteen, giving my consent from beneath a magnificent Chantilly lace veil, naïvely unaware of what would come next."

Mauro preferred not to dwell on that, and so asked:

"What about your sister?"

"She never forgave me."

The rustle of her silk skirt told him that underneath the magnificent material she was uncrossing her legs, only to cross them again in the opposite sense.

"Once we realized what was going on, and seeing that at first Edward seemed equally attracted to both of us, Inés began to think of it far more seriously than I did. She began to get her hopes up and almost to take it for granted that, since she was the older one, the one who was more settled and serene, possibly even more beautiful, she would eventually become the definitive object of the affections of our suitor once the rather childish courtship of the two of us ended. Before then, we had both taken this very lightly, although he hadn't."

"Your grandfather?"

"No, Edward," she corrected him quickly. "He took the challenge of choosing a bride very earnestly. His first wife, left an orphan by a rich importer of hides from Canada, had died of tuberculosis nine years earlier. He was a widower in his late forties, passionate about wine, and the owner of a prosperous wine business he had inherited from his father. He spent his life traveling to arrange deals; his son meanwhile was brought up by some maternal aunts in Middlesex. They were spinsters who turned him into a spoiled and selfish little monster. Each time Edward came to Jerez on one of his twice-yearly visits, our house was the closest thing he had to a home, and it was one long celebration. With our grandfather as his staunch business ally, and the ne'er-do-wells of my father and uncle as his closest friends despite the contrast with his Victorian bourgeois morality, all that was lacking was for our bloods to be mixed through marriage."

She uncrossed her legs again, this time to get up from the armchair. She went over to the table the maid had pointed out earlier, the one on which stood the delicate lamp with its shade painted with tree branches and long-legged birds. Taking a long cedar match out of a silver box, she lit the lamp, and a warm glow spread over the study. Still standing, she blew the match out and, holding it between her fingers, continued her story.

"He soon decided I was the one; I never asked him why."

She walked over to the big window and went on talking with her back to him, perhaps so as not to reveal such intimate details to his face.

"The fact is, he made a great effort to cut this state of affairs short. He could see what a difficult situation it was: two sisters taken out of the shop window and forced to compete without wishing to, at an age when neither of us was sufficiently mature to understand much of what was going on. Then came the night before the wedding. The house was full of flowers and foreign guests; my wedding dress for some reason was hanging from a chandelier. Inés, who as far as anyone could tell had accepted this unexpected choice quite calmly, was lying in the bed next to mine in the room we had always shared, which is the one you are sleeping in now. Suddenly, she broke down in a fit of inconsolable weeping that went on until dawn."

Sol returned to her armchair and leaned back in it. Now, even though she was revealing her innermost feelings, she did look him in the face.

"I was not in love with Edward, but I was naïvely seduced by the esteem he began to show me. And by the world that I imagined was at my feet," she added with a hint of bitterness. "A magnificent wedding in La Colegiata, a splendid trousseau, a maisonette in Belgravia. Trips back to Jerez twice a year, up-to-date with the latest fashions, and surrounded with new things. A paradise for the unthinking, pampered, and romantic creature I was then, a foolish young thing who had no idea of how bitter my uprooting would be, or how hard it was going to be in those first years to live far from my family with a stranger nearly thirty years older than me and who brought an insufferable son to our marriage. A dizzy young woman who never once imagined that this commitment she had fallen into almost by chance would sever once and for all the relationship she had with the person to whom she had been closest since birth."

Mauro Larrea was taking in every word. He did not drink, eat, or smoke.

"In spite of everything, I learned to love Edward. He was always attractive, attentive, and generous. He got on extraordinarily well with people, was a good conversationalist, knew the world, and behaved impeccably. I realize now, though, that I loved him differently from the way I would have loved a man I myself had chosen."

Although she did not mean to, her words sounded harsh and unsettling.

"In a completely different way to how I would have loved you."

He scratched at the scar on his hand until it almost began to bleed.

"But he was always a good companion on my journey. With him I learned to swim in both calm and stormy waters, and it is thanks to him that I am the woman I am today."

Now it was the miner who rose to his feet. He had heard enough and refused to listen to more. He did not want to continue corroding his soul as he imagined what it would have been like to have spent all those years at Soledad's side. Waking up next to her every morning, sharing common dreams, filling her fertile womb with daughter after daughter.

He went over to the window, which she had moved away from a few moments before. The rain had ceased, and the gray sky was beginning to clear. In the square, a few scruffy children were splashing in the puddles, running and laughing with pleasure.

That's enough, compadre. Cut loose from a past that cannot be brought back and from an imagined future that will never exist. Get back to your life at the point where you left it. Get back to your pathetic reality.

"The devil knows where that Gorostiza woman has got to, trying to cause us more trouble," he muttered.

Before Soledad could react to this sudden change in topic, a voice rang out in the room.

"I think I know."

Startled, they both turned their heads toward the doorway. In it, accompanied by Palmer, stood Nicolás.

"Santos Huesos has just come back from combing the streets for her, and told me."

He stepped confidently into the room. His clothes were soaking.

"He told me you were desperately searching for a relative of the Gorostizas' who had arrived from Cuba. A flamboyant-looking woman whose appearance was different from the ladies around here. I didn't need any more information to remember: I met her in . . . in Santa María del Puerto?"

"El Puerto de Santa María," they corrected him as one.

"No matter: I saw her early this morning at the quay. She was about to cross to Cádiz on the same steamship I had just arrived on."

CHAPTER FORTY-SEVEN

I t was completely dark by the time he raised the brass door knocker in the shape of a laurel wreath. He adjusted his cravat; she straightened the bow on her hat. They both cleared their throats at almost the same time.

"I understand that the lady from overseas who came looking for me might be here."

Genaro, the aged butler, said nothing but showed them into the office, the room Mauro had been received in when he first disembarked and arrived at the Fatous' house with a letter of recommendation from Calafat. Since that morning he had not set foot inside this room reserved for customers and for business; he had quickly become a welcome guest and had a comfortable bedroom placed at his disposition, as well as the family room and the dining room where every morning they had served him hot chocolate with churros beneath the unchanging gaze of bearded ancestors. Now, however, he was back at the starting point again: here he was seated on the same pinwale-upholstered chairs, surrounded by the same engravings of motionless schooners. As if he were once more a stranger, lit by the dim lamps of this outer room. The only difference was that this time he was accompanied by a woman.

"Fatou is a fourth-generation shipping merchant as well as a com-

mission agent and a government supplier," Mauro said quietly to Soledad. "He ships goods throughout Europe, the Philippines, and the
Antilles, including a lot of sherry. He owns his own ships and warehouses and also lends money for big ventures."

"That's not bad."

"I'd give my right arm to own a fifth of it."

Despite the tense atmosphere, they both almost burst out laughing.
An untimely, uncouth guffaw to free themselves from all the accumulated anxiety and recharge their spirits to confront all the uncertainties
ahead. Unfortunately, this did not happen, because at that very instant
the owner of the house appeared.

He did not greet him with the simple "Mauro" with which he had
bidden the miner farewell a few days earlier: a solemn "Good evening
to you" showed them that the situation was likely to be as taut as the
skin of a drum. Sol Claydon was presented as the cousin by marriage of
Carola Gorostiza, and then Fatou, plainly stiff and uncomfortable, sat
down opposite them. Before saying a word, he carefully straightened
the fine pin-striped material of his trousers over his knees, concentrating on that trifling task in order to gain time.

"Well, now . . ."

The miner preferred to spare him his embarrassment.

"My dear Antonio, I'm truly sorry for the problems this unpleasant
turn of events may be causing you." Using Fatou's Christian name was
of course deliberate. By doing so, Mauro was hoping to reestablish the
cordial links between them. "We came as soon as we suspected that
Señora Gorostiza might be here."

Where else could that madwoman have gone, he had thought as soon as
they learned from Nicolás that her destination was Cádiz. *She doesn't know
anyone in the city; all she has is a name and address written on a scrap of paper,
because that's what she had when she left Havana in search of me. It was at the
Fatous' house that they gave her vague directions to where I was in Jerez, and*

that's the only place she can possibly return to. Those were his thoughts, and so that was where they headed without a moment's delay. They told Nico, who would have preferred a hundred times to accompany them, if only to have something to do, to go and inform Manuel Ysasi, who as usual was busy with his appointments and visits. And to await any reply from the possible purchasers from Madrid. *It's really important to us,* Mauro warned Nico as he squeezed his forearm by way of farewell. *Be careful, because both our futures depend on what they finally decide.*

Soledad and he had weighed up the different possibilities of what to do next. They chose one of the most straightforward ones: to demonstrate that Carola Gorostiza was a greedy, unstable outsider not worthy of an ounce of trust. This was the idea they had in mind when they arrived at Calle de la Verónica and found themselves seated in this room dimly lit by two feeble lamps.

Waiting before they gave Fatou their own slanted version of the story, they listened first to what he had to say.

"This is certainly a rather unpleasant situation. And as you can imagine, it has put me in a very difficult position. This lady is making very serious accusations against you, Mauro."

He was using Larrea's first name again: that was a good sign. But it was of little use against the veritable cannonade that Fatou fired pointblank at him immediately afterward.

"Keeping her imprisoned against her will. Unlawful appropriation of goods and properties belonging to her husband. Underhanded use of wills and testaments. Illicit deals conducted in houses of ill repute. Even slave trading."

God almighty. That madwoman had even thrown the brothel at El Manglar and the abominable deals done by Novás the crockery seller into the mix. Mauro could sense Soledad stiffen but preferred not to look directly at her.

"I trust you did not give the slightest credence to her claims."

"I should dearly like not to have to call your honesty into question, my friend, but there are numerous facts that go against you, and not all of them are insubstantial."

"Did the lady in question also tell you what she hoped to achieve by these absurd allegations?"

"For the moment, she has asked me to accompany her tomorrow to present a complaint against you at the court."

Mauro snorted incredulously.

"I imagine you have no intention of doing so."

"I don't yet know, Señor Larrea." It did not escape Mauro's notice that Fatou had returned to using his surname. "I don't yet know."

Footsteps could be heard; the door that Fatou had closed as a precaution burst open without anybody knocking to request entry.

Her dress was a discreet vanilla color, with a much less revealing neckline than she usually wore. Her black hair, often loose and adorned with flowers, ringlets, and other embellishments, was now pulled back in a tight chignon. The only thing that had not changed were those eyes of hers, which he already knew so well: burning like two candle flames, a sign of her determination to commit any barbarity.

She dominated the scene in a carefully prepared role. A role he had not been expecting and that therefore caught him unawares: that of the distraught victim. *You cunning vixen,* he muttered under his breath.

She did not greet him, as though she had not seen him.

"Good evening, madam," she said from the threshold after studying Sol closely for a few moments. "I suppose you must be Soledad."

"We have already met, even if you don't remember it," Sol replied calmly. "You fainted in my house soon after you arrived. I was looking after you for quite some time. I put rosemary alcohol compresses on your wrists and rubbed your temples with jimson oil."

Paulita, Fatou's young wife, was struggling to push past to get into the room, but Carola Gorostiza would not budge.

"I doubt very much that I fainted by chance," said the Mexican woman, finally stepping inside the room with the look of a much-maligned heroine. "I think it's more likely that you somehow caused it with the intention of keeping me there. Then you shut me up in that filthy room. But as you can see, much good it did you."

She sat down in one of the armchairs with a regal air. Mauro Larrea stared at her in astonishment. He had been mentally preparing to meet the Carola Gorostiza he had always known: haughty, tough, arrogant. Someone to confront openly, face-to-face, in a shouting match if need be. If that had been the case, he had no doubt he would have come out on top. But Zayas's wife had had more than enough time to work out her strategy and, of all those available to her, she had chosen the least predictable and perhaps the most intelligent. To pretend she was a martyr, the poor little victim: a grandiose display of hypocrisy that if he was not careful could allow her to win hands down.

As an unconscious reaction he stood up, possibly anticipating that being on his feet would help make what he was about to say more convincing. As if a simple posture could withstand the devastating armory she had at her disposal.

"Do you really believe, my friends, that I, a prosperous mine owner in whom your Cuban agent Don Julián Calafat placed his complete confidence, could have been capable of—"

"Capable of the worst villainy," she interjected.

"Capable of carrying out such abuses with a lady I hardly know, who has pursued me across the Atlantic for no good reason, and who in fact is the younger sister of my own son's future father-in-law?"

"My gullible brother has no idea what kind of family he is getting mixed up with if he allows his daughter to marry somebody of your kind."

The Fatou couple had been having lunch when the arrival of a weeping stranger was announced. She was begging for help, using as pretext not only her family connections with the Calafats in Cuba but even with the banker's wife and daughters, with whom she claimed to move among the cream of Havana society. She was fleeing Mauro Larrea, she gasped between sobs. From that soulless brute, that savage. And she provided details about him that made the couple hesitate. Didn't it seem odd to them that he should come from the Americas simply to sell some properties he wasn't even familiar with? Didn't it seem suspicious that he should rid himself of them without even knowing what they consisted of? By the time the miner came looking for her several hours later, she had the gentle wife in her pocket and the husband teetering, unsure of where he stood.

"Do you know, dear friends," she said now, "what this individual is hiding beneath his smooth exterior and fine suits? One of the biggest swindlers ever seen on the island of Cuba. A ruined adventurer, an unscrupulous manipulator, a . . . a . . ."

Mauro muttered, "For the love of God" as he stroked his old scar.

"He scoured the streets of Havana looking for any opportunity to lay his hands on some cash. He tried to get money out of me behind my husband's back for a very dubious business venture. Then he inveigled him into risking his inheritance on a game of billiards."

"None of that is true," he refuted.

"He dragged him to a house of ill repute in a neighborhood full of riffraff. He used trickery to fleece him of all his money and then embarked as quickly as possible for Spain before anyone could stop him."

He planted himself in front of her. He could not allow her to sink her teeth into his dignity like a starving vixen, dragging him through the dust without letting go.

"Would you care to stop spouting all this nonsense?"

"And if I followed him here from Cuba," Carola Gorostiza went on, "it was solely to demand that he return to me what is lawfully ours."

The miner drew a deep breath, anxious as a cornered beast. He could not let her get away with this, but losing his temper would only confirm her claims.

"All the deeds to the properties are in my name, confirmed by a notary public," he said firmly. "Never at any moment for any reason or in any way did I commit the slightest illegal act. I did not even betray any moral code, something I am not sure you can claim. You should know, my friends . . ."

Before getting started on his accusations, he glanced quickly around the room. The young couple were witnessing everything wide-eyed, bewildered and terrified at this bitter struggle that threatened to spatter the carpets, curtains, and wallpaper with its mud. This was predictable: it would have been strange if the Fatous had not been astonished by this fierce row more suited to a dockside tavern than to that respectable Cádiz residence where the word *scandal* had never had any place.

But what he could not figure out was the reaction of the third witness. What was Soledad's viewpoint? To his amazement, he could not see what he had been expecting on the face of his closest ally. She had not moved: she was still sitting upright, shoulders stiff, hardly shifting since they had arrived. It was her big eyes that had changed. A change he immediately noticed. A shadow of suspicion, a wary look, was threatening to replace what until that moment had been a rock-solid complicity.

Mauro Larrea's priorities changed in an instant. His worst fears suddenly ceased to worry him: the probability of having to face a Spanish court, the threat of being ruined for the rest of his life, even the foul Tadeo Carrús and his accursed threats. All this became of secondary importance, replaced by a far more urgent and important task: to recover a trust that had been broken.

His muscles tensed; his jaw hardened as he gritted his teeth. His voice resounded through the room, and even the windows seemed to shake.

"That's enough! You must proceed as you see fit, Señora Gorostiza," he continued firmly. "And let it be resolved by whoever has the authority to do so. Make a formal accusation against me, present a judge with the evidence you have, and I will determine how to defend myself. But I demand you cease calling my integrity into question."

A tense, prolonged silence took hold of the room. It was torn apart by the voice of Zayas's wife, as sharp as a barber's razor.

"Excuse me, but no." Little by little she was abandoning her role as the outraged martyr and returning to her natural self. "It's nowhere near over yet, sir; I still have a lot more to say about you. A lot that nobody here is aware of, but which I'll make it my business to report. Your negotiations with the crockery seller on Calle de la Obrapía, for example. You all should know that this ignoble wretch here was dealing with a slave trafficker in order to obtain rich profits from the despicable trade in African flesh."

Not even the fact that Mauro had not answered all her accusations could prevent the Gorostiza woman from spreading her filthy gossip. She clearly intended not only to recuperate her husband's inheritance but to seek revenge for the way she had been treated in Jerez.

"He arrived in Havana without a penny to his name, unable even to hire a carriage, as decent people there," she went on feverishly. Her hair was coming loose from its neat chignon, her cheeks were aflame, and her generous bust was straining at the neckline. "He intruded in balls where no one knew him; he lived in the house of a quadroon who had been the lover of a Spaniard and with whom he shared glasses of rum and heaven knows what else."

As she continued spewing her poison into the air, the world came to a standstill for Mauro Larrea. All he was interested in was one person's reaction.

He silently tried to convey the only thing that mattered to him at that moment.

Don't doubt me, Soledad.

It was then that she decided to intervene.

CHAPTER FORTY-EIGHT

❧

"Well, now, I think that this lamentable spectacle has gone on far too long."

"What are you talking about, you hussy? What is it you dare say about me? Because I'm not going to admit a thing, you can count on that. This man has not been the only source of my misfortune, because long before he came into my life, you were already there."

Carola Gorostiza screamed this at the top of her voice: her nerves were finally getting the better of her. The long, sleepless night before she could escape, the days she had spent shut in, her anxiousness. As all of this rose to the surface, the role of a submissive victim burst like a soap bubble.

A tense silence descended on the room once more.

"None of this would have happened if you hadn't always been on my husband's mind. If Gustavo hadn't been so afraid of meeting you again, he would never have allowed himself to be robbed of his inheritance."

Mauro Larrea's mind flew back to La Chucha's turquoise room: images and moments piled on top of each other. Zayas risking his return to Spain with a cue and three balls, deciding his destiny on the outcome of a game of billiards with a stranger. Fighting to defeat him while at the same time wishing to lose; obsessed with a woman he had not seen for more than twenty years but who ever since he had crossed the ocean he had not stopped pining for. A strange way to behave: to let chance have the last word. If he had won, he could have returned with money and a position to a place he had been expelled from following the drama he himself had caused: a return to face the living and the dead. A return to Soledad. If he lost and did not gain the amount he needed to return in a viable position, he handed over the family properties to his adversary and washed his hands forever of his forebears' house, vineyard, and winery. Of guilt and the past. And, above all, of her. It was truly a strange way to decide things. All or nothing. Like someone risking the future on a suicidal game of heads or tails.

Carola Gorostiza meanwhile began to search in vain for a handkerchief in the cuffs of her dress. Ever attentive, the young Señora Fatou offered her own, which the other proceeded to dab at the corners of her eyes.

"I've spent half a lifetime fighting your ghost, Soledad Montalvo. Half a lifetime trying to make Gustavo feel an ounce of what he never ceased feeling for you."

She addressed Soledad with the stark familiarity of someone revealing the unhappiness of a lengthy marriage starved of affection: the despairing cry of an unloved woman.

Something stirred deep inside Sol Claydon, but she resisted showing it. She sat as still as a caryatid, straight-backed, head held high, and hands folded on her lap. Both her rings were visible: the engagement ring that showed her acceptance of the irrevocable decisions made by the great Don Matías, which had crushed her cousin's youthful passion, and the one with which she married a foreigner and tore herself away from her sister and her world. Soledad Montalvo remained apparently icy-faced with the other woman's lament. Even though her heart had crumpled like parchment, she refused to let her reaction peep through the façade of fake indifference.

Finally she spoke, calmly and solemnly.

"I wish it had not come to this, but given the circumstances I'm afraid I must reply to you with painful frankness."

Her words had the effect of a painter's brush, splashing a look of intrigue across all their faces.

"As you will have observed during all this time we have allowed Señora de Zayas to speak, her mental health has deteriorated considerably. Fortunately, my cousin has made the whole family aware of this."

"You and your cousin uniting yet again behind my back!"

Sol pretended not to have heard her, and went on.

"That is the reason why recently, on medical advice, we preferred to keep her in her room. Unfortunately, taking advantage of a momentary lapse by our servants, and driven on by her maniacal fantasies, she decided to leave on her own account. And to come here."

Unable to believe her ears, Carola Gorostiza tried to leap from her chair. Antonio Fatou immediately stopped her, in a commanding voice he had not previously adopted.

"Be still, Señora Gorostiza. Continue, Señora Claydon, if you please."

"Dear friends, your guest is suffering from a profound emotional imbalance: a neurosis that transforms her vision of reality, distorting it impulsively and leading her to adopt the kind of extremely wild behavior you have just witnessed."

"What are you saying, you trollop?" shrieked Carola.

"That is why, and at her husband's request . . ."

Soledad slid one of her long hands into the bag she still had on her knees. Out of it she took a small brown suede pouch and began emptying its contents with an excruciating lack of haste. The first thing she placed on the marble table was a small glass vial half filled with a cloudy liquid.

"This is a mixture of morphine, chloral hydrate, and potassium bromide," she explained in a low voice. "It will help relieve her crisis."

The miner struggled to breathe. Far more than an ingenious ruse or a magnificent challenge like the one she had confronted the possible buyers with in the winery, this was sheer recklessness. On the evening when her stepson had kept them prisoner she had told him that she always carried her husband's medication with her, just in case. Now, in an attempt to calm the insane fury of this female hurricane, she was proposing to inject those substances into a completely different organism.

In a rage, Carola Gorostiza finally got up and tried to snatch the vial from her. As though released by the same spring, Mauro Larrea and Antonio Fatou immediately grabbed hold of her arms. She resisted as though possessed by all the devils in hell.

Soledad meanwhile was calmly taking the hypodermic syringe out of the pouch. She fixed a hollow metal needle to it with all the skill of someone who had practical experience in the maneuver.

The two men managed to immobilize Carola on the sofa. Her hair was disheveled, her bosom had almost burst free of her dress, and rage was imprinted on her face like a sailor's tattoo.

"Could you push up the sleeve of her dress, please," Sol instructed Paulita. The young wife obeyed timorously.

Soledad went toward the sofa. A couple of big drops of liquid fell from the end of the needle.

"The effect is immediate," she said in a low, solemn voice. "In twenty or thirty seconds she will be asleep. Paralyzed. Inert."

The expression of furious defiance on Carola Gorostiza's face gave way to a terrified grimace.

"She will lose consciousness," Soledad continued gravely.

Overcome with fear, Carola's body went limp. She was panting; her lips were two taut white lines. Beads of sweat appeared on her forehead.

Soledad had decided to stake everything on this. Even at the cost of dismissing Gustavo's probably genuine emotions toward her as crazy. Even using the same weapons she had employed to counteract the perverse sickness that had destroyed her husband's mind and devastated her own life.

"Then she'll go into a deep, prolonged stupor."

Bewilderment hung in the air of the room like a dense fog. Fatou's wife was looking on in complete terror. The two men were tense, awaiting Soledad's next move.

"That is, unless . . ." Soledad whispered, holding the needle a handbreadth from the arm of the supposed lunatic. She paused for a few moments. "Unless she manages to calm down by herself."

Her words had an immediate effect on Carola. She closed her eyes and, after a few moments, nodded. A slight movement of her chin, nothing more. But that tiny signal indicated she had surrendered.

"You can let her go."

The mixture of drugs that Edward had been absorbing into his body over years did not enter Carola's veins. The fear of being neutralized by chemical substances did.

The miner and Soledad avoided looking at each other as she neatly returned the instruments to her pouch, and he let go of Carola's limp body. They both knew they had just played a dreadful, underhanded trick. But there was no other way: they had no other cards to play.

Either you stop or I'll put a stop to you, Sol had just warned her cousin's wife. And Carola, despite her anger and desire to get even, had understood. No longer dangerous following their silent pact, she allowed herself to be led upstairs by the men. The two other women watched her climb the steps. Dignified and stiff, biting her tongue so as not to confront them again. Proud despite the tremendous blow she had just received. Sol put her arm around the shoulders of poor Paulita; overwhelmed by a mixture of dread and relief, the young woman had burst into tears. After the two men accompanied Carola to a guest bedroom and locked the door, Fatou gave orders to his servants.

"It's better to keep her on her own, although I don't think she'll have another crisis. She'll sleep soundly, and tomorrow will be perfectly relaxed," Soledad assured them when they reappeared downstairs. "I'll come early in the morning to see how she is."

"You may spend the night here if you wish," suggested Paulita in a faint voice.

"Many thanks, but we have friends waiting for us," Soledad lied.

Still in a state of shock, neither of the Fatous insisted.

"I'll make sure to book her passage on the next boat for the Antilles," said Mauro. "I understand there's a mailboat leaving quite soon. The quicker she returns home, the better."

"Yes, the *Reina de los Angeles*, but that's only in three days' time," said Paulita, dabbing the corner of her eye with the tip of her handkerchief. She was obviously horrified at the idea of having this time bomb beneath her roof until then. "I know, because some female friends of mine are going to San Juan."

Antonio Fatou hesitated a few seconds, then said, "We have a ship moored in the port that has a cargo of two thousand sacks of salt. It is leaving at dawn on the day after tomorrow, in little more than twenty-four hours, heading for Santiago de Cuba and Havana."

Mauro had to stop himself from crowing: even if she reached the Caribbean converted into salt fish, the important thing was to get that woman out of Cádiz as quickly as possible.

"The ship is supposed to take only cargo," Fatou explained, "but in the past it also used to have a few passengers on board. I seem to remember there are a couple of small cabins with some old bunks that could be made decent. It doesn't call in at either the Canary Islands or Puerto Rico, and so will arrive long before the mailboat."

Soledad and Mauro contained their impulse to embrace him. What a great man Antonio Fatou was. A worthy son of the legendary Cádiz bourgeoisie, a gentleman from top to toe.

"Will she be in a fit state to . . . Perhaps she ought to see a doctor," Paulita cautiously suggested.

"She's as fit as a fiddle, my love. She'll be fine from now on, you'll see."

They agreed to finalize everything the next day, and the Fatous accompanied them to the entrance. The two women walked in front, the men behind. Soledad kissed the young wife on both cheeks; Fatou shook Mauro Larrea's hand and offered a heartfelt apology.

"I'm truly sorry, my friend, that I ever doubted your honor."

"Please don't trouble yourself about the matter," the miner replied with shameless nerve. "You have both done more than enough by enduring this nasty business in your own house even though it doesn't concern you in any way."

He and Soledad took deep breaths of the sea air as the butler came out to light their way with an oil lamp.

"Good night, Genaro, and thanks for your help."

The only response was a couple of coughs and a slight nod of the head.

They set off, seeing themselves as a pair of unscrupulous crooks walking down the deserted streets in the middle of the night. They had taken only a few steps when they heard the voice of the elderly servant behind their backs.

"Don Mauro, Señora."

They turned to look at him.

"You'll be well looked after in the Cuatro Naciones Inn, in Plaza de Mina. You needn't be anxious: I'll keep an eye on the foreigner and my master and mistress. God be with you."

They walked on in silence, unable to squeeze so much as a drop of joy out of this bitter triumph that had left them feeling jarred, with a taste of bile in their souls.

CHAPTER FORTY-NINE

෴

He leapt up when he heard a loud knocking at the door. Daylight and early morning noises were filtering in through the half-open curtains from the square.

"What's this, Santos? Where did you spring from?"

Hardly had he said this than the events of the past two days came flooding into his mind. Starting with the latest.

They had been received at the inn with the offer of two adjoining rooms with no questions asked, and a meager meal served in a corner of the plain dining room. Cold beef. Cooked ham. A bottle of pale sherry. Bread. They said little, drank little, and hardly ate, despite the fact that they had put nothing in their stomachs since breakfast.

After climbing the stairs together, they walked along the corridor side by side, each carrying a key. When they reached the bedroom doors, both of them found it hard to get out the words "Good night." Not being able to speak, she stepped toward him and leaned her head on his chest, burying her beautiful face between the lapels of his frock coat. She was searching for shelter, comfort, or the solidity that both of them were starting to lack and that only together, supporting one another, did they seem able to regain. He pushed his nose and mouth into her hair, breathing it in like someone drawing his very last breath. Just as he was about to embrace her, Soledad took a step back. She raised a hand to his jaw and caressed him for a brief moment. Then came the sound of her key turning in the lock. As she disappeared behind the door, Mauro felt as if he had been flayed alive.

In spite of all his accumulated weariness, he found sleep hard to come by. Perhaps because his mind was full of scenes, voices, and faces that were as violent and disturbing as a cockfight. Or possibly because his body was desperately crying out for the person who on the far side of the wall was silently stepping out of her clothes, loosening her hair around her bare, angular shoulders, and then slipping between the covers, preoccupied by the fate of a man who was not him.

To brush against her, feel her breath on him, warm himself beside her in the dark early hours. He would have given what little he now had, the fortune he once had, and whatever fate might offer him in the future, just to spend that night clinging to Soledad Montalvo. To roam over her body with his hands, to curl up between her legs and have her embrace him. To bury himself in her, hear her laughter in his ear, feel her mouth on his mouth, become lost in the folds of her body, and taste her sweetness.

Instead, he surrendered to the arms of Morpheus when the bell of the nearby San Francisco church struck half past three. And it was not yet eight o'clock when Santos Huesos came into his room and unceremoniously roused him.

"Dr. Ysasi needs you to return to Jerez."

"What's happened?" asked Mauro, sitting up in the untidy bed.

"The Englishman has appeared."

"Thank God. Where has the idiot been?"

He began dressing in great haste; one foot was already in the leg of his trousers.

"Yesterday evening he was left for Don Manuel to attend to right outside the hospital. He'd been attacked, it seems."

Mauro uttered a curse. "That's all we need," he growled.

"I'll fetch you a pitcher of water," said his servant. "I can see the *patrón* has not awakened in the best of moods this morning."

"Wait a moment. Where is he now?"

"I think he spent the night at the doctor's house. But I don't know for sure, because as soon as I heard, I took it upon myself to come and look for you."

"Was he badly wounded?"

"Only a little bit. More scared than anything."

"What about his possessions?"

"In his attackers' saddlebags, I guess; where else? He didn't have a single coin on him. They even stole his hat and boots."

"Did his documents vanish, too?"

"That would be asking a lot for me to know, wouldn't it, *patrón*?"

He finally brought him the water and a towel.

"Now go and get me paper and a pen."

"If it's to leave a note for Doña Soledad, don't trouble yourself."

He looked at Santos in the mirror as he was struggling to comb his unruly hair with his hands.

"She was up much earlier than you. I met her as I came in. On her way to the Fatou house, she told me: that was where I had just been, asking after you."

As Mauro continued dressing, he felt his pride was wounded as if a sharp nail had been driven into it. *You ought to have been more alert, you fool,* he told himself.

"Did you tell her about her stepson?"

"From beginning to end."

"What did she say?"

"That you and Don Manuel should deal with him. That she would stay here and look after Doña Carola. That you should send the woman's baggage as quickly as possible so that she could be put on board."

"That's fine. Let's go."

Santos Huesos, with his lustrous hair and the poncho over his shoulder, did not move from the spot.

"She also mentioned something else, *patrón*."

"What?" Mauro asked, searching for his hat.

"That you were to send the mulatta as well."

He found his hat in a corner on an umbrella stand.

"So?"

"So Trinidad doesn't want to go. And her mistress promised."

Mauro recalled the strange pact the slave girl had mentioned as she wept the day her mistress left: that if she helped Carola to escape, she in turn would grant her freedom. Knowing the Gorostiza woman as he did, he very much doubted she had the slightest intention of keeping her side of the bargain. But the innocent girl's head had been filled with fantasies. And Santos Huesos's as well, apparently.

Mauro turned to face him as he buttoned up his frock coat. His faithful servant, his companion in so many trials and tribulations. The quiet Indian who had come into his care when he was no more than a boy down from the mountains. And now here he was, as fierce as a stallion over Trinidad.

"Blasted women . . ."

"Forgive me for saying so, *patrón*, but lately you're hardly the one to teach me lessons on that score."

That was certainly true. Not to him or anyone else. Especially when the woman innkeeper told him on the way out that the lady had already paid their bill. The nail digging into his manly pride sank in a little deeper.

He had still not managed to recover his composure by the time they reached Jerez a few hours later and turned into Calle Francos.

"The Englishman didn't see you, did he?"

"Not even a whisker, I swear."

"It's better, then, that he doesn't see me, either."

A coin was the answer. The one he gave to a boy idling in the street for him to go to the doctor's house.

"Tell Don Manuel I'm waiting for him in the small tavern on the corner. And you, Santos, go and find Nicolás."

It took Ysasi barely three minutes to appear, his brow still furrowed at the unpleasant situation he found himself in. Sitting at the table farthest from the counter, they brought each other up to date over a plate of crushed olives and two glasses of cloudy wine from the barrel. Ysasi had no need to give a complicated medical report on Alan Claydon's state.

"He's black-and-blue, but there's no serious damage."

He told him the same story as he had told Santos, but in greater detail.

"The victim of a gang of robbers of the sort that hold people up every day on the roads of southern Spain. Their mouths must have watered when they saw his magnificent English coach without even a miserable shotgun rider to protect him. The unhappy subject of Queen Victoria doesn't yet know how things stand in our country. They robbed him of everything, coach and coachman included. They left him half-naked among the thorn bushes and cactuses at the bottom of a ravine. Fortunately, a muleteer passing by at nightfall heard him shouting for help. He only understood two words: *Jerez* and *doctor*, but Claydon managed to use gestures to describe my beard and thin frame. And the man, who knew me because some years ago I treated him for sunstroke, which by some miracle he recovered from, took pity on him and brought him to the hospital."

"What about the documents?"

"What documents?"

"The ones Claydon was demanding Soledad sign when he had them locked in the bedroom."

"In the same fire that the highwaymen cook their stew, I imagine. Those vandals don't even know how to sign with their finger, so you can imagine how little they would be interested in documents written in English. Anyway, even without those papers, I'm sure Edward's son has many other ways of accusing her. This incident might have delayed him for now, but as soon as he gets back to England he'll find a way to counterattack."

"So the longer it takes him to reach there, the better."

"Yes, but the solution is not to keep him in Jerez. The best thing would be to send him back to Gibraltar; by the time he arrives, recovers, and organizes his trip to London, we'll at least have gained a few days so that the Claydons can find refuge from him."

By now it was midday, and the small tavern with bare beams, earthen floor, and bullfight posters on the walls was filling with customers. The voices became louder and glasses clinked. Behind the counter, two waiters with a piece of chalk behind their ear were busy pouring out glasses of wine from the neighboring wineries.

"I suppose there's no news of the father."

"I passed by the convent last night and went again this morning. As was to be expected, Inés refuses to see me."

One of the waiters came to their table with two more glasses and a plate of lupine seeds, offered by yet another grateful patient. Ysasi waved his thanks to a figure in the distance.

"Soledad explained the reasons, more or less. But it doesn't seem that the stone wall she has for her sister would change even if she were blasted with dynamite."

"She simply decided to cut us out of her life. That's all there is to it."

The doctor raised his glass in a toast.

"The magnetism of the Montalvo sisters, my friend," he said sarcastically. "They get into your bones, and there's no way of getting them out again."

Mauro Larrea tried to conceal his confusion by gulping down his wine.

"The same attraction that you now feel for Sol," continued Ysasi, "I felt for Inés as a youth."

The amber liquid burnt Mauro's throat. *Good God, Doctor.*

"First she said yes, then no, then yes again, and then she rejected me once more. She thought she was in love with Edward, but it was too late. He had already made his choice."

"Soledad told me about it."

That grandfather would not have minded which granddaughter the Englishman chose: the only thing that mattered to him was to cement the commercial links with the English market as securely as possible. The old rogue.

"Afterward, when the incident with Matí happened in Doñana only a few days following Edward and Sol's wedding, Inés begged me not to abandon her. She swore she had been wrong to lavish her affection on the man who was now her sister's husband. She said she had been confused, that she had been carried away by a fantasy. One evening after another she poured her heart out to me on the benches of the Alameda Cristina. She promised she would come and live with me in Cádiz, or Madrid, or anywhere in the world."

A shadow of melancholy flitted across the doctor's dark eyes.

"I still loved her, heart and soul, but my poor wounded pride was as fierce as a bull out in the fields. And so at first I refused, but then I thought it over. When I came back to Jerez for Christmas I was ready to accept, but by then she had taken the veil. I never saw her again until two nights ago."

Draining his glass of wine, Ysasi stood up. When he spoke again, his tone of voice had completely altered.

"I'm going to feed the Englishman and have them take Gustavo's wife's things to Calle de la Tornería. Let's see if in the meantime you can come up with one of your ruses to get him out of my house so we can put an end to this wretched pantomime once and for all."

He banged the glass back down on the table, then walked off without saying good-bye.

Half an hour later, Mauro sat down to eat with Nicolás at the Victoria Inn, the same place he had been taken to by the notary the day he arrived in Jerez, before he became caught up in this spider's web that seemed humanly impossible to extricate himself from. He was seated with his son at the same table, by the same window.

He let Nicolás prattle on about the marvels of Paris while they shared a stuffed chicken. He would gladly have skipped the meal to dedicate himself to the endless list of emergencies he was facing: to go to the convent to see whether he had any better luck than Ysasi; decide what to do with the stepson; go back to Cádiz to make sure everything was going well at the Fatous. To plan the embarkation on the salt ship, to rush back to Soledad. All of this was threatening him like a vulture circling around a dead mule in Veracruz, and yet at the same time he was aware that he had a son whom he had not seen for five months and who demanded at least a bit of his attention.

This was why he nodded occasionally while Nico was talking, and from time to time asked about some trivial detail so as to disguise the fact that his mind was miles away.

"By the way, did I tell you I met Daniel Meca at a performance at the Comédie-Française?"

"Sarrión's partner, the one with the coaches?"

"His eldest son."

"Wasn't he already working for his father?"

"Only at first."

Mauro raised a forkful of potato to his mouth as Nico went on.

"After that, he came to Europe. To begin a new life."

"Poor Meca," said Mauro without a hint of irony, recalling his companion during endless conversations in the Café del Progreso. "He must have been really disappointed at seeing his heir apparent take flight like that."

He was still racking his brains to try to find solutions to his own problems, but this news about former colleagues in Mexico took his mind away for a moment at least.

"I suppose it must have been painful," his son went on, "but it's understandable as well."

"What is understandable?"

"That children do not meet up to expectations."

"Whose expectations?"

"Their fathers', of course."

Mauro looked up from his plate and observed his son with uneasy curiosity. There was something he was missing.

"What are you driving at, Nico?"

The young man drank deeply from his glass, doubtless to give himself courage.

"At my future."

"And where does your future start?"

"By not marrying Teresa Gorostiza."

Their eyes fixed on one another.

"Don't talk nonsense," growled Mauro.

His son's voice was steady in his reply.

"I don't love her. And neither she nor I deserve to be tied to an unhappy marriage. That's why I came: to tell you that."

Calm, compadre. Stay calm, Mauro told himself while he struggled not to bang his fist on the table and shout at him at the top of his lungs: *Have you gone out of your mind?*

He managed to control himself and talk calmly. To start with, at least.

"You don't know what you're saying. You don't know what you'll lose if you renounce that marriage."

"Her affection or her father's fortune?" was the acid retort.

"Both of them, for the love of Christ!" bawled Mauro, brutally slapping the tablecloth.

The diners at the nearby tables immediately turned their heads in unison toward these eye-catching Indianos who had been the center of attention from the moment they came in. The two of them fell silent, aware of being watched, but continued to eye each other like wary hounds. It was only then that Mauro Larrea saw someone he had not seen before. Only then did he start to understand.

Sitting opposite him was no longer the frail creature of the first months following the death of Elvira. Nor was he the mollycoddled little whelp of his early years, or the impulsive, lively adolescent who took his place. When he managed for a moment to confine his own worries to a corner of his brain—when he was able properly to observe his son for the first time since he had arrived—he found sitting on the far side of the table a youth endowed, rightly or wrongly, with a solid determination. Someone who in part resembled his mother, in part took after him, and yet at the same time was entirely his own man, with an effervescent personality that could not be controlled.

One fundamental thing was missing, however. He needed to know something that at first Mauro had wanted to keep from him at all cost. Although by now it hardly mattered. That was why he laid down his knife and fork, leaned forward, and said in a hoarse voice, slowly and menacingly, "You cannot . . . prevent . . . that . . . wedding. We . . . are . . . ruined . . . *ruined.*"

He almost spat these last syllables, but they seemed to have no effect on the young man. Perhaps he had intuited it. Or perhaps he didn't care.

"You own properties here. Make them pay."

Mauro snorted with contained fury.

"Don't be so stubborn, Nico. Think it over; take your time."

"I've been thinking it over for weeks, and that's my decision."

"The banns have been read, the entire Gorostiza family is anticipating your return, the girl even has her wedding gown hanging in her wardrobe."

"It's my life, Father."

A strained silence descended on them once more, which the other diners were immediately aware of. Until Nicolás spoke again.

"Aren't you going to ask me what my plans are?"

"To carry on living the high life, I suppose," Mauro replied harshly. "Except you no longer have the means."

"On the one hand, you're mistaken. On the other, I already have a project."

"Whereabouts, if I may ask?"

"Between Mexico and Paris."

"Doing what?"

"Opening a business."

He gave a bitter laugh. A business. A business, his Nico. For the love of God.

"A business buying and selling artwork and fine furniture from other periods between the two continents. They're known as antiques. There's a fortune in it in France. And the Mexicans are crazy about them. I've made contacts, and have a partner lined up."

"Wonderful prospects . . ." his father muttered, head down as he pretended to concentrate all his attention on separating the skin from a piece of meat on a chicken drumstick.

"And I'm also waiting," the young man went on, as if he hadn't heard him.

"For what?"

"There is a woman I am in love with. An expatriate Mexican who is anxious to go back, if that reassures you."

"Perfect. Marry her, give her fifteen little Mexicans, be happy," Mauro said sarcastically, still busily cutting up the bird.

"I'm afraid that's impossible at the moment."

Mauro finally raised his eyes from the plate with a mixture of dismay and curiosity.

"She is about to marry a Frenchman."

The miner's rage was on the verge of turning into loud laughter. To top all his ridiculous nonsense, Nico was in love with a girl engaged to somebody else. *Aren't you going to get a single thing right, flesh of my flesh?*

"I don't know why you're so surprised at my choice," Nico went on wryly. "At least she hasn't already been to the altar, or have a sick husband shut in a convent, or have four daughters waiting for her in another country."

Mauro took a deep breath, as if the air contained particles of that patience he so sorely needed.

"Enough, Nico. That's enough."

The young man took his napkin from his lap and brusquely left it on the table.

"I think it would be better for us to finish this conversation some other time."

"If what you're after is to seek my approval for your stupidity, don't count on it now or at any other time."

"I'll take care of my affairs on my own, then, don't worry. You have more than enough to do to sort out the mess you've got yourself into."

Mauro watched him stride out angrily. Left alone at the table facing an empty chair and the carcass of the half-eaten chicken, he was overcome by a sense of desolation. He would have given his life to have Mariana there to intercede between them. *Why on earth did I insist my son go to Europe just before he got married?* he reproached himself. What were the two of them doing in this foreign land that only ever offered them uncertainty upon uncertainty? How and when had the firm alliance between the two of them begun to break down—an alliance that had begun during the dreadful days in the mines, and continued amid the splendors of the Mexican capital? Despite his adolescent revolts, this was the first time that Nicolás had openly challenged his authority as a father. And he did so with all the force of a cannonball crashing into one of the few remaining walls of his nearly depleted stamina.

CHAPTER FIFTY

⌒

After leaving a generous amount on the table without waiting for the bill, Mauro quit the inn to return to the mansion. Carola Gorostiza's baggage was piled up in the doorway.

"You take that side, Santos, and I'll lift here."

By this stage, he could not have cared less if anyone in Jerez saw him lifting and carrying like a vulgar porter. *Ready: one, two three. That's it.* Everything was sinking fast, slipping through his fingers: What did a little more shame matter?

The last thing he did before leaving was to send old Simón with a note to the doctor's house. *Beg you to accompany you-know-who to Cádiz, Plaza de Mina,* he had written. *The Cuatro Naciones Inn. We'll meet there tonight to decide how to proceed.*

He was convinced Fatou would help them find a way to dispatch the Englishman to Gibraltar as quickly as possible. Until then he had no more tricks up his sleeve: all he could think of was to put the stepson in a hotel. He could wait close to the port for his transport. Meanwhile, they would send the Gorostiza woman back to Havana on the salt ship. After that, God would decide.

When they arrived in Cádiz at nightfall with Trinidad, the young slave, was still sobbing like a babe in arms. Unusually sullen, Santos Huesos had only responded in monosyllables to his *patrón's* questions along the way. *That's all I need,* Mauro had muttered under his breath.

"Go for a walk and say good-bye to each other," he said as they approached the studded door in Calle de la Verónica. "And find some way to calm her down, Santos: I don't want any scene when she sees her mistress."

"But she promised me . . ." said Trinidad, bursting into tears once more.

Her sobs were so loud and bitter that several of the passersby turned to look. Shutters behind several windows in the elegant houses nearby were opened as prying eyes peeped out.

Mauro looked daggers at them. The last thing he needed at that moment was to add unnecessary problems to the long list of favors he already owed Fatou. And if he didn't put a stop to it quickly, this scene from an operetta in the middle of the street would do just that.

"Make her shut up, Santos," he growled before turning his back on them. "By all that's holy, shut her up."

He was greeted once more by Genaro and his polite coughs.

"Come in, Don Mauro, they're waiting for you."

This time he was not ushered into the company office but into the sitting room on the main floor where he and his hosts had chatted over coffee and spirits. The married couple, their faces still marked by shock despite their attempts to hide it, were now seated on a damask sofa beneath a pair of still life paintings full of crusts of bread, clay jugs, and freshly hunted partridges. Sitting near them in an armchair, apparently calm, Soledad greeted him with a slight nod of the head that only he perceived. Beneath the exterior calm, however, Mauro Larrea knew she was still dueling with a host of disturbing devils.

Let's go—let's get out of here, he wanted to tell her when their eyes met. *Let's board a ship at the dock: any one that will take us far from here, somewhere we're not overwhelmed with disasters. Far from your problems and mine, from the lies we've told together, and the deceits each of us has committed. Far from your demented husband and my chaotic son. From my debts and your frauds, from our failures and our pasts.*

All he said, though, was: "Good afternoon, my friends; good afternoon, Soledad."

It seemed to him as if she, with an almost imperceptible gesture, were replying, *If only I could. If only I had no burdens or ties. But this is my life, Mauro. And wherever I go, my troubles must go with me.*

"Well, it looks as if everything is being resolved."

Antonio Fatou's words burst his absurd reverie.

"I am anxious to hear the news," said Mauro, taking a seat. "I beg you to excuse my delay, but I had to return to Jerez on important business."

Fatou told him of the arrangements made: as soon as the salt from the Puerto Real marshes had been loaded, he arranged for the small cabins to be prepared, sorting out all the necessary details. A thorough cleaning, mattresses, blankets, additional provisions of water and food. And, thanks to Paulita's charitable spirit, a few luxuries as well: cooked ham, English biscuits, cherries in syrup, tongue with truffles. She even added a large bottle of eau de cologne. Everything that might help soften the deplorable conditions on board an old cargo boat that no one would imagine carried deep in its hold a proud lady whom everyone wanted to keep as far away as possible, like a dog with the mange.

Even though the ship would not set sail until the following morning, they had decided to put Carola Gorostiza on board that night. In the dark, so that she would not completely realize what was going on until Cádiz had disappeared in the distance.

"She won't enjoy the comforts of a cabin passenger on a proper ship, but I trust it will be an easy enough crossing for her. The captain is a trustworthy Basque from Vizcaya; there is only a small crew, and they are peaceful sorts; they won't disturb her."

"And her maid will be going with her, of course," said Sol.

"Her slave," Mauro corrected her.

The same girl who had wept disconsolately and begged him to let her stay with Santos Huesos. And sobbed over her freedom, agreed in a pact as fragile as a film of ice.

"Her slave," the others agreed with some embarrassment.

"Her baggage is ready, too," Mauro added.

"In that case," said Fatou, "I think we can get on with the embarkation."

"Would you allow me to talk to her in private first? I'll try not to be long."

"Of course, Mauro, as you wish."

"And if you'd be so kind, I'd like a pen and some paper."

Carola Gorostiza received him with apparent restraint. She was wearing the same dress as the day before, but her hair had been scraped back and she was wearing none of the adornments or rice powders she had been so fond of in Cuba. She was sitting by the balcony in the guest room decorated with toile de Jouy, and lit only by a dim lamp.

"It would be hypocritical of me to say I'm sorry that nothing worked out as you had hoped."

She turned her head to peer out of the window at the encroaching night. As if she had not heard him.

"However, I trust you will arrive in Havana without any great problems."

She remained unmoved, although doubtless she was fuming inside and would dearly have loved to curse him.

"There are a couple of matters I wish to raise with you before you depart. It is up to you whether you choose to cooperate with me or not, but that will determine the state in which you disembark. I imagine you wouldn't think much of the idea of arriving in Havana harbor looking like a scarecrow: exhausted and filthy, not having changed your clothes in weeks. And without any money to your name."

"What are you talking about, you wretch?" she said, rousing herself from her feigned lethargy.

"Everything is ready for you to embark, but I have no intention of returning your things to you until we have settled two questions."

She turned to look at him.

"You're the son of a whore, Larrea."

"Seeing that my mother abandoned me before I had reached my fourth birthday, there's no way I can contradict you," he replied, moving toward the small writing desk in a corner of the room. On it he placed the sheet of paper, the freshly cut quill pen, the glass inkwell, and the blotter that Fatou had just provided him with. "Well, the less time we lose, the better. Please come and sit at the desk and prepare to write."

She made an attempt to resist.

"May I remind you that it's not only your wardrobe that's at stake here. There's also the money of your inheritance that you brought sown into the lining of your petticoats."

Ten minutes and any number of insults later, and after many refusals and reproaches, he finally managed to get her to transcribe one by one the words he dictated.

"Let's carry on," he said, blowing on the fresh ink on the sheet of paper. "The second question has to do with Luis Montalvo. What I want to know is the complete truth, Señora."

"That blessed Little Runt again . . ." she said sourly.

"I want to know why he ended up naming your husband as his heir."

"What's that to you?" she spat.

"You're running the risk of all Havana knowing about the sorry state you arrived in after your great journey back to the mother country."

She dug her nails into the palms of her hands and closed her eyes for a few moments, as if trying to control her fury.

"Because that was how justice was done, Señor," she eventually said. "That's all I have to explain to you."

"Justice for what?"

Weighing up whether to continue or to keep her mouth shut, Carola bit her lip. He stared at her with folded arms. Unyielding, waiting.

"For my husband having assumed someone else's guilt for more than twenty years. And for this having meant being uprooted, being scorned by his family, and being condemned to isolation for the rest of his life. Doesn't that seem enough to you?"

"Until I understand what guilt you're talking about, I couldn't say."

"The guilt of being the person who caused his cousin's death."

A heavy silence fell on them until she realized she had no other recourse than to finish her story.

"He never fired that shot."

She turned to look again through the window.

"Go on."

She pursed her lips until they went white, refusing to comply.

"Go on," he repeated.

"It was Luisito who fired it."

It seemed to him as though the light from the lamp was wavering. *What?*

"The spoiled child, the poor little sick boy, the youngest of the family," hissed Carola Gorostiza.

The pieces were coming together, starting to fit.

"Matí and my husband were arguing. They had dropped their shotguns and were shouting and cursing one another like never before. And Little Runt, who never took a weapon when he went hunting with them, grew nervous and tried to intervene. He picked up one of the guns, perhaps only to fire it into the air, or to scare them, or heaven knows why. By the time the closest hunters reached them, Gustavo's fired shotgun was on the ground, Matí was bleeding to death, and Little Runt was crouched over the warm body in a hysterical fit. My husband tried to explain what had happened, but everything was against him: his shouts and curses had been heard by everyone, and it was his weapon."

Mauro had no need to insist she go on: she seemed to have decided to pour everything out.

"When he saw the state of his older brother, the dwarf could not or would not say a word. And instead of being seen as the killer he was, he was treated as a second victim. There was never any formal complaint against Gustavo: it was all kept within the family. Until the grandfather put a bag of money in his hand and forced him to go abroad."

He never thought he was worthy of the inheritance due to him. That was what Manuel Ysasi had told Mauro at the social club when he asked about Luis Montalvo's chaotic, dissolute life and his lack of interest in the family's business and properties. At that moment he had not been able to interpret the doctor's words. But now he could.

"Seeing that you're pulling words out of me like that tooth-puller on Calle de la Merced, let me tell you something else. Do you want to know why they were arguing?"

"I can imagine, but confirm it for me."

"Of course. As ever, the great Soledad was at the heart of it. Gustavo was distraught because she had just married the Englishman. He accused his older cousin of not preventing that romance while he was away: at that moment he was living in Seville. He called him a traitor, accused him of being disloyal. Of having collaborated with the old man so that the cousin he had been in love with ever since he could remember turned away from him."

Carola Gorostiza was in full flow, as if wanting to go on to the finish now that she had started to unravel things.

"Do you know something, Larrea? A lot of water has flowed under the bridge since my husband told me that: when the phantoms would wake him in the early hours, when he was still talking to me and forced himself to pretend he loved me just a little bit, even though the accursed shadow of another woman lived with us constantly. But I never forgot that that was the moment when Gustavo's life was cut short. That was why I wrote to Luis Montalvo over the years. That was why I welcomed him in our house and plantation like an affectionate relative, telling him my husband was anxious to see him again, when in fact he had not the remotest idea of what I was up to. All I wanted was to revive his spirits, to help his blood course through his veins after carrying the weight of somebody else's guilt on his shoulders for so long. I thought I could do so by reminding him of the scenes of that happy world his family had expelled him from. His family home, the winery, the vineyards he had known as a child. So first of all I succeeded in tempting Little Runt from Spain so that they could make up. Then, without my husband's knowledge, I convinced him to change his will. That's all."

A sour grimace spread across her face.

"All it cost me were a few fake tears and an unscrupulous notary. You can't imagine how easy it is for a good-looking woman to change the mind of a dying man with an uneasy conscience."

Mauro preferred not to dwell on this impudent boast: he had to bring the matter to a close as soon as possible. The Fatous and Soledad were waiting anxiously in the living room; everything was ready. But Mauro, buried up to his neck in the ruins of the Montalvo family, refused to let her leave without fully understanding.

"Continue," he ordered once more.

"What more do you want to know? Why my husband was so foolish as to stake everything on a game of billiards with you?"

"Exactly."

"Because I was wrong through and through," she admitted with a regretful twist of her mouth. "Because his reaction was not what I had expected; because I didn't manage to give him hope as I had wanted. I thought I could offer him a promising future for both of us: we could sell our properties in Cuba and come to Spain together, start all over again in the land he missed so much. But far from what I was hoping, when Gustavo learned after his cousin's death that he owned everything, instead of feeling relieved, he fell into his habitual inability to decide. And this only increased when he learned Soledad had returned to Jerez with her husband."

There were noises outside: the sound of steps, and people arriving. The night was slipping by; someone had come looking for him. But when they heard them talking, whoever it was decided not to interrupt.

"Do you know what was worst, Larrea, what was saddest of all? To confirm that there was no room for me in his intentions; that if in the end he decided to return, he wasn't going to bring me with him. That was why he made no plans to sell our properties in Cuba, neither the house nor the coffee plantation, so that I could survive on my own, without him. And do you know what he was aiming for by keeping me out of everything?"

She gave him no time to make any suggestion.

"His only aim, his only thought, was to win back Soledad. And to do that he needed something he didn't have: ready money. Money to return in triumph and not as a failure begging to be forgiven. To return with a project, an optimistic plan: to restore his legacy, to start to rebuild it."

He recalled seeing her at the ball in Casilda Barrón's house, asking for his complicity in the midst of the luxurious vegetation in the garden, all the time shooting nervous glances toward the ballroom.

"That was why I was so anxious he had no knowledge of what you were bringing me from Mexico: because that was all he needed to take the final step. Capital to return to Spain in triumph, not as a failure. To show his worth to her, and abandon me."

Tears, this time real ones, began to roll down her cheeks.

"And why bring me into your machinations, if I may ask?"

The combination of bitter tears and a cynical grimace was as incongruous and as obviously sincere as the story that had been pouring out of her.

"That was my big mistake. To bring you into this by inventing all that nonsense about your supposed affection for me; that was a stupid idea. All I wanted was to give Gustavo a different kind of concern, to see if at least he reacted when his public dignity as a husband was called into question."

Her expression became even more bitter.

"But the only thing I managed to do was hand him the rope he needed to hang himself."

At last. At last it all made sense to the miner. Now the pieces were recognizable and had their place in this complex game of lies and truths, passions, defeats, plots, and frustrated loves that neither the years nor the oceans had succeeded in eclipsing.

All he needed to know was there in front of him. And there was no time for anything more.

"I'd like to be able to respond to what you've said, Señora, but considering everything we need to deal with urgently, I think it would be best for you to start getting ready."

She looked out over the balcony once more.

"I've nothing more to say anyway. You have already swept away my future, just as Soledad Montalvo ruined my present for so many decades. The two of you can be satisfied."

Mauro left, intending to head for the living room, still dazed from what he had heard. He had to act quickly. *Ready? Let's go,* he was going to tell Fatou; he would have time to think things over later on. But he found his way was blocked: something was curled up on the floor in the dim light of the corridor. A skirt spread out on the floorboards, a back leaning against the wall. Head sunk in her shoulders, arms folded to protect herself. The sound of the soft crying of another woman. Soledad.

So it had been her footsteps he had heard outside while Carola Gorostiza was vomiting her pent-up agonies. She was the one coming to tell him they had to hurry up, and who had come to a halt outside the door when she heard the brutal revelations from her cousin's wife.

Now, curled up in a ball like an orphan beset by nightmares, she was weeping for all she had not known of the past. For the guilt of others, and her own. For what had been hidden from her, for all the lies. For bygone days, happy or heart-rending, depending on which year and which moment. For those who were no longer there, and for all she had lost along the way.

CHAPTER FIFTY-ONE

When they arrived, the port was dark and silent, filled with ships moored by thick cables to the bollards, sails furled on their masts, with no sign of life. Schooners and feluccas rocking on the nocturnal waves, sloops and fishing boats quietly asleep. There was almost no sign of the usual piles of crates, barrels, and bundles from all over the world, nor of the noisy stevedores, or the carriages and crowds of people who every day came and went through the Puerta del Mar. Only the sound of the water beating dully against the hulks of the ships and the stone walls of the quay.

Fatou, Mauro Larrea, and his servant accompanied the women in the rowboat out to the salt ship. Paulita stayed at home, preparing egg punch, she said, for when they came back with dampness in their bones.

Soledad watched their silhouettes depart from behind a shutter in a room on the main floor of the Fatou house. Mauro Larrea had picked her up from the floor, holding her close, and had taken her to a nearby room, struggling hard not to be overwhelmed by the demands of his body and his feelings, trying to act with a clear head and icy reason. *I'll take care of everything, then I'll be back,* he whispered in her ear. She nodded her agreement.

She did not say a word to Carola Gorostiza; there was no time. Or possibly there was nothing to say. What sense did it make now to send any message to Gustavo through his wife? How could a few hasty words possibly erase twenty years of unjustified guilt, more than two decades of a bitterness as terrible as it was unjust. That was why Soledad decided to remain in the room as they left, the tips of her fingers pressed against the windowpanes and her eyes brimming with tears. How could she say good-bye to the woman who, despite the bonds of matrimony and the long years of living together, had never succeeded in displacing her in the heart of a man who, at another time and in another place, she had not succeeded in dismissing, either.

Dignified and composed, Carola Gorostiza did not open her mouth during the short crossing. Trinidad said next to nothing, either, seeming resigned to her situation, while Santos Huesos spent the whole time staring at the silver lights of the city.

If, when they boarded the old cargo ship, Carola suspected this was not a place for a lady of her stature, she concealed her feelings behind a distant scorn. She simply said a curt good evening to the captain and demanded that her belongings be transferred immediately to her cabin. It was only when she found herself shut in a room that despite the efforts of the Fatou couple was still oppressive and cramped that her cry of anger could be heard up on deck.

He was about to rid himself of a burden that weighed like a leaden sack on his shoulders, and yet Mauro Larrea's sense of relief was mixed with a contradictory emotion. Ever since he had used threats to drag the most intimate secrets out of her, something had changed in his view of this woman who, with her scheming and lies, had turned his life upside down. He still saw the woman who at first light would begin her return to the New World, the woman behind the game of billiards that had completely altered his destiny, as a twisted, deceitful, and selfish person. Now, however, he knew that behind her behavior was hidden something that until now he had not even suspected, something beyond the mere desire for gain that he had at first imagined. To a certain extent that redeemed and humanized her, and left him slightly disconcerted: the desperate need to feel herself loved by a husband whom he now saw differently, with painful splinters in his heart.

At any rate, it made no sense to keep going over the reasons and the consequences of everything that had happened between Carola Gorostiza and him since he met her at that ball in Havana's El Cerro. Now that she was installed in her less-than-luxury cabin, there was only one thing left for him to do. And so, while Fatou and the captain were finalizing details on the bridge, Mauro Larrea called Santos Huesos aside. His servant pretended not to have heard him and remained seated on a coil of rope in the prow of the ship. Mauro called him again, but again there was no response. He took six steps toward the Indian, grasped him by the arm, and forced him to his feet.

"Will you listen to me, you rogue?"

They were standing in front of one another, both with their legs spread wide even though the sea was completely calm on that night. The servant refused to raise his eyes.

"Look at me, Santos."

Instead, he peered beyond him at the black waters.

"Look at me."

In all the long years they had known each other, Santos had never refused an order from his *patrón*. Except this once.

"Is it really so hard for you to leave me even a moment's peace?" his servant asked.

"So much the worse for you if you don't want to hear that the lady kept her promise."

At this, Santos raised his gleaming eyes.

"The girl is free," said the miner, feeling for the sheet of paper in the inside pocket of his frock coat. "I'm going to give the captain the document; he will make sure it reaches Don Julián Calafat."

In the name of Almighty God, amen. May it be known that I, Carola Gorostiza y Arellano de Zayas, in full possession of my faculties at the time of composing this document, declare to be free of any subjection, captivity, or servitude, María de la Santísima Trinidad Cumbá, who has no other family name. I grant this freedom gladly and without financial reward so that she may as a free person enjoy all her rights and desires.

This was what Mauro had forced her to write at the desk in her room: the emancipation of the young girl that so troubled Santos Huesos.

"When you are ready, Mauro." Fatou's voice behind them prevented Santos from giving any reply.

"Run and tell Trinidad that she must fly to the banker's house as soon as they dock in Havana," Mauro added, lowering his voice. "As soon as he reads this document, he'll know what to do."

His stunned servant did not know what to say.

"We'll arrange for you two to meet again when the moment comes," said Mauro, clapping him on the back as if to rouse him from his stupor. "Now hurry, and let's get off this ship."

～

They were not expecting anyone to be waiting for them on the dockside, but from the rowboat they spied a dark silhouette carrying a lantern. As they drew closer, they saw it was a youth. A porter hoping for one last load that night, a street urchin or a lover contemplating the bay as he sighed over his unrequited love; nothing to do with them, surely. But as they were about to disembark, they heard him call to them.

"Does one of you gentlemen go by the name of Larrea?"

"Your servant," said Mauro as he stepped on to dry land.

"They say you're wanted at the Cuatro Naciones Inn. As quickly as possible."

He had no need to ask why: something must have gone wrong between Ysasi and the Englishman.

"We'll say good-bye here for now, my friend," he said, extending a rapid hand toward Fatou. "I'm immensely grateful for all your generosity."

"Perhaps I could go with you . . ."

"I've taken advantage of you far too much already; I had better let you return home. But, please, would you mind informing Señora Claydon where I've gone? And now I beg you to excuse me; I'm afraid this may be no trifling matter."

"This way, Señor," said the youth impatiently, waving the lantern. He had been told to accompany them to the inn as rapidly as he could, and he did not want to lose his promised sovereign. The miner strode after him, followed by the still-bemused Santos Huesos.

They left the port, taking Calle del Rosario and then El Tinte alley, seeing no one apart from the occasional poor soul in rags sleeping in a doorway. But they didn't reach the inn: they were stopped by someone who emerged from among the fig and palm trees in the middle of Plaza de Mina.

"Here," said Ysasi, holding out a coin for the boy. "Give us the lantern and be on your way."

They waited until he had been swallowed up by the shadows.

"He's leaving. He's found a boat to take him to Bristol."

Mauro knew the doctor was referring to Alan Claydon. And he knew this was disastrous news, because it meant that in eight days, ten at most, the stepson would be in London, poisoning the family affairs yet again. By then, Sol and Edward would barely have had time to seek refuge.

"I brought him from Jerez. He was convinced I was helping him to get to Gibraltar, but unfortunately in the dining room of the inn we ran into three Englishmen, three sherry importers from Bristol who were celebrating their last night in Spain with a hearty dinner. They were seated a few tables from us and were talking of barrels and gallons of oloroso and amontillado, of the excellent deals they had done, of qualities and prices, how keen they were to get it all on the market as soon as they could."

"And Claydon heard them."

"Not only that, he went over and started talking to them."

"And asked them to take him straight to England."

"In a sherry ship loaded with wine to the gunwhales. They agreed to meet again at five this morning."

"Damned bad luck."

"That's exactly what I thought."

You fool, he said to himself. *How could you have suggested to the doctor that he accompany the stepson to a public place in a city where there were so many of his countrymen?* Obsessed as he had been with making sure Carola Gorostiza boarded her ship, distracted as he was by the possible imminent sale of his properties and by Nicolás's exasperating decisions, he had overlooked this detail. And now it had become a huge blunder.

They were standing in the semidarkness of the square that had once been the garden of the San Francisco convent, talking in low voices with the collars of their capes turned up, beneath an iron framework covered in bougainvilleas no longer in flower.

"These Englishmen are not simply wine merchants who happened to be passing through. They are well established and have good contacts here," Ysasi went on. "They knew Edward Claydon and do business in the same circles. So as they travel to Great Britain together, they will have more than enough time to hear all that Alan wishes to tell them, and for him to spread his lies."

"Good evening to you."

Mauro's skin prickled when he heard this female voice a few steps away. Soledad was coming up behind them, wrapped in her velvet cloak, the quick tapping of her feet resounding in the square. She seemed determined and concerned, and had brought Antonio Fatou with her. They greeted one another briefly and quietly, not moving from the shady garden. This was probably the safest place. Or the least compromising.

As soon as she was beside him, Mauro could make out traces of the bitter tears she had shed. Hearing the terrible confessions that Carola Gorostiza had made about her cousin Gustavo had demolished at a stroke the elaborate edifice her family had constructed on the foundations of a cruel, unjust version of reality. It could not have been easy for her to accept the disturbing truth more than twenty years later. *But life goes on,* Soledad seemed to be telling him in a fleeting, silent exchange. *Pain and remorse cannot hold me back now, Mauro; the moment will come when I have to deal with them. For now, I have to go on.*

An almost imperceptible nod showed his agreement, but he seemed to be wondering what Fatou was doing there, since they'd already caused him enough trouble. She reassured him, arching an eyebrow, and he understood that if she had brought him with her, there must be a good reason.

The doctor explained the problem to her in a few short phrases.

"This means our plans are useless," murmured Sol.

What plans? thought Mauro. During the tumultuous day they had just experienced, they had never once had the chance to plan anything.

Now Fatou spoke, and what he said explained his presence among them.

"Forgive my interfering in other people's business, but Señora Claydon explained her family's unfortunate situation to me. In order to help resolve it, I offered her the possible solution of sending her stepson in a coastal cargo boat as far as Gibraltar. But that is only scheduled to leave the day after tomorrow."

So that's why you're here, my dear friend Antonio, the miner said to himself with a wry grin. *You, too, have blood in your veins, and have also been ensnared by our Soledad.* She had forged ahead, as ever: the last of the Montalvos never wasted a second. Mauro Larrea now understood why she had spent the whole day in Cádiz. To test Fatou, subtly persuade him, seduce him as she had done Mauro himself. To make sure the trader was on her side. With the sole aim of sealing Alan Claydon's fate, along with her own and her husband's. Naturally.

The silence was augmented among the date palms and magnolia trees lining the square. They heard the night watchman with his pole and lantern call out "a quarter to twelve" at one side of the square. Huddled together, four minds struggled in vain to find an answer.

"I'm afraid this is slipping through our fingers," Ysasi concluded with his habitual tendency of always seeing the glass as half-empty.

"Of course it isn't," Sol insisted.

The head emerging from the folds of an elegant Parisian cloak had just made a decision.

CHAPTER FIFTY-TWO

❧

W hat followed was complete upheaval. The sound of hurried footsteps, orders being given, a stream of misgivings and doubt. Perhaps they were making a huge mistake, or perhaps this was the most audacious way of removing Alan Claydon from the scene for a while. In any case, the approaching dawn was breathing down their necks like a hungry beast, and if they didn't make haste, Bristol would win the day.

They instantly decided who would carry out which tasks and functions. In Calle de la Verónica, Paulita was told to pack a small travel bag with a few items of men's clothing. Four trustworthy sailors were dragged fresh from their beds; old Genaro made up a few extra food parcels. The clock had barely struck one when the doctor returned to the inn.

"Be so kind as to rouse the gentleman in room six, if you please."

The attendant gazed at him with sleepy eyes.

"I was told four thirty, sir."

"Pretend that is the hour that has just sounded," said Ysasi, slipping a coin over the counter. He was sure that Claydon had no way of knowing exactly what time it was; luckily for them, his fob was the first thing the brigands had fleeced him of.

Minutes later, the stepson emerged into the central courtyard, both thumbs bandaged and a cut on his cheek. His usually clean-shaven, well-groomed face was now showing the strain of a day spent at the bottom of a ravine, with clear signs of the humiliation he had suffered in this fanatical, extravagant, southern land, one of whose daughters, much to his vexation, his father had decided to wed. Everything that had befallen him during his brief stay in Spain had been crazy, brutal, violent: the presumed lover of his stepmother bursting into his father's room, the Indian calmly breaking both his thumbs, the assault by highwaymen who had stripped him of everything but his name. The pace at which Ysasi saw him approach betrayed his eagerness to leave that wretched country.

However, he frowned when he saw no sign of the merchants from Bristol.

The doctor reassured him. They had gone on ahead to the docks to sort out a few final details, he said in the faltering English he had learned from the Montalvos' governesses. A glimmer of suspicion appeared on Alan Claydon's face, but the doctor parried before he could give it a second thought.

"Come on, my friend."

They had decided that Ysasi and Fatou alone would accompany him. The doctor was key to the plan, for he had earned Claydon's trust. As for the young heir to the shipping company, hypnotized by Soledad's ineffable charms, he had resolved to side with her come what might, despite the many arguments proffered by both his wife and his own common sense.

Two moored boats awaited them at the quayside, each with a pair of sailors at the oars; all of them wondering what had possessed Master Antonio to offer them a silver coin each for rowing out to sea at this hour. Obviously Fatou did not introduce himself by name to the young Claydon but behaved in a convincing manner, addressing the newcomer in English, the language he used daily in conducting his business transporting goods from the Iberian Peninsula to Britain. A throwaway observation about the nonexistent changing winds, or an unlikely morning mist, a couple of allusions to the gentlemen from Bristol who had supposedly already left to join the sherry ship anchored in the bay, and the urgent need for Mr. Claydon to accompany them immediately. A parting handshake, a thank-you here, a thank-you there. With no time to express any doubts or to change his mind, the stepson installed himself as best he could in the tiny boat. The dark night did not prevent them from seeing the unease on his face when the mooring rope was untied. Ysasi and Fatou contemplated him from the quayside as the oarsmen began to row. *God be with you, my friend. May you have a safe voyage.*

They gave him a few minutes so as not to spoil the crossing out to the vessel. They were sending him to the Antilles, without hesitating and without his knowledge. To a crowded, hot, troubled, pulsating Caribbean island, where the Englishman would be treated as an unwanted intruder and from which, with no money or contacts, they were sure it would take him an eternity to find a way out. When they reckoned he was at a safe distance, the remainder of the company emerged from the mist to complete the performance. Genaro, the butler, and a young house servant loaded the provisions onto the second boat: water barrels, food, mattresses, blankets, an oil lamp. Soledad joined Manuel Ysasi and Fatou to exchange last thoughts, while Mauro Larrea ordered Santos Huesos to come over to a canvas awning near the seawall.

"Just a minute, *patrón*, let me finish helping."

"Come here, we haven't a moment to lose."

He approached, a sack of beans on his back.

"You're going with them."

Santos Huesos let the bundle fall to the ground, taken aback.

"I don't trust that Englishman an inch," said Mauro.

"Are you really asking me to go back to Cuba without you?"

His mainstay, his place in the world, and the impetus behind everything he did. This was the significance of the man who had plucked him from the depths of the silver mines that had claimed him out of pure necessity when he was little more than a slippery kid, a sack of bones inside a coppery body.

"I want you by that sonofabitch's side during the entire crossing; don't let him out of your sight," he continued, grasping Santos Huesos by the shoulders. "Attend him as best as you can, and try to steer him clear of that Gorostiza woman. If they exchange conversation, which I doubt, as neither of them speaks the other's language, stick to him like glue, do you hear?"

Santos Huesos nodded, dumbfounded.

"Once you dock in Havana," he went on without pausing for breath, "you must take Trinidad and disappear, so that they can't find you. Calafat will tell you where to go. Deliver this letter to him the moment you arrive."

I beg you, my dear friend, to protect my servant and the freed slave girl by giving them refuge outside the city. I will let you know my whereabouts in due course and will recompense you accordingly for the favor, the letter said. He had ended the brief missive with an ironical reference, which he knew the old banker would appreciate. *With thanks in advance from your Spanish protégé.*

"Take this as well," he added.

The last of his money, which he had been keeping at Fatou's house: now he would need to sell his inherited properties quickly, otherwise he would be forced to eat into the countess's capital.

"This is yours," he said, thrusting the bag into Santos Huesos's midriff. The servant remained speechless. "Use it wisely, as there's no more. And take care while on board: Don't let that fire in your loins get us into any more trouble. Afterward, make your own life, wherever you wish. You know you will always have a place by my side, although I'll understand if you decide to stay in the Caribbean."

Something trickled down the Chichimec Indian's face beneath the crescent moon.

"Don't go sentimental on me, lad," Larrea warned him, with a forced guffaw aimed at relieving the shared instant of emotion. "I've never seen a man from the San Miguelito sierra shed even half a tear; don't be the first."

Their embrace was as brief as it was sincere. *Off with you now; get on the boat. Stay alert, and don't lose heart. Take care of yourself. And of her.*

He wheeled around as soon as he heard the splash of oars, preferring not to contemplate the anguish, immense as the sky, on the face of the lad who had grown into a man under his tutelage as, rocked by the black waters, he sailed toward the anchored vessel. It had been bad enough to watch Nicolás walk away from him earlier that day; he had no wish to receive another blow to the heart.

The group set off in silence toward Calle de la Verónica, each struggling with his or her conscience over the outrage they had just committed. As they reached the entrance to Calle del Correo, Soledad slackened her pace and plucked something from the folds of her dress.

"These two letters arrived this morning: Paulita asked me to give them to you in case she didn't see you."

Pausing for a moment beneath the light of a streetlamp, he made out the tattered appearance of the two envelopes that had crossed valleys, mountains, islands, and seas to reach him. One bore the familiar writing of his agent, Andrade. The other, the faded return address of Tadeo Carrús.

He thrust the one from Carrús in his pocket, then broke the seal of the other without hesitation. It dated from a month earlier.

After a day and a half of difficult labor, wrote Andrade, *your daughter, Mariana, gave birth to a healthy baby girl who inherited her grandfather's strength, judging by her lungs. Despite the mother-in-law's stubborn insistence, Mariana refused to call her Úrsula. The girl will be named Elvira, after her grandmother. God bless them and you, my brother, wherever you may be.*

Mauro gazed up at the stars. Children departing, and the children of children arriving: the cycle of life, nearly always incomplete, nearly always accidental. For the first time in many years, Mauro Larrea felt a foolish desire to cry.

"Is everything all right?" a voice beside him asked.

A weightless hand rested on his arm, melting away his unease as he returned to the reality of the port city, to the only thing he could be sure of now that his last defenses had fallen.

This time he was incapable of containing himself. Seizing her by the wrist, he led her around a corner, where no one would see them should they turn to look, wondering where the devil they were. He cupped her face in his big, rough hands, slid his fingers down her slender neck, then drew her close. With a primitive hunger, he pressed his lips against those of Soledad Montalvo in a sublime kiss, to which she yielded willingly. A kiss that contained all the desire accumulated over those past days, all the dreadful anguish suffocating his soul, and all the relief in the world, for among all the calamities that dogged him, one thing at least had turned out well.

They went on embracing, protected by the early morning mist and the shadow of the bell tower of the San Agustín church, enveloped by the scent of the sea, leaning up against the stone wall of one of the many buildings. With uninhibited, passionate abandon; clinging to each other like two castaways beneath the towers and rooftops of a city foreign to them both, flouting all rules of public decency. The dignified, cosmopolitan, married lady from Jerez and the returned adventurer whom the wind had carried across the sea, entwined beneath the light of streetlamps, as if she were a simple, unattached woman and he a rough, indomitable miner, unfettered by fears or armor of any kind. Pure desire, pure hunger from within. Pure skin, pure heat, flesh, breath.

His hungry mouth roamed over Soledad's neck until he found the soft haven of her shoulder beneath the cape. Uttering her name in a hoarse voice, he longed to rest there without end, feeling the immediacy of her whole body, and her heart, entwined in his.

A few steps away, out of sight, they heard Genaro's rasping cough, alerting them that he had been sent to look for them.

Her slender fingers stopped caressing his jaw, already covered with stubble at that late hour.

"They're waiting for us," she whispered in his ear.

But he knew this wasn't true. There was no one, nothing waiting for him anywhere. The only place in the world where he longed to remain was in Sol Claydon's embrace.

CHAPTER FIFTY-THREE

⟋ℛℒ⟍

Despite their fatigue, none of them managed to fall asleep during the return journey to Jerez. Soledad rested her head against the side of the carriage, eyes closed as she was rocked by the jolting of the wheels over the bumps and dips in the road. Next to her, Mauro Larrea tried in vain to rally his thoughts in a logical way. Between them, beneath the folds of her skirts and shielded by darkness, two hands were clasped together, like converts to a private faith, while outside, beyond the windows, the world was clouded and gray.

Sitting opposite them was Manuel Ysasi, severe beneath his black beard and his endless burden of impenetrable thoughts.

They expected to reach Jerez by dawn, when the city was still rubbing the sleep from its eyes, preparing for what might have been a morning like any other: domestic servants entering the grand houses, laborers leaving for the fields or vineyards; pealing church bells; mules and carts setting off on their working day. Less than half a league from this anticipated hustle and bustle, the promise of a routine day had already vanished.

Protected inside the carriage behind the oilcloth curtains, they were oblivious to the furious approach of hooves, nor did they see the face of the rider crossing in front of them. Only when the horses abruptly slowed their pace did they sense that something was wrong and draw back the curtains to try to see out. Mauro Larrea opened the door. Amid clouds of dust, whinnying horses, and general confusion, he recognized an incongruous figure sitting astride the newly arrived steed.

He leapt out of the carriage, slamming the door behind him, shielding Soledad and the doctor from whatever he was about to hear from Nicolás's lips.

"The convent."

The youth gestured toward the north. A plume of smoke the color of rat's fur was rising above the rooftops of Jerez.

Soledad opened the carriage door.

"May I ask what's going on . . . ?" she said, descending nimbly by herself.

Observing the stony expressions of Mauro and his son, she turned her head in the direction they were gazing. Her face froze in an anguished grimace, even as the fingers that before had clasped his in a warm embrace now dug into his arm.

"Edward," she murmured.

He had no choice but to nod.

A few moments of tense silence passed before the doctor, who had also stepped out of the carriage and realized what was happening, began to fire questions. *When? Where? How?*

"It started sometime after midnight in one of the cells, caused, they think, by a simple candle stub or an oil lamp," Nico began. His hair, face, and boots were soiled with ash. "The neighbors have been helping all night, thank goodness. The flames didn't reach the church, but all the nuns' cells have been destroyed. Someone raised the alarm at the Claydons' residence, and the head butler, unsure what to do, roused me. I accompanied him there, and between the two of us we tried . . .

we tried . . ." Leaving the sentence hanging in the air, he changed tack. "The fire is practically out now."

"Edward," Soledad repeated softly.

"They managed to save the nuns. They've been taken in by local people," the lad went on. "Only one is unaccounted for, it seems." Then, lowering his voice, he added: "No one said anything about a man."

Memories of Inés Montalvo, of Mother Constanza, mingled with the early morning cold.

"Let's not waste any time," said Larrea, urging them all back into the carriage.

Soledad stood rooted to the ground.

"Come along, Sol," the doctor insisted, placing an arm around her shoulders.

She didn't respond.

"Come along," he repeated.

Just then, the bay stallion Nicolás was riding whinnied. It was the same horse she had mounted when they first visited La Templanza, and, on hearing it, Soledad shook her head quickly, appearing to return to the present. To take the reins, as was her custom. This time, in a more literal sense.

Approaching the animal, she patted its rump. The three men instantly understood, and none of them dared oppose her. Nico helped her mount. No sooner had she set off, cloak flapping in the air, than they piled into the carriage, urging on the driver to follow amid the dust and kicked-up earth, deafened by the thunder of hooves and the iron wheels jouncing over the stones. The galloping bay easily outpaced the carriage, with Soledad Montalvo's slender figure growing smaller in the distance as she entered the city alone.

Foam dripped from the horses' mouths by the time they reached the convent. Despite their shouts and threats, the carriage was forced to stop before it reached the small, crowded square. They leapt out: father, son, and doctor elbowing through the throng of people who were still gathered there in the early morning. Three nearby wineries, they heard as they continued to push their way through, had brought water pumps to fight the fire. As Nico had already reported, the flames had not reached the church. The convent itself was another matter.

Strewn about the ground, amid pools of water and mounds of rubble, they stumbled over upturned wooden buckets, earthenware jugs, even bowls from the kitchens of terrified neighbors who, forming human chains, had spent the night handing water from the wells in their courtyards. Finally the trio managed to reach the front of the convent: scorched and devastated by a fire that by now had been reduced to embers. Opposite the ruins, a circle had opened among the crowd. In the center stood the exhausted stallion, nostrils aquiver, a tired, disheveled-looking Palmer holding its reins. Next to him, motionless at the sight of the destruction, Soledad.

Jerez was, in the end, a small place where everyone knew everyone else, where yesterday and today merged into one. And, if not, there was always someone able to make a connection. And so, at the sight of this dignified lady contemplating the bleak panorama with her fists clenched and her face clouded with anxiety, rumors began to spread. In whispers and murmurs to begin with, then brazenly. *She's a sister of one of the nuns,* some asserted. *Both high-class ladies. Look how graceful and elegant she is; that velvet cloak must have cost a fortune. Granddaughters of one of those fancy wine producers. Their father's a scoundrel, remember him? I think she's the one who married the Englishman. Maybe she's the sister of the mother superior, the one they say is missing. Who knows?*

They flanked her like a praetorian guard, Ysasi on her right, the Larreas on her left: shoulder to shoulder in the face of the devastation. Breathless, perspiring, inhaling the filthy air in short gasps, incapable of taking in the full extent of the tragedy. Above their heads, flakes of ash and black plumes still floated, while the last cinders crackled around their feet. None of them were capable of uttering a sound. As the muffled cries and whispers of the locals and onlookers gradually died out, silence descended over the scene like a vast blanket of dreadful calm.

Suddenly they heard a terrifying sound, like the branches of an enormous tree breaking off, followed by a cascade of falling stones and rubble crashing into one another. "Part of the cloister has collapsed!" cried a lad, darting out from one side of the building. Soledad clenched her fists again, the tendons bulging in her neck. Mauro Larrea glanced sidelong at her, sensing what she was going to do next.

"No!" he cried emphatically, his arm shooting out horizontally in front of her, thwarting the step she was about to take.

"I have to find him, I have to find him, I have to find him—"

The words streamed from her mouth feverishly. Aware that Larrea's arm would remain like a barrier blocking her path, she turned to the doctor.

"I have to go inside, Manuel, I have to—"

Her friend's reaction was equally firm. No.

Common sense suggested that the two men were right. Although the flames had abated, the destruction they had wrought was no less dangerous. Still. Even so.

It was then, with catlike agility, that she wriggled free from Mauro's arm, clasping his wrists with the force of an animal trap, forcing him to look straight at her. Incongruously, as though swept along by a raging river, Larrea's mind and body dissolved in a flood of sensations. The impassioned kiss that had brought them together only a few hours before, insatiable and glorious amid the shadows; his mouth hungrily exploring hers, she yielding utterly; her fingers moving eagerly over his face and becoming entwined in his hair—these fingers now gripped him like a vise, and Mauro Larrea's soul and desire, oblivious to the surgical coldness the moment required, came alive once more, like a fire rekindled by a pair of gigantic bellows. *Stop behaving like a fool, you idiot,* he reproached himself pitilessly.

"I have to find him . . ."

He had no trouble guessing what would come next. Perhaps somewhere in the convent, in a corner that had been spared the fire, or in a nook mercifully untouched by the flames, Edward might be clinging to a glimmer of hope. *He might still be alive, Mauro. If you won't let me go in, then find him for me.*

"For God's sake, man, have you gone raving mad as well?" thundered the doctor.

CHAPTER FIFTY-FOUR

❧

"A pail of water," he cried out. Others took up the cause. A pail of water, a pail of water, a pail of water. Within seconds there were three at his feet. Tearing off his frock coat and cravat, he doused his handkerchief and wrapped it over his nose and mouth. He'd witnessed a few fierce blazes in his time—fires were inherent in mining. Several friends, fellow miners——entire teams—had met their deaths in the bowels of the earth engulfed by the flames, burnt or suffocated, crushed beneath collapsed supports. On more than one occasion, he himself had escaped by the skin of his teeth. That was why he knew how to act, and was fully aware that what he was about to do was reckless in the extreme.

The doctor continued to upbraid him to no avail: the locals uttered words of warning. *Take care, Señor, fires can be treacherous.* A few women crossed themselves, one recited the Lord's Prayer, while a crooked old lady fought her way through the crowds to touch him with the image of a Virgin. Nico considered accompanying him and began to take his coat off. "*Get back!*" Larrea cried, driven by sheer animal instinct: the sort that compels a father to protect his young against cruelty and misfortune.

The image that remained fixed in his mind before he ventured into the blackness was the terror in Soledad's eyes.

He advanced amid the smoke, treading on embers, his feet sinking into the still-hot ash, letting himself be guided by instinct alone. Scarcely any light entered through the slits in the walls. Soon his eyes began to smart. He tripped on a mound of rubble, managed to lean on a stone column to steady himself, uttering a curse when he realized how hot it was. He crossed what had doubtless been the chapter house, the roof of which was partially caved in, the wooden bench circling the inner wall reduced to blackened cinders. Raising the wet handkerchief covering his face, he inhaled deeply, exhaled, then pressed on. He supposed he was approaching the most secluded part of the convent. He trampled over stones, splintered wood, glass. Taking occasional gulps of air, he passed through what looked like the nuns' cells but found no signs of life: only a few broken wash bowls, charred bed frames, and from time to time a scorched prayer book or toppled crucifix. Finally he reached the end of the long passageway and then, gasping for breath, started retracing his steps. He had scarcely covered a few yards when he heard a tremendous crash behind him. He quickened his pace without looking back: he preferred not to see the stone wall that had just collapsed, leaving a gaping hole open to the skies. If it had it fallen mere seconds before, it would have crushed his skull.

He returned to the communal area bathed in sweat, his own breath ringing in his ears. Passing through the refectory, its elongated table and benches burnt to a crisp, he made his way blindly through to the kitchens. The handkerchief shielding him had become clogged with soot, and he was starting to choke. He groped in the darkness for bucket of water in which to plunge his head, but found none. A partition had fallen onto a large earthenware jar, spilling cooking oil over the tiled floor; he slipped, collided with a stone bench, then let out a fierce howl as he fell onto his left elbow.

A few hellish moments passed, the pain so intense that it prevented him from breathing. Then he dragged himself through the slippery pool of olive oil and managed to sit upright, arm clasped to his body as he leaned back against the remains of a wall. He pressed his arm gently and let out another howl. His elbow bone was dislocated, jutting out obscenely. Ripping off his shirtsleeve, he twisted it into a ball and bit down on it with all his might. His jaw and teeth firmly clenched, breathing heavily through his nose, he began to manipulate his forearm—gently at first, to lull himself—and then yanked it as hard as he could. Tears started from his eyes, forcing him to lurch to one side. He spat out the cloth and, as one might exorcise the devil from one's soul, puked his guts out.

He waited for several minutes, eyes closed and legs stretched out in the puddle of oil. The stench of burning and of his own vomit a few inches away from him filled his nasal passages. He cradled his elbow in his free hand, just as he had done countless times with Mariana and Nico when they were plagued by childish nightmares. As he would do with the warm tiny body of newborn Elvira once misfortune no longer dogged his steps.

Gradually his head stopped pounding, his breathing returned to normal, and the pain subsided with the dislocated elbow back in its socket. It was then, as he was struggling to get up, that he thought he heard a noise that was different from the sounds that had accompanied him since he entered the convent. He slumped back onto the floor, closed his eyes again, and listened hard, frowning as he heard it a second time. Once more and he was in no doubt. The weak yet unmistakable sound of someone desperate to get out of a place they were trapped in.

"Can anyone hear me?" he shouted.

In reply, the dull echo of rapping on wood.

Drenched and covered in oil, he began to move toward where the sounds were coming from: a side corridor, which doubtless linked the kitchens to another, smaller room, a pantry, a bakery, perhaps a wash-room. In any event, there was no way in: a pile of rubble blocked the entrance.

He managed to lift the fallen rafters, moving them in the darkness inch by inch, using one shoulder or the other depending how they lay. Then he started to shift the stones with his good arm. He had no idea how long it took him to clear the entrance: half an hour, an hour, an hour and a half. At all events, he succeeded. Until then, not a sound had come from the other side, and he preferred not to speculate as to whom he might find. From time to time he was aware of the anxious knocking of someone eager to return to the light.

"I'm coming in," he warned as he removed the last of the rubble.

But he didn't have to pull the door. Before he could even touch the handle, it swung open with a pitiful groan to reveal a haggard face crowned by a head of cropped hair, a grimace of infinite dejection etched on its features.

"Get me out of here, I beg you."

The voice was cracked, the lips two white lines.

"What about *him*?"

She shook her head slowly, squeezing her eyes shut. Her skin was the color of wax, and she had a jagged burn on one cheek.

"I don't know," she murmured. "May the good Lord forgive me, I don't know."

CHAPTER FIFTY-FIVE

❧

J ubilant cries rose from the crowd. *It's a miracle! A miracle!* the women declared as one, clasping their hands to their chests and raising their eyes to heaven. *The blessed Rita de Cascia has produced a miracle! The Infant in the Silver Manger has produced a miracle!* There was clapping and hallelujahs. Young boys jumped for joy, blowing through whistles made from dried apricot stones. A rattle seller whirled his merchandise wildly.

Only Soledad Claydon, along with the two men by her side, stood silently as they held their breath.

The figures emerging from the darkness grew steadily clearer. Mauro Larrea, bare-chested and covered in soot, was leading Mother Constanza, the former Inés Montalvo. He was helping her to avoid burning her bare feet on the still-smoldering embers. He had improvised a sling with the remains of his filthy shirt to support his injured elbow. Both of them were squinting in the glare of the morning light.

No, was the answer he gave from a distance, wordlessly, to Soledad's grief-stricken face. *I couldn't find your husband. Alive or dead. He isn't there.*

He parted company with the nun, noticing Nico at his side greeting him joyously. Someone handed him a jug of cold water, from which he drank greedily; then his son tipped a bucketful over him, which cleaned away the film of ash, oil, and sweat from his skin but could not dispel his great uneasiness.

In the midst of all this, he hadn't been able to take his eyes off her. Off them. The two sisters. A few paces, a man's love, and half a lifetime spent living beneath different flags separated the Montalvo sisters. One wore elegant clothes, the other a scorched raw linen nightshirt; one wore her hair swept up in a chignon, which, though disheveled, gave her a natural elegance; the other, without her wimple, had a shaven head and a bad burn that would leave an ugly scar.

Despite the yawning differences in their appearance, at last he could see how alike they were.

The two women were gazing straight at each other, motionless. Soledad was the first to respond, taking a hesitant step toward Inés. Then another. And a third. The crowd had fallen silent, withdrawing to give them space. Manuel Ysasi had swallowed his disquiet like a bitter medicine; Palmer looked as if he was about to lose his composure at the continued lack of any news about his master. An intrigued Nicolás, who understood little of what was going on, tried desperately to make sense of it all. Mauro Larrea, the water from a second pail still streaming down his hair and chest, nursed his throbbing elbow even as he wondered where on earth her deranged husband might be.

The slap resounded like a whiplash, provoking gasps from the onlookers. Inés Montalvo, her face turned by the stinging blow, began to bleed from her nose. A few agonizing moments passed before she slowly raised her head upright and the two women were facing each other once more. She didn't move another inch. She didn't even lift her hand to her reddened cheek or utter a single word of protest or murmur of pain. She understood what the blow had meant, the reason for this outburst of violence. A few drops of thick blood trickled down her nightdress.

It was then that Soledad, having given vent to her rage, spread her arms out wide. Those long arms that fascinated him, seduced him, that he never tired of contemplating. Those arms that had embraced him in Cádiz, under the shadow of the San Agustín tower. The ones that had spread like a seagull's wings when she showed him the Montalvos' gaming room, that had rested on his back when they waltzed together what seemed like ages ago. Or was it just a couple of nights? Her arms, in any case. Weary now, numbed by the tension of the past few days and hours. She flung them about her older sister's neck. Locked in their embrace, the two women began to weep, for the old times and for the sorrowful present.

"You must come at once, Don Mauro."

He swung around. A wad of ash and saliva remained stuck in his throat.

It was the old servant, Simón, standing at his side, who was speaking to him.

"This instant, master." Beneath his cropped head and behind a weather-beaten face that looked like an old wineskin, the man appeared terrified. "Come home at once, for God's sake."

Larrea thought he understood what Simón was saying. The lump where his Adam's apple was seemed to grow bigger.

"Should the doctor come with us?"

"I think so."

Once more they made their way through the crowd, leaving the square without a word, using all their energy to push on. A few heads turned, astonished at his appearance. Calle de la Carpintería, de la Sedería, Plaza del Clavo. And finally Calle de la Tornería.

A distraught Angustias was waiting for them at the mansion entrance. The three men standing beside her were obviously upsetting her, but they couldn't be the reason why the old servant had come looking for him.

"Larrea, my dear fellow, at last! We bring good news!"

The triumphant smile vanished from the fleshy lips of the land agent, Zarco, when he glimpsed Larrea's demeanor. Behind him, the men from Madrid also appeared startled. *My goodness, what on earth happened to the man? Where is he coming from with that dreadful aspect, with no shirt on under his frock coat, covered in dirt and oil, reeking of smoke, eyes bloodshot? Is it possible we came here to sign an agreement with this individual?* they seemed to be saying as they exchanged glances.

Larrea, in the meantime, struggled without success to remember their names.

"I tried telling these gentlemen that now wasn't a good time to speak with you, master," Angustias mumbled by way of apology. "I said to come back this afternoon. I said this morning we have . . . we have other matters to attend to."

Had Mauro paused for a few minutes to gather his thoughts, he might have acted differently. But the accumulated pressure got the better of him. Or perhaps it was fatigue. Or his fate, which was already written.

"Get out of here."

The land agent's dewlap quivered.

"Look, Don Mauro, these gentlemen are here to close the deal. They've brought the money."

"Out."

The potential purchaser and his secretary stood contemplating him. *What's going on here?* they muttered. *What has happened to this gentleman who seemed so genuine and determined?*

Zarco's face had turned bright red, beads of sweat the size of peas glistened on his brow.

"Look here, Don Mauro . . ." he repeated.

Through the fog of his mind he dimly recalled that his man was simply an honest broker whom he himself had hired. But that must have been in a different life. An eternity ago.

The agent drew near, lowering his voice, as though attempting to gain his trust.

"They're willing to pay what the lady asked," he said almost in a whisper. "The most favorable transaction that has occurred in these parts in a long while."

Zarco might as well have been speaking in Aramaic.

"Please leave."

Without uttering another word, Mauro walked into the courtyard.

"The man must be drunk," he thought he heard the secretary whisper to his boss. "He looks as if he's been rolling around in a pigsty." Those were the last words Mauro heard. And he couldn't have cared less.

Behind his back, the potential buyer adopted an expression of utter contempt. "These people from the old colonies in America, so eager to break away from the mother country, and look how they've turned out. Unstable, frivolous, boastful. They'd be singing a different song if they hadn't been so rebellious."

Visibly upset, the portly Zarco mopped his brow with a large handkerchief.

The doctor was the last to speak.

"Go and get some fresh air, my good man, before you suffer a seizure. As for you, my friends, you heard what Señor Larrea said. Please respect his wishes."

They marched off in a rage, and with them went all his plans and hopes. The money to return to Mexico, salvage his properties, his status, his past; to see Nico married or not. To return with pride and pick up the mantle of the man he had once been. Doubtless, once his mind was less clouded, he would regret his actions. But there was no time for that now; other, more urgent matters were at hand.

"Lock the door, Simón!" Angustias cried shrilly.

Despite her weary, arthritic bones, no sooner had the visitors departed than she leapt up the stairs like a hare, hiking up her skirts and revealing her scrawny calves.

"Hurry, Señores, hurry, hurry . . ."

They ran up the stairs behind her. The aged servant stopped dead in her tracks as she reached the doorway to the former dining room, crossing herself before loudly kissing her thumb and forefinger. Then she stepped aside, allowing them to contemplate the scene.

He was sitting with his back to the door. Upright, in one of chairs at the head of the Montalvos' magnificent dining table. The same table where lunch had been served at his own wedding, and where he and old Don Matías had signed all their deals over the finest oloroso sherry in the house. The table where his best friends Luis and Jacobo had made him roar with laughter at their japes, and where he had exchanged flirtatious glances with two adolescent beauties, one of whom was to become his wife.

The men entered the room with cautious steps, observing him at first sideways: noble, angular features, aquiline nose, mouth half-open. *Like a Norman aristocrat,* the doctor had described him. He still boasted a thick head of blond hair streaked with silver; not an ounce of fat on his lanky frame, ill-clad in a rumpled nightshirt. His limp, sinewy hands lay outstretched on the table. They approached slowly, maintaining a respectful silence.

Finally they contemplated him head-on.

Two deep hollows surrounded his eyes. Blue, glassy, wide-open.

His chest was drenched in blood. A triangular shard of glass protruded from his neck.

Both the doctor's and Larrea's hearts froze.

Freed from the burden of logic and reason, Edward Claydon, either due to his disturbed mind or in an irrational act of surrender, had taken his own life, severing his jugular with surgical precision.

They stood looking at him for a few long seconds.

"Memento mori," murmured Ysasi.

He walked over and gently shut Claydon's eyelids.

Mauro Larrea walked out into the gallery.

Placing his hands on the balustrade, he leaned over until his head was resting on the stone, feeling its coldness. He would have given his life to be able to say a prayer.

By water or by fire I see someone leave, a toothless old Gypsy woman had told him when she read his palm. Was it only a few nights ago? What did it matter? Soledad's husband had started a terrible fire, then fled to the ramshackle old house where years ago he had been happy, on a path of no return. Where there was no awareness, reason, or fear. Or was there?

Without straightening up, Mauro Larrea rummaged in his pockets for a handkerchief, but all he found were a few scraps of damp, illegible paper. On the front of what had been a letter bearing the name Tadeo Carrús, there was now only a smudge of ink and oil. He crumpled it between his fingers without looking, letting the fragments drop to his feet.

He noticed a hand on his arched back. He hadn't heard the steps approaching. And then, the doctor's voice.

"Let's go."

CHAPTER FIFTY-SIX

❧

September brought his first grape harvest, and with it the winery sprang back to life. Carts bearing the juice from the pressed grapes trundled in and out of gates open day and night; the floor was permanently wet, and the cellar was filled with voices, bodies, and busy feet.

A year had gone by since those Yankee women dressed like crows had arrived at the house in Mexico that had once belonged to him to announce his ruin, setting him on a path toward the unknown. Looking back, he could not help feeling that several centuries had elapsed between then and now.

Despite his initial resistance, it was the countess's money that had helped him take the first few steps toward reinstating the Montalvo legacy; after all, what the old lady had wanted was to make a profit, and he would give it to her all in good time. Mariana had supported him from afar. *Forget about trying to become what you once were. Look toward new horizons. Wherever life takes you, on this side of the world we will be proud of you.*

Tadeo Carrús died three days after Larrea failed to pay the first of his four-month installments. Contrary to the moneylender's wishes, his son, Dimas, far from reducing the house to rubble, had not broken a single tile or pane of glass. To the astonishment of the entire capital, a week after giving his father a miserable burial, he installed himself permanently in former palace of the Count of Regla, with his withered arm and a pack of scrawny hounds.

Mauro Larrea's link to La Templanza had begun in late fall, amid the vines and within himself. In December he hired workers, in January it was sowing time, in February the days grew longer; March brought showers and in April the green buds started to show. May filled the chalky earth with tender vines, June was the time for pruning, and throughout the summer they raised the vine trellises to air the clusters of fruit and keep them from touching the hot earth. In August they witnessed the miracle of the budding fruit.

Even as his eyes feasted on the fields of white hills squared off by the rows of vines, Mauro started to appreciate the different stages and methods of cultivating a vineyard. He began to learn about the different parcels of earth and about clouds, to distinguish between days when the dry heat of the levanter from Africa ruffled the calm of the vines, and those when a benign, humid *poniente*, rich in sea salt, blew in off the Atlantic. And, in tune with the seasons, hard work, and winds, he also sought advice from those who knew. He listened to old hands, day laborers, and winegrowers. With some he shared tobacco in the taverns, stores, and businesses run by men from the northern mountains. With others he shared a seat beneath the shade of the vines, listening as they mashed gazpacho in a wooden bowl. Occasionally, very occasionally, when he needed answers or was assailed by doubts, he would enjoy piano music and fine cut glass in the tapestried salons of the big wine producers.

The same eyes that for decades had dwelled in darkness became habituated to long hours of harsh sunlight; the hands that had clawed the earth's entrails for veins of silver now plunged amid the vines to test the fullness of the grapes. A mind filled with myriad ambitions and projects remained focused on a single, precise, tangible objective: to put things right, to begin again.

He purchased an Arab stallion, which he rode on track and road, recovered the strength in his injured arm, grew a thick beard, and adopted a couple of hungry stray dogs. On rare occasions he would stop off at the social club and converse with Manuel Ysasi for a while, but most of the time he lived immersed in an absolute silence, to which he became effortlessly accustomed. After shutting up the mansion on Calle de la Tornería, he made his home in the old ranch at La Templanza vineyard, and in the hot season he would spend many a night sleeping out in the open, beneath the same glittering firmament that in other latitudes also shone on those whom he struggled in vain to forget. Despite this, he learned to live with the different light, air, and moons of this corner of the Old World, to which he never thought he would return.

On the morning before the last day of the grape harvest, Larrea was listening intently to his foreman's assessment of the quality of the vintage in the noisy cobbled yard, his sleeves rolled up, arms akimbo, hair disheveled from all his labors. Until Don Matías's former employee, a lithe, elderly fellow whom he had kept on, glanced over Larrea's shoulder and paused in midsentence. He wheeled around.

Nine months had passed since Soledad had walked out of his life, leaving Jerez. Without her husband, there was no reason for her to hide at the mouth of the Duero River, in Valletta, or in some remote French château. And so she had done the simplest, most sensible thing: she returned to London, to her world. The most natural decision. They did not even manage to say their farewells in those days of sorrow and agitation following Edward Claydon's demise: all Larrea received by way of good-bye was one of those impersonal notes, edged with black, that she sent to friends and acquaintances alike, thanking them for their condolences. Two or three days later, accompanied by her faithful servants, a multitude of trunks, and her grief, she had upped and left.

Now here she was again, striding toward him with her usual confident gait, glancing from side to side to contemplate the comings and goings of the workers transporting the must and the barrels; life returning to the old winery. The last time he had seen her she was dressed in black from head to toe, a thick veil over her face, at the funeral Mass in the San Marcos church. Gathered around her were her friend Manuel Ysasi and the big wine-producing families of which she had once been a member. He kept his distance from the cortège, a solitary figure standing at the back of the church, his arm in a sling. He spoke to no one, and no sooner had the priest recited the *requiescat in pace* than he slipped away. In the eyes of the city, thanks to Dr. Ysasi's maneuvering, the English wine merchant had died in his sleep of natural causes. The demonic word *suicide* was never uttered. Inés Montalvo was absent at the last farewell; only later did Mauro learn that she had moved to a convent on the central plateau without giving any reason.

Soledad had now exchanged her grim widow's weeds for a pale gray chintz dress with buttons down the front; on her head there was no black veil but a simple yet elegant hat. As they stood facing each other, their bodies maintained a seemly distance. Her hand clutched the ivory handle of her parasol while he stood motionless even as a knot appeared in his stomach and the blood coursed through his veins as though driven by a mallet.

To avoid being overwhelmed by the memory of this woman at every turn, to prevent the piercing nostalgia, and to find some reprieve from her absence, Larrea had simply immersed himself in work. Twelve, thirteen, fourteen hours until he dropped like a deadweight at day's end. To cease probing his mind in search of the times they had spent together; to stop imagining what it would have been like to warm each other on winter nights or to make love to her slowly beneath an open window in springtime.

"A glorious harvest this year, I've heard."

So it seems, he could have retorted. *And although the winds have brought great miracles, as you taught me, I struggled to cooperate as I played my part. After recklessly telling the Madrid buyers to go to hell, I accepted that I had lost everything I left behind in Mexico, and decided not to return there. But if you ask me why, I fear I have no answer. Perhaps it was due to sheer cowardice, to avoid confronting the man I had once been. Or the thrill of facing a fresh challenge when I believed all my battles were lost. Or because I did not wish to leave this land where always, lingering in each sound and smell, I find your presence.*

"Welcome, Soledad" was all he said.

She glanced around her again, appreciating the busy clamor.

"How reassuring to see this again."

Larrea also gazed over the surroundings. Both were trying to buy time, but one of them had to take the first step. He did.

"I trust that everything turned out for the best."

She shrugged with that natural grace of hers. The same eyes, like a beautiful foal, the same cheekbones and slender arms. The only difference he noticed were her fingers; one in particular. The ring finger on her left hand was bare: the two rings confirming her attachment were missing.

"I had to deal with some heavy losses, but I finally succeeded in untangling my web of lies and deceptions before Alan returned from Havana. Following which, I decided to narrow my options and concentrate solely on sherry."

He nodded sympathetically, although this wasn't exactly what interested him most. *How are you, Sol? How does it feel to be back? How has it been living without me all these months?*

"Otherwise, I am relatively well," she went on, as if reading his thoughts. "The business and my lively daughters keep me busy; they help me to bear the absence of the dead and the living."

He lowered his head, running a grubby hand over the back of his head and neck, wondering whether he might be one of those absences.

"That beard suits you," she went on, changing her tone and the direction of the conversation. "But you still look like a savage."

He perceived the characteristic twist of irony at the corners of her mouth, although she was right: his face, arms, and chest, weathered by a life in the vineyards beneath the unforgiving sun, bore witness to the fact. His half-open shirt, the close-fitting trousers he wore to give him freedom of movement, and his old boots caked in mud scarcely gave him the look of a landed gentleman.

"May I steal a minute of your time, brother . . ."

A bald older man wearing gold-rimmed spectacles approached hurriedly, eyes fixed on a bundle of papers. He was about to say something when he caught sight of her:

"Excuse me, Señora," he said, startled. "Forgive the intrusion."

"Please, there's no need to apologize," she said politely as she let him kiss her hand.

So, it's her, thought Elías Andrade, contemplating Soledad with the utmost discretion. *And she's back. Blasted women. Now I'm beginning to understand.*

He disappeared after a minute on the pretext of some urgent task or other.

"My agent and friend," Larrea explained as they watched him go. "He sailed across the ocean to try to persuade me to return, and since his mission failed, he is staying here with me for a while."

"What about your son and Santos Huesos? Did either of them come back?"

"Nico is still in Paris; he came to see me recently before going on to Seville in search of some baroque paintings for a client. Contrary to my gloomy predictions, he is doing well. He has gone into partnership with an old acquaintance of mine in the antiques business and has fallen in and out of love for the umpteenth time. As for Santos, he ended up settling in Cienfuegos. He married Trinidad and they have brought a child into the world; I would wager it was conceived in our good doctor's house."

Her feminine laughter rang out like a bell amid the virile voices and manly bodies, the loud activity and sweat. Then she changed her tone and direction once more.

"Have you had news of Gustavo and his wife?"

"Not directly, although Calafat, my Cuban contact, tells me they are still together. Going from one event to the next. Surviving."

She paused for an instant, as though hesitating.

"I wrote to my cousin," she said at last. "A lengthy missive, asking his forgiveness in my name and in memory of our forebears."

"And?"

"He never replied."

Silence descended on them once more as the workers busily fulfilled their tasks. And the shadow of a man with watery eyes arose between them, the same one who had built castles in the air that the cruel winds of fate had blown away ruthlessly; the one who had clung to a billiard cue in a final, reckless attempt to find a final, reckless solution with no way back.

Soledad broke the hush.

"Shall we go inside?"

"Yes, forgive me, of course."

Wake up you fool, he reproached himself as he ushered her through the dark wooden door, wiping his hands on the sides of his trousers in a futile gesture. *Watch your manners: you may shun the society of humans, but you don't want her to think you've turned in to a wild beast.*

Inside the winery they were enveloped by a fragrant gloom that made her close her eyes and take a deep, nostalgia-filled breath. Grapes, wood, the promise of a full-bodied wine. As she did so, he took the opportunity to contemplate her fleetingly. There she stood, the being who had walked into his life on a fall morning, and whom he had thought he would never see again, now reencountering the smells and sights of the world in which she grew up.

They started to stroll amid the cool darkness, down long aisles flanked with wine barrels. The thick whitewashed walls kept the mid-morning heat at bay; patches of mildew close to the floor revealed the never-ending humidity of the place.

They exchanged a few pleasantries as they walked over the wet yellow ground, aware of the muffled sounds of ceaseless activity around them. *We're lucky it hasn't rained so far. We had a terrible heat wave in London in July. Your grandfather's vines are promising a fine vintage this year.* Until they both ran out of things to say, and he peered down at the beaten earth floor, scuffing it with the tip of his boot.

He said at last: "Why did you come back, Soledad?"

"To propose that we join forces once more."

They came to a halt.

"The English market is being swamped with outrageous compe-tence. Sherry from Australia, Italy, even from the Cape, for God's sake," she added. "Real sherry substitutes that are discrediting our Spanish wines and wrecking our business; it is downright intolerable."

Mauro Larrea leaned against one of the old black-painted barrels and folded his arms across his chest. With the composure of someone who had thought all was lost. With the patient longing of someone who glimpses a crack of light through a shutter he thought had been closed forever.

"And where do I come into this?"

"Now that you've decided to become a *bodeguero*, you are part of this world. And when a war breaks out, we all need allies. That's why I came: to suggest we fight together."

A shudder ran down his spine. She wanted them to be accomplices again—partners—each bringing the weapons they had to the fray. She with her strong intuition, he with his few certainties, to overcome, side by side, future challenges, future hurdles.

"I hear that the postal service between here and Great Britain is excellent. It must be because we are so close to Gibraltar, I imagine."

She blinked at him, puzzled.

"I mean, if you wanted to propose a business deal with me, you could have done so by mail."

Soledad reached out a hand toward one of the barrels and his eyes followed it. She ran her fingers over it absentmindedly, gathering her strength until finally she was ready to reveal her truth in all its particulars.

"God only knows I've struggled hard with myself all these months to get you out of my head. And out of my heart."

At the overseer's harsh shout, the men working inside the winery gave a loud sigh of relief and stopped their toil: time for lunch and to wipe away the sweat, give their muscles a rest. What Soledad said next was largely lost amid the noise of tools being laid aside and the voices of the hungry men as they passed nearby.

Only a few words remained floating in the air amid the fragrant motes of old wine and fresh must. But enough for him to catch: *Me with you here, you with me there.*

And thus, among the towering racks of wine barrels, an enduring alliance was forged. What Mauro Larrea then told her, and how she replied, would soon become apparent in a future filled with comings and goings, and on the subsequent labels adorning the bottles that from that same month of September were to leave the winery year after year bearing the words *Montalvo & Larrea, Fine Sherry.* Contained inside was the essence of the fruit of that pale southern earth bathed in sunlight and tempered by a westerly breeze, mingled with the passionate tenacity of an emigrant forced to cross the ocean twice and a heiress in dire circumstances who reinvented herself as a merchant.

ACKNOWLEDGMENTS

I n an enterprise that crosses an ocean, travels in time, and delves into worlds with profoundly different local essences—most of which have ceased to exist—many people have lent me a helping hand in recreating elements of the past as well as ensuring language, setting, and plot accuracy and credibility.

In keeping with the geographical order of the novel itself, I would like first to extend my gratitude to Gabriel Sandoval, director of Planeta Mexico, for his prompt and generous assistance; to the editor Carmina Rufrancos, for her knowledge of dialect; to the historian Alejandro Rosas, for his documentary precision; and also to Fernando Macotela, director of the Book Fair at the former Palacio de Minería in Mexico DF, for allowing me free access to every part of that magnificent neo-classical building where Mauro Larrea one day set foot.

For revising the chapters set in Cuba with his acute eye and nostalgic sense of the old Havana, I wish to thank Carlos Verdecia, veteran journalist and former director of *El Nuevo Herald* in Miami, currently a collaborator on literary projects that I hope will bear fruit one day. I also thank my colleague Gema Sánchez, professor in the Department of Modern Languages at Miami University, for helping me to access the archives of the Cuban Heritage Foundation—and for inviting me to eat mahimahi in the balmy south Florida night.

Crossing the Atlantic, I would like to express my gratitude to Professors Alberto Ramos Santana and Javier Maldonado Rosso of Cádiz University, specialists in the history of the Jerez wine and sherry trade, for their wonderful research on the subject, and for agreeing to let me fire a thousand questions at them; and also to my friend Ana Bocanegra, publishing director at the same university, for facilitating the meeting with them over a feast of sea urchins and prawn omelet.

Venturing into the universe that perhaps once encircled the Montalvo family, I should like to extend my gratitude to a handful of people from Jerez who are connected to those mythical nineteenth-century winegrowers: Fátima Ruiz de Lassaletta; Begoña García González-Gordon, for her infectious enthusiasm and her wealth of detail; Manuel Domecq Zurita and Carmen López de Solé, for their hospitality at the splendid Camporreal palace; Almudena Domecq Bohórquez, for taking us around the vineyards that could very well have been home to La Templanza; Begoña Morello, for tracing literary journeys and keeping secrets; David Frasier-Luckie, for letting me imagine that his beautiful house belonged to Soledad, and for allowing us to intrude on it repeatedly. And a very special thanks to two people without whose help and collaboration the Jerez connection would have lost much of its magic: Mauricio González-Gordon, chairman of González-Byass, for welcoming us to his legendary vineyard both singly and en masse, for having agreed to be master of ceremonies at our first coming out in society, and for his wonderful kindness; and Paloma Cervilla, for enthusiastically arranging these meetings, and for showing me with her generous discretion that friendship comes before journalistic zeal.

Beyond these personal contacts, I have immersed myself in many written works and extracted both sweeping portraits and minute details with which to give the narrative its flavor. *Por las calles del Viejo Jerez,* by Antonio Mariscal Trujillo; *El Jerez de los bodegueros*, by Francisco Bejarano; *El Jerez, hacedor de cultura*, by Carmen Borrego Plá; *Casas y Palacios de Jerez de la Frontera*, by Ricarda López; *La viña, la bodega y el viento*, by Jesús Rodríguez; and *El Cádiz romántico*, by Alfredo González Troyano. Two classics on the subject of sherry's remarkable international success have been essential to me: *Sherry*, by Julian Jeffs, and *Jerez-Xérez-"Sherish,"* by Manuel María González Gordon. I must also mention José Manuel Caballero Bonald, the great writer from Jerez, and the evocations he traces with his magisterial prose—a delight for any reader. For their descriptions of atmospheres and settings viewed through female eyes, as avid (and almost as foreign) as my own, I must mention four volumes filled with wit and sensitivity, penned by four women from another era, who, like me, found themselves seduced by other enticing worlds: *Life in Mexico, 1843*, by Francis Erskine Inglis, Marquess of Calderón de la Barca; *Viaje a La Habana*, by Mercedes Santa Cruz y Montalvo, Countess of Merlín; *Headless Angel*, by Vicki Baum; and *The Summer of the Spanish Woman*, by Catherine Gaskin. Although I may inadvertently have overlooked mentioning some titles here, all are very much present.

Returning to reality, a nod as always goes to my family—those who are still with me in the day-to-day, as well as those who left our side while I was writing this novel, leaving a huge gap in our lives that we will never be able to fill. A nod is due also to the friends who accompanied me to various places during the writing; those who applauded when the corks popped; and all those whose names, backgrounds, or ways of looking at life I have borrowed to transplant them into my characters.

I am grateful to Antonia Kerrigan, who is already threatening to convert half the world's readers into aficionados of the Jerez vintages, and to the wonderfully capable staff at her literary agency.

I find myself ending these acknowledgments only a few days after the departure of José Manuel Lara Bosch, chairman of the Planeta group, without whose vision and tenacity this novel might never have reached the bookshops—or, if it had, it might have arrived in a radically different way. In his memory, and to all those he trusted for nurturing hundreds of authors and their works, I extend my deepest gratitude. To the new editorial team who are looking after me: Jesús Badenes, Carlos Revés, Belén Lopez, Raquel Gisbert, and Lola Gulias, I say thank you from the bottom of my heart for your kindness and immense professionalism. Over the telephone, in daily emails, beneath the morning light in Plaza de la Paja, in your offices in Madrid and Barcelona, during walks through Cádiz, Jerez, and Mexico City—even late at night in the wonderful night spots of Guadalajara—you have always been accessible, solid, dependable. Thanks to my splendid press officers Isa Santos and Laura Franch, for once again having turned what could have been an exhausting promotional tour into something more akin to a pleasure trip; to the magnificent design and marketing teams; to the sales networks with whom I shared a few surprises; to the painter Merche Gaspar for bringing to life Mauro Larrea and Soledad Montalvo with her wonderful watercolor.

To all my readers in Mexico, Havana, Jerez, and Cádiz who are so familiar with all the settings around which I have woven my tale, I express the hope that you will forgive the small artistic licenses and liberties I allowed myself for aesthetic purposes and in order to make the narrative flow.

Thanks to the magnificent Atria Books team, led by their wonderful captain, Judith Curr, for their enthusiasm and support for my novel: Paul Olsewski, Suzanne Donahue, Mirtha Peña, Melanie Iglesias Pérez, and the fantastic sales team; and to my editor, Johanna Castillo, Atria's Latina force.

And, finally, thanks to all those in any way associated with mining and wine-making. Despite being a fiction from start to finish, this novel aims to pay sincere homage to the miners and wine-makers, small and large, of yesteryear and of today.